one

"please tell me you're not looking at him again."

"i'm not," harry sighed, blinking and turning towards the blonde boy walking next to him. the hallway was incredibly crowded, so every time he took a step a shoulder would bump into him.

"you know, it's really weird that you have a crush on my stepbrother."

"i don't have a crush on him, niall. i wasn't even thinking about him before you brought him up," harry lied. but he couldn't help but take one more glance at the shorter boy dressed in a white tank top and black skinnies, topped off with black vans.

"i didn't even say his name and you knew who i was talking about," niall pointed out, rolling his eyes, but he was smiling.

sometimes niall confused harry. he never could make up his mind over whether or not he agreed with harry's major crush.

the bell rang, and it seemed as if the whole hallway cleared up in a second.

"shoot, i'm late," harry mumbled, dragging his black high-top converse to the next class. niall called a quick goodbye before heading off in the other direction.

the teacher didn't seem to notice his late arrival, which he was extremely grateful for. he already had enough trouble in math, a bad relationship with the teacher would just make it worse. so he hunched over and walked to his desk, sliding into a seat with a deep sigh.

"hey mate." harry jumped at the deep voice in his ear, and whipped his head quickly to the left.

"oh," harry said, relieved, when he realized it was his friend zayn speaking to him. "hi zayn."

and then zayn leaned in closer, and harry wanted him to stop because the teacher was talking and he didn't want to get in trouble. but he didn't say that.

"you going to niall's after school?" zayn whispered and harry nodded quickly.

"it's friday. course."

"good."

the rest of the class was spent staring at the confusing equations on the board and trying to find how it all made sense. but no matter how much he contemplated; he couldn't understand it.

he let out a sigh of relief as the bell rang for dismissal, and it seemed everybody agreed as they made similar noises.

harry smiled at zayn as they walked out of the classroom and into the busy hallway. it smelled of sweat and hairspray and harry scrunched up his nose. "it smells in here," he frowned.

zayn nodded in agreement but didn't say anything, and harry looked away as he maneuvered his way through bodies that were almost all shorter than him.

but then he was frozen as he looked up ahead and saw the boy with shaggy brown hair and a slight frown as he walked.

louis.

"what're you doing man? niall is waiting for us."

of course he was. niall's last class was at the very front of the school, which meant he was always the first one waiting at the end of the day. harry was extremely jealous, as he had to walk forever until he finally got into the fresh air.

and that thought almost, *almost* distracted him from the fact that louis was coming closer, his blue eyes trained straight ahead, and his books held in one arm by his waist, in a loose way that was very different than harry's. harry held his to his chest tightly, as he was very bad about getting bumped into and he didn't want to drop his stuff.

louis looked extremely bored but also beautiful, and harry could feel his face heating up as they walked by him, and ducked his head so his curls were covering his face when louis slightly bumped into him.

"sorry," he whispered, but louis couldn't hear him, instead he rolled his eyes at the younger boy and strode away.

"that was rude," zayn noted, but harry ignored him, and instead trained his eyes on his locker.

"hurry," zayn groaned as harry struggled to stuff his many books into his backpack and harry resisted the urge to roll his eyes.

because harry wasn't mean. that was probably his main goal in high school. to be nice to everyone, no matter what they did. so, he bit his tongue as zayn continued to say impatient words.

"almost done." his voice came out soft, and he was surprised zayn could hear him.

he finally swung his backpack over one shoulder and gently closed his locker door. it annoyed him terribly when people slammed their doors, because it was pointless, and it gave him a headache.

zayn didn't seem to think the same way, as he had earlier slammed it so hard that harry could feel his locker door shaking.

"done," harry smiled softly at zayn. besides niall, zayn was his best friend. although his impatience and occasional door slamming, he was a good person. it seemed niall and zayn were the only people in this school that cared about him, but that was enough.

"okay, let's go!" zayn grinned, bumping his shoulder into harry's and laughing a bit as they walked quickly to the front doors of the high school.

they finally arrived at niall's car. he always drove them on fridays, because they always went to his house.

harry, per usual, was the most excited. going to niall's meant seeing louis.

louis was niall's stepbrother, and he was two years older than all of them. harry knew he didn't have a chance with louis, first because while louis was a senior, he was a sophomore.

another reason was louis' small hatred towards him and zayn.

niall still apologized to the two of them for louis' cruelness, and harry always pretended it was okay, even though it wasn't.

harry knew louis could be nice. he sometimes watched him at lunch, eating with his only friend, liam, and he noticed how he always was smiling brightly and laughing and talking.

he wondered why liam was the only person louis tolerated. (well, besides niall.)

niall was confused why harry liked louis, because he was so mean to him. harry didn't know himself. something about his feminine features and loud laugh, and his joking attitude whenever he talked to niall, caused his stomach to get butterflies.

"harry, get in the car you twat," niall teased, looking at harry through the window.

harry jumped, blinking a bit before realizing he was, indeed, standing by the car like an idiot, and he needed to get in.

"sorry," harry said sheepishly, climbing into the backseat.

zayn and harry always rotated the front seat every friday. today was zayn's turn and harry didn't mind. he needed to think a bit, because he always needed to think before seeing louis. that was why he was so caught off guard when they bumped into each other in the hallway.

harry partially listened to zayn and niall's conversation about why girls should be allowed to wear shorts to school. he honestly didn't care, which he knew his friends would understand. they knew he was gay.

he hadn't exactly come out, but he wasn't hiding it either. in sixth grade, when the three boys became friends, they had asked him and he hadn't hesitated to tell them that yes, he was gay.

they had completely accepted him, which harry was extremely grateful for.

so now, while they continued to rant about the 'has to be past your knees' policy, harry pushed his ear buds in his ears and let himself bob his head to the soothing music.

his mum had found it weird that ever since harry was a kid, he had insisted on listening to classical music, and harry thought it was odd as well.

but he didn't mind. if he had to deal with the horrible music taste of this generation, so be it. as long as he had the violins and flutes to relax him, it was fine.

"we're here!" zayn screeched and harry slowly pulled his ear buds out as they pulled into niall's endlessly long driveway.

niall's parents were extremely rich, as one was a doctor and the other a plastic surgeon. harry couldn't help but be a bit jealous, because his house was small and average just like everyone else's.

niall laughed as zayn rambled on about what they were going to do and harry smiled along.

this was why he loved his friends. they accepted that talking wasn't his thing, and they still always tried to make him feel included.

he had to give himself credit though. he was a good listener.

the talking between the two never seemed to end as they strolled up the stairs of the house and into niall's large room. harry commented on things a few times, and niall always seemed to laugh like it was the funniest thing in the world, which harry liked about the blonde boy.

"louis, we're home!" niall called, cracking his door slightly, and harry leaned forward to listen to louis' voice from where he was sitting on niall's bed.

"don't be loud and tell your friends not to speak to me!" louis called back.

and even though what louis said was mean, harry couldn't help but smile foolishly and stare at the ground at louis' high, sweet voice that he had grown to love.

"what're you smiling 'bout, h?" zayn nudged his knee, and harry shot his head up.

"nothing."

"you sound so believable," zayn teased. "really, why are you giving that signature harry smile that we so rarely see?"

it was true. harry did smile, but it was rare that he did a real, large smile where he showed his teeth and his eyes crinkled up at the sides.

because, although harry was a nice, happy person, he wasn't particularly... content. there seemed to be something missing from his life. he loved his friends, but that was it. his sister gemma was away at college and his mum seemed to never be home.

and although it was selfish, harry wanted somebody who would pay attention to him, and only him.

he just didn't know who.

so, harry decided not to answer zayn, instead raised his eyebrows and said, "i will never tell you."

he expected zayn to continue and bug him about it, but zayn just winked and pulled his phone out of his pocket.

harry glanced around the room and realized that niall was missing.

"hey zayn, where's niall?" harry asked, slipping his backpack off his shoulders and plopping it on the floor.

"probably went to go get some snacks," zayn chuckled, and harry leaned forward to look at his phone screen.

he was playing 2048, a game that still confused harry. he didn't understand why it was so enjoyable. it had something to do with math, and he hated math.

zayn was right about niall, as a few seconds later niall came in with a bag of chips in one hand and three mountain dews in the other.

"give me one of those!" zayn laughed, throwing his phone down and holding his hands out.

it was a lousy toss from niall, and the mountain dew instead spiraled through the hair and hit harry right in the head, causing harry to let out a little squeak.

"oh my god, harry i'm so sorry!" niall rushed, covering his mouth with his hands, but harry could see him giggle a bit.

"s'not funny," harry whined, rubbing the side of his head and wincing a bit.

"it kinda is," zayn cut in, and harry glared at him.

"no, it's not!"

and then zayn opened his mouth to speak when the door swung open and harry stared blushing like an idiot because it was louis, and he was now shirtless, his tank top probably on the floor of his room.

"what's up lou?" niall asked, gently placing the bag of chips on his bed before turning back to the shorter boy.

"mum's not gonna be home for dinner, so i'm supposed to ask you guys what kind of pizza you want," he sighed, and harry frowned when he pointedly looked at him with a glare on his face.

"and don't say cheese," louis rolled his eyes just as harry opened his mouth. zayn had already requested pepperoni along with niall.

and harry sat there with his mouth wide open, because louis was talking to him. it was a rarity for his attention to be on harry, and when it was harry always turned into a blushing mess.

"uh, uhm," harry stuttered. "anything you want."

"well, i wanted pepperoni, but we're getting two pizzas and i want you to choose the second one."

apparently what louis had said there was too nice as he looked away with his cheeks flushed, biting his lip in a way that made harry squirm.

"cheese?" harry squeaked, ready to face palm, but then louis laughed.

and it was the most musical, beautiful sound harry had ever heard.

"did i not just tell you not to say cheese?" and louis voice sounded teasing, and harry didn't know what to do.

"uhm, i guess, if you-"

"okay, fine! i'll order cheese." louis' smile wasn't on his face anymore, as if realizing his mistake of teasing around with harry.

then he left and harry looked at his hands and tried not to grin.

because even though louis had been mean to him, he had also been nice.

it was a start.

two

all the boys ended up falling asleep on the floor, covered by random blankets that were strewn across niall's room.

zayn nor niall found it odd that harry stripped off all his clothes once he was hidden by the blanket, instead rolled their eyes fondly and laid their heads on their pillow. harry blushed a bit, and he was embarrassed, but he wasn't going to stop. clothes restrained him in his sleep; he could never fall asleep when he was wearing them.

niall turned off the lamp with a sigh, and suddenly it was completely dark.

so, he cowered further into the blankets, until his head was the only thing showing. the room was black and quiet now, and all harry could hear was the soft breathing of his friends. so, he let that relaxing rhythm echo in his mind until his thoughts ceased, and he drifted into sleep.

***

"wake u-"

harry's eyes flew open as he felt a sudden coldness all over his body. his hands automatically moved between his legs and he cringed against the light.

"oh my god, i'm so sorry, oh my god."

and then the situation got so much worse, because that was a voice that harry would never mistake. a high, raspy voice that seemed to always be on his mind lately.

once he had finally adjusted to the light, he realized that louis was still standing there, mouth wide open, staring.

"i... i sleep naked," harry mumbled, embarrassed.

"this isn't even your house!" louis said, but harry's heart leaped when he started laughing.

"i'm sorry, but why are you still-"

"oh," louis shook his head, but didn't move.

"are you just going to sit here?" harry blushed, reaching over to grab the blankets.

louis bit his lip and harry swore that his eyes scanned over his chest for a few seconds, and then the shorter boy whipped around and stumbled out of the room.

***

when harry went back to school on monday, something felt different.

and it wasn't that the gym was getting remodeled, nor was it the fact that zayn hadn't been there to pick him up this morning. (he had swimming practices really early in the morning before school, starting today) it could've been that niall was sick but harry just felt that wasn't it.

and then his confusion was suddenly answered.

louis was walking in front of him, wearing his signature black skinnies and white tank top, along with his worn-out pair of black vans.

harry loved that louis wore the same thing every day. niall said that he had seven pairs of each thing he wore, and that made harry laugh.

but seeing louis wasn't the unusual thing. often, harry would secretly follow him and hide behind bodies, sometimes stopping to listen to louis discuss his weekend with liam. he knew it was creepy, but he didn't care.

this time, louis was slowing down. and he was walking next to harry and harry suddenly couldn't breathe.

he decided to not say anything about the odd situation. instead, he clutched his books tighter to his chest and continued walking, and he hoped louis couldn't hear his racing heart. he was afraid he would drop his books because he was shaking so bad.

louis didn't speak either, just walked next to him in silence, and it wasn't awkward because the quiet was filled by the shouts and laughs of their classmates.

harry tried not to be obvious when looking at louis. his hair was pushed across his forehead in a way that said "i didn't fix it, but it still looks perfect." it was shaggy in the back and harry blushed as images of running his hands through louis' hair flashed through his mind.

they finally arrived at louis' locker, and harry sighed in a mix of relief and sadness when louis glanced at him, his blue eyes glowing brighter than ever, and turned to face his locker.

he must've stood there awkwardly for about ten seconds before blinking and rushing down the hallway a few strides to where his locker was.

and if he wasn't mistaken, he heard louis chuckle a bit.

and then there was a little smile on harry's face, and he stared at the ground and bit his lip to hide it.

"you have a beautiful smile."

and harry jumped, shooting his head up to see louis, but just as quickly as he was there..

he was gone.

***

"he called you *beautiful?*" niall stared at harry in disbelief.

he had returned to school on thursday, after a horrible case of the stomach flu followed by a cold.

and that whole time, harry was waiting in anticipation to tell the blonde boy what happened on monday.

"he didn't call *me* beautiful; he called my smile beautiful."

"still" niall said suspiciously. "i think my brother likes y-"

he was cut off by a rough force bumping into harry, and niall's eyes widened. harry stumbled and looked to see who it was. and it was a blue-eyed boy in a white tank top, and he felt his heart drop.

"sorry," louis shrugged, and harry's breath caught in his throat. "watch where you're walking." and then he was glaring at him and harry suddenly felt like crying as he stalked away.

"well it *seemed* like he liked you," niall sighed. "he is so confusing!"

harry nodded in agreement. that was very true, and he was probably the most confused out of everyone.

he stepped into his class just as the bell rang, and he breathed in the relaxing smell of chemicals and paint.

he was in art, his favorite class.

"hi harry."

harry smiled at her voice.

"hi eleanor." he sat down in the chair next to the brunette girl. her hair was fixed in a messy ponytail and she had a soft layer of makeup. harry thought she was beautiful, but he would never think about dating her.

"you actually came to class on time," she teased, bumping harry's shoulder with hers. he chuckled a bit and pulled a pencil out of his binder.

"i'm always on time," he said sarcastically, and eleanor opened her mouth to respond when the teacher interrupted from the front of the classroom.

"today, we're working on the hair of our portraits. i hope you have a picture of the person you're drawing with you, because it's hard to get it down unless you have a visual to help you. same with the eyes.

harry leaned closer and examined the eyes he had drawn. it looked quite nice, although the pencil could never bring out the vibrant color.

with that, he sharpened his pencil and placed the point on the paper, closing his eyes and letting each stroke draw itself.

he didn't need a picture. he had already memorized it all.

and when he finally fully opened his eyes, he smiled happily.

the perfect shagginess.

he could see the boy in the drawing clearly now, although it was just eyes, a face shape, and hair. he added a few hairs to brush into louis' eyes the way it always did.

that was one of harry's favorite things about louis. his hair. and his eyes.

"that's really good," eleanor commented, squinting her eyes and nodding as she looked over harry's paper.

"can you guess who it is?" harry asked shyly and lowered his voice in case someone could hear him.

"uhm.. i recognize him. i just can't think of who it is!" eleanor groaned, slapping her forehead.

"it's looks exactly like him." harry blushed, realizing he had complimented himself.

"is it... oh! louis tomlinson!"

"shhh!" harry hissed, widening his eyes and covering eleanor's mouth with his hand.

she glared and ripped his hand off of her lips. "get your large hand off of me. and harry, everybody knows you have a crush on that boy, just letting you know."

harry frowned. "nuh uh. i only have told zayn and niall."

"and? doesn't mean we don't know. you literally stare at him during every passing period."

"do not!"

eleanor raised her eyebrows, and harry stuck his tongue out at her.

"did you know that you have perfect teeth?" she asked and harry raised an eyebrow at the random question.

"not really.. they're not perfect.."

"harry, all you have to do is smile and louis will love you."

"already tried that," harry mumbled, shading a few strands of louis' hair darker.

***

and the rest of harry's day was uneventful. he tried not to look at louis' locker for the rest of the day, because apparently people *did* notice those things.

did louis notice?

did he know that harry was totally in love with him?

hopefully not.

he sighed deeply as he finally walked out of school. everybody hated mondays, but personally he hated thursdays. not because anything bad happened, but because you were waiting for friday and that wait was so slow.

"see you actually got clothes on now."

harry jumped at the voice behind him, whipping around and feeling his backpack slide a bit down his shoulders.

"why wouldn't i?" he murmured, feeling his cheeks burn.

"because you don't sleep with them."

and his voice was teasing but harry didn't know if he was trying to be nice or not.

"what do you want?" he stumbled over his words, and it seemed the older boy could notice.

"what's wrong with you?" his tone of voice sounded like he didn't care, but his words did.

"why are you so mean to me?" harry lifted his head and his breath caught when he came face to face with a vibrant shade of blue.

"because."

his breath was hot on harry's face, and it smelled like mint, and harry was trying not to smile but at the same time he was freaking out.

"because why?" the harry whispered.

louis pulled back, a smirk on his face that harry could not interpret the meaning of.

"i just said. *because*."

harry glared at him, anger and annoyance and confusion burning in his heart. and louis glared back, just as hard, and they sat there for a few minutes.

"why do you have such a huge crush on me?" louis finally spoke, his glare turning into amusement when harry blushed deeply.

"what are you talking about?" harry asked quietly, avoiding louis' intense blue eyes.

"harold it's obvious."

and harry wanted to respond, he really did, but his heart was melting, and he couldn't stop smiling because louis called him harold and he said it in his perfect voice, and it was really nice.

"why are you smiling like that?" louis asked, grinning, and his voice was really loud, and it caused harry to smile wider.

"i don't know," harry whispered. "but i don't have a crush on you." the smiles vanished from both their faces in a second.

"yes, you do."

"no i don't."

"yes, you do."

"no I *don't!*" harry shouted, and louis looked taken aback, pausing for a few seconds before "that's the loudest i've ever heard you speak," he chuckled, and it was supposed to be mean, but it caused harry to giggle.

"really harry. i've never realized this, but you're so quiet."

harry didn't respond, instead stared at his hands.

"see? this is what i'm talking about!" louis rolled his eyes and harry swore he could see him hiding a smile.

but it was probably his imagination, just like every other dream he had about louis.

"you're really mean," harry said quietly.

hurt flashed in louis' eyes for a few seconds before his amused expression reappeared.

"you need someone to be mean to you. there's something wrong with you, i'm only trying to help."

it felt like a stab in the heart. the words weren't that uncommon to hear, as many people thought he was mental in some way due to his lack of talking, but the fact that the words had escaped louis' lips made it much worse.

so, he gathered himself and left, biting his lip and only letting the tears fall when he started driving away from the school.

three

for once, harry was not looking forward to going to niall's house on friday.

he even requested they go to his house instead, but the other boys declined. harry didn't have much to do at his house, while niall had a flat screen tv and every type of gaming system there was.

so, the curly lad had no choice but to get in niall's car on friday afternoon, after the bell had rang and all the students had flooded out of the school.

"c'mon h, it won't be that bad," zayn said sympathetically, climbing into the backseat while harry plopped in the front.

"yes, it will!" harry cried. "he hates me! i know it!"

he knew that the boys agreed, although they didn't want to say it.

"it's going to be fun, harry. just ignore him," the blonde lad comforted, reaching over to turn on the radio, and they bobbed their heads in silence for a few minutes, until they finally pulled into niall's driveway.

"i have a bad feeling about this," harry murmured, reluctantly stepping out of the car and dragging his black converse towards the door.

niall and zayn followed behind him, each sending harry nervous looks but at the same time having a conversation.

he finally reached the large wooden door, and he turned the knob. it was locked.

"hey ni, it's locked," harry called behind him, and niall fished through his pockets for a few moments before coming up empty.

"shoot, i forgot my key," niall groaned. "just knock, louis might be in there to answer."

harry's eyes widened, but niall just nodded in encouragement.

the curly boy hesitantly hit his knuckles against the thick wood, and he cringed at the loud noise it made.

after about twenty seconds of waiting, the door swung open, and there stood louis. he was still dressed in the clothes he was wearing to school, but there was a grey beanie sitting upon his messy hair in a way that made harry's heart stop for a second.

his blue eyes stared into harry's with burning intensity, and the younger boy could faintly hear niall asking louis why he locked the door.

louis didn't answer, just stared at harry, and harry couldn't tell whether it was a mean glare or not.

he settled on nice when a small smile ghosted across louis' lips for a few moments, leaving harry a blushing mess as he walked away with a wave of his hand.

"what was that?" zayn asked in harry's ear, and harry shrugged, flustered.

and then they walked past the kitchen, and when harry heard a clattering noise, he glanced around the wall to see clearly into the dimly lit room.

louis was there, his eyebrows furrowed in concentration as he poured a few pills into his small hands, and harry tried to see what the pills were, but he couldn't tell from so far away.

"h, what are you doing?"

harry blinked and fled away from the doorway just as louis whipped around, and he couldn't tell whether the older boy saw him or not.

"nothing," he mumbled, his heart racing.

the two other lads made suspicious eye contact but then just shrugged, ruffling harry's curls as they pounded up the stairs towards niall's room.

and harry couldn't help but wonder: what were those pills?

"hey niall?" harry asked hesitantly as they put their backpacks on the floor of niall's room.

the blonde boy raised his head from where he was turning on the tv, a small smile on his face.

"yeah?"

and harry wanted to ask him, to ask him what medication louis was taking, but he just couldn't.

"nothing," he whispered.

niall raised an eyebrow at harry, only turning to hand zayn an xbox controller.

"you know you can ask us anything, right?" niall walked over and placed a hand on harry's shoulder and harry again felt thankful to have such good friends.

"yeah, i know," the curly boy said, forcing a smile.

niall gave him one last curious look before sitting down in one of his huge blue beanbags. and then nobody was talking except for the occasional groan whenever zayn or niall died on the game they were playing.

to be honest, harry wasn't interested in games like that. he wanted to do something, more, fun.

which brought him back to his discontentment. he loved his friends to death, but they didn't like to do the things he did.

"i'm going to go the bathroom," harry said quietly, and his friends just nodded in acknowledgement.

he sighed, rising from his place on the floor, his knees popping. the noises of the game faded behind him as he stepped into the quiet hallway, and he took a deep breath, closing his eyes for a second.

and he wasn't trying to be quiet as he went down the stairs. nope.

the tile was cold even through his white socks, and it send a slight shiver through harry's body.

or maybe it was the hot breath on his neck that made him shudder all over.

"what are you doing?"

"going to the restroom," harry whispered, hoping that louis didn't see the goose bumps running across his arms.

the older boy didn't respond, even when harry turned around so they were facing each other. the house was unbelievably silent, the only sound coming from the clock on the nearby wall, a gentle ticking noise that somehow relaxed harry. he squirmed uncomfortably under louis' gaze, and louis didn't smile.

instead, he pushed harry hardly.

"what makes you think you have the right to just go looking through my house?" louis sneered.

"i wasn't, i wasn't looking. i just needed to go to-"

"i know."

harry cringed back as louis leaned closer. his blue eyes were so bright, so blue that harry's mind went blank for a few seconds.

"why do you hate me so much?" harry whimpered, hugging his arms around himself and willing his tears not to fall.

his hands were shaking, shaking so much that he had to push them in his pockets in an effort to get them to stop.

louis didn't reply to harry's comment, instead answered with a question himself.

"are you scared of me?" he looked curious and harry couldn't help but notice how long his eyelashes were.

"no," harry replied, biting his lip and looking everywhere *but* louis. he noticed the blue paint on the wall and the fancy chandelier hanging above their heads.

"look at me," louis said softly, so softly that harry wanted to smash his head into a wall.

not because it wasn't a beautiful sound, louis' voice. because one-minute louis was yelling at him and being rude and the next it seemed like he actually *cared* about him.

harry finally turned back to face louis, and he felt a pang in his chest at how flawless the older boy looked. there was a bit of hair brushing his eyelashes, and his eyes fluttered a bit at the touch. and there was a bit of stubble across his chin, and his nose was like a pixie's and his features were so feminine and unique and just so *pretty* that harry's heart pounded in want.

"you are something else," louis murmured, and harry flinched as the older boy stuck his hand out and gently ran it across his cheek.

harry's breath caught in his throat, and he didn't know what to say, and all he knew was that he didn't want louis to stop.

but the minute harry bit his lip and finally let his eyes meet louis', louis shot his hand back to his side and a frown appeared on what used to be his peaceful face.

"what's wrong?" harry asked, although he didn't want to break, well, whatever *this* was.

louis' frown deepened as his eyes ran across harry's face.

and since harry was very, very good at reading people, he could tell louis was sad.

he didn't know why, he wasn't *that* good, but the shiny, faraway look in louis' beautiful eyes was heartbreaking.

it looked like he was trapped.

"why are you staring at me?" louis growled, stepping back.

"you, you were staring at me t-"

"just finish what you said you were going to do. stop being creepy."

harry's heart shattered for what felt like the millionth time, and he stared at the ground as he walked towards his original destination.

when he finally arrived in the large, master bathroom, he sat on closed toilet seat and put his head in hands, feeling his long curls fall over the top of his fingers.

he could feel it, that rock in your chest he got when you cried, but there were no tears coming out.

and all that escaped his lips was a whimper, but that was all that harry would allow. he bit his lip hardly until he tasted metallic.

he slowly stood up and stared in the large mirror. his lip was bleeding, his curls messy. and his eyes were shining with tears that would never allow themselves to fall.

he quickly relieved himself and stepped out into the cool, air-conditioned room, turning off the bathroom light behind him and licking the bit of blood from his bottom lip.

and when he heard footsteps, he looked around for somewhere to hide.

but there wasn't anywhere.

so, he braced himself for the many mood swings of louis tomlinson.

"is your lip bleeding?"

harry sighed, licking his lips once more.

"yeah," he murmured, looking up to see louis once again, this time holding a glass of water in one hand and his phone in the other.

"why aren't you in niall's room?"

"i told you. i was in the restroom. i'm going back now." harry stepped forward, trying to go around the older boy but louis just stepped back, in his way again.

"you're talking more than usual," louis noted.

and harry did have to think about that. because it was true. he used to only speak a few sentences in the course of a whole day, and he had already said much more than that.

someone's paying attention to me.

the thought crossed his mind before he could stop it, and it brought a grin to his face.

"you're freaking me out, harold," louis said, but his voice was teasing and there was a hint of a smile on his lips.

someone who is terribly confusing.

harry was still pondering whether or not louis hated him.

"why am i freaking you out?" harry asked, and his voice was raspy, and he hoped to god that louis liked it because he did it on purpose and if he didn't like it then that would just be embarrassing.

who was he kidding? he would never, ever be attractive. no matter how much time spent on his hair and how long he took to pick out his clothes, he would never be good looking.

nope. he didn't care if niall and zayn disagreed.

they said he was a handsome lad, and always got mad at him about his insecurities, but it was normal, wasn't it?

to think he was extremely unattractive?

he hoped so. because when he looked in the mirror, all he saw was a mess of curls and eyes that told a story that nobody could read.

and it was after he finished his long, sad thought that he realized louis was speaking.

"sorry, what was that?" harry asked, blushing.

"i said, you're freaking me out because you keep going into these trances and you keep smiling for no reason."

and he smiled again.

louis rolled his eyes, the corners of his mouth turning up slightly.

"harry? where are you?"

harry jumped at zayn's loud voice echoing down the stairs and through the room that he and louis were standing in.

"i, uhm, gotta go," harry stuttered, pointing his thumb towards the stairs.

louis nodded and harry frowned at what he said next.

"okay? i don't care."

of course he didn't.

four

harry woke up before his friends, who had stayed up until two in the morning while he went to bed quite early.

he yawned loudly, stretching his arms above his head. the room was surprisingly cool, a perfect temperature.

he kicked the blankets off his legs and stood up, before slipping on some shorts but leaving his shirt off.

"harry?" a groggy voice called from niall's bed and harry looked to see zayn. his eyes were bleary from sleep and his hair a mess on his head.

"yeah?" harry whispered, careful to keep his voice down so he wouldn't wake niall, who was scrunched up into a ball and emitting large snores.

"where you going?" zayn asked, blinking the sleep out of his eyes.

"i was going to get a glass of water," harry lied, scratching behind his head.

"can you bring me one too?" zayn collapsed back onto the bed when harry nodded, and the curly lad shut the door quietly behind him before stepping into the silent hallway. thankfully, the floor didn't creak beneath him when he went down the stairs and into the large kitchen.

but he stopped in the doorway when he heard louis' voice and what sounded like his mum talking.

"-i'm not trying to, and i feel so bad-"

"louis, please just take the medicine they *prescribed* to you. what you're doing is dangerous, and you can't do it anymore."

"it's the only thing that helps."

"obviously, it doesn't help. you keep snapping at him-"

"i know, okay! you don't have to rub my problems in my face!" louis yelled, and of course harry had to slip on the wall and face plant in the middle of the kitchen right then.

"harry?" jay asked, her voice shaky and scared.

"sorry. totally tripped," harry murmured, gathering himself and slowly standing up.

louis' eyes were wide open, as was his mouth. and harry didn't know what to do, because he was standing like a fool in the middle of a kitchen that wasn't his and he probably ruined any chances of being with the only person he had ever loved.
so he stood there, blushing and crossing his arms so each of his hands were on the opposite hip over his bare stomach.

"honey, did you, uhm, hear anything?" jay cleared her throat and looked at harry with a worried look in her eyes.

"what are you talking about?" harry asked, and it was obvious he was lying, because he was such a horrible actor.

"oh thank god," jay sighed, and harry raised an eyebrow. she believed him.

it didn't seem louis believed him though.

in fact, the older boy strode up to him and pinned him against the wall and harry couldn't help but gasp loudly.

"louis!" jay shouted, and harry would be surprised if it didn't wake up everyone else in the house.

"what did you hear?" louis growled, placing both his hands on harry's chest and pushing him harder.

and harry couldn't help but grin, despite the situation, because louis' hands were on his chest, and they were so small and warm and *soft* and he didn't want him to stop. but the thought quickly left his mind when louis pushed him further into the wall and he could feel his back throbbing from the pressure.

"stop smiling," louis spit, and harry gulped and tried to listen but then louis' was smiling too and he was gently being lowered to the floor and jay was just standing there with a confused look on her face.

"you always freaking smile and ruin everything," louis sighed, biting his lip, but it didn't conceal the little grin on his face.

"i didn't do anything," harry said quietly, his heart still racing and fear coursing through his veins.

"yes, you did. you smiled when i was *trying* to tell you that it's rude to eavesdrop, it really is, and i'd appreciate if you *didn't* do it anymore." his tone was slowly getting more angry, and harry was frantically searching through ideas on how to get him back to the playful mood that he liked.

jay seemed to know how to calm him down, as she placed an arm around his shoulders and squeezed him too her tightly.

louis closed his eyes at the touch, leaning into the mother and finally looking at her with a torn look on his face.

"i'm trying so hard," louis whispered, so quiet that harry could barely hear it.

"i know baby, i know you are."
and harry stood there awkwardly, still shirtless and flustered.

"it's, i just, harry get out," louis said, his eyes widening as he quickly pulled away from his mum.

"wha-"

"get out. now. please."

and then harry's heart broke, because louis was now whispering and there were tears in his eyes.

"please," he said softly, his face crumpling as he broke down in front of harry.

and harry wanted to leave, to listen, but his feet were frozen to the ground as he stared at the boy that he had been in love with for his whole two years at high school.

and he found himself walking towards louis, unable to watch from so far and not do anything.

jay shook her head in warning, but harry ignored her and pulled the sobbing boy into his arms.

"it's okay," he whispered, and louis shook his head against harry's chest, choking on his tears.

"no, it's not, i," louis hiccupped, unable to get the correct words out.

"just don't talk. i'll hold you, it's okay."

and harry felt so out of his element, because he was never the one to speak this much or to comfort someone. he seemed to be the one who always needed comfort, not zayn or niall.

but either way, it felt right at the same time. he hesitantly placed his hand in louis' hair, the hair that he had wanted to touch forever.

"this is your fault," louis whimpered, and harry sighed in defeat when the boy lifted his hands up and pushed harry off of him.

"i know," he whispered. "i know."

"just leave me alone. stop freaking acting like we're friends, because we're not."

harry tried not to cry,
especially when jay gave him an apologetic look.

"what is wrong with you?" harry asked, so quietly that he could barely hear himself.

louis glared at harry, as if about to say something, but harry decided to run away and save himself from more hurtful words.

and he never let himself cry, even when he ran into a room with the two people he trusted the most. he just held it in.
"where's my water?" zayn asked. he was now sitting on the floor, phone in hand.

"sorry, i didn't get it," harry mumbled, squeezing his eyes shut and trying to swallow the huge lump in his throat. "uhm, is niall awake?"

"yeah, he just woke up a few minutes ago," zayn said skeptically, and the blonde boy popped his head from under his blankets.

"niall's awake!" he called, and harry forced a smile.

"hey h, what's wrong?" niall furrowed his eyebrows, the smile fading from his lips the minute a whimper escaped harry's lips.

"louis, he, i don't even know." harry stared at the ground, his voice cracking. niall and zayn both stood up and walked towards him, wrapping him in a tight bear hug that made him cry even harder.

"mate, i know you don't want to hear this, but you need to give up on him. he's got issues," zayn comforted, and harry could practically hear niall's glare.
"hey. that's my brother we're talking about."

"*step*brother," zayn corrected, and harry buried his face further into his chest.

and while his best friends said comforting words to him, all he could think about was the fact that louis did have a problem, a problem that needed medicine and help.

they finally let go of the teary-eyed boy, and zayn sat on the floor with a frown.

"i'm still thirsty," he complained, and harry immediately shot up.
"i'll get it."

"you know harry? you are so eager to help, it's odd," niall observed. the curly lad shrugged, going out the door of the hallway and praying that he wouldn't see a certain blue-eyed boy in black skinny jeans and a tank top.

and his prayers were not answered, for the minute the passed the bathroom the door swung open and he ran straight into that boy.

"sorry!" he cried, backing away. louis' eyes were swollen and bloodshot, and when harry looked down at his hands he gasped.

there were white bandages wrapped around his wrists, but the worst part was the red color seeping through.

"louis," harry gasped, grabbing at his hands.

"don't touch me, okay? we don't even know each other, you're my little brother's creepy *friend,* so please just mind your own business and quit trying to run into me everywhere you go!" louis screamed. he literally screamed. his voice was so loud that harry had to step back in surprise, and he felt a pang in his chest at the cruelness in louis' tone.

"why did you-"

"why did I *what* harry?"

harry did notice the way that louis hid his hands behind his back, and he also noticed that he was shaking, and his bottom lip was trembling.

"why would you hurt yourself?" harry whispered.

louis glared at him, tears falling from his eyes.

"i'm not hurting myself. i don't know what you're talking about. either way, you should leave me alone."

harry nodded, pushing past the older boy to walk down the stairs.

"i need to get zayn a glass of water," he said softly, his bare feet sinking into the white carpet of the stairs.

he froze when he finally poured the glass of water and he heard a sniff beside him.

"why did you follow me?" harry breathed, staring at the water sloshing in the glass.

"you look pretty when you cry," louis noted, and harry suddenly remembered that his eyes were probably all red and shiny and there was nothing he could do about it.

"no i don't," harry murmured, taking a sip of zayn's water and avoiding louis' intense stare.

"well then again, you look pretty all the time," louis continued, ignoring harry's incredulous look. "and i like when you smile. that's really nice too."

and harry didn't know what to say, because louis had just gone on a rant about how much he hated harry and now he was complimenting him.

"what's with your mood swings?" harry questioned, leaning up against the fridge.

"that's none of your business," louis replied, but harry could tell he wasn't as mad as before.

"well, the least you could do is tell me why you cut y-"

"don't ask me that, harry. please don't make me mad, i, i don't think i can handle that," louis said, looking at the curly boy with pleading eyes, and harry tilted his head.

"can you explain to me why that is?"

and he was still reeling over the fact that he was having a legitimate conversation with the one and only louis tomlinson, when first of all he never spoke, and second louis looked really good when his hair was messed up.

"i can't tell you that harry," louis sighed, placing his head in his hands.

"are you bipolar, or-"

"no, i'm not bipolar."

harry groaned in frustration. that was the only answer he had to louis' crazy mood swings and it was already wrong.

he decided he was done talking. he had already said enough words for the day; he was already feeling unnatural.

"it's kinda hard, sometimes, when everyone thinks you're crazy and you're really not." harry lifted his head and stared at louis, waiting for him to continue.

the older boy was standing there, eyes straight forward and arms wrapped around himself, and if they were in any other situation harry would've thought it was cute.

but right now he was looking for clues. he noticed the way louis fidgeted and frowned.

"Where's my water Harold?!"

harry jumped at the loud voice yelling down the stairs but smiled slightly when he realized it was zayn.

"coming!" harry called, glancing once more at the zoned-out louis before walking away.

"wait!"

harry froze, slowly turning around to face louis.

"what?"

louis stared at him for a second, and it had harry squirming under the heavy gaze of his eyes.

"never mind." louis looked away and shooed harry off with his hand.

"bye."

five

harry walked into school monday morning fretting over his math test and the fact that louis was walking next to him *again.*

he was also thanking the world because he had decided to wear his favorite cologne today, and he hoped louis noticed.

and it ended up happening. when they arrived at louis' locker, he felt something grab his hand. he looked down and saw that louis had wrapped his delicate fingers around his. he felt his breath catch and he lifted his head to look into louis' blue eyes.

"yeah?" he breathed out, but it was so quiet that harry was surprised louis could hear him.

"you smell really good today." louis smiled at harry, and harry could feel his heart melt.

"thank you," he whispered.

and harry walked away to his locker, a blushing mess.

***

"remember to write your name, and you can use a calculator," mrs. lancaster, the math teacher, called as she placed tests on everyone's desk.

harry cringed the minute the paper hit his desk. the numbers seemed to all blur together, and every formula he had ever learned retreated his mind.

"i freaking hate math," he mumbled, running a hand through his curls with a large sigh.

and since it was multiple choice, he went through and circled letters he thought looked right. when he finally finished, he slowly got up out of his seat and grudgingly handed his failed math test to mrs. lancaster. she gave him a suspicious look before pulling the pen out from behind her ear.

and harry didn't wait for her to grade it. he just stumbled back to his desk and sat down, laying his head on the cold metal of the desk.

he was almost asleep when he felt something shake his shoulder. "harry."

he shot his head up, blinking to the sudden change in light. "yeah?"

"harry, do you want a tutor? i highly recommend it." he cringed when mrs. lancaster gently placed the paper on his desk, and it was marked with a large, fat F.

"i guess? i mean, i could try harder, i guess, uhm yeah," harry sighed.

"well, i've already talked to liam payne about it, and he said he would."

harry resisted the urge to roll his eyes. she already found him a tutor before she even asked him. but then who she said would tutor him finally processed through his mind, and he felt his heart jump.

"so liam's my tutor?" he tried to contain his excitement. he could learn more about louis from liam.

"yep! i really think he can help you." she patted him on the shoulder and harry stared at his math test with a frown.

***

"okay! get your book out!"

harry grunted as he pulled his large math book out of his backpack and slammed it on the table in front of a smiling liam.

"aren't you excited?" liam grinned, slapping his hand on harry's book before pulling it open.

"yeah." harry forced a smile and met eyes with liam. his hair was curly, not as much as his, and it was a caramel color. it was styled in a fringe across his forehead. his eyes were dark, chocolate brown, and warm. harry automatically liked him, but that didn't make him any happier.

and so for the next three hours, harry tried to pay attention while liam went over every problem with him carefully. it was much easier, because liam was a better teacher than mrs. lancaster.

"can we be done?" harry groaned after they had completed another page full of notes.

"i guess," liam sighed, slamming the book shut and reaching over to ruffle harry's curls.

"see harry? you're smart, you just learn differently."

harry smiled gratefully at the older boy. he could see why louis was friends with him.

"so, we have about thirty more minutes until we're *supposed* to be done. so what do you want to do?"

"you want pizza?" harry offered, stuffing all of his books in his backpack and zipping it up.

"sure!" liam beamed, standing up out of his chair and stretching. so harry got up and walked to the kitchen, where the phone was. after he had found the number in the phone book, he ordered a cheese pizza, watching as liam sat on the counter next to him.

"ten minutes? okay, thanks," harry said quietly into the phone before hanging up.

"so do you know my friend louis?" liam asked curiously, and harry felt his heart stop for a second.

"uhm yeah." he cleared his throat.

"do you like him?"

"what?! no, no i don't like him! why would you think that?" harry blushed.

"well, i meant as a friend, but now i can tell it's something more," liam grinned, jumping off the counter and walking closer to him. "how long have you liked him?"

harry didn't think his cheeks could get any redder, and he looked everywhere *but* liam.

"harry, it's okay," liam said, placing a hand on the curly boy's shoulder. "i think louis kinda, well. i know he's *interested* in you."

harry shot his head up, a smile beginning to form on his lips. "what do you mean he's interested?" he tried his best to sound casual.

"well, he's talked about you a few times," liam looked like he had said too much, and a guilty look crossed his face.

but harry didn't care. "what'd he say?" he rushed, grabbing liam's wrist and trying not to jump up and down.

"he said that you always smile, and it frustrates him because, he has this condition.." liam trailed off before slapping a hand over his mouth. "i was *not* supposed to say that."

"what!?" harry scoffed. "now you have to tell me."

liam just shook his head and harry let out an exasperated sigh.

"he's interested in you, okay? that's all you need to know," liam groaned. he seemed torn between whether or not he should tell the younger boy.

and just as harry opened his mouth, the doorbell rang.

"that's the pizza," he muttered, dropping liam's wrist and digging for his wallet as he ran to the door.

"that'll be eight pounds," the pizza guy mumbled, handing harry the box, and harry paid him quickly before rushing back into the kitchen with the pizza.

"that smells so good," liam sighed, closing his eyes for a few seconds. harry smiled at him and opened the box on the counter. he grabbed a piece and bit the tip off, moaning a bit at the amazing taste.

"you know i gotta go in about ten minutes," liam frowned, chewing his pizza.

"you wanna, maybe, sleepover?" harry asked shyly.

"it's monday," liam bit his lip, as if deep in thought. "but okay."

harry immediately dug through his mind for the best questions to ask the senior boy.

"can you please tell me why louis takes medication?" was finally the question he decided on.

liam's eyes widened and the pizza fell out of his hand.

"how did you know he took medication?" he asked, his voice lowered although there wasn't anyone else there.

"i saw him. and he wouldn't tell me what was wrong with him." harry bit his lip and stared at the ground.

"well, i can't tell you. maybe we can invite him over and he might tell you if i'm here," liam suggested.

"you'll have to invite him and say it was your idea," harry replied, looking at his half-eaten pizza.

"'course. he's my best friend, it doesn't matter."

and harry tried to ignore the jealousy burning in his heart.

***

the pizza was halfway done when the doorbell finally rang.

"probably mum, or louis," harry mumbled, but jumped when his phone buzzed. it was a text from his mum.

COMING HOME REALLY LATE TONIGHT, LIKE TWO A.M. TOOK A LATE-NIGHT SHIFT AT THE GAS station.

harry wasn't trying to smile, he really wasn't, but louis, him, and liam were going to have the whole house to themselves tonight.

"aren't you going to answer the door?" liam raised an eyebrow at the grinning curly lad, who blinked a bit and ran to the door.

"sorry, i was la-" harry began as he opened the door, but immediately stopped when he saw louis.

he was wearing a grey beanie over his messy, side swept hair and his normal apparel. but the different thing was the prominent smile on louis's face.

"hi, harry."

harry almost lost his balance right there. louis' voice was raspy and low, a husky tone that proved that louis was, in fact, sex on legs.

"hi louis," he said sheepishly, opening the door wider so the shorter boy could walk in.

harry bent his knees a bit so he wasn't towering over the boy.

louis gave him a questioning look and harry shivered when their shoulders brushed.

"louis' here!" harry called out, leading louis into the kitchen.

liam was biting into yet another piece of pizza, which made harry roll his eyes.

"ooh, pizza!" louis cried, in a childish tone that caused harry to smile fondly at him.

"have as much as you want," liam offered.

"hey! i'm in charge of the pizza here!" harry teased, laughing. and then louis laughed too, and then they were all laughing for no reason.

harry about died from stomach pains when louis took the rest of the half of the pizza in his hands and pressed it into his face.

"i'm hungry!" the louis groaned, and when he pulled the pizza away, his face was covered in sauce and cheese.

"oh my gosh, louis," harry giggled, rushing to get him some paper towels.

this is the louis I have a crush on, harry thought, then shook the mean words from his head. he liked all of louis, whether he had problems or not.

louis gratefully took the paper towels and wiped the red sauce off of his face, which harry thought was quite beautiful, especially because he was smiling.

and when louis ruffled harry's curls, liam looked surprised, but harry couldn't breathe.

***

everything was going perfect until harry hugged louis.

and no, he didn't do it out of random. louis and he had teamed up against liam on capture the flag when they were playing xbox, and they had won. so harry, being excited and also being totally in love with louis at the moment, decided to jump out of his seat and pull a cheering louis into a hug.

louis immediately froze, pushing the giggling curly boy away from him.

harry braced himself, knowing what was coming. liam stood up and pulled louis away just as louis had growled, "don't you dare touch me like that."

"louis, it's okay," liam said calmly, holding louis' wrists and staring into his icy blue eyes.

was it wrong that harry wished that he was liam? the one who knew him so well that he could calm him down and touch him and call him his best friend.

but he just sat on the couch awkwardly and tried to ignore louis' evil glares.

"he acts like we're friends, we're not," louis huffed to liam, his warm eyes now mean.

liam frowned and harry could tell he felt guilty when he said, "i know. i know he's not."

"finally. someone who understands. he's the most annoying little twat i've ever spoken to," he whispered, but his bottom lip was trembling, and he looked torn.

"and he keeps freaking *smiling*!" he shouted, making both of the other boys jump.

but the fact that louis said that, despite his mean words before, made harry smile.

his heart was hurting, but when someone tells you not to smile, it's kind of impossible to listen.

so he sat there smiling but he was also crying, and everything felt so messed up because louis was laughing and liam was looking between them and it was so confusing that harry didn't know what to think.

it seemed his smile was the only thing that could save him.

six

"harry. harry wake up, i'm cold."

harry sat up, blinking a bit when he realized louis was hovering over him, his hair blowing from the fan behind them.

"what?" he asked groggily, looking at the clock, and it read two in the morning.

"i'm cold. why do you keep a fan on?"

harry frowned at him sympathetically, as he was only wearing a tank top and boxers. it reminded him of when they were going to bed.

louis had slid his pants down his legs, his short tan legs, and harry had blushed, unable to look away.

"i can't sleep without the fan," harry sighed, running a hand through his hair. louis rolled his eyes, his eyes that were glowing light blue in the dark room. the only way he could see was the moonlight shining through his open window.

they both stopped talking when liam, who was sleeping on the floor, shot up in bed.

"give, give it back," he slurred, running his hands all over the floor. "i don't want it, give it to mum," he said, his voice getting louder. harry raised an eyebrow at him, before looking at louis.

"he talks in his sleep," louis explained, before looking back at liam.

"where is it where is it where is it," liam blubbered, before falling back into bed and emitting loud snores.

and then louis and harry met eyes, smiles on both of their faces, before they burst into laughter while trying to stay quiet at the same time.

"i'm still cold," louis snickered, still trying to calm himself.

"oh my gosh, fine, just close your eyes," harry whispered, trying not wake liam up.

louis complied and harry threw his covers off his legs and got out of bed, and the air on his lower regions felt quite weird.

"are you still closing your eyes?" he asked nervously.

"no," louis laughed, and harry whipped around. "your bum is quite cute."

harry could feel his cheeks burning. "stop looking!" he whined, before quickly grabbing a large grey sweatshirt and hurling it at the older boy as hard as he could.

"ow!" louis said loudly, and harry's eyes widened.

"shh! liam's still sleeping!"

"don't worry. he won't wake up. he's practically dead right now."

harry rolled his eyes and hopped into his bed, immediately covering himself in blankets, and then louis was slipping his sweatshirt over his head.

when it was finally on, harry couldn't help but smile like a fool, because louis was wearing his oversized sweatshirt and it looked adorable.

"there. now go to bed," harry grinned, biting his lip and trying to hide the fact that his heart was beating a million beats per minute.

"don't tell me what to do."

harry cringed, preparing himself for louis' next mood swing and feeling overwhelming sadness at the fact that their perfect moment was going to be ruined.

"i didn't tell you what to do, i just-"

"yes, you did."

"okay, just stop being mean!" and harry's voice came out louder than expected, so loud that even liam woke up.

"what are you guys doing?" he breathed, yawning.

"i'm not being mean! just, i-" louis' voice cracked, and he looked troubled and mad at himself.

"smile."

harry looked at him questioningly.

"wha-"

"i can't do this," louis groaned, slapping himself in the forehead.

"louis, just take a deep breath. let yourself think," liam said calmly from behind harry.

surprisingly, louis listened, taking a deep breath through his nose and closing his eyes, and harry thought he looked beautiful.

"this is so hard," he whispered, and harry was confused as to who he was talking to.

"what's so hard?" he asked curiously, blinking as a few of his messy curls fell in his face.

louis' eyes widened and he looked at liam, actual *fear* in his eyes.

"you have to tell me," harry begged. "you don't even realize how hard this is for *me*. you keep being nice to me and then acting like you hate my guts."

"did i not tell you to stay out of my business? do you still think we're friends?"

"well, yeah, kinda," harry admitted, biting his lip in embarrassment.

"why?" and louis actually sound curious and confused about the fact that harry thought of him as a friend.

"because i like you, and you're sometimes nice to me."

and harry hoped he didn't imagine the tiny little smile that ghosted across louis' lips.

but then he was frowning again. "key word. sometimes."

***

liam had practically pulled louis out of harry's house when they finally got up in the morning. apparently it took louis forever to get ready for school, and harry didn't understand as he wore the same thing every day and fixed his hair the same.

harry, however, was standing in front of the mirror and trying to tame the mess that was his curls. his eyes were bleary and tired from lack of sleep and his lips were a deep shade of red due to the fact that he was constantly biting them.

and there was only one thing on his mind.

no, it wasn't louis, because he had sworn off louis from his mind the minute louis had laid back down in bed and fell asleep.

so currently, he was thinking about the fact that his hands were shaking, and he felt like crying but he wasn't letting himself think about the thing he wants to think about.

it was confusing, but yeah.

"harry! i'm here!"

harry made himself smile in the mirror once more before walking over to where zayn was standing in the doorway.

"whoa, mate. you look.."

"what? fat? pathetic? ugly?"

"rough." zayn frowned at the curly boy, holding his arms out for a hug. "c'mon. give uncle zaynie a hug."

harry didn't roll his eyes, just fell into zayn's arms with a sob, his arms pressed to his sides and his body hunched.

"what did he do this time?" zayn sighed, holding harry tightly to him and placing his hand in his curls.

harry shrugged, unable to speak without bursting into tears.

"c'mon. let's go to school so nialler can cheer you up," zayn comforted, moving harry so his arm was wrapped around his shoulders.

harry sniffed, embarrassed as he let zayn lead him to his car.

***

"i am going to kill him. i made him swear he would be nice to you before you went over," niall growled, glaring at louis, who was tiredly pulling books out of his locker. harry watched him longingly, his heart hurting.

"he *was* being nice," harry defended him. "there were only a few times he was being mean, the rest, well, i don't know." he frowned, watching the way louis swept his bangs across his forehead and bit his lip, and he blushed.

"hey, harry? can you keep a secret?"

harry perked up, looking at niall and nodding.

"louis has a problem. he can't control it. but that's all jay told me. she said not to take it personally if he was mean to me. but she didn't tell me what the problem was."

"but he isn't mean to you. or liam. just me."

"that's because he doesn't know you that well. i think," niall sighed. "it's so frustrating to not know anything."

harry nodded in agreement, following louis with his eyes as the older boy walked to his classroom.

"you think he can change?" harry asked quietly, but when he turned his head niall was gone.

***

"louis wants to know if you want to go to his party on friday," liam said at their next tutor session at harry's kitchen table.

"what?" harry asked in disbelief, shaking the curls out of his eyes.

"i know. you don't have to, and i'll understand if you don't want to. louis was kinda being a jerk last night, and i shouldn't be making excuses for him, but he's trying to be nice. he just can't."

"you know, i would be more understanding if you could tell me why that was," harry said flatly, writing down the next math problem slowly and neatly on his notebook paper.

"harry, i just can't tell you," liam groaned, putting his face in his hands. "and i want to tell you so bad."

"it can't be *so* bad that nobody but you and jay can know. i'm a good person! i'll understand! i swear it! if he has a disease, that's okay. it's not his fault."

"i'm not the one who doesn't think anyone should know. i would love to tell you. but louis doesn't want anyone to know. if he were to tell somebody else, it would probably be niall, because he's beginning to trust him."

"so it's about trust," harry clarified.

"i guess, yeah. so do you want to go to the party?"

"you're trying to change the subject." the curly boy narrowed his eyes.

liam held his hands up in surrender. "i just wanted to know."

"okay, fine. i'll go," harry sighed, pulling his calculator towards him and beginning to solve the problem.

"good. now do you understand this?" liam asked, leaning in to see what harry had written. "good job. you're actually doing really well."

harry smiled, proud. he had already gotten a c on his last test, instead of his usual f.

"thanks so much for this, liam," harry said sincerely, closing his math book once he had finished his problem.

"hey. i like tutoring you. you're quiet and sensible and i like that. some people i tutor won't stop speaking and distracting themselves from their work."

"i don't know. i'm usually quiet, but with louis.. i don't know." harry bit his lip.

liam rolled his eyes. "louis makes everyone like that. he's extremely loud and cheeky, and it seems to rub off on people."

and harry couldn't help but smile fondly as images of louis laughing and joking flashed through his mind, reminding him that he really did like louis. a lot.

"stop smiling like that. it's gross," liam teased, reaching over and ruffling harry's curls.

harry giggled and looked at the table, his cheeks burning.

"are you guys having fun without me?"

both liam and harry jumped as the voice reached both their ears.

"niall!" harry grinned, while liam yelled, "louis!"

"hey boys," niall said in a girly voice, leaning up against the wall dramatically. "niall's here."

"so is louis!" louis yelled, strutting up from behind the posing blonde boy.

"how did you guys get in here?" harry smiled, scooting his chair back so he could get up.

"we let ourselves in, duh," louis said rolling his eyes, and harry suddenly couldn't breathe when the older boy went up to him and patted his cheek.

"how you doing haz?" he asked, his voice lowered and his eyes more vibrant than ever.

harry about choked on air.

"good," he finally responded, wanting louis to stop standing so close to him but at the same time hoping he would come even closer.

"sorry about last night."

harry's eyes widened. louis had never apologised before for being mean to harry.

"it's, it's okay," he stuttered, shuffling his feet and trying to make himself short, because louis was so small, so freaking small that his head reached harry's chest.

harry wondered why he was so terrified of louis sometimes, as he was so tiny.

well, his sass and personality made up for it.

"do you want a drink?" harry asked, remembering his manners as he stepped towards the cupboards.

"yeah, i do!" niall called, looking over from where he was talking to liam.

"you want beer?" harry winked, and niall laughed, and he blushed when he heard louis mumble, "you're charming."

"mountain dew," the blonde boy finally requested.

"what do you want?" harry asked louis, opening the fridge.

"you."

harry froze, staring straight ahead as the word replayed over and over in his head.

"i'd like a coke," louis said softly, and harry realized that he was now right behind him, his chin on the younger boy's shoulder.

"okay," he breathed, reaching his hand in and pulling out the two sodas. niall immediately grabbed his, shaking it up like an idiot. harry wanted to tell him to stop, as when he opened it, it would spill over, but he couldn't speak at the moment.

he handed louis his coke and was about to run to the bathroom and scream into a towel when louis grabbed his hand.

"you have big hands," he commented, smiling.

harry just gulped and nodded.

and then he was comparing the size and harry felt himself smile fondly when he realized that louis' fingers were extremely small and delicate.

"do you want your sweatshirt back?" louis asked randomly, pulling his hand away to open his coke, and harry tried not to stand there foolishly and shook himself out of his trance.

"no, it's fine. you can keep it," he responded.

"good. because i was gonna keep it anyway," louis grinned.

harry smiled, but then he jumped back when louis' can was finally opened and coke began to run over the edges.

"oh my god! you shook this up!" louis accused, holding the coke away from his body.

"no i didn't'!" harry defended, eyeing niall's can and wishing that it was the can that this was happening to.

"why you have to ruin everything!" louis spit, slamming the can on the counter and storming out of the room.

and harry just stood there, staring at the spot where louis had earlier been holding his hand.

seven

harry was extremely nervous for the party. he was so nervous, in fact, that all he could do was stand in zayn's full-length mirror and watch his shaking, sweaty hands.

"are you going in that harry?" harry watched as zayn appeared behind him, sporting a black band t-shirt and black skinny jeans along with his red high tops.

harry looked at his outfit. he was wearing his pajamas, literally.

when he had got home, after taking tests all day, he had stripped out of all his clothes and thrown on a pair of plaid pajama pants and a light blue t-shirt.

"no." he responded, looking at zayn hopefully. "i was wondering if i could wear something of yours?"

zayn sighed. "you look like the white V-neck and black skinnies kind of guy."

harry just watched him quietly as he dug through his closet, throwing outfit after outfit into a pile on his bed.

"here. i never wear this, so it's clean and nice and yeah."

harry gave him a grateful smile, taking the clothes into the bathroom attached to zayn's small room.

and when he had finally pulled the clothes on, he couldn't help but smile. zayn had styled his hair into a quiff, a look he thought only zayn could pull off. and white actually looked really good on him, as zayn said.

"harry! i have shoes for you to wear!" zayn called and harry stepped out of the bathroom before frowning sadly at his black converse.

"i thought i was gonna wear-"

"no. you wear those things every day. try these." harry flinched as zayn threw the shoes at him, lifting them up to see a pair of faded brown boots.

"boots?" he scrunched his nose up.

"yes, boots. my mum bought them for me, but they will look better on you," zayn smirked, looking harry up and down. "speaking of that, i can't wait until louis sees you. if i was gay, i'd think you were hot."

harry smiled. "thanks."

"well, let's go to the party!" zayn cheered, wrapping his arm around the curly lad and leading him out of the house and into his beat-up blue car.

***

the party was more crowded than harry expected.

and that was not a good thing, no, it wasn't.

zayn just came along because harry begged him to. zayn was more into small get togethers with a few people.

when they walked into the hot, humid room that was louis and niall's house, harry immediately cringed at the smell of alcohol.

he felt disappointed when he saw louis holding a red solo cup in his hands, laughing along with a few girls that harry was immediately jealous of.

"oh my gosh, i did not know perrie edwards was here!" zayn said excitedly, shaking harry's shoulder. the curly boy looked up at zayn questioningly. "harry, please let me go talk to her, please! i swear it'll only be an hour of so."

harry nodded, rolling his eyes, and then zayn was gone, and he was alone in a room full of people bigger and more confident than him. so he cowered down, although he was quite taller than most of them, and slowly made his way to the drink table.

thankfully, there were water bottles there and he immediately grabbed one, holding it against his flushed face.

"you look hot."

harry jumped, pulling the water bottle off of his face and whipping around to see louis tomlinson.

he was wearing his usual tank top, but his hair was sweaty and messy, and his eyes were a sparkling blue and there was a goofy smile on his face.

harry blushed at louis' compliment, staring at his boots that he had already grown to like.

"why don't you always wear that. i mean, you don't even look hot. you look beauti-"

"hey! louis, you know someone is in your bed right now?"

never had harry been so mad at niall in his life. he sent him a glare that probably made him look constipated, but he didn't care.

louis almost called him beautiful.

and now his heart was melting, and his hands were shaking, and he couldn't stop smiling.

"who. i want to know who the heck is sleeping in my bed." louis was grinning though, and it confused harry a bit.

"it's taylor and ed," niall laughed, punching louis' shoulder.

"oh my god. i knew it," louis said, his mouth wide open, and harry giggled.

"what. you think that's funny?" louis teased, looking at harry and smiling, a bright eye crinkling smile, and harry never wanted him to stop.

"no," harry lied, watching as amusement flickered in louis' blue eyes.

"you're a terrible actor harry, i swear," louis laughed. and then he reached over and start massaging his hands through his curls. "i love your hair. so curly."

harry didn't think his cheeks could get any redder, especially when louis took one of his hands out of his hair and put it on his waist and pulling him so they were hip to hip.

"'s not that curly," harry mumbled. he was flustered and he couldn't think of anything to say.

"yes, it is. and soft."

harry was practically purring, putting his head on louis' shoulder as he pulled his fingers through his curls.

"uh, what are you doing?"

harry finally realized how ridiculous they probably looked when niall's voice pulled him out of his trance.

"feeling harry's curls, you wanna make something of it?"

harry tried to pull his head off of louis' shoulder but smiled widely against it when louis held him down.

"it's okay, harold, don't listen to him."

"are you drunk?" niall laughed from beside them.

"no! i've only had a sip," louis defended, chuckling.

"well let the poor boy go. look at him. he's miserable."

harry wanted to shake his head and say no, he wasn't miserable, he was enjoying himself.

but louis gently pulled him away and tugged his hands through his hair once more before laying his arms at his sides.

"that was fun."

and all harry could do was nod and replay the moment in his head so he would never forget it.

"harry! come with me!" niall cried, grabbing the curly lad's wrist and tugging him away from louis.

"what the was that?" niall whispered loudly when they had finally got far from louis.

"i don't know," harry breathed, his heart racing.

"i'm sorry, but louis needs to decide whether he likes you or not. because he can't keep leading you on and then breaking your heart. because even though he is my brother, i don't want to see you get hurt."

harry just nodded, his mood dimmed a bit at the reminder that louis was only nice sometimes.

"i wish i knew what was wrong with him," he said quietly.

"i wish that all the time, trust me," niall replied, wiping a few sweaty strands of blonde hair off his forehead.

***

harry spent the next hour of the party making small talk with niall and watching louis. he could also see zayn and perrie kissing, which he guessed was a good thing.

louis' bright smile never seemed to leave his face, which harry admired about him. harry seemed to always have to force smiles.

he also loved the way that louis was drinking, but he only had a few sips the whole hour. he hated when people got drunk. because what was the point of going to the party if you weren't even going to be fully aware the whole time?

it seemed louis finally realized that harry was staring at him, as they made eye contact in an intense way that made harry's hands shake.

niall was still speaking as this happened, talking about a football game that harry honestly couldn't care less about, and he didn't seem to notice that harry was dying on the inside.

louis' eyes were brighter than ever, an energized, beautiful smile on his wet, dark red lips.

harry wished that he could get a picture of this exact louis and stare at it forever.

to his surprise and horror, louis started to walk towards him, throwing his cup away in a nearby trashcan on the way there.

"louis' coming over here," harry whispered, his eyes widening as he turned and looked at niall.

"if he's mean to you i'm taking you away from him," niall warned, touching harry's shoulder in a comforting way.

"why're you staring at me?" louis asked when he finally reached the two nervous boys.

"i-i don't know what you're talking about," harry stuttered, avoiding louis' eyes.

"c'mon love, we all know you were," louis teased, but harry had stopped breathing at the word *love.*

"hey! leave him alone!" niall said defensively, standing in front of harry.

"i wasn't being mean, i was just-"

"look. me and harry are freaking tired of your games. either be nice to him or not but stop treating him like a punching bag."

"i was kidding," louis said quietly, hurt shining clearly in his eyes.

"okay, maybe not this time, but every other time," niall clarified, and harry wanted to defend louis, but honestly he agreed with the blonde boy.

so he just stood there like a coward behind his best friend.

"niall, you know it's not my fault, i-"

"no. i don't care if you have some 'mental disease' or whatever, harry has cried and worried because of you, and i'm tired of it."

harry appreciated what niall said, but that was a bit embarrassing. so he cowered farther away from the boys.

"niall, i know. don't you think i freaking *hate* myself every day for it? i don't want to be mean, it's just..." louis trailed off when he realized that people had stopped talking and started listening in on their conversation. "will you please mind your own business?" he sassed, putting a hand on his hip and narrowing his eyes at the curious teenagers.

harry finally built up enough courage to step in. he nervously walked forward and grabbed louis' wrist, dragging him into a nearby bathroom and shutting the door behind them.

"i deserve an answer," he said quietly, his voice shaking.

"i know, i just can't. you don't realize how hard it is right now for me to,"

"for you to what? stay calm and not turn into a jerk who i know isn't you?"

"yeah," louis muttered, looking at his hands, and harry could see his bottom lip trembling. "i'm so sorry," he whispered.

"i would understand if you would just tell me. i know you're taking medication for it," harry said hesitantly, reaching out to touch louis' arm.

"the medication i'm taking isn't for it. it's over the counter, i can buy it at any drug store," louis replied.

"so basically you're abusing drugs?" harry accused, his stomach churning.

louis didn't answer, just took in a shaky breath and leaned slowly against the bathroom sink.

"i can't believe this." harry ran a hand through his hair and sighed deeply. "so now will you tell me what you have?"

louis' eyes widened and he looked at the younger boy, before shaking his head slightly.

"you were born with it, louis. do you honestly think i'll blame it on you?" harry stepped closer to louis, who flinched away.

"don't touch me," he said, his voice scarily calm.

"i'm not trying to hurt you," harry whispered, placing his hand on his shoulder.

"don't you dare freaking touch me," louis repeated, shoving harry away. harry held in a gasp, and then an idea came to his mind.

smile.

so he gave a nervous, hesitant smile, closed mouth, but wide enough that his dimple was showing. and when louis met harry's eyes, at first louis looked confused, but then he started smiling back.

it worked, harry thought, and he was so relieved that he couldn't help but let out a little laugh.

"thank you," louis breathed.

"for what?" harry asked.

"you smiled."

eight

after louis and harry had left the bathroom, harry wandered off, and he couldn't remember anything after that.

and he ended up waking on the floor of louis' room.

he checked his phone and it said it was seven in the morning, the usual time he woke up. so, he stretched his sore arms over his head-sleeping on the floor wasn't comfortable-and blinked a bit before looking around the room.

he saw zayn, snoring loudly next to him, and louis on the bed.

harry admired him fondly, watching him take soft breaths, and he loved the way louis looked so innocent and vulnerable.

he couldn't help himself from crawling a tiny bit closer and looking at his thin pink lips, and his heart beat a bit faster.

he threw himself backward when the older boy's eyelashes fluttered a bit, and he immediately winced as the carpet rubbed harshly against his elbows.

and even though he was holding his elbow in pain, with his mouth in a silent o, he could still hear louis' adorable yawn.

"harry? what are you doing?" louis asked groggily and harry closed his eyes for a second before looking at louis.

"nothing. just woke up."

"really? you look like you've been awake for a while," louis observed, and harry tried not to look guilty.

"no, i-i just woke up," he stuttered, staring at the floor.

"hey! shut up."

then harry felt a pillow hitting his head.

he looked to see zayn, who was face down in a pillow now and his arm was still outstretched in the air from when he threw the pillow.

"hey. don't throw pillows at curly," louis scolded, before turning to harry and giving him a small smile.

harry bit his lip, unable to respond.

"i can throw as many pillows as i want if he doesn't shut up," zayn muttered, and harry jumped when he heard a groan on the other side of the bed.

"quiet, liam! stop complaining!" louis leaned over and looked on the side harry wasn't on and harry tried his best to avert his eyes from his bum, but it was quite hard.

"i know you're staring, harold."

zayn let out a chuckle into his pillow while harry blushed like an idiot, awkwardly sitting on the floor and playing with his fingers.

"you didn't respond. that means you definitely *were* staring."

harry didn't think his cheeks could get any redder.

"no i wasn't," he mumbled, and when he saw louis turning around, he quickly ruffled his curls and pushed his messy fringe to the side with two fingers. his quiff had fallen out over night, after much touching from louis. and he wasn't complaining.

"i think i've said this before, but you're a terrible liar." but he was smiling, with bleary tired eyes from lack of sleep and hair that went every direction.

"i'm terrible at social skills," harry mumbled, and immediately regretted it, and he hoped louis wouldn't ask anything about it.

"so am i, harry, it's okay," louis grinned, climbing out of his bed and sitting down next to harry, who was now sitting crisscross on louis' white carpet.

"how did we get in your room?" harry asked quietly, looking at the many band posters and some posters with depressing things that made harry wonder what exactly what was wrong with louis.

"okay, long story. so. first liam asked if he could sleepover, and that's why he's here. zayn was drunk, so i didn't let him go home. and you were just standing there all innocently and you looked half asleep, so i carried you up here, and i put you in my bed but you said you didn't want to take up any room, and i said no, you're sleeping in the bed, and when i fell asleep you *were* in my bed. but i think you were being stubborn, and you crawled out when i was sleeping."

"Will you wankers shut-up?!" zayn groaned, and liam grunted in agreement. harry looked at them curiously, smiling a bit.

"this is my room, i'm in charge," louis replied, and harry giggled a bit.

"what're you smiling about?" louis laughed, his eyes sparkling as he touched harry's hand.

"nothing," harry whispered, and he felt so happy and right, and he had never felt that way before. especially since he didn't have very many friends.

"you have to tell me. you can't just say nothing, and then do a little harry smile that i know means you're thinking."

since when did louis know me so well?

harry didn't respond, because honestly he couldn't think of what to say.

so he just played with his fingers and twisted the ring around his right hand. he loved wearing rings, but he didn't know why.

after much teasing and begging from louis, harry finally said that he was smiling because he thought louis was funny. louis didn't seem to buy it, but still let it go.

"so. it's saturday. how about me and you hang out?"

harry could practically hear zayn and niall shaking their heads and telling him it was a bad idea. in fact, his mind was doing the same thing.

but the thought of being with louis was so tempting.

it was worth it, even when louis was mean, wasn't it?

hey. he had problems too, lots of them. louis just needed to work on his.

and yeah, harry didn't know what that exact problem was, but he felt that things were going to get better.

he just had to keep smiling, no matter what.

***

harry had just watched louis bite his lip and look at the sky when they were trying to think of what to do, instead of actually helping. because how could someone look so perfect all the time?

louis had finally decided that of all the choices, they would go shopping.

"you like shopping, right?" louis asked, patting harry's cheeks, and harry just blushed and nodded.

"you're shy, harold. i like it."

i'm not just shy. that's not all it is, harry thought, and shook the thought away immediately.

"you have money, right?" louis asked, when they had finally walked into the air-conditioned mall. harry reached into his pocket and pulled out two twenties that his mum had reminded him to bring.

"yeah" he said, and shoved the money back into his pocket. "where are we going first?"

"wherever our feet lead us," louis called loudly, holding his hands ahead of him, and harry smiled, although he was a bit confused.

"where's that?" he asked, just as they walked into forever 21. he scrunched up his nose. "this is a girl store."

"and?" louis asked, raising his eyebrows.

the curly boy shrugged, running his fingers across the soft fabric of vintage shirts.

"it's not like we're gonna try anything on or anything," louis mumbled, and harry looked at him, and then they were both smiling at each other.

louis ended up strutting out in a white dress that would've been really pretty on a girl, but he didn't have any boobs.

although he did have curves. his hips were hugged perfectly, as well as his abnormally large bum, and harry let out a little giggle.

"you think i should buy it?" louis said in a girly voice, turning back and forth in front of the mirror and snapping the straps on his shoulders.

"yes," harry laughed, and then they were both giggling hysterically and neither of them cared that everybody could hear them.

"excuse me, but you're distracting other customers," a voice came from behind him, and harry whipped around along with louis. a young woman was standing there with an annoyed look on her face, which was caked with makeup.

"i'm just trying on a dress. are you against cross dressers or something?" louis said seriously, placing a hand on his hip.

the woman rolled her eyes, obviously not putting up with louis' crap.

"i'm against the fact that ya'll are giggling and being annoying, so please be quiet or get out."

"that's it. let's go harold. we don't have time for these losers," louis shouted, so everyone in the store stared at them.

harry burst into laughter when louis stripped off the dress to his boxers and then threw his clothes on, despite everyone else's reactions.

and then louis was grabbing harry's hand tightly, even intertwining their fingers, and tugging him out of the large store.

and they ended up in sephora.

"is it weird that i feel like a girl today?" harry muttered, looking at the rows and rows of makeup everywhere.

"okay, i'm serious this time when i say we're not trying anything on," louis laughed, still out of breath.

so they roamed around for a little before louis claimed that he couldn't stand it anymore, and that he wanted a pretzel.

harry followed beside him willingly to the "world's best pretzels,", and played with his fingers while louis ordered his pretzel and was very specific about how he wanted it.

louis did not seem shy in public at all, which was exactly the opposite of harry.

and louis looked a bit disappointed when his pretzel fell in half the minute they handed it to him.

when louis finally got his pretzel, they sat down at the table, and harry couldn't help but notice that the older boy was frowning.

"louis, what's wrong-"

"harry, i'm begging you, please don't talk to me right now. i'm not in a good mood."

"why? nothing happened, we're having fun."

"just shut up, harry! okay? just leave me alone, before i say something i regret."

you already have, harry thought, trying not to let louis' words hurt him too much.

"louis, please tell me what's wrong," harry begged, and his voice was louder than it had been for a while.

"harry! shut your freaking face! okay! you're so annoying, you don't know when to leave someone alone! you're so socially awkward and annoying and stupid and-"

harry burst into tears. literally. in the middle of the food court, where everybody was.

"i can't believe you said that," he breathed, images of doctor's appointments when he was little flashing through his mind and reminding him of why he was such a screw up.

"stop crying, i know you're just trying to make me feel bad," louis said weakly, and harry just kept crying.

it wasn't just because of what louis said, it's because it was true.

he tried so hard to fit in, but he just couldn't.

and he thought that with louis he could, but every single time they started to get close louis would snap at him.

why was everything so hard?

and when louis kept saying mean things he tried to smile through the tears, he tried so hard to smile but he just couldn't.

"okay! just stop!" louis shouted, attracting the attention of the nearby table. harry burrowed his head further into his arms, hot tears wetting his cheeks.

"hey, harry," louis whispered, touching harry's arm, and the curly boy flinched away.

"don't touch me," he said quietly, pushing the curls out of his face.

and louis just gave him this look, this sad, regretful look that told him that he didn't mean it.

he just didn't know why, and that killed him.

so they sat there, staring at each other, and harry would usually turn all awkward and break eye contact and start playing with his hands but louis' blue eyes just pulled him in and then louis was kissing him and he couldn't breathe.

he wanted to pull away, because if he had any self-respect he would, but louis' lips, the lips he had just been looking at all morning, were on his and they felt really nice and he didn't want him to stop.

and he wasn't the one who pulled back first. it was louis, who immediately rubbed his fingers over his lips before looking at a flustered harry.

"oh my god, harry, i'm so sorry. i didn't mean to, i mean i don't even deserve you," he breathed, and harry just sat there staring at him.

louis had taken his first kiss, and the minute before he was reminding him of the reason he could never succeed in this world.

he had asperger's syndrome.

nine

harry and louis had driven home in silence, neither of them knowing what to say after they had kissed.

well, it was silent except for louis groaning in frustration and running his hands through his hair every few seconds, as if it was the worst thing he could've done.

"louis, it's okay," harry said quietly, as they stopped at a red light on the highway.

"no, it's not!" was all he replied, blowing air out through his lips.

"you know this would all be better if you could explain your random outbursts," harry whispered, shaking his curls around before brushing them across his forehead. and all louis could do was sigh and rest his head on the steering wheel.

"okay, i'll tell you."

harry waited, but louis never said anything.

"lou-"

"let me think!" louis yelled, slamming his hand against the wheel and emitting a loud honk, and both the boys jumped.

"okay," harry breathed, biting his lip and closing his eyes, trying not to take everything too personally.

why did he even like louis when half the time he was getting hurt?

"harry, i'm-"

"*Just stop!*" harry screamed, covering his ears and squeezing his eyes shut. he felt like he was five years old again, trying to block out the taunting of his classmates when they told him he was weird, and he cried too much.

the younger boy flinched when louis placed a hand on his arm, giving a gentle squeeze, and then his whole body seemed to relax from louis' warm touch.

"harry, uncover your ears," louis said softly, moving his hand up his arm and into his curls.

the curly boy hesitantly removed his hand from his ears and opened his eyes, and the only thing he could feel was louis' light touch as he tangled his fingers through his hair.

"harry, talk to me," louis whispered, continuing the small movements.

and harry wanted to speak, but he couldn't bring himself to.

"harry," louis sang, and when his voice cracked harry couldn't help but smile a tiny bit, but it immediately turned into a frown.

"harry styles, hazza, curly, harold!"

and harry found himself grinning like a fool and trying not to laugh because louis was now patting his cheek and doing stupid baby noises.

"who's a good boy? who's a cute boy?" louis cooed and harry was about to die because wow louis was cute and louis was now touching his lips with his short, delicate fingers.

"bpd," louis finally sighed, casually resting his hands back on the steering wheel and staring straight ahead.

bpd? harry thought, running it over and over in his head before remembering to look it up.

and soon louis was dropping harry off at his house with a sad smile and harry gave a shy wave before sprinting up to his room and pulling his phone out of his pocket.

he clicked on the google app and typed in bpd.

Borderline Personality Disorder

Symptoms Include: Mood swings, depression, self-harm...

the curly boy jerked back, his mouth wide open as he threw his phone out of his hands.

louis... he told him.. louis had borderline personality disorder.

and then all he could do was bury his head in his pillow and squeal and kick his legs like an idiot because louis *told* him and that meant that he trusted him and now he knew *why*.

harry found himself typing in liam's number and pushing the phone to his ear excitedly.

"hello?" liam answered.

"bpd he has bpd!" harry yelled, louder than he had been in a while.

"he told you," liam replied, and he could practically hear him smiling.

"yeah, he told me, and you didn't have to!"

"congratulations, you found out why louis can be a jerk sometimes," liam mumbled, and harry felt his heart burn a little bit.

"louis isn't a jerk," he frowned, looking through the website and reading about the disorder.

"he can be," liam muttered.

"it's not his fault," harry defended, gripping his phone tighter. liam was louis' best friend, how could he not understand?

ever since he was little, he seemed to be more understanding than most people. maybe it was because he was observant or maybe it was because he had a problem himself, but he did.

and now he understood why it was so hard for louis.

"harry, he isn't even taking his medication for it."

the two were silent, and harry blinked tightly, because he felt like he was about to cry.

"i'll get him too," harry said quietly, before pressing end on the phone and sighing, laying his head on his pillow.

***

when harry walked into school on monday, he felt happier, and less confused. and he was so much happier, in fact, that when he passed louis, he walked over and did something he would probably regret later.

he grabbed both sides of his waist and pulled him in for a hug, because he liked hugging better than kissing.

and louis melted into him, first he looked surprised but then he was smiling and harry loved that the older boy just leaned against his chest because he was shorter, and everybody in the hallway was staring but he didn't care.

"thank you for telling me," harry whispered, then leaned so close that his lips were brushing the shorter boy's ear. "i have asperger's."

louis just nodded, pushing his forehead against harry's chest and tugging him closer.

"i know," louis whispered, and harry felt his heart stop for a second.

he knew? how?

and everything felt so perfect. because they both knew each other's deepest secrets and louis was wearing his white tank top and black skinnies, and his hair was messy and long like always. harry was dressed in the white shirt gave him and he had matching black skinnies and he had his favorite black converse on. his mum had recommended an old bandana they had so he had that on too, and he had actual felt confident walking through the hallways.

"let's go on a date," louis mumbled, his fingers gripping harry's hips tightly, and harry just nodded before pulling back.

literally everybody was gaping at them, but the people he noticed most were zayn and niall. the blonde boy actually looked mad, while zayn looked... proud?

harry shook his head and strolled down the hallway and tried to ignore the many people's stares.

he jumped when he felt someone grab his shoulders and whip him around.

it was niall.

"mate, what the heck was that? why did you just like hug my stepbrother?" niall's eyes were wide as he stared at harry, and harry didn't know what to respond.

"because he wanted to."

and louis was standing there, his blue eyes shining and a bright smile on his face. his legs looked short and cute and harry just loved to stare at them.

"louis, why are you here?" niall sighed, standing in front of harry almost protectively, and harry glared at the blonde boy's back.

"i'm here because you need to stop telling what to think. just because he's quiet doesn't mean he can't take care of himself," louis spit, stepping closer to niall. "i feel like i'm the only one who truly understands him, so will you stop making him think i'm such a horrible person? i'm not, okay? i'm not.." he trailed off, now looking at harry.

"harry." louis smiled and reached his hand out, pulling one of harry's curls just for it to spring back into place. "hi."

"hi louis," harry bit his lip and looked at the beautiful blue-eyed boy standing in front of him, his heart beating incredibly fast, and niall seemed to disappear for a moment.

"has anyone told you that you have breathtaking green eyes?" and his voice was low and raspy, such a pretty sound that harry squeaked, despite his embarrassment.

louis laughed a bit, which made it obvious that he did in fact hear the younger boy, which made harry blush.

the bell rang just as niall opened his mouth to speak and harry quickly rushed to class.

***

"so, i hear you and louis were doing stuff in the hallway," eleanor smirked when they sat down at their table in art.

"we just hugged," harry sighed, pulling out his unfinished portrait of louis from the drawer in the table and staring at it.

"really?! oh my god that's so cute!" eleanor squealed and harry gave a little smile he hoped the brunette girl couldn't see.

"i think he kinda likes you," she added, reaching over and ruffling harry's hair.

he didn't respond, just started to add the blue in louis' eyes that he didn't notice until today. he also turned louis' frown into a smile.

"i see you're making him happier," eleanor commented, before frowning at her picture of herself. her hair looked straight, even though it was in fact curly.

"because i've always been scared of him." harry paused and admired his picture. "now i'm not."

"there is something weird going on between you two and i wanna know what it is," eleanor giggled, tapping louis' nose on the paper.

"i wish i knew too," harry sighed, before pulling out his headphones.

that was another thing he loved about their art teacher. she let them listen to music, as it was known to give inspiration.

so he twisted the ear buds in his ears and put on his classical music, letting the rhythm soothe him as he drew every little feature he remembered about louis. he drew the tiny bit of stubble on his chin and the curve of his eyebrows.

ever since harry was little, he had loved to draw. it was the only thing he was good at, so that's what he did all the time. his favorite drawing ever, besides this one, was the picture of the flower he drew for his mum.

it was when his parents weren't divorced, and his mum wasn't working every hour of the day just to keep them alive. she was bubbly and happy and carefree, but the night harry drew the flower, she wasn't.

it was the day harry had missed the bus, and instead of telling his mum, he burst into tears and made himself walk to school.

when he finally arrived, all his classmates laughed at him and called him a baby.

the teacher had to call his mum and explain the situation, and she was really upset when she picked him up.

when they got home, she held harry and put her hand on the back of his head, pressing soft kisses to his head. he was crying, like always, and he couldn't see anything because it was so blurry.

she knew he had asperger's, she just hadn't told him yet.

but then it became too much for her, thinking about how hard it would be on her son, and she broke down crying right in front of harry. so harry ran off and grabbed his special paper that she had gotten him for christmas, and then three crayons. one was pink, one was yellow, and one was green.

and he drew her a flower. of course, since he was only eight, it wasn't the best, but he carried to his mum who was still crying on the couch, and he handed the paper to her.

she saw the picture and started crying harder, telling him it was beautiful and that she would keep it forever.

she wasn't lying. every time harry came into her room, he would see the pink flower in a frame on her bedside table, and he would smile.

but ever since then, harry was obsessed with drawing, and making him mum feel better.

he taught himself how to draw faces, at first drawing his favorite celebrities and then drawing zayn and niall.

and his last creation was louis, his favorite person of all.

now all he had to do was figure out how to keep the smile on louis' face.

ten

as a person with asperger's, harry did not like when things were done differently than usual.

he ate the same cereal everyday-cheerios- and no matter what he went to niall's house on friday.

his bed had to be made a certain way, and his room was always spotless. he only did chores on sundays, and he had to brush his teeth at a certain time twice a day. he preferred wearing his black converse with white socks, and his hair was almost always in a curly fringe across his forehead. he needed to be wearing his silver watch he got for christmas two years ago whenever he was awake, and his phone has had the same background ever since he got it-a picture of louis, actually.

he was a freshman and louis was a junior when his mum had finally decided that he could have his own cell phone. he had already been crushing on the older boy, watching him in the hallways and "accidentally" brushing hands with him when they passed. louis looked a lot different then. he wore a red beanie every day, with red sweatpants and a big grey sweatshirt. he had the same method of dressing the same every day, except with different clothes.

harry liked how soft louis looked with all his big baggy clothes and his fringe sticking out from beneath his faded beanie. louis' hair didn't used to be styled as much, and it looked like he combed it across his forehead before throwing the beanie on.

his face was more like a baby face, clean shaven, with innocent blue eyes and a bright smile that reminded harry of sunshine.

and harry wanted a picture of that sunshine.

so the day he received his phone, on his birthday, actually, it had a plain neutral background that he absolutely hated. so he opened up the camera during lunch and aimed it at louis. it was an iphone five, so the pictures were extremely good quality. louis was sitting at the table right next to theirs, and harry had a perfect view of his face.

he seemed like a stalker, and he hoped nobody noticed.

when louis finally showed his beautiful smile when liam said something funny, harry snapped a picture.

and it turned out amazing.

his eyes were crinkled up at the sides and his hair was brushing against his long, coal black eyelashes, which framed a pale blue. the picture was clear and perfectly taken; harry had felt like a photographer.

louis was wearing his usual sweatshirt and sweatpants, which meant the hood of the shirt folded around his face in an adorable way, and his lips were dark red as he had just drunk from his water bottle.

and harry ran his thumb over every feature with a smile on his own face, and then he set it as his lock screen and his background.

it'd been that way ever since.

and, being harry, and wanting everything to go exactly the same, the younger boy loved watching louis come in wearing the same clothes. it seemed louis could read his mind, knowing that those slight changes bothered him.

another thing that harry liked about louis was his hands.

he never really got close enough to really admire his hands, but he could from afar. when louis was talking to someone and he put his hand on the locker, or when he was running them through his hair, harry would grin and look at them, because they were perfect.

everything about louis was perfect, except for his mood swings.

those, he could handle, now that he knew what caused them.

so, when louis showed up at his front door, he wasn't as nervous as he used to be.

he was on his phone, staring at the picture and going over every feature as if he hadn't done it a million times before, and the bell rang. he took his time going to the door, as he had to put his phone on the charger and then put some socks on his feet. he never answered the door barefoot, it was a rule of his that even he didn't understand.

when he finally arrived at the small wooden door of their house, he could see louis through the windows on the side.

he opened the door with a smile, and louis smiled too.

"hi harry."

"hi louis," harry responded, making sure that louis took off his shoes when he walked in the house before looking back at the boy. "what are you doing here?"

"i need to talk to you," louis said, but harry wasn't scared because he didn't seem mad or nervous, just relaxed.

"okay," was all harry said, before walking into the living room and sitting on the couch, and louis sat down next to him.

louis, to his surprise, wasn't wearing his tank top and black skinny jeans, and it bothered him a bit.

he was dressed in a purple jack wills sweatshirt that looked eerily similar to his, and grey sweatpants that reminded him of freshman year.

"is that my sweatshirt?" harry asked quietly, biting his lip and trying not to look at the way the sweatshirt slid down a bit and showed a bit of louis' collarbone, his beautiful, wonderful collarbone.

"yeah. you left it at niall's a while back, and he let me keep it."

and harry couldn't help but blush.

"you look different," he said softly, nonchalantly scooting closer to louis. luckily, louis didn't seem to notice.

"i know that." louis nudged harry's knee with his, and harry let his curls hang in front of his face to hide the redness dusting his cheeks.

"what did you want to talk to me about?" his voice came out raspier than he intended it to, and he started playing with his fingers to avoid eye contact with louis.

"you know what's wrong with me," louis sighed. "and it's bothering me that you haven't said anything about it yet."

"borderline personality disorder," harry breathed. "you can't help it, louis."

"i know, i can't really completely control it. but i can help it, and i'm not, i just can't take the medication." louis' voice was lowered to a whisper, a quiet whisper that had the curly boy leaning in to hear him.

"why can't you take the medication, if it helps?"

"i want to fix it on my own. i want to be myself, not something that meds make me into. have you seen the side effects for that stuff? it gives you more depression, and i already have a lot of that. it gives you mood swings, which doesn't make sense, because that's what they're trying to fix." he groaned in frustration. "i need your help to fix it."

"what am i supposed to do? i'm just some freak. a kid with asperger's, who doesn't even know how to be social," harry muttered, ignoring the fact that his therapist he went to a few years ago said he was the exact opposite. she said he could be outgoing, he just needed to try.

he didn't believe that.

"you're not a freak, harry. don't say that. you're just special."

and harry couldn't help but flash back to the faces of his classmates, when they whispered the word freak and didn't hang out with him. the laughter used to haunt his dreams; their words so common that the sting in his heart finally became bearable.

he was so broken before zayn and niall.

he still was, but not as bad.

and when louis put an arm around him, he broke down crying.

"harry, please don't cry," louis begged, tugging harry tighter to him and wrapping warm, soft, arms around him, in a perfect hug that gave harry butterflies.

neither of them spoke, both just thinking.

"i think it's cute that you're so quiet," louis whispered, nudging his nose in harry's curls.

"really?" harry lifted his head, feeling his eyes burn from the tears that leaked from his eyes, but staring at louis nonetheless.

"yeah. i know i say otherwise when i'm being mean.." louis lowered his voice. "but don't listen to me when i'm like that. i hope you know that anything i say when i'm mad like that i don't mean. well, most of the time."

"why do you say them? why say things you don't mean?" harry asked, genuinely curious, and louis smiled at him when he sniffed a bit.

"when i'm like that, all i want to do is hurt the person i'm with. now don't take this in a weird way, but i'm only mean to them when i'm having a problem with them."

harry raised an eyebrow. "what was your problem with me?"

louis didn't respond, just stared ahead and played with the fabric on his jack wills sweatshirt.

"louis," harry pressed, putting his hand on the older boy's shoulder.

"harry, please don't make me mad," louis replied quietly, brushing harry's hand off of him and continuing to look ahead.

harry actually listened this time, leaning back on the couch and watching the way louis licked his lips and furrowed his eyebrows instead.

they sat there for about two minutes until louis finally spoke.

"i think you know the answer to that question, harry," was all he said.

"no, i don't," harry whispered.

"this is the problem," louis breathed, and then louis' lips were on harry and they were soft and gentle and it felt perfect.

harry kissed him back, with as much passion as he could muster, and he couldn't believe that louis, the boy he loved for two years, was kissing him.

and louis had *initiated* the kiss.

they kissed until their lungs were burning and their lips were sore. harry's heart was racing a million miles per hour and his hands were shaking and sweaty. he hesitantly placed his hands on louis' chest, feeling the soft fabric of his sweatshirt beneath his fingertips.

louis' eyes had darkened to a color that harry would describe as the ocean at nighttime, with stars reflecting on it and the sea foam glowing in the dim light.

harry looked down to see louis' hand on his waist.

he finally realized with a blush that he was wearing the pajama pants with the ducks on them that gemma had gotten him for his birthday last year.

he was surprised louis had commented on them yet.

and he was caught off guard when louis started kiss him again, now fully wrapping his arms around harry's thin waist and pulling him closer, and harry kept his hands on louis' chest, curling his fingers against the soft shirt.

they finally pulled back, breathless, and harry pushed his forehead against louis' as he struggled to catch his breath.

louis was smiling, and that caused him to smile.

"remember when i told you that you have a beautiful smile?" louis whispered, his breath tickling harry's lips.

harry nodded shyly, his heart fluttering.

"well, i'm just reminding you."

"you're smile is sunshine," harry breathed, before pulling back and covering his mouth.

he did *not* mean to say that.

but now louis was giving his sunshine smile, reaching his hand forward and intertwining his fingers with the curly boys.

"you really think so?" he asked, but harry's heart was beating much too fast to actually answer the question. so he just nodded and tried not to pinch himself because this felt like a dream.

"harry, you're such a good person, and i feel bad because i keep treating you like crap," louis frowned.

harry was going to say it was okay, but really, it wasn't.

he liked louis, a lot, and he really liked kissing him, but that didn't mean louis could speak to him like that.

and just because a smile stopped it, didn't mean he wanted it to start in the first place.

"i think, if you try hard enough, you can control it," harry said confidently.

louis shook his head. "i've tried pretty hard before."

"yeah, but try harder. when you get mad, smile so much that you feel ridiculous and think of something that makes you incredibly happy"

and then louis looked at harry with this knowing smile and harry about fainted.

eleven

the saddest moment in harry's life used to be when he was about fourteen and him and gemma got in a fight.

it was a stupid reason; he couldn't even remember why they were fighting in the first place. but he could remember how much hatred he had felt towards his family, but more towards himself.

he told gemma he hated her. he said that he wished she was never born. and he screamed. there was so much going on his mind. his stomach was hurting, hurting so much, and he couldn't breathe and there were tears running down his face and all he do was bite his lip as hard as he could and squeeze his eyes shut.

and gemma wouldn't stop yelling at him, yelling out insults that she knew would hurt him the most.

and they did hurt. they hurt and he screamed at her until their mother came up and started shouting at harry, while gemma ran away to her own room, and she wasn't crying like harry was.

and then he was being yelled at by his own mother, and all he could do was run past her and out the door, into the cold air as it was late at night and he was so tired. she didn't even follow after him. he laid down on the cold concrete of the sidewalk outside their house and fell asleep, he fell asleep to the sound of passing cars and the comforting, dim light from the streetlamp nearby.

he woke up with an aching back and his face hurt and his eyes were burning from the tears he had shed.

and he swore to himself that he hated his life, that it couldn't get any worse. he knew it was the saddest moment that would ever happen.

when he went back inside that morning, his sister was acting as if nothing happened and his mother was ignoring him.

he could practically hear their thoughts.

it's okay. it's the asperger's, not him.

but asperger's wasn't the reason his heart was hurting; it wasn't why he cried himself to sleep.

he was unhappy.

and it was like that until the day louis kissed him, for real, and it was his first kiss and he didn't know what to do with his hands because he was inexperienced.

when louis left later that day, harry was smiling, he wasn't crying, and he was happy. louis made him happy.

but only sometimes.

which led to the saddest moment in his life.

it was a whole week after louis had visited him at his house and kissed him senseless.

that whole week was spent shamelessly flirting and giving long hugs in the hallway and harry was walking around with butterflies in his stomach and hearts in his eyes.

which was why when louis changed it hurt more than ever before.

harry had just finished drawing louis' collarbones on his portrait. he decided to draw him in his signature white tank top, which meant he could draw his collarbones. they were one of harry's favorite things about louis.

eleanor was bugging him about how harry should ask louis out but harry felt that louis should ask *him* out instead. because louis seemed more likely to do it, as he was more confident and more in charge.

so eleanor advised harry to drop subtle hints about being louis' boyfriend, which harry thought was a good idea.

but when he arrived at louis' locker after the seventh period bell rang, he was brought back to when he was fourteen. the hallways were empty, because he had spent about ten minutes trying to think of the right things to say to louis. what if he sounded dumb? stupid?

and then, right as turned into the seniors' hallway, where louis' locker was, he froze.

louis and liam were screaming at each other, but nobody was there so nobody heard them. well, except for harry. it was more louis screaming at liam, in this angry, aggressive way.

at first he hid behind the corner, feeling tears pool in his eyes because things were going so perfectly this week and also because he was a crybaby.

liam was trying to calm louis down, telling him to breathe. and harry felt as if liam were talking to him, because he couldn't breathe either. louis scared him when he was mad.

"you're such a freaking screw up! why can't you just stay out of my life?!"

harry wished that he knew what louis was mad about, and he finally found out when he heard liam's quiet, calm response. "you're such a freaking screw up! why can't you just stay out of my life?!"

"i didn't mean to rip up your book, it's not that big of a deal."

"not that big of a deal? that book... that had everything."

louis wrote? what did he write about?

"it had everything in it, liam. everything."

and harry listened as louis broke down crying, so loud and so heartbreaking that the younger boy had to cry with him. he slid down the wall and felt his stomach churn and his hands shake as he listened to louis.

"louis, i'm so sorry."

"just go! leave me alone liam!"

and harry was surprised to hear liam walk away, his footsteps quiet and slow, and harry watched his shadow as he disappeared down the hallway and into the main entrance of the quiet, deserted school.

the younger boy hesitantly stepped into the hallway, and he jumped when his converse squeaked loudly on the tile floor.

louis' head shot up and harry watched as his eyes darkened the minute they landed on him.

"harry," louis said, his voice eerily quiet. "why are you here? you need to leave, you need to.." he trailed off.

"what was in your book?" harry whispered, a tear trailing down his cheek, and he quickly wiped it away.

"why are you crying?" louis stood up and harry felt himself back away. a hurt look flashed across louis face for a moment and harry was shaking all over and he couldn't stop.

"what was in your book?" he asked again.

louis just shook his head. "i can't tell you."

and then louis was apologising, rambling on in words that didn't make any sense, and harry just covered his ears and whispered comforting words to himself because he wasn't happy anymore and he wanted to be happy.

"i hate my life i hate my life i hate my life," he whispered, over and over, hoping that his heart would stop hurting and just go numb for a second.

and yeah, he was hurting today, but when he repeated i hate my life, images of his whole, horrible life flicked through his mind in black and white.

"harry, harry snap out of it," louis said, his voice growing louder, and harry cringed as louis placed a hand on his cheek.

"he's going to have episodes. and he won't snap out of it, you just need to hold him, hold him until he falls asleep."

"don't try to talk to him when he's like that, anne. he's stuck there until he sleeps."

"just leave him be. it's part of the disease. people with asperger's have episodes, they can't snap out of it. they can't. don't try, and don't you dare egg him on."

the voices of the hundreds of doctors he had visited wouldn't stop, they just crumbled together in his mind and he opened his mouth to scream and he squeezed his eyes shut but nothing came out.

that's when he realized louis was holding him, rocking him.

"shhh, it's okay," louis whispered, and harry held his hands to his ears tighter because no, louis couldn't be here. he couldn't. louis was bad, louis was mean, and he wanted to hurt him.

"i hate my life i hate my life i hate my life," harry breathed, letting out loud sobs into louis' shoulder.

"shh, no you don't, baby it's okay."

harry was shaking, literally shaking all over and he wanted to stop, he just wanted it all to end. he couldn't do it anymore.

"i deserve to die," harry choked out, and he was gasping for air because he couldn't breathe, and his stomach felt like there were a million rocks in it.

"you're only human. you mean so much to me harry, you mean so much to me. it hurts me to see you like this. i'm sorry for scaring you," louis said softly, and harry fell limp in his arms the minute louis started to gently tug on his hair, and he was pulled tighter to louis' body.

"hold him until he falls asleep."

and he could feel his eyes closing. he was exhausted, so exhausted, and he had literally just used all his energy.

and through heavy lids he watched the lights dim and sparkle because of his tears, and all he could feel was louis, louis' warm, firm, strong, and soft arms wrapped around him tightly, and harry buried his head in his chest.

"you're okay, harry. you're a beautiful, wonderful human. i'm sorry i'm such a messed-up person. it's all my fault."

"harry's episodes are caused by fights. yelling, screaming fights."

harry had hated the doctor that told his mum that. because he had acted like harry was never there, acted like harry was some problem that his mother had to learn the instructions to, but couldn't fix.

he couldn't help but wonder how louis was diagnosed with borderline personality disorder. did he go to a lot of doctors?

and then all harry saw was black, and louis arms seemed to squeeze him tighter as his exhaustion took over.

twelve

harry woke up to a pleasant, wonderful smell.

no, it wasn't pancakes or frying bacon. it wasn't his freshly changed sheets or a new air freshener.

it was a musky, yet sweet smell that harry just wanted to breathe in forever. his eyes were closed so he didn't know what it was, but for some reason the beautiful scent caused butterflies to flutter in his stomach.

he couldn't place it until he felt his body shift, and he was suddenly aware of the warmth surrounding him.

he felt his eyelashes flutter, giving him a small glimpse of bright light that pressed harshly against his eyelids.

"harry?"

the voice was sweet and soft as honey, a melody. harry felt his lips turn up in a small smile, a smile that caused the person holding him to laugh.

"harry. open your eyes."

harry hesitantly let himself open his eyes, staring at the ceiling tiles before he saw bright blue.

"louis," he whispered, before looking at his arm and seeing that the older boy was holding his fingers, gently rubbing his thumb over the top of harry's hand. "where am i?"

he could feel the dried tears on his cheeks, the aching of his eyes, and the hollow feeling in his stomach.

louis gave him a sad look, a frown prominent on his worried face.

"oh," harry replied knowingly, nodding his head. he couldn't remember, but the way he felt and the look on louis' face told him that he had one of his episodes.

and then he was blushing, his cheeks burning as he averted his eyes from louis.

"harry? are you okay?"

"yeah, yeah i'm fine," the curly headed boy muttered, lifting himself from louis' arms, and the older lad loosened his hold around him.

"so do you wanna leave school now? i don't' wanna be in here anymore than i have to."

harry nodded, his eyes widening when louis stood up then reached down to grab his hands. "let's go, curly."

they walked down the hall in silence, except for the sound of the boy's breaths.

harry finally broke the silence, surprisingly. "louis?"

"yeah?"

"how did you know how to.. uhm.. handle me?"

"i wasn't 'handling' you. i love holding you."

harry turned to look at louis, who was now blushing and biting his lip as if he said too much.

"i just kind of guessed. i felt as if you fell asleep, when you woke up you wouldn't be as upset."

the younger boy nodded, licking his lips as they reached the parking lot.

"zayn took me home, and now he's gone," harry said quietly. he felt a little hurt that zayn didn't even go look for him, but he was gone for about two hours.

he flinched a bit when louis gently draped his arm around his shoulder. "i'll take you home. don't worry."

they quietly walked to louis' small car, harry trying to recall what happened before he broke down and wondering what louis was thinking.

"the book," he finally whispered to himself, and hoped louis couldn't hear him.

but he must've, because he responded. "it's about me, and..." louis trailed off, opening harry's car door for him, and harry smiled at him sheepishly before climbing into the passenger seat.

"and what?"

louis plopped into the driver's seat and turned the key, waiting until the car roared to life before speaking.

"and i'm not telling you. you don't need to know everything harold."

the word harold never ceased to cause harry's heart to race and turn his mouth into a dimpled smile.

he felt a pressure on his arm, and he looked down to see louis touching him right where his sleeve ended, and his pale skin began.

"why're you smiling?" louis' grin screamed fond, a perfect, flawless look.

"nothing."

and that was the end of it.

***

harry got home at seven o'clock, his arms wrapped around himself and a foolish smile on his face.

his mum was surprisingly at home, and exhausted smile on her face as she greeted harry with a hug.

"hi baby," she sighed. "i haven't really talked to you in forever."

harry buried his face in anne's shoulder. he could still smell what he did when he was little; flowers and sweetness and honey. but now it was mixed with the smells of the gas station, like smoke and donuts. he didn't like it very much, it was different.

"how have you been feeling honey?" anne shook harry slightly, before pulling back and holding harry at arm's length.

"i had one of my.. uhm.. episodes today."

anne's eyes widened. "are you taking your medicine?"

harry shook his head. "you haven't got my new prescription for a long time. probably, uhm, eight months?"

his mother gasped and harry was surprised to see her lip trembling and tears welling up in her eyes.

"harry, i've been working so hard that i have been ignoring you."

harry found himself crying with her.

he missed his mum, he missed her so much. every day he came home he was alone. his sister was away at college and she was the only sibling he had.

"are you okay, harry? are you okay?"

harry nodded, biting his lip. he was okay.

"i feel like something's changed."

he nodded. "louis."

"tell me about him."

anne reached out and put her hand on her son's shoulder, leading him out of the entryway and into the living room, where they sat on the couch.

harry blushed, looking at his black converse and closing his eyes for a second.

"he's perfect," he whispered, but then he shook his head. "no, no he's not perfect. he's actually the opposite of perfect. but that's what i love about him."

anne's eyes widened and harry covered his mouth.

love?

was that love?

were two shared kisses and hesitant conversations where harry found himself a blushing mess... were they love?

were the late-night phone calls where harry was crying and louis was upset, the phone calls that they refrained to speak about or acknowledge... were they love?

that's when harry realized that his mum was talking, but he was so confused, and he didn't know what to do.

"... does he make you happy? does he make you smile?"

harry looked at her, at her tired but loving eyes.

"he holds me." he paused. "until i fall asleep."

harry, having asperger's, wasn't very good at reading people, but sadness was clear on his mum's face.

"mum? what's wrong?"

"it must be so hard for you."

the curly lad didn't know what to say, so he just stood up and walked to the kitchen, grabbing a pack of macaroni out of the king-sized box on the counter. it was what he ate every night, even if he grew tired of it.

he could practically sense his mum standing behind him, and he whipped around.

"what?" he asked, wiping a tear from his eye and hoping she didn't see it.

"i have to work in two hours.. can you make me some of that?"

he nodded, pouring the noodles into a bowl of water before carefully placing it in the microwave.

"thanks."

***

and when harry was finally cuddled up in his bed at exactly nine o'clock, his phone rang.

he slowly reached over and grabbed it off his bedside table, glancing at the picture of louis' smiling on the caller id before holding it up to his ear.

"hello?" he said slowly, holding in a yawn.

he heard louis clear his throat over the phone, a sound that was usually odd, but it sounded beautiful when it came from louis.

"hi harry."

"hi."

"hi."

then they both started laughing, and really it was mostly harry burying his face in a pillow and giggling while louis chuckled.

"how are you harry?" louis finally breathed out, in this tired, husky voice that caused harry to squirm.

"i'm fine," harry said quietly, adjusting his pillow so he could sit up against his headboard. "have you been writing in your book?"

he hoped that he didn't sound too obvious.

"uhm, yeah, how'd you know?"

harry smiled. "i didn't."

"oh."

and then louis brought up what he had for dinner, which led to a conversation about macaroni and cheese, which led to school lunches, which led to school.

and harry found himself dying of laughter throughout the whole phone call, especially when louis was complaining about the cheerleaders.

louis was unbelievably funny, and he hadn't said anything mean the whole time.

when they finally hung up, it was one in the morning.

and harry didn't care that it was against his nightly routine.

thirteen

harry couldn't sleep after he hung up.

no, he wasn't upset, which was usually the reason he stayed up late with heavy lids but too much on his mind.

he was just.. excited. shocked.

and all he could do was stare at his phone and smile softly, running his finger over the screen as if he could touch louis' sunshine smile in some way. louis' voice was repeating over and over in his head, like a pretty instrumental song that you listened to really loud on your headphones. a classical one.

which brought him the idea of listening to his classical music, in an attempt to calm him his mind and bring him sleep.

so he rifled through his drawer next to his bed, until he pulled out some tangled white headphones and he plugged them into his phone. he clicked on the music app before playing a pretty classical piece that he had heard on the radio on the while back, and absolutely loved.

and then he switched off his lamp before resting his head on his pillow, a soft, squishy pillow that he had bought himself for his birthday.

thankfully, the soothing violins and flutes blocked out all of his giddy thoughts, which revolved around louis tomlinson, and he closed his eyes tightly, hoping that he could finally sleep.

he would be tired the next day.

a few minutes later, he was asleep.

***

harry woke up on saturday morning with his ear buds tangled in a mess next to him and bleary eyes. his hair was blowing in his eyes due to the fan next to his window, and his phone was still clutched tightly in his hand.

when he checked the time it said eight o'clock, and he bit his lip, irritated and frustrated.

he *always* woke up at six, every morning, no matter what. how could he have slept through the alarm?

then last night all came rushing back to him, and the irritation left his mind. because louis was just that perfect.

he grudgingly got out of bed, slipping on some sweatpants and a red sweatshirt before dragging himself downstairs. although he was surprisingly happy, he was tired.

the cheerios were almost empty when he poured them in the bowl, and he made a mental note to buy some more later.

just as he had taken his last bite of cereal and he was holding the bowl up to his lips to drink the milk, he heard a loud knock on the door.

the pounding noise gave him a headache, and he sighed deeply before standing up from his chair, his knees popping loudly, and he trudged to the door with a sour frown on his pale face.

his spirits uplifted a little bit when he saw a grinning niall. his blonde hair was messed up, as if he had just woken up, and he was dressed in black skinny jeans with white high tops and a white t-shirt.

"hi niall." harry lifted his hand in a small wave, opening the door wider so the blonde boy could come in.

"we've come bearing gifts," niall laughed, and harry raised an eyebrow. we?

"they're getting the coffee right now. i take it your tired? louis practically fell out of bed this morning and he hasn't fully opened his eyes yet. he figured that you would want some coffee too."

harry was biting his lip and trying not to smile when louis, zayn, and liam burst through the door. well, zayn and liam. louis just shuffled behind them with a lazy grin.

"hey, harry," they all said, and then harry was handed a large coffee from zayn, who pat him on the back and ruffled his hair.

"is this just an excuse to see me?" harry teased, taking a large gulp of the warm liquid.

all the boys shook their heads, except for louis.

the tired boy had this smirk on his face, and his hair was all over the place as he nodded his head, stepping closer to the younger lad.

"yes, it is an excuse to see you," he said softly, and harry smiled when he saw louis was holding a cup of tea, not coffee.

and although what louis said left him flustered, he came up with a response. "don't like coffee, huh?"

louis scrunched up his nose. "ew. no. tea is much better. *yorkshire* tea."

zayn made fake gagging noises, and niall and liam rolled their eyes in unison, an action that made harry laugh a bit. "i like both," he shrugged.

"good." louis glared hardly at the three other boys. "those twats don't know anything."

"hey! i'm your best friend!"

"used to be," louis corrected, and harry thought he was kidding until he saw the hurt look on liam's face.

the group of five were silent for a few moments, until, of course, niall broke it.

"what do you guys want to do today? we're all together right now."

harry stared at the ground, because he never had good ideas. he felt louis nudge his hand a bit, and his heart fluttered when the older boy intertwined their fingers. a blush immediately when across his cheeks, and he hoped the other three wouldn't notice.

liam, louis, and zayn immediately started shouting out suggestions to niall, who nodded and grinned like every idea was the one he agreed with.

"bowling!"

"swimming!"

"skydiving!"

and it went on for a minute or two, while harry just stood there, and the only thing he could think about was the fact that louis was *holding his hand.*

niall finally let out a loud scream, which harry thought sounded like a girl, and all the boys went silent.

"putt putting!"

while everyone cheered, millions of movie scenes and crazy ideas flooded harry's mind.

he could just imagine louis standing behind him, his arms wrapped around him and their hands over each other, and then louis would swing them gently and hit the ball.

and then harry was smiling foolishly and nodding his head, squeezing his sweaty hand tighter with louis'.

"sounds good."

***

they ended up stopping at mcdonalds, because zayn was complaining and niall was making odd moaning noises because he was hungry.

harry, who had just eaten a bowl of cereal, only ordered a chocolate chip cookie and a water.

louis, on the other hand, got a cheeseburger, fries, a coke, and then another order of fries.

"how can you eat all of that? didn't you just have breakfast?" the younger boy asked quietly, trying to avoid watching louis' lips as he took a sip of his coke.

"no, i didn't have breakfast, harold. i was too busy going to get you coffee and drowning in my exhaustion to eat."

harry nodded at the odd answer, smiling a bit and taking a bite of his cookie.

louis and he had ended up sitting at the end of the table, right across from each other.

liam seemed to be having more fun than ever, as him and niall really bonded well and zayn was crying he was laughing so hard.

"what do you think they're laughing about? people usually laugh at *me*." louis pointed to the other three, holding a fry up to his lips.

"niall probably farted or something," harry muttered, and he beamed when louis started laughing.

"probably," louis chuckled, shaking his head. "how about we act like we are laughing really hard?" then he rolled his eyes, as if he said something wrong. "take that back. i'll make you laugh really hard. i like your laugh."

harry shook his head quickly, because he hated his laugh.

but louis just nodded, a smile creeping onto his face. "do you think cheesy pick-up lines are funny?"

harry shrugged, blushing at the way louis was staring at his face.

"okay, get ready." louis paused, looking up in the sky and biting his lip, an action that made harry squirm.

"are you a burger? because you can be the meat between my buns."

and then harry burst out laughing, covering his mouth and putting his head down, and louis was laughing with him, a loud beautiful laugh that was quite unique.

harry loved louis' laugh.

niall, liam, and zayn all looked over with curious faces, confused smiles on their faces.

"mind your business," louis said with a wave of his hand, before putting his face closer to harry's. "i have another one."

"what is it?" harry grinned, and he was holding his cookie so tightly that it crumbled in his hand. he frowned, brushing them into a napkin before meeting eyes with a smirking louis.

"we're having a penis-measuring contest over there. do you have a yardstick that we could borrow?" to add to it, louis gestured over to a group of old men that were all chewing on their hamburgers wordlessly.

harry didn't think he could laugh any harder.

he laughed so hard in fact, that there were tears coming out of his eyes and his stomach felt like it was going to explode.

and louis was gasping for air, but he could still say another one.

"my name is louis." he paused. "remember that, you'll be screaming it later."

harry didn't think he could take anymore, especially when the rest of the group scooted over and begged to know what they were talking about.

louis, obviously not wanting them to hear, got up from the table and put his lips unbearably close to harry's ear.

he giggled a bit before talking. "if you and i were the last men on earth, i bet we could do it in public." his voice was a low, husky whisper, a noise that caused harry's heart to stop for a few seconds.

and when louis and harry started to roll on the floor with laughter, niall finally spoke up.

"let's go putt putting, yeah?"

harry blushed and got up, his hands literally shaking because he was so happy and buzzed.

***

the putt course wasn't very far away, so the drive was quite short.

"i still want to know what they were talking about," zayn grumbled as louis went up and paid so they could have their putters and golf balls.

harry just shrugged. he loved hearing the lines, but he would never say them himself. and he liked having an inside joke with louis. it felt nice.

they were halfway through the course when it happened. louis was in the lead, harry was in fourth, and zayn was falling behind in last. niall, although in third place, acted like he was winning.

harry didn't want to be upset, because it was just a game and they were playing for fun, but he was embarrassed that it took him so long just to hit a ball into a hole.

he couldn't help but groan in frustration when he hit the ball for the fifth time, and it rolled to the place where he had started.

"that's it! i can't take it anymore!" louis cried, jogging from where he was waiting at the next hole and standing behind harry. "i'll help you." his voice was now soft, as if he was telling a secret he only wanted the younger boy to hear.

harry held in a smile while louis did exactly what he had imagined. he draped his arms over harry's, then placed his hands on top of his.

then he swung their arms and the contact made a small click and harry watched as the ball rolled incredibly close to the hole.

"so close!" louis moaned and harry could feel blood rushing to between his legs because that *noise*.

"do you think you can handle this one?" louis asked quietly, and harry nodded bashfully.

he walked towards the ball and lightly tapped it, smiling widely when it plunked into the hole.

"good job."

harry looked up to see louis giving him his sunshine smile that he only saw sometimes, and the rarity of it made it much more beautiful and wonderful.

***

"two more holes, and you guys can't beat me! that means i win!" louis screamed, and it echoed into the warm air of the afternoon.

while zayn, niall, and liam grumbled, harry watched him fondly with a weird feeling in his heart.

and it was all going perfectly until harry clumsily tripped and knocked into louis the minute the older boy had swung backwards to hit.

"what the heck was that?" he cried, and harry's eyes widened as he stepped back.

"i didn't mean to, i-"

"don't give me that 'i didn't mean to' crap. how would you feel if i shoved you?"

and then louis placed his hands against harry's chest and pushed him backwards, so hard that the curly boy landed on his butt in the middle of the grass. he watched through tear filled eyes as liam rushed over to louis and started yelling at him.

zayn and niall rushed over to harry. niall looked mad while zayn looked sympathetic and sorry.

"it was all going so well for you guys," zayn said sadly, helping harry up, and niall just shook his head.

"i hate my brother sometimes," he growled, glaring at louis before pulling harry into a hug. "it's okay. he's not worth it."

harry just shook his head, biting his lip. he was trying not to cry too hard, but a few tears had to slip past and slide hotly down his cheek, leaving a burning trail in its path.

he looked over niall's shoulder to see louis, tugging his hair with both hands as liam talked calmly with him. and his heart hurt a bit when they met eyes, and louis was crying.

"i'm sorry," he mouthed, and harry didn't say anything, just pulled back from niall and averted his eyes to the ground.

niall immediately stood in front of the younger boy when louis started to walk towards him.

"niall, i won't hurt him, i swear."

"how can i believe that?" niall looked extremely angry.

"i didn't mean to. i just get mad like that sometimes and-"

"that's no excuse louis. this is your last freaking chance, and if you hurt him one more time, i won't let you speak to him ever again."

"you can't do that!" louis shouted, throwing his putter on the ground. "i can't control it!"

"just take your medicine," harry mumbled from behind niall, wiping away his tears with his fingers.

louis' face changed drastically, a sad look that was worse than the mad one.

"harry, you know i can't."

they were stepping closer to each other with every word and harry forgot that the other three were there.

"please. i know you're not meaning to hurt me," harry whispered, now so close that their feet were touching.

louis reached his hand down and took harry's, a gentle touch that made harry's heart race.

"i'm not. i like you a lot harry."

"then prove it. don't act like i'm out to get you all the time. we both know you didn't mean to shove me."

both of them looked surprise that harry was speaking so much.

"okay. i promise i won't hurt you again. and if i do, i'll take my medicine."

"don't promise that louis, i know you'll break it," harry sighed, holding onto louis' hand tighter.

louis look intensely into harry's eyes, and harry squirmed nervously.

"fine. but if i do, i promise to take my medicine. i *can* keep that promise."

harry nodded, and was completely caught off guard when louis leaned forward and pressed his lips into the younger boy's.

it was a warm, gentle kiss that felt amazing, especially with the cool breeze blowing on them and the way louis was holding his hand.

it had to end when liam cleared his throat.

and when harry pulled back, louis just reached out and caressed his cheek.

"you remind me of a twinkie. every time i bite into you, you cream in my mouth."

and then they were laughing all over again.

fourteen

confidence isn't something you just have.

even the most beautiful of people can be insecure about themselves, although beauty is known to radiate happiness and courage.

confidence is all about how you feel, not what you look like.

and harry was the exact opposite of that.

every time he looked at himself in the mirror, he wanted to take a straightener to his unruly, stubborn curls.

he wanted his eyes to look like louis'; blue and beautiful and sparkly.

his lips looked like a girls, which he didn't like at all.

and his nose was too big.

but no, that wasn't the only thing that lowered his confidence.

if he was in a large group, he felt so incredibly small. like every person in there could crush him with one word. he felt as if everyone secretly hated how quiet he was, how thoughtful and shy he was.

he could practically hear their thoughts, telling him that he's a crybaby and he's too sensitive.

and yeah, he had started off high school with two amazing best friends, the greatest, most caring best friends you could ever ask for, but when he walked through the hallways on the first day, he thought he was going to cry.

until he saw louis tomlinson.

then, it wasn't about him. it wasn't about his insecurities and awkwardness and clumsiness. it was about louis. louis and his sunshine smile and his baggy sweatpants and long, shaggy hair. and his plaid boots that harry happened to own the same pair of and his loud laugh that he could hear from a mile away.

so his confidence, although low, didn't seem to matter much until niall and zayn became more popular and started forgetting harry, even though they slept over together every friday they talked about people that harry dreamed to be.

harry, being watchful and thoughtful, noticed how niall started bleaching his hair blonde and how he started to dress more like the popular kids. he saw how zayn styled his hair into a quiff and began to say phrases that didn't even sound like himself.

he noticed how they went to large high school parties that harry only saw through pictures on twitter.

but he didn't say anything. his confidence just went down, lower and lower, until the day he started talking to louis for real.

the fact that louis actually took time out of his wonderful life to speak to harry was unbelievable.

and that made harry feel just a little bit better.

and for a week, there was a smile on his face more than half the time, which was quite different than usual. he felt like he had laughed more that week than he had in a whole year.

but the best moment, the biggest burst of confidence, was when they walked into school on monday morning.

louis and liam were on his left, with louis with a hand on his waist. niall and zayn were on the right, and he couldn't help but smile, because he, awkward weird quiet harry, was in the middle.

and louis was touching him.

zayn had volunteered to drive all of them to school when they had finally left the putt putt course. harry was very eager to agree, as was the rest of the boys.

so harry felt like he was on mean girls, strutting down the hallway in the black skinnies and white t-shirt that zayn had let him borrow again, and a beanie upon his curls. louis and he were almost matching, except for the fact louis was wearing his usual tank top, but their beanies were the same color and louis was the one that had styled his hair.

everyone in the hallway either stared at them or did a double take when they saw the group of five, and harry just blushed and looked at the ground, especially when louis tightened his arm around the younger boy's waist.

niall and zayn seemed oblivious, laughing and joking around as if they weren't being stared at. liam just looked ahead with a small smile on his newly shaven face.

but all harry could do was first look at louis' hand on his right hip, and then lift his head and stare with wide eyes at louis, at his calm, relaxed face and his vibrant blue eyes that were framed by coal black lashes.

liam was the first to leave the group, and then louis. and then it was like old times. harry, zayn, and niall.

harry's confidence immediately crashed.

because that's what louis did. you couldn't help but feel proud and confident when there was a beaming, adorable, popular, and unbelievably beautiful boy standing next to you.

***

harry was brought back to primary school the minute he walked into the lunchroom.

niall was the only one out of harry's four friends that didn't have the same lunch as him. so it was only liam, zayn, and louis sitting together.

he had brought his own lunch. it was his usual peanut butter and jelly sandwich with a bag of baked lays chips, along with a mountain dew he bought from the vending machine every day.

he had just gotten halfway to the blue lunch table in the middle of the lunchroom in which is friends were sitting at when he felt something bump into him hardly.

it was stan lucas.

harry knew quite a bit about stan lucas.

he knew that him and louis used to be best friends when they all went to primary school. he knew that stan was probably the biggest jerk at their school and he was a sad boy on the inside but let out his feelings by hurting others.

it wasn't easy for harry to figure that out. it took a lot of staring during lunch and passing periods, and lots of thinking.

and now stan lucas was standing right in front of him, with an annoyed look on his face and his hands clenched in fists.

and all harry could do was shake and stare at the ground, scared out of his mind. stan *punched* people. stan *hit* people.

"where do you think you're going?" the older boy asked, and harry flinched when he felt stan grab his arm.

"i'm going to eat lunch," he whispered, quieter than he had been in a while.

"yeah. i know that you retarded dolt. *where* are you eating lunch?"

"at a lunch table," he replied, confused and fearful.

"don't be smart with me." stan leaned in closer, so close that harry could feel his hot breath hitting his face. "*who* are you sitting with?"

"zayn, liam, lou-"

"louis? really?"

the curly haired boy nodded.

"why? he doesn't even like you. in fact, he told me that he thinks you're weird and mental and that you freak him out."

harry didn't want to believe it. but he could imagine louis saying it, and that's what hurt the worst.

it hurt so bad that he actually had to step back and drop his lunch, wrapping his arms around himself as he felt his lips tremble.

"i freak louis out?" he whispered to himself, squeezing himself tighter and tighter and he couldn't breathe.

"i see why he said it. look at you. you're a freak."

harry could feel it taking over. he could feel the blood rushing through his veins and the quivering of his legs.

"i'm a freak, i'm a freak." he squeezed his eyes shut, blocking out stan's rude comments and the curious stares of nearby classmates.

it seemed as if stan could hear what harry was repeating, as he started saying it with him.

"you're a freak, you're a freak, you're a freak." he was laughing now, a horrible sound that gave harry a headache.

his eyes hurt and his legs were going numb, and he couldn't feel anything.

stan kept doing it, he wouldn't stop, and harry just had to scream. he screamed so loudly that everybody in the lunchroom stopped talking and watched him. he couldn't see them, but their stares were practically burning holes in his head.

he started shaking harder when he heard zayn and louis' voices.

"i know what to do, okay?" it was zayn.

"no. i do. let me do it, okay? i've done this before!" louis voice wasn't so sweet anymore. harry didn't want to hear it, after what he had said.

then there was silence and harry let out a whimper when he felt arms wrap around him. they were warm and they were soft, but there wasn't any fabric, which meant they weren't wearing sleeves.

then harry could smell that musky, beautiful scent that he used to love but now it hurt his head.

"go away," he breathed, squirming in louis' arms and opening his eyes. "go away!"

his voice sounded so loud in the silent room, it echoed, and he was so embarrassed and scared and he didn't know what to do as he looked around.

their wide eyes, some filled with sorrow and some even scared, made his heart hurt worse than before.

"get off of him!" zayn yelled, and then louis was being yanked away from harry and never had the curly lad been more thankful for his best friend.

"i'll hold you, baby, i'll hold you. just go to sleep."

zayn's voice was more comforting than louis' had been, because louis thought he was a freak and he didn't like it.

zayn's arms weren't' as warm and tight around him as louis' had been, but it was okay because he wasn't mad at zayn.

it took him longer to fall asleep, but he finally did when zayn carried him out of the lunchroom, and he could hear louis following them, but he didn't think about that.

he just cried silently, because his stomach was hurting and he couldn't breathe.

his sleep wasn't that peaceful, but it was sleep.

***

he woke up in a room that smelled like new shoes and hand sanitizer.

he scrunched up his nose and opened his eyes, to a bright light that was hovering above his head.

there was a curtain around the bed he was laying in, and when he saw the posters all over the walls he realized he was in the nurse's office.

he decided to just stay awake until someone noticed, and about five minutes later, the curtain was pulled back and in walked the nurse.

she was dressed in a blue shirt with khaki pants, along with a lab coat that harry knew she didn't actually need.

"hi harry. how are you feeling?"

the curly haired lad shrugged, because he couldn't remember anything.

the only thing he could think of was that louis thought he was a freak.

louis tomlinson, the person he loved the most in this world, thought he was a freak.

and that hurt.

"are you tired, hun? you can stay in here until you're feeling better."

he shrugged again, not really knowing what to say.

"do you want me to get your friend zayn?"

he nodded, pulling his legs to his chest and picking on the loose thread by his ankle.

"harry?"

harry lifted his head and shook his curls out of his face.

"hi zayn," he said quietly, looking back at his shoes with a frown.

"hi h. how you feeling?"

"i've already been asked that," he sighed. "i don't know."

"louis wants to talk to you." zayn looked scared as he shuffled back and forth next to harry's bed.

the younger boy immediately shook his head, his long curls flying and his eyes wide open.

"no. no i will not speak to him. he hates me anyway." he mumbled the last part, but zayn could obviously hear him.

"no he doesn't! why would you say that?"

"he said i was a freak and that i was annoying and weird," harry whispered.

"did stan tell you that?"

harry nodded.

"well, don't listen to him, he's-"

"hi harold."

and then harry was blushing and he didn't know what to do because louis was standing in the doorway. but now he was holding harry's lunchbox and his hair was messed up, as if he had run his hands through it a lot.

he didn't respond to louis, even when he repeated himself and sat on the edge of his bed.

"love, i know you can hear me. you're sitting right there, and you look like you've seen a dying cow."

harry tried not to smile, but louis was too funny and adorable and he had to.

"please don't speak to me."

he wanted to sound mean, but his laughing betrayed him.

louis didn't seem very happy though, as there were tears welling up in his eyes.

"harry, i don't know what i did wrong, but i am so sorry, i-"

"i know i'm a freak. but the least you can do is tell me to my face."

harry rose from the bed and walked out of the room, just as louis had opened his mouth to respond.

but honestly, he didn't care what louis had to say.

fifteen

harry checked his big silver watch on his pale wrist, watching it tick slowly by the three. that meant school was almost over.

words couldn't describe how frustrated he was. his whole schedule was messed up and there was anger bubbling on the surface and ready to burst, so much that he would have another episode, except much worse.

he cringed when the bell rang, walking as fast as possible to his locker and ignoring the looks and comments from his classmates.

"do you need a ride home?"

harry lifted his head to see niall and was surprised that his eyes were rimmed red and there was a bruise on his cheek.

"niall," harry gasped quietly, reaching his large hand out and putting it on the blonde boy's cheek, who flinched away.

"ow, harry," he laughed flatly, gently pushing harry's hand out of the way. "still tender."

the curly haired lad blushed, shutting his locker softly and squinting to see niall's bruise closer. "what happened?"

"nothing," niall dismissed, wrapping an arm around harry. "i just fell."

"he's not going to believe that."

harry immediately froze, his feet stopping and his books almost falling out of his hands. his heart was beating unbelievably fast and he just wanted louis to *go away.*

niall whipped around, causing harry to trip from how they unlinked their arms, and fall painfully on his bum in the middle of the hallway.

louis gave him worried eyes and stepped forward, offering a small delicate hand and a shaky smile.

harry glared at his hands and instead let niall help him up.

the look on louis' face was unreadable, but it wasn't good.

"tell him the truth niall," louis said, his voice cracking.

"he doesn't want to hear it," niall said quietly, and harry's eyes widened.

"of course i want to hear it," he argued.

"stan.. he punched me in the face. but it was my fault! i pushed him first because he was being a dick."

harry tried not to laugh but when that word came out of niall's adorable mouth it was impossible.

he could see louis smiling at him, a fond sunshine smile that used to make him melt but now just hurt, and he tried his best to avoid louis' pale blue eyes.

and niall looked between the two of them, confused at the tension. "did something happen between you two?"

"he thinks i'm a freak," harry whispered, so quietly that he was surprised he could even hear himself. "i freak him out."

niall's face immediately changed and he stepped in front of harry.

"harry isn't a freak," he growled, and louis' eyes widened.

"i never said that!"

there was a group gathering around them, even though some of the people probably had a bus to catch that they were missing.

and all harry could do was cover his red face with shaky hands, wishing they could leave him alone for once because this was so *hard,* and he couldn't handle it.

"make it stop, make it stop," he muttered, blocking out niall and louis' voices as they got louder and louder.

and when niall started to look at harry, he broke down. he let his knees buckle as he fell on the dusty floor of the hallway, listening to his new boots squeak.

"harry," niall mumbled, but then it was louis holding him, his small hands splayed out across the younger boy's back and his nose buried in his neck.

"don't touch him!" niall yelled, and the muffles surrounding them got louder and louder, until eleanor's voice stuck out.

"everybody freaking leave right now or i'm personally putting tampons up every single one of your nose holes."

and harry's blurry was vision from tears and all he could smell was louis, but he was laughing, and it hurt his stomach especially when louis stood up slowly, one of his arms under harry's knees and another around his waist tightly.

niall let out a sigh of defeat. "all you do is hurt him, and you expect him to just love you."

louis stopped and harry knew because now he was aware of louis' steady breathing instead of the soft, soothing footsteps they were taking earlier.

"that's because i love him back."

it was a small, weak whisper, and that's what made harry's heart break the most but at the same time it fluttered in his chest.

he repeated those words over and over in his head like a soothing classical song until he fell asleep, his cheek laying against louis' chest as the older boy carried him out of the school.

***

harry woke up in a moving car, because of the gentle bumps turned into a big bump.

"where am i?" he yawned, sitting up in the very soft leather and blinking the bleariness out of his tired eyes.

"you said you would go on a date with me."

harry whipped his head to the right and looked to see louis in the driver's seat, a smug smile on his wonderful face.

"i said that a long time ago," he mumbled nervously, his cheeks burning. "before i knew how much you hated me."

"dang it harry!" louis shouted, banging his hands on the steering wheel and causing them to swerve a bit. "i don't hate you! stop saying that!"

harry jumped, biting his lip and ignoring the throbbing of his heart.

"i wish you would stop believing everything anybody ever tells you; it's really freaking annoying! like literally, stan tells you i think you're a freak, and you just assume he's right! you don't even know half the story. you don't know.." he trailed off.

"i don't know what?" harry whispered, his bottom lip trembling as he felt his eyes blur from the wetness gathering.

"where do you wanna go on the date?"

"don't change the subject!" harry yelled, his voice incredibly loud in the small car, and both of the boys jumped.

louis looked at him with wide eyes before turning back to the road. "your voice sounds sexy like that."

and harry was mad, fuming mad in fact, but there was blood rushing to his cheeks and between his legs and he was so flustered that he couldn't speak.

"do you like rollercoasters?"

then there was full blown smile on both their faces, and they were grinning at each other foolishly and harry was trying to frown but louis' crinkly eyes and his perfect teeth were too contagious.

so he just nodded and bit his lip, and he could feel his dimple prominent on his face.

***

"it's not crowded at all. aren't you excited harold?"

harry shrugged, nervously eyeing the many twisting roller coasters that were caged by a large barb wire fence.

"don't worry. it's just carts rolling on steel. nothing too scary."

harry took in a shaky breath, flinching away when louis tried to grab his hand.

louis blinked a bit, before giving harry an awkward smile that seemed so incredibly fake, and then they walked up to the entrance and louis paid for both their tickets.

"i'll pay you back," harry offered quietly, sticking his hands in the pockets of his black skinny jeans. louis shook his head silently. it was slightly breezy out, and it blew through his curly hair gently, along with louis'. they walked in silence to the first rollercoaster, a blue one that had tons of loops and was upside down.

"this one first?" harry asked nervously, looking down at louis, who laughed.

"yep," was all he replied.

and then they were walking through the empty queue lines, louis cheering and saying random stuff and harry trying to calm his nerves.

the employee had a bored face as he buckled them side by side on the coaster, and he continued to stare at them tiredly as he sent them off.

"oh my gosh we're upside down we're-" louis began, before he turned to look at harry. there was already blood rushing to his face, bringing a glowing pink to his cheeks, and his hair was suspended in the air. "harry," he whispered.

harry looked at louis, completely embarrassed at their position. "what?" he licked his lips nervously.

"you have no idea how beautiful you are, do you?"

harry would've blushed but all the blood was already in his cheeks, so he just averted his eyes to where louis' hands were clinging tightly to the handlebars as they rose up the hill.

"curly," louis giggled, and then he unlatched one of his hands from the blue handles before reaching out and tugging gently on one of harry's crazy curls that were hanging all over the place.

"i'm losing oxygen," harry breathed dramatically, which caused louis to burst out laughing.

"ow, ow that hurts. don't laugh," louis gasped, and they were finally relieved when they were falling down the hill quickly and they turned right side up for a few seconds.

harry couldn't help but scream, but for once his scream wasn't a terrified, sad scream. he was rushed with adrenaline and butterflies and *louis* and he felt like he could finally breathe.

"i love roller coasters," he whispered, but louis couldn't hear them because the wind blowing in their ears and the extremely high pitched screeches coming from the older boy.

after a couple more loops the ride was slowing down and the boys were turned right side up and harry was breathless because now they were both laughing like drunk, foolish teenagers and louis was holding his hand.

***

"the last one!" louis exclaimed, sticking his hands out and gesturing to a large coaster with an extremely tall, steep hill, and harry watched as the train shot off the beginning very, very fast.

"i'm scared," harry whimpered embarrassingly, flinching as a person brushed past him.

there weren't very many people there at all, which louis thought was great and harry thought was odd.

"don't be scared, harold. you'll be fine."

what he said was proved wrong when someone came out of the exit and puked all over the concrete, followed by a crying little girl.

"i can't do this."

although harry had grown to love coasters, this one was too hardcore for his first day riding them.

"ride the freaking coaster!" louis shouted and harry was scared that he was changing moods but then he smiled with all of his teeth and nudged his shoulder into the younger boy's, proving him wrong.

when harry didn't answer, louis leaned in closer, so close that harry could feel his warm breath on his lips.

"okay?"

"okay."

then they were getting strapped in and harry was hyperventilating and trying not to scare the few people sitting behind him and in front of him.

"baby breathe."

when louis said that, it just made it worse and now he *really* couldn't breathe because he called him baby.

"i'll try," he squeaked, his knuckles white as he clutched tightly on the lap bar pressing against his legs.

harry looked nervously at the countdown clock next to them.

5..

4...

3....

2....

1....

and then harry was faintly aware of louis screaming and pulling harry in, so close, and then they were done and all he could feel was his windblown hair in his eyes and the blood rushing through his veins and louis' mouth wrapping around his.

sixteen

it wasn't until harry stumbled into his house when he realized his mistake.

yeah, it had been wonderful. after they had gotten off the roller coaster they each had a piece of pizza and ice cream.

and when they finally got home, exhausted from a whole school day and a trip to the amusement park yet buzzed at the same time, louis had threaded his fingers through harry's messy curls and smiled softly. then he pushed his forehead into harry's for a moment before pressing their lips together gently.

"bye harold," louis whispered. "my quiet, shy, curly harry."

and all harry could do was nod and blush, and he had practically fallen through the front door after louis kissed him once more.

it was when he could finally breathe again, and louis had driven away when he remembered his problem.

louis now had to fulfill his promise and harry forgot to tell him.

of course he did.

whenever harry was with louis his mind became clouded with butterflies and hearts and he felt so in love and half of his words didn't make sense, so harry wasn't surprised that he forgot to tell louis that he had to take his medication now. louis had yelled at him again in the car, and it hurt. but harry, being harry, let it go.

so he let out a groan and ran a hand through his curls that louis had been touching before walking past the kitchen and into his room.

it was spotless, like always, and his bed looked unbelievably perfect. his legs were shaky from walking so much and his head was throbbing from all the new information he had processed in one day.

so he plopped onto the soft mattress and closed his eyes, listening to the soothing sound of the ceiling fan spinning around and the hum of the air conditioner.

his mum had written a note on the fridge that she would be gone until eleven that night, so harry had the house to himself.

he jumped when his phone rang, pulling it out of his pocket and holding it to his ear.

"hello?"

"hi harry."

"hi zayn," the curly haired lad sighed, trying to hold in a yawn as he leaned against the headboard of his bed.

"are you busy on friday?"

"i'm going to niall's house, duh," harry said, confused.

"oh." zayn paused. "do you mind skipping?"

harry shrugged before he realized zayn couldn't see him. "does niall care?"

"he's going out with louis, jay, and bobby. apparently bobby got promoted and they need a celebration dinner."

"oh."

"yeah. so i was wondering if you wanted to hang out. go bowling or something. perrie's coming."

harry loved zayn, but third wheeling did not sound fun.

"nah. how about you and perrie go alone?" harry yawned, his eyes hooded as he relaxed further into his pillow.

"are you sure? do you just wanna stay home alone?"

"yeah, it's fine," he sighed. "see you later, zayn."

"bye h. you sound tired, go to sleep."

all harry could do was nod and hang up, plugging his phone in the charger and taking his clothes off, folding them and putting them away before cuddling up underneath his blankets.

a few minutes later, he was sleeping, louis tomlinson on his mind.

***

the wait to friday was unbearably slow. louis didn't talk to him more, just sometimes gave him a small smile as they passed in the hallway or ruffled his curls when they saw each other at lunch.

it wasn't until friday that harry gathered up enough courage to tell louis about what he promised when they went putt putting.

it was at lunchtime, and harry reluctantly sat down next to louis, holding his lunch box and mountain dew. his hair kept falling into his eyes, as if reminding him that he needed a haircut soon. louis looked surprised at the younger boy, yet he still moved his lunch over a bit so harry could put his down. they were both quiet for a few seconds, before louis spoke. "hi." and he looked into harry's eyes with his bright blue ones and gave him the sunshine smile and wrapped a small arm around harry's thin waist.

"hi," harry whispered.

louis tightened his grip, causing fireworks to explode in harry's stomach. he blinked quickly and unwrapped his peanut butter and jelly sandwich, taking a small bite and chewing quietly.

"why did you decide to sit by me today harold? not that i mind, i'm just wondering."

harry glanced around at the table. there were all the popular kids sitting there, too caught up in their own conversations to actual listen to the two boys, which harry was grateful for.

"i wanted to make sure you kept your promise," harry said quietly, listening to the pop and hiss as he opened his mountain dew.

louis looked a bit confused for a moment, before realization washed over his features and he frowned.

"did i hurt you at all?" he didn't sound mad, just a little sad and scared.

harry didn't want to speak, his hands were shaking, and he had to put down his mountain dew so it wouldn't spill everywhere.

"you yelled at me in the car," he whispered, gauging louis' reaction.

"oh," louis sighed, putting his head in his hands before spreading his fingers and peeking at louis. "i'm sorry."

the younger boy nodded nervously, hoping that louis wouldn't get too mad at him. "you have to take your medication now. you promised."

louis' eyes widened and harry flinched as he squeezed his waist unbelievably tight.

"ow, that hurts," he whimpered, looking at louis' knuckles turn white from where they were wrapped around his hip.

but louis didn't let go, just squeezed harder and harder until harry could barely breathe and he was cringing in pain and begging for louis to stop.

"louis, stop," harry breathed, tears gathering in his eyes. "please stop, it hurts." louis turned his head to look at the younger boy, and harry closed his eyes as a few droplets rolled down his cheeks.

louis finally released his death grip, and harry shot up out of his chair, grabbing his lunch and throwing it in the trash can.

"harry, oh my god i'm so sorry," louis whispered, reaching his hand out to the crying boy. "harry, i hurt you again, god what is wrong with me?" he groaned, pushing a hand through his hair, and harry stood there next to the table, feeling stares on him.

"i'm so messed up, i don't deserve you, just please, i'm so sorry," louis whimpered, and then he started pushing on his wrists with his thumbs.

harry's eyes widened and he looked closer to see the many bracelets on louis' wrists, and then a red mark underneath. where louis had hurt himself.

"louis, stop!" harry screamed, his heart throbbing in pain as louis continued to push on his cuts, tears appearing in his eyes and his lips trembling. harry watched as liam got up from the table, because he was sitting on the end talking to a group of girls who harry didn't know the names of.

"louis, louis, louis stop. louis stop. louis stop. louis stop," harry repeated, sitting back down and trying to pull louis' hands off of his wrists.

"harry, go away."

harry didn't listen, even though his mind was screaming at him to do as he was told because that's what he always did.

"harry, i'll handle this." harry lifted his head to see liam standing there, a concerned and sad look on his face. "just go talk to zayn. i've got this."

"no, he's hurting himself. make him stop," harry's breath caught as he struggled not to cry to hard, and he squeezed his eyes shut because he didn't like this.

"okay harry. i'll make him stop," liam comforted, and harry watched as liam leaned down and whispered something in louis' ear, and then he reached over and pulled louis' hands apart like it was nothing.

and then there were hands wrapped around harry, pulling him away from louis and liam, and he didn't scream because he wanted to go, he didn't want to watch this.

"c'mere, come with me," zayn said softly, and harry followed him to their table, where he sat numbly.

after a few minutes, when the commotion had died down and everyone had resumed eating, harry finally let himself look at louis.

he was sitting there, staring straight ahead as liam spoke to him. his eyes were rimmed red, and the other people at his table were looking at him curiously.

harry could still see the ugly, red cuts on louis' wrists.

"harry?" zayn asked hesitantly, after taking a sip of his bottled water.

"if louis hurts himself, that hurts me too," harry whispered, wiping away the tears that still weren't leaving. "i want him to stop."

"i know you do," zayn said gently, reaching across the table and placing his warm hand on top of harry's. "he will."

"you don't know that."

zayn didn't respond, and the two of them sat there in silence, and harry's stomach growled because he had thrown away his lunch, but it was good. because if louis didn't feel good, if louis wasn't happy, then he wasn't either.

***

zayn and perrie sat in the front seat when they had driven harry home, and zayn looked very worried when he dropped the curly haired boy off.

"be careful harry," zayn called after him as harry walked silently into his quiet house. he could see his mum was home because her purse sitting on the table and the lights on in the kitchen.

he missed his mum, and he loved her, but he could barely speak at the moment.

so he just sat down on the living room couch, flicking the tv on and flipping through the channels. nothing good was on, but that didn't matter. he was too upset to actually pay attention to the show anyway. so he just faintly watched cartoons while millions of thoughts swam through his mind.

this was the first friday night since he met zayn and niall that he was spending friday night alone, and it wasn't fun. he could hear his mum in the kitchen talking on the phone and the loud voices of the cartoon characters on the tv, but it still felt like it was silent.

it was when he ran over the lunchroom scene over in his mind for the hundredth time that he finally got up off the couch and walked quietly to his room. there was a bathroom attached, where he immediately went.

the only thing on his mind when he broke his razor on the bathroom sink and picked up one of the sharp blades was louis' wrist, hidden by bracelets.

and just as he had hesitantly put the edge of the blade on his pale, clean wrist, he heard a voice come from the hallway.

"harry, i'm home!"

he dropped the blade, his eyes wide in fear and his hands shaking.

"gemma," he whispered.

he kicked the blade, so it was hidden behind the toilet, and let his trembling legs lead him to where gemma was in her room, plopping her suitcase on her bed.

"hi gemma," he said quietly from her doorway with a soft smile, his hands hanging awkwardly at his sides. he hoped she wouldn't notice his watery eyes.

"harry!" she whipped around with a bright, beautiful smile, and it reminded harry how much he missed her.

and when she rushed towards him and pulled him in for a warm, tight hug, harry couldn't help but burst into tears.

"harry, sweetums, what's wrong?" gemma pulled back and looked at harry, who was choking on his tears. hugs were the worst things when was upset.

"i just missed you," harry said. he wasn't lying. he did miss her, and that was part of the reason he was crying. the other part was louis, but he wasn't going to tell her that.

"oh, harry, i missed you too. mum called a week ago and asked if i could come down this weekend, and i said of course! i want to see you! how are you holding up?"

harry just shrugged, sniffing and trying to stop crying.

"well, we'll talk about it over dinner. we're going for dinner, just me and you."

"what about mum?" harry cringed as his voice cracked.

"she's working in an hour." gemma paused. "is she overworking herself?"

harry nodded, biting his lip and wishing that his mum could be home more.

"well, i'm going to have a talk with her. now go get ready."

harry was about to say that he was ready, when he looked at his outfit. he wasn't dressed very nice. grey sweatpants, a baggy football shirt he had stolen from niall, and his black converse.

so he just nodded and trudged to his room, his wrist burning from where the razor had almost cut him.

and seeing it there, laying behind the toilet, was tempting, but he ignored it as he ran a brush through his curls and brushed his teeth.

he decided to wear a white shirt with a blue flannel over it and black skinny jeans, with his pair of boots that were already fading.

and when he walked out, gemma's eyes widened. "you look different! you always dress like that?"

harry shrugged. "sometimes," he mumbled, and she gave him a smile.

"let's go."

***

she took him to olive garden, which she knew was harry's favorite restaurant.

"when did you get so much money gems?" harry teased, and she rolled her eyes.

"i'm the best waitress where i live. people tip me all the time," she giggled.

gemma had three jobs, which showed how hard she worked to pay for her college. their mum was helping, but she paid for most of it.

the waiter sat them down at their table and harry ordered a water because he didn't want gemma to pay for his soda.

gemma got a water too, and after their drinks arrived and they decided on what they were going to eat gemma finally brought up a conversation.

"how's school been going?"

"okay," harry whispered. "i like someone."

he was surprised that he was already telling her this, but she always used to talk to him when they were little about the crushes she had, so he knew she wouldn't make fun of him.

and after they had gotten over talking about how perfect louis' looked and how he was so funny, they moved on to the rough stuff.

harry was very reluctant to tell her that he had borderline personality disorder, but he did. and she kept asking questions, and it felt nice that someone actually cared enough to listen to his problems.

their conversation paused when harry's spaghetti and gemma's ravioli arrived.

and when the waiter left gemma went on a long rant about what harry should do and harry only half listened because what she said was exactly what he had been thinking, but he was too upset to think about it much longer.

when gemma finished, harry decided to turn the conversation on her, and she began to talk about college and her new boyfriend and harry just ate his spaghetti and listened to her voice because he missed her so much.

but no matter how much gemma talked about herself, harry couldn't stop thinking about louis.

seventeen

niall had called and told zayn and harry that they would have their usual sleepover on saturday instead, and both boys agreed happily.

harry was planning on telling his two friends what gemma had told him to do.

although it hurt, it hurt so bad, he had to do it.

"i totally agree. he deserves to be treated like crap for once," niall scoffed, and harry, although upset, let his friend say that.

but zayn didn't. "niall, he treats *himself* like crap every day. i don't like this. have you seen his wrists?"

harry couldn't help but hold his breath and bite his tongue, because thinking of the way that louis had pushed on the cuts on his wrists and grimaced in pain would always be too much for him.

"harry are you okay?" it was niall, climbing off of his bed and going to the floor where harry was sitting crisscross in big red t-shirt and baggy grey sweatpants.

harry just shrugged, squeezing his eyes shut so the tears wouldn't fall past onto his pale cheeks.

"you don't have to do this, actually i'd prefer if you didn't. louis doesn't like being ignored."

and the three sat in silence, consumed by their own thoughts. well, harry just watched his friends.

they didn't seem to notice as he lifted his head and gauged each of their reactions before standing up, pulling his t-shirt farther down so that it was hanging past his knees.

and then he quietly walked out of niall's room and into the hallway, the cool, quiet hallway where he could finally hear his own thoughts. and he shut the door behind him, a tiny click.

"i didn't know you were here."

harry closed his eyes, just listening to the way louis' voice ended in a whispery tone, to how his footsteps sounded so small on the white carpet.

and he didn't respond. because that's what gemma said. ignore him until he realizes what he's been missing.

"harry?" louis said quietly and harry opened his eyes to look at louis. he was dressed in a soft sweatshirt with soft sweatpants and soft socks and he looked so *soft* that it hurt. he even had these glasses that were sitting upon his nose, and he looked so perfect.

but harry just bit his tongue, although for once he wanted to speak.

only louis made him *want* to speak.

so he just slid down the back of niall's door, feeling his eyelashes flutter against his skin as he struggled to close them.

maybe, if he couldn't see louis, it wouldn't hurt as bad.

but it was hard not to look when there was a soft, beautiful person standing close to you.

and when he finally had sat down and pulled the red shirt over his knees and rested his head against the door, focusing on his breaths instead of louis, the older boy finally spoke.

"harry, angel, stop that."

angel.

angel angel angel angel.

harry bit his lip, images of louis' wrists and his bright blue eyes flickering through his mind like a movie, a bittersweet movie.

and louis seemed surprise that he said that as well. he whispered it again to himself, a pretty sound that caused a tremor in harry's heart.

"angel," he whispered, raising his voice a little bit, and harry listened to the creak of the floor as he walked closer. "my angel."

harry opened his green eyes, and he could hear zayn and niall speaking through the door, but it was too muffled for him to hear anything. so he just looked at louis, who was now standing over him, and it was weird because louis was usually shorter than him and now he could see how beautiful louis' eyelashes really were and the way his sweatpants were really tight around his thighs and how small his feet were.

"why aren't you saying anything?"

gemma's voice echoed in his ear like she was still here.

"don't speak to him. don't speak until he apologises," she breathed, giving harry a comforting smile before putting her hand on the back of his head and leaning in, kissing his forehead so gently, so gently that harry could barely feel it.

"okay," harry said quietly, watching as gemma walked away to her car and gave one more wave before driving away.

and now her words didn't make so much sense anymore, when soft louis was standing in front of him with his purple socks and glasses that framed his pale blue eyes.

but niall told him that it was a good idea, so then he had to listen. well, he had to listen until louis apologised. or in gemma's word, fell to his knees begging for forgiveness.

for some reason, harry didn't think that could happen.

harry snapped out of his thoughts when he felt a warm, gentle touch on his wrist. he lifted his head and fully opened his eyes, although it was a bit dark in the hallway and he couldn't see much. all he could hear was him and louis' soft breaths and niall and zayn's murmurs from behind the door.

but louis was sitting on the floor next to him, his knees bent, and his feet tucked under his bum and his glasses slipping a bit on his nose.

"harry." louis' voice was light and airy, a teasing tone in it that caused harry to smile a tiny bit before forcing a frown again. "harold, curly!"

and harry was trying not to smile, he really was, but louis was lightly running his fingers up and down his wrist and he was nudging his nose into his cheek in a way that reminded the younger boy of a baby kitten.

"why don't you speak to me? are you mad at me? i'm sorry if it hurt you on friday. i couldn't think."

"you pushed on your cuts," harry whimpered, and louis pulled back a tiny bit, flickering his eyes over harry's face. "you tried to hurt yourself. and that hurts me too."

louis had a weird look on his face that harry couldn't place. he couldn't tell whether it was sadness or surprise or anger or *what*.

so he just stared back, watching the way louis held his lip between his teeth before releasing it, and how his eyes were slightly hooded, and his eyelashes were brushing the tips of his fringe.

"harry, i didn't think you knew that i-"

he stopped talking when harry wrapped his long fingers around louis', before pulling his wrists closer so that their hands were rested on harry's knee. and then he gently, carefully moved louis' bracelets down his arm so that they hit his elbow, and now louis' wrist was bare.

and the cuts looked even more ugly, and jagged, and swollen and red and painful.

harry could feel wetness gathering in his eyes and burning, and they rolled down his cheek and left a stinging path behind them.

"it hurts me," he whimpered, lightly touching the cuts with his thumb before holding louis' wrist up to his cheek.

louis was looking at harry with an intense look, tears pooling in his eyes, and harry watched as one finally slipped past.

"i tried to but gemma stopped me," harry whispered, showing louis the small mark that the imprint of the blade had left on his right wrist.

louis' mouth dropped open for a few seconds before he looked up at harry and started crying, really crying. "this is all my fault. please don't hurt yourself, just because i do. please don't do that to yourself. you mean so so much to me."

harry felt a weird aching in his heart and his stomach was churning and his breaths were uneven as he stared into louis' eyes longer than he ever had with anyone else.

"i won't if you won't."

it was like a quote harry had read when he was scrolling through twitter. *if you jump, i jump.*

"harry, i can't just stop, i can't-"

"yes, you can."

harry moved their hands and threaded their fingers together, a bold move that he was surprised he was making.

"i won't if you won't," harry repeated, and he jumped when the door pushed against his back painfully.

"dude, stop!" louis yelled, wrapping his arms around harry and pulling him away from the door. "harold is sitting there!"

"oh my god, i'm so sorry," niall giggled, before he realized that louis was still holding harry tightly to him and harry was just staring at the way louis' legs were intertwined with his.

"harry!" niall cried, a disappointed look flickering across his face. "did he apologise?"

"what?" louis asked, and harry blushed. "what do you mean 'did i apologise?'"

"he said that he wouldn't talk to you unless you apologised," zayn sighed, appearing behind the blonde boy in the doorway with his phone in his hand. "obviously you did."

"no he didn't," harry said quietly, embarrassed but still incredibly happy that louis and he were still laying on the white carpet of the hallway together.

"what? you just forgave him!?"

"i didn't do anything!" louis exclaimed and harry frowned.

yes you did, was what he wanted to say, but he didn't. niall did it for him.

"yeah, you actually did louis. harry doesn't realize that he needs to stop letting you do what you want, because you keep hurting him and i'm getting real freaking tired of it."

"yeah," zayn said weakly, locking his phone and pushing it in his pocket. "why don't you just say sorry?"

harry hesitantly climbed out of louis' arms and resumed his crisscross position on the floor, trying not to look to expectant when he looked at louis.

"harry, i.. this is so hard," he groaned, running a hand through his hair and closing his eyes. he paused for a few moments before speaking again. "i'm sorry? okay? i'm sorry and i care about you so much and you mean so much to me. just please don't ignore me. i can't take that."

"it hurts when you yell at me," harry whispered, wrapping his arms around himself as niall sat down next to him and pat his back.

"i'm sorry."

and they all looked at each other. well, harry didn't know what niall and zayn were doing but louis and he were looking at each other and everything felt a bit messed up.

"i think we need to go to bed now. i'm really tired and harry you look like you're about to fall asleep," zayn finally said, yawning and walking towards harry. harry didn't even move when zayn put his hands under his arms and lifted him up into the air.

"let me do it," louis said quietly, and zayn gave him a skeptical look, while at the same time niall groaned and walked into his room.

and then louis was putting his arms under harry's back and legs and lifting him up, and harry could barely keep his eyes open, so he just licked his lips a bit and leaned his head against louis' chest, his eyelashes fluttering as he finally let himself close his eyes and fall asleep to the steady walking of louis.

it wasn't until all he could hear was louis' soft voice in his ear when he realized that louis had carried him to the room down the hall, not niall's.

he was in louis' room.

eighteen

it was raining.

a pounding rain, the kind of rain that brushed across the window loudly and tapped on the roof. there was bright, blinding lightning that flashed through the windows and was followed by thunder that shook the house and made harry cringe where he was sleeping.

he was covered in a soft blanket, so soft that all he could do was rub the fabric against his cheek.

and it smelled amazing. a musky, warm scent that he couldn't stop smelling. so he just closed his eyes and breathed it in until he finally recognized it.

he stopped acting like a fool when he realized that he was in a room that wasn't familiar, but it was really dark so he couldn't tell.

where am i?

he jumped and his heart started pounding when he heard a whimper beside him, and it was so quiet that he couldn't place who it was.

at this point, he was starting to freak out because he was in a bed and he didn't know whose it was.

but then there was another round of thunder, a cracking noise that caused harry to cringe and cower beneath the soft blankets.

"make it stop," a whisper sounded, and the voice was so close to his ear and he found himself leaning into it because he knew that voice. that was louis.

"louis?" harry whispered, holding in a sigh of relief when he realized that he was still wearing sweatpants and red shirt.

"i hate thunderstorms," louis grumbled, and he sounded more angry than scared. "they're trying to test my temper."

harry couldn't help but giggle, a quiet giggle that he could barely hear over the loud storm.

"it's not funny," louis muttered, but harry could hear his smile in his voice. "they're scary." and when another boom of thunder echoed into the boys ears, louis was cowering into harry's chest and harry froze.

all harry could do was hold his breath and hope that louis would lay there forever. he hesitantly placed his arms around louis', feeling incredibly awkward because now louis was sleeping, mouthing against his shirt with soft breaths.

well, harry thought he was asleep until louis let out a sigh and then said in a hoarse whisper, "relax."

so he slowly let his tense muscles unclench, until his arms were resting on louis' waist, and louis' head felt heavy on his chest and he couldn't focus on the storm anymore. his eyes fluttered shut right when he heard louis' murmur something, and then he was sleeping.

***

he was so incredibly warm, but not so warm that he was sweating, and his left arm felt like it was tingling. there was an incredibly sweet, perfect scent in his nose.

basically, he woke up feeling comfortable but confused.

so he glanced down at his chest, and almost jumped out of bed when he saw louis' head lolling as harry breathed, and his lips were parted slightly, and his hair was messed up and shaggy and soft. harry stared at his eyelashes, how they rested so delicately against his skin and how they were incredibly long.

the younger boy flickered his eyes to his stomach, where he saw louis' arm was thrown over his hip, his fingers lightly brushing harry's bum in a way that made harry' heart beat rapidly.

and then there was a click, and he realized that louis' door was opening. he hastily pushed himself away from the sleeping boy, who grumbled a bit and yawned before relaxing into the soft bed again.

he pulled his legs to his chest and tried to look natural as niall and zayn walked in.

"what happened here?" zayn finally spoke, rubbing his groggy eyes with his fingers before letting his arms hang at his sides and revealing his morning appearance. his eyes always were dark in the morning, as if he had put lots of mascara on and eyeliner. harry was confused why it was.

niall had a major case of bedhead, and his cheeks were dark red like he was blushing, and his clothes were incredibly wrinkled.

"why did we let you sleep here?" niall asked, his voice regretful as he eyed the blue eyed boy on the bed with a frown on his face.

harry just responded to both of their questions with a shrug, trying his best not to look too fond when he stared at louis.

"well i have to go to my cousin's graduation party today," zayn murmured, stretching his arms above his head and sighing. "then tonight i'm going on a date with perrie."

harry frowned in disappointment. he really wanted to hang out with zayn today. "what about you niall?" he asked, nonchalantly moving his arm just so his fingers were brushing louis' hair.

"footie game," niall said, with a sad smile on his face, and harry groaned.

"what am i going to do?"

"why don't you stay home, watch movies?" zayn suggested, and then covered the side of his face that niall could see before wiggling his eyebrows and looking at louis, then winking at harry.

harry blushed, his cheeks burning, and he shot his hand away from louis and placed it on his knees.

"i think i'll just do that," he said quietly, and niall smiled at him.

"i gotta go get ready. the game's in an hour."

harry raised his hand in a wave, and he sighed when zayn followed niall back into the hallway and shut the door behind them.

apparently the click behind them was loud, as louis stirred in his sleep, and harry watched as his eyes fluttered for a few seconds before opening.

harry tore his gaze away from the boy, staring at the wall and awkwardly playing with his hands.

"good morning," louis' light voice sounded from beside him, but it was hoarse and raspy and tired and harry took a sharp breath.

"morning," the younger boy whispered, blinking when a few of his curls fell into his eyes.

"did you sleep good?"

harry nodded, hesitantly lifting his head and looking into louis' blue eyes, and he was so tempted to look away, but louis' smile kept him there.

"me too. you make a good pillow."

red dusted harry's cheeks and he laughed a little, licking his lips and smiling.

"thanks," he said softly, and he stopped smiling when louis reached out with both hands and started pushing his curls around.

"what are you doing?" he breathed, and he was trying to keep himself from purring.

"your hair is messed up."

and then he started fixing his hair, rearranging it and brushing it skillfully across harry's pale forehead, then smoothing it down in the back.

"better!" he cried, patting harry's cheek and then kissing his lips.

and all harry could do was sit there like a fool, watching as louis laughed, and he reached his fingers up to lightly brush his tingling lips, his eyes wide. and louis was just looking at him, watching as he bit his lip and finally let a smile break out on his lips.

"you like that, curly?"

harry nodded, ever so slightly, and louis beamed.

"i thought so."

harry held his breath when louis leaned in, holding his face gently and smiling softly before pushing their lips together, moving them softly together that had harry wanting more.

he didn't know what to do, so he just led louis lead and he hesitantly placed his large hands on louis' small waist.

louis was now pushing his forehead against harry's and kissing him harder, wrapping his mouth skillfully around the younger boys and slipping his tongue across harry's closed lips.

and harry just went along with it, and before he knew it he was practically hugging louis' small body to him, his fingers gripping louis' waist tightly and his legs intertwined with the older boy's.

he tasted like bubble gum, probably because the night before harry saw him brushing his teeth with bubble gum toothpaste, and there was a slight tint of morning breath but surprisingly it wasn't as bad as niall and zayn claimed.

and just as louis slipped his hand under harry's shirt and put it against harry's hot skin, the younger boy realized that he was *kissing louis tomlinson.*

the boy he had a crush on all of high school.

the boy that had a sunshine smile.

the boy on his lock screen.

the boy with borderline personality disorder.

and harry was a shy, awkward lad with asperger's and a low self-esteem.

***

"have you ever been to starbucks?"

it was a simple question, really, but harry didn't know whether louis wanted him to answer yes or no.

they were driving in louis' car, because louis had insisted on going out. and of course harry followed along. he couldn't really say no to the boy, now that his lips were chapped and swollen, and his heart still wasn't beating at a normal pace.

"harry!" louis called, and harry snapped out of his thoughts.

"no, i haven't been," harry finally muttered out, closing his eyes and hoping that he wouldn't disappoint the senior boy.

"me neither."

then he was laughing, a cute little chuckle that gave harry butterflies.

every single thing about louis was flawless.

harry just watched louis' face as he drove, and louis just kept talking and talking and rambling about things that harry honestly didn't care about, but he liked the way it sounded so it was okay.

they finally pulled into the parking lot of a building that harry had never been before. he titled his head to see the other side and beamed when he realized they were at a pool.

"my mum owns this place," louis commented, before yanking open his door, and right as harry had laid his hand on the handle louis sprinted across the front of the car and opened his door for him breathlessly.

all harry could do was blush, like always, and follow behind louis into the building, which was very open, and the tiles were covered with water.

"i didn't bring a swim-"

"i know. i did though."

harry raised an eyebrow.

"i brought two," louis explained, opening the drawstring bag on his back and revealing a blue and a green swimsuit.

the younger boy nodded, watching as louis flashed a white name tag, and then he was grabbing harry's hand and pulling him into a doorway, which looked like a bathroom.

"hurry up, change, i'm really hot and i wanna go swimming."

"it's not even that hot," harry laughed, noting the warm spring air that surrounded them. "but okay."

louis handed the curly headed boy his green swimsuit and harry shyly walked into a stall, hastily pulling his pants and boxers down before slipping on the swim trunks.

he frowned when he realized they were a bit too tight, so they hugged his hips snuggly and his flat bum, but he didn't mind.

it was better than them falling down.

he walked out and crossed his arms over his chest, and his cheeks burned when louis let out a whistle.

"those look better on you than they do on me."

harry shook his head in disagreement, trying to look everywhere but louis' tan, perfect torso. he had a few tattoos that had harry's head spinning.

"you look pretty," he whispered, and louis must've heard him because he looked up from where he was tying the strings and gave him a cocky smile, his curved eyebrows wiggling.

"and you look beautiful," he responded casually, but it most definitely *wasn't casual.*

after louis had fixed harry's hair again, they walked outside.

well louis' strut while harry followed shyly behind him.

"let's go swimming!" louis screeched, and before harry knew it he was being lifted up bridal style and all he could do was let out a little squeak but then he was engulfed in freezing water and bubbles and he squeezed his eyes shut.

right when he resurfaced a large splash sounded beside him, spraying him with water that smelled of chlorine and chemicals.

so while harry shook the water out of his curls, louis popped up out of the water choking on laughter and water and all harry could do was admire how beautiful he looked with wet hair.

"your curls are finally straight!" louis giggled once he had calmed down, and then he was grabbing the younger boy and kissing him fiercely.

harry kissed him back for a few seconds when he realized that they were at a public pool.

he tried not to be obvious when he pulled back, and they both looked around. there were a few people here and there, but that's all.

"what, are you embarrassed to kiss me?" louis scoffed, backing away from harry, who's legs were shaking severely in the water.

"no, i-"

"you pulled away." louis waded closer, his head tilted down as he looked up at harry through his eyelashes, and he looked mad but incredibly hot. "you don't pull away from me, harry."

harry's eyes widened. he could hear the warning tone and anger in louis' calm voice. so he just held his breath and braced himself.

"and you kissed me first, anyway!"

harry wanted to scream, *no i didn't!* but he couldn't.

"stop coming onto me! just stop!" and then louis was swimming out of the pool, and harry looked closely to see that louis was crying, his lips trembling and he was letting out little whimpers as he stalked out of the pool area and into the building.

he looked hurt.

and all harry could do was stand there, the pressure of louis' lips still lingering on his.

it wasn't until he heard a car screeching away that he got out of the pool and ran to the front.

louis' car was gone.

he broke down into tears right there, regretful and embarrassed and *so mad*.

and although he could barely see through his blurred vision, he ran to the bathroom and pulled his phone out of his sweatpants pocket, dialing zayn's number and trying to hold in the pathetic whimpering noises escaping his lips.

"hello? h?"

"zayn, i need you to pick me up," harry choked, his tone breathy and he was practically gasping.

"h, what happened? oh my god, tell me what happened. what's wrong?"

"i-i need you to p-pick me up," harry hiccupped, squeezing his eyes shut as tears leaked from his eyes.

why did this always happen? whenever things were going perfect, louis had to get mad or someone had to ruin everything.

"okay, harry, i will, but you're telling me everything, okay? just breathe. i'm coming."

nineteen

harry found himself sitting on his couch, an old beach towel wrapped around his shoulders and a cup of tea warming his shaky hands.

and zayn was pacing back and forth, ranting about how stupid he was and how harry should never forgive louis.

harry wasn't trying to ignore him, no he wasn't.

he just was tired, that was it.

and when zayn called louis some bad, vulgar names, there wasn't a burn in his heart and a rock in his stomach. nope.

he just took sip after sip of steaming tea that zayn had made him. zayn hadn't been that upset about missing his cousin's graduation party to pick the younger boy up, but he still was planning on going to the date with perrie.

harry didn't mind. all this groaning was giving him a headache.

it made him so upset, in fact, that he politely asked zayn if he could be alone for the rest of the day.

"are you sure?" zayn asked, pausing in his steps to look at the wet, shivering boy sitting on the couch. harry nodded, biting his trembling lip as he went over the scene in his head for the millionth time. he wasn't going to cry, no matter how much it hurt.

"call me if you need me, h. i'm just down the street."

the younger boy nodded again, staring at the tea sloshing in his cup and letting the steam rise against his face, creating moist droplets on his nose and cheeks.

he was distracted when zayn took the cup out of his hands and placed it on the table, before reaching his arms around harry and pulling him to his feet. harry could barely hold in his tears when zayn held him to his chest, whispering goodbye and hugging him tightly.

"bye," harry whispered, sitting back down on the couch as zayn exited through the front door.

and then he decided to sleep, letting his damp curls hang in front of his face, and closing his eyes.

but right as all of his sad thoughts fleeted his mind, his phone went off, jolting him from his half sleep.

he dug around in his pocket lazily, only opening his eyes halfway when he muttered a, "hello?"

"i'm sorry. i'm so freaking sorry and i just ditched you.."

harry pulled his phone back as louis' phone sounded loud in his ear, and he let his thumb linger over the red button for a few seconds before he took a deep breath and shook his head.

louis was still rambling when he put it back to his ear, about how sorry he was and how he *still* wasn't taking his medication. harry frowned in disappointment and played with a loose thread on his beach towel as he listened to louis.

"louis," harry finally said, his voice quiet and low and tired. "just stop."

louis, and they were both so quiet that harry could hear louis' soft breaths and he sounded a bit worn out from talking so much.

"are you still mad at me?"

harry closed his eyes, because they were burning from the tears building up in them.

don't cry.

he was lost for words, because he could never be mad at the person he loved the most in this world. but he didn't want louis to know that, because if he wanted to have any self-respect he would wait until louis started taking his medication and being nice until he forgave him.

so he just stared ahead at the wall, listening to louis say his name.

"harry. please. are you mad at me? i'll understand if you are... i just.. please reply."

"are you still hurting yourself?" harry asked, and he knew it was random, but he needed to know before he replied.

louis sighed, a low, sad sigh, and harry knew that he *was* still hurting himself.

"harry, it's hard to just 'go clean.' it takes time. i'm trying, okay?"

harry shook his head, his wrist itching, and he could practically feel the razor laying behind the toilet pressing into his skin.

"harry, don't you dare even think about it," the older boy warned, traces of worry in his voice. "please don't do that. i could never forgive myself."

"it doesn't seem as if you would care," harry murmured. "you obviously think i'm obsessed with you and i'm just an annoying friend of your little brother's. nothing more. you've said it more than a few times."

louis took a sharp breath.

he was crying.

"harry you know i don't mean that."

"no. i came onto you in the pool. sorry i just can't help myself," harry said sarcastically. "and i keep following you everywhere. sorry about that."

"harry, stop."

"and how *dare* i even speak to you when your pretzel falls apart at the mall? and how freaking *dare* i fall in love with you?! is it such a problem?"

never had it been more silent.

and harry was sitting there waiting for louis to answer until he assumed the boy had hung up.

and just as he was about to turn his phone off to get some rest, louis' voice came through the phone, gentle and sad and regretful.

"you fell in love with me?"

harry's breath caught in his throat, and it felt as if a million butterflies had been released in his stomach.

"yeah."

"i fell in love with you too."

"okay," harry said.

***

it was nice to finally eat his normal dinner of macaroni and cheese.

harry surprisingly wasn't as sad and irritated as he had been in a while, maybe it was because louis said he was coming over.

and harry told him to bring the medication his mum had bought him a while back, because maybe the louis would take it if he was with him..

so just as he had scrubbed his dishes clean and put them neatly in their place, the doorbell rang.

he quickly put his socks on, like always, then he walked slowly to the door while rubbing his eyes. sunday was going by unbelievably slow, and it was only six o'clock.

when he opened the door, louis was standing there clutching an orange bottle in his right hand tightly and his other arm was open wide.

and he gave his sunshine smile, so all his teeth were showing, and his eyes were crinkled up at the sides and his eyebrows were raised.

"hi," harry said, his heart beating at an abnormal pace.

louis just sat there, his arm still open, and harry hesitantly stepped towards the older boy and pushed his forehead into his chest, although he had to duck a bit. and he just sat there, his head against louis' shirt and he smelled like lemons and honey and something perfect, and he let his arms hang at his sides while louis tightly put his arm around harry's shoulders.

"hi angel," louis breathed, and harry loved the way it felt when his chest rose and fell against his cheek.

"hi louis," harry whispered, finally moving his arms so they were around louis' curvy, soft waist.

they sat there for a minute or two, until the pills in the bottle louis' was holding made a small clicking noise as they knocked against the plastic sides and reminded harry of why louis came in the first place.

so he pulled back and nervously took louis' hand, and he was shaking because he knew he was doing something wrong. he always did things wrong.

but louis was looking at their hands and grinning like a fool, it wasn't his sunshine smile, but it was almost as beautiful.

harry led them into the kitchen and jumped on the counter, his legs swinging back and forth as he looked at the older boy. that was all he did lately, was stare at louis and wonder how someone could be so flawlessly amazingly lovely.

louis' blue eyes were piercing and pale as he stared at harry, and his hand holding the pills was shaking.

"go on," harry whispered, and he was afraid he said too much when louis threw the pills on the ground and took a shaky breath, running a hand through his long, messy hair.

"i'm not going to even be the same."

"if you get worse, you don't even have to take them. i promise."

louis looked so vulnerable when harry jumped off the counter onto two long, lanky legs, and bent over to pick up the pills. he unscrewed the cap after reading the label and shook a pill into his hands. then he got a glass of water and handed it to the older boy.

"you need to take one of these every day."

louis didn't move when harry held out his hand. so the curly headed boy decided to uncurl one of louis' fists and gently push the pill into his hand, and louis sat there with wide eyes.

about three minutes of them waiting in silence, louis put the pill between his lips and took a few gulps of water.

harry had the urge to clap, because it was a huge accomplishment, but he feared it would be the wrong thing to do, so he kept his hands hanging at his sides.

so instead, he used his words. "i love you."

but louis wasn't listening. there were tears running down his cheeks and his breathing was heavy, and he looked so upset that it hurt.

"louis. louis," harry said, and he felt like their roles were switched today because louis was usually the one comforting him.

"why did i take that wretched pill?" the blue eyed boy shook his head and harry grabbed his shoulders.

"i love you," he said again. the words sounded so odd coming out of his mouth because he never thought he would say them in a romantic way to anyone, ever.

louis just looked at harry, and then he reached his hand out and brushed harry's wrist with his fingertips.

"you shouldn't love me. i should love you but you shouldn't love me."

harry blinked, staring at the ground.

"i love you," was all he said.

and then there was a pressure under his chin, gentle and soft, and he lifted his head to see louis' face incredibly close to his, and their foreheads were now touching. harry could now see the bit of green that was touching louis' irises and it was surrounded by blue, and it reminded him of *his* green eyes.

"i'm trying," louis whispered.

"so am i."

then louis' lips were on harry's, warm and soft, and it felt really nice.

louis' hands were now wrapped around harry's neck and harry knew he was standing on his tip toes because louis wouldn't be able to reach him if he wasn't.

so to help him out, he snaked his arms tightly around louis' waist and lifted him so that his toes were barely touching the ground.

louis apparently liked it, because he giggled against harry's lips and kissed him harder, but it was closed mouth and innocent, perfect.

perfect.

twenty

the note stuck to the refrigerator was not big enough nor bright enough for harry to see.

it was a white sticky note and it had a message in his mum's tiny handwriting telling him that she would be home early that night.

and since harry didn't know that, anne walked in on harry and louis kissing deeply, louis' hand tangled in harry's curls, and the younger boy hoisting louis' legs around his waist with his hands on his bum.

he didn't hear her walk in. she let out a gasp, quiet and surprised, and harry almost dropped louis. he pulled away, breathless, and louis hastily jumped to the ground, and they were both flushed with swollen lips and harry's legs were shaking.

"hi mum," harry mumbled, right when anne had asked, "who's this?"

then they were both looking at louis, who was smiling widely for some odd reason. he just stuck his hand out and walked confidently towards anne, shaking the hair out of his eyes and crossing his ankles. "'m louis."

"hi louis," anne said skeptically, shaking his hand softly while raising an eyebrow at harry. "i'm anne."

harry took a moment to look over her face, at her dark hair pulled into a messy bun and the small hoop earrings on her ears. she didn't look as tired as usual. she almost looked happy.

"what's the occasion?" harry asked, stepping around louis to pull his mum into a hug, and she smelled so much like perfume that he knew she didn't work today. she went out.

"i went on a date," anne smiled, brushing a strand of hair behind her ear. "but the real question is why i just walked in on you kissing another boy."

harry looked at the ground, and immediately started blushing when louis wrapped his arm around harry's shoulders.

"i'm not just any boy, anne. i'm louis tomlinson."

a laugh escaped harry's lips as he watched his mum's face.

"and why are you so special?"

"because i am."

harry laughed harder, because louis was so confident and funny.

"who do you think you are?" anne asked, but she was giggling as she looked at louis, who was wiggling his eyebrows and leaning his head on harry's shoulder.

louis sighed dramatically. "we already went over this."

then they were all laughing and harry found himself leaning against louis so hard that they fell against each other onto the counter, which made them burst into another fit of giggles.

"okay, okay boys. i'm serious. i need you to explain to me what just happened. because that was not acceptable."

"what? this?"

and harry's eyes widened as louis grabbed his face and pushed their lips together in a quick kiss.

"louis!" he exclaimed, avoiding his mother's eyes, but he couldn't help but smile.

but there was a happy look on anne's face as she glanced at the two boys.

"do you two want to have a movie night?"

***

harry found himself scrunched into a ball on his couch, holding the hem of his shirt under his watering eyes, and louis' legs were laid across his lap.

anne was sitting on the other end of the long couch, a tissue tucked in her fist and a faraway look in her eyes.

the movie was over.

and harry was such a crybaby, as well as anne. it was a romance movie that anne had rented a week ago at a store that sold old films, and all the characters had died, and it was so cheesy yet so sad.

"that movie was so lame," louis finally said, breaking the silence as the three of them watched the credits roll across the screen. "the plotline sounded like a twelve year old made it."

harry glared at louis and pushed his legs off his lap, trying to blink the tears out of his eyes and look mad.

"your heartless," he frowned, and louis' face screamed fond when he leaned in a wiped a tear away from under harry's eye with his thumb.

"i'm not heartless. i just don't put my heart into every little thing."

harry had to think about that for a second before he understood.

so he just nodded, rubbing his shirt over his eyes once more before moving his attention to anne. "you alright over there, mum?"

"hanging in there," she laughed. "just haven't seen a sad romance movie in a while. it's so tragically beautiful."

while louis rolled his eyes, harry listened intently as his mum began to talk about what she thought of the movie.

and just as he had burst into tears once more, louis yawned loudly and grabbed harry by the waist and pulled him to his chest. "'m tired," he mumbled. "can i sleep here tonight?"

harry never knew that one sentence could get him so flustered.

"i'll, i'll ask mum," he stuttered, blushing deeply as he turned to look at his teary mother. "can louis sleep here?"

she narrowed her eyes. "just sleep?"

harry's cheeks burned as he nodded. "yeh."

"don't worry, anne styles. i will keep your wild child controlled."

harry buried his face in louis' chest, unable to breathe because there were so many emotions going through his head at once. happiness, embarrassment, excitement, and nervousness.

"you better. now i'm going to bed. be good."

harry lifted his head and watched as anne walked slowly to her bedroom, tightening her robe around her shoulders and shutting the door behind her quietly. then it was silent, except for the hum of the air conditioner and the crickets chirping outside.

"do you own a tent?" louis asked out of the blue, drumming his fingers along harry's hip.

"uhm, a small one, why?"

"we're going camping."

harry's eyes widened. "no! we have school tomorrow!"

louis rolled his eyes. "in the backyard, silly harold."

"oh."

***

"where did you learn to do that?"

louis had popped up the blue tent skillfully and quickly, and now he was piling all of the pillows they had collected from around the house into the small space.

"me and niall and bobby go camping all the time."

"okay," harry nodded, handing louis a bag of chips and also his stash of gummy bears he hid under his bed. "well i never go. i'm not even sure why we have this tent in the first place."

"well, it's a good thing you do."

louis flicked on a flashlight, shining it painfully in harry's eyes and causing him to cringe.

"ow," harry mumbled, squinting his eyes and putting a hand across them. "stop."

"get in the tent and i will."

"but there's bugs," harry frowned, deciding to just turn so louis' blinding light was on his back instead. "and it'll be uncomfortable."

"uncomfortable?" louis scoffed. "and why do you say that when there's a million pillows here?"

"it's just," harry paused, feeling awkward since he was standing up and facing the other direction and louis was all cuddled in the tent. "we're outside."

"and? back then house's didn't exist, curly."

harry just shrugged, turning around hesitantly ducking to walk into the tent. louis held out the bag of gummy bears and he took a small handful, placing one in his mouth and chewing quietly and louis began to ramble on about his camping experiences with niall and bobby. he talked about bears and big fires and raccoons raiding the cooler, and the way he told stories was so intriguing. he spoke fluently and softly, and it left harry wanting more. there was a whispery, sweet tone to his voice that harry had never heard anywhere else. so he just cuddled into his warm flannel blanket, watching how the flashlight brought out louis' feminine features more than ever as he spoke, and his lips were wet because he licked them all the time and his eyes were darkened to a royal, deep blue. they both were wearing a pair of harry's pajamas. harry was wearing his duck pajamas and louis had borrowed some blue pajama bottoms and a white shirt that was much too big for him. but the only thing harry could think when he saw louis walk out of harry's room wearing all the baggy clothes with a bright smile and messy hair and tired yet excited eyes, was that he was the personification of beauty.

"...and then niall threw the bag of hot dogs at that bear, and it just sprinted away. it was so hilarious, niall was literally choking because he was laughing so hard. and bobby looked like he couldn't breathe because he's one of those people that laughs really hard but it's silent, you know what i mean?"

"yeah," harry giggled, playing the scene in his head like a movie. "yeah, zayn does that a lot."

"so harry, i've talked for about an hour. and it's," louis paused, clicking the lock button on his phone before meeting eyes with harry again. "midnight. so how about some midnight story telling from the lovely harry styles?"

harry blushed. "'m not lovely."

"harry, don't even try to pull that crap with me. we both know you're beautiful."

harry bit his lip while trying not to smile, playing with a loose thread on a pillowcase and avoiding louis' honest, clear eyes that were shining against the bright light of the flashlight.

"now tell me a story. i want to listen to the wonderful voice that i so rarely hear."

harry actually didn't like his voice. it was low, quiet, and slow.

but he decided to listen this time.

"what do you want me to say?"

louis looked up in thought, a beautiful expression that harry could only watch as his heart fluttered.

"tell me one thing about yourself that no one knows," louis said softly, scooting closer to harry and crossing his legs. "it can be anything. just think about it."

harry searched his mind for something nobody knew, until a minute later he finally came up with something.

"i like to sing," he said shyly.

"really?" louis was looking at him in surprise, although there was a smile playing on his lips. "why don't you sing something for me."

harry groaned. why did he have to say that? now louis' going to insist on hearing something.

"i'd rather not," he mumbled, because heck if he was going to embarrass himself in front of the person whose opinion of him meant the most. "how about we just keep talking? tell me more about camping."

"harold, you suck at changing the subject. just sing something, it doesn't even have to be that long."

harry probably sat there in scared silence for a minute or two until he opened his mouth hesitantly to sing. at first, nothing came out. and then, he finally sang the song "never say never," by the fray.

and at first his voice was shaky, so quiet that even the crickets were louder than him, but as louis started watching him with wonder in his eyes and a smile on his lips, he grew more confident and lifted his head up, singing with the beat louis made as he tapped his foot against the floor of the tent.

he stopped when he reached the end of the chorus, and louis just sat there, staring at him with his sunshine smile.

"that was so wonderful harry. your voice is so pretty, so lovely."

harry didn't know how to respond, because he never worked well with compliments. so he just smiled shyly and looked at his bare feet.

"tell me another thing about yourself," louis said, gently. "because that was a pleasant surprise."

"ehm..." harry cleared his throat as he thought and thought. "ehm, i guess.."

louis nodded, encouraging him to continue.

"i miss my mum," harry whispered. "i miss her so freaking much."

louis furrowed his brows. "she's home right now, harry. i don't understand."

harry frowned. "this is the first night in a year that she's been home. she works so hard.. and all her money is to pay for my medicine."

"for your asperger's?" louis asked quietly, and the younger boy nodded.

"everything will be okay, harry," was all louis said after a few minutes of silence.

and then harry remembered that his mum had just come home from a date. and maybe if she would get married someday, then they would have enough money and he could actually spend more time with his mum, and they would be a real family again.

the thought brought a hopeful smile to his face, until he was aware that louis was watching him.

"i like when you smile, harry."

that sentence brought harry back to when louis was being extremely mean but then he would smile, and everything would be okay.

so he smiled wider.

"screw it," louis mumbled, and harry couldn't smile any wider because now louis was kissing him, moving their mouths together gently and then they were both laughing, and their teeth clashed together. harry had to pull back, giggling, and louis just grabbed the back of his head and threaded his fingers in his curl and kissed him again.

he tasted like gummy bears, a sweet wonderful taste, and his hair was so soft and harry could smell louis but also himself and the mix was too wonderful.

"i'm so sorry," louis breathed against his mouth, and harry paused, pulling back, and he watched in shock as a tear ran down louis' cheek.

"louis, what's-"

"i'm sorry. for all the times i yelled at you and hurt you and i'm sorry for cutting and for being such a screw up."

he apologised.

louis apologised.

so harry just nodded. "okay."

and they were kissing again, and louis grabbed under the younger boy's thigh and hoisted it onto his hip, pushing their lips together even harder before slipping his fingers under his shirt and leaving a burning path on harry's skin.

and just as harry couldn't breathe and he was growing squeamish because the blood rushing to between his legs, louis pulled away.

"we have school tomorrow, harold. go to bed, sweetums."

harry glared, and his cheeks were flushed, and he was so *warm* all over.

but he listened, turning off the flashlights and cuddling up under the blankets, sadly a bit far away from louis.

"tease," he muttered.

"c'mere," louis said in a warm voice. "c'mon angel."

the word never failed to cause harry's breath to catch and his body to tingle all over.

and he crawled towards louis, and louis cuddled him close so that harry's back was against the older boy's chest. they were spooning and harry was on the inside although he was taller, and he loved it so much.

"you are my sunshine, my only sunshine. you make me happy, when skies are grey. you'll never know dear, how much i love you, please don't take my sunshine away," louis sang quietly, in his ear and his voice was so lovely and clear and sweet.

sunshine.

and louis' sunshine smile was the only thing on harry's mind the whole time he slept.

and it was what he woke up to the next morning.

twenty-one

perfect.

it was all going perfect, that monday morning after louis and harry had slept in the small tent together.

math class wasn't so bad.

because instead of reading the complicated math equations mrs. lancaster scribbled on the board, harry stared off into the distance and went over that whole night and morning, over and over and over.

it felt like it was happening. he could still feel his tingling lips and shaky legs, he could still feel the rush that shot through his body and veins he got when he kissed louis.

and he was smiling like a fool as he thought about it.

right when he had almost fallen asleep, when his eyes were closed and his breathing was more even, louis had spoken. his voice was groggy, tired. it was almost a whisper, but a little less quiet than that. and it was right next to harry's ear, the breaths tickling and making his eyes shoot open.

"mine," was all he had whispered.

at first, harry, in his sleepy and hazy state, had no idea what louis had meant by that simple word. but as he fell asleep, his thoughts and dreams answered it for him.

he longed to walk through school with the older boy, hand in hand and confident, giggling at louis' stupid jokes and blushing over the ridiculously dirty things he would always say. he longed to kiss him hard when they finally got home, and it not be weird. he wished that louis could be, to put it simply, his.

and maybe that would happen. because that one "mine" gave him hope.

so when he woke up the next morning, he first was confused about why he was extremely hot and why there wasn't a rotating ceiling fan above his head. but then he could see louis' hands resting gently around his waist, and he could hear louis' soft, steady breaths.

which brought him to the night before, and a small smile ghosted across his lips as he turned to look at louis.

his eyes were closed, his eyelashes brushing his tan, glowing skin, dark and long. his red lips were parted slightly and harry longed to kiss them.

and he just sat there staring, examining ever single feature of the boy with his green eyes as if he hadn't memorized them all.

it was when louis' eyes fluttered open that he turned back into his old self.

he stumbled backwards, letting out a puff of air as he landed on his back. his cheeks were burning as he scrambled to get into a natural sleeping position, but sadly, he was a bit too late.

"you're a very jumpy sleeper."

never had harry been so flustered.

because louis' voice was incredibly, sexily low, a low grumble to it that wasn't usually there. and he was caught staring at him, which was mortifying.

but when he turned to look at the boy, he was smiling with an amused light in his tired eyes.

"let's go to school, harold mccurly."

then they ate a breakfast of cheerios and milk, and then harry had watched as louis reluctantly put a pill into his mouth, a sad and hesitant look on his face.

"this is for you, harry."

and harry repeated that sentence over and over again in his mind as he watched the hand on the clock tick by, a quiet noise that you could only hear if you listened for it.

"harry? are you having fun over there?"

harry shook his head quickly, blinking out of his trance before looking at mrs. lancaster, who stood with a marker in her hand and a disappointed look in her eyes.

"'m sorry," he mumbled. "just don't get it, is all."

"are you still doing your tutoring lessons?"

harry didn't want to answer, because he was so utterly embarrassed and ashamed as all of his classmates stared at him. he was actually quite irritated that the teacher had asked him that in front of everyone.

"you should ask him that after class," a voice came behind him, and harry was extremely grateful when he realised it was zayn.

mrs. lancaster didn't even look mad at zayn, actually she seemed regretful as she thought over what he said in her head.

"oh," she breathed, shaking her head and blushing. "i'm sorry. harry, pay attention."

harry didn't know whether to be happy or not when he listened to the chuckles of his classmates.

***

the walk to lunch seemed incredibly long because he was so excited. louis invited him to sit at his table, and it was quite nerve racking.

but he had to take a bathroom stop first. because heck if he was going to take a bathroom break when louis was there. nope. not happening.

so he asked a couple of classmates to watch his lunch box and mountain dew before taking a few strides to the restroom. but right before he hit boots to the blue and white tiles, he heard a noise. it sounded like choking and gagging and..

puking.

harry's stomach churned at just the sound, and he was about to run out before he heard the person whimper a pathetic, "ow."

he knew that voice.

it was the voice that he ran over and over in his mind at math, the voice that sounded so beautiful in the morning and the voice that made shivers run up and down his body.

"louis?" he asked quietly, his voice cracking.

the sound immediately stopped, and that confirmed that it was, in fact, louis.

and that hurt harry's heart, it hurt it a lot.

"louis," he repeated shakily. "what are you doing?"

"just felt a bit sick," louis croaked, and harry stepped a bit closer.

"is this because of the medicine?"

when louis didn't reply, harry knew he was right. so he just shook his head, banging his fists on the wall near him before resting his head on it. it was cold, which felt a bit nice on the headache that was worsening with every breath he took.

he was shaking, and he wanted to stop because it wasn't normal and normal people didn't have panic attacks and he *wanted* to be normal.

so he took deep breaths, not letting the panic take over his body, because he wasn't going to have an episode there. not with louis so freaking close and the whole group of people sitting just outside the doorway.

he didn't even lift his head when he heard the stall open, a small creaking noise that was quiet but so loud and it hurt his head.

"harry?"

"shut up," he whispered, fisting his hands together to keep them from shaking.

louis threw up the medicine. that medicine did so much the night before, louis wasn't even mean to him once and louis had promised and now he was just throwing that promise down the toilet.

"harry, i'm sorry. but it just feels so unnatural to take it and i don't feel like myself and-"

"shut up!" he shouted, before lowering his voice. "go away, please."

 he flinched when he felt a warmth on his bare arm, it was warm and soft, and he knew it was louis' hand.

"i said go away," he whispered. "just leave me alone. i don't want to talk to you. please leave."

"harry, i won't throw it up anymore, i swear-"

"you're lying!"

his voice was quite loud, so loud and he could hear some people near the restrooms murmuring about him.

"you lie," harry whispered. "you lie all the time and i'm so tired of it and you don't realize that you're hurting me *too*." he fisted his shaky hands against the wall tightly and slowly, squeezing his eyes shut and clenching his teeth, because his mind was blanking.

"okay," louis said, defeated. "i'll leave."

it was another lie.

because harry could hear his footsteps stop when louis got outside into the lunchroom, but then they stopped. he could see the older boy's shadow and could hear his quiet breaths.

it's as if he was there just to be there.

and that made him even more upset, because louis lied again and he couldn't have one minute alone to calm down, and he was trying so hard, but he could feel his emotions taking over.

he never knew that if he shook hard enough, if he cleared his mind blank enough, that he would pass out.

he fell, and he could feel pain on his bum and his elbows, but he couldn't even breathe.

he could also feel louis.

but again, he couldn't breathe.

***

"harry, wake up. lunch is over, you don't wanna be late to class."

harry's eyes shot open, and they were burning.

"zayn," he said softly as he saw the tan, dark haired boy looking down at him with his arms outstretched. "zayn what happened?"

"long story," zayn sighed. "i'll call you after school and tell you."

"no," harry argued. "tell me now."

zayn ran a hand through his hair. "harry, you passed out, i don't know why. louis wouldn't tell me-"

"wait. louis?"

"yeah. he was, uhm, crying, and he told me to come to the bathroom. and then when i got here, he left."

and all harry could remember was louis throwing up all the pills. the rest was all a blur. but he could tell from the dry skin of his cheeks and the stinging of his eyes when he blinked that he was crying.

"did he say anything?"

"he said that you hated him," zayn said quietly.

harry's heart dropped.

he didn't hate louis.

he loved him.

but he just took a shaky breath as his lips trembled, trying not to cry again as zayn led them out of the bathroom, through the cafeteria, and into the crowded hallways.

and right before harry walked into biology, he could see louis' eyes, clear and blue, staring at him from across the hallway.

and heck if his heart didn't race.

***

"aren't you excited? our portraits are done! and mine actually looks *decent*!"

harry leaned over and looked at eleanor's portrait of herself. it was quite big, except her nose was a different size and shape than before and her hair still wasn't the right amount of curliness.

but he just nodded. "that's great."

eleanor smiled happily and gave harry a quick hug. "now let's see yours."

harry slid his paper over slowly, watching his other classmates have conversations to distract him from the picture. because looking at louis, even if it was just a drawing, hurt too much.

but eleanor didn't notice. "harry, i am so jealous. oh my gosh, it looks exactly like him! when are you going to give it to him?"

harry shrugged, taking the paper back and turning it over before carefully sliding it in his binder, making sure there were no wrinkles or folds.

"give it to him today, after school! it'll be so cute! you *have* to tell me his reaction," she gushed, sloppily shoving her paper in her backpack and zipping it up hastily. "he'll love it, i know it."

"okay," harry whispered.

maybe he would. because the best way to make someone feel bad is being nice. he could remember gemma talking to her friends in the living room when he was only a nine year old.

"kill him with kindness."

and that's exactly what he would do.

so he thought.

***

his knock on niall's door wasn't even that loud, but the blonde boy answered it immediately.

"harry!" he exclaimed, laughing and pulling the younger boy into a hug. "what brings you here?"

"is louis here?" was all he said, and he was nervous that his legs were shaking, and his breaths were rushed.

niall raised an eyebrow. "uhm, yeah. i think he's in his room."

harry kept louis' picture behind his back, hoping niall wouldn't notice his awkward, scared stance. "okay, thanks."

he pushed past niall, ignoring his confused stare, and quietly walked up the stairs. the house was actually loud, as he could hear jay and bobby talking in the kitchen. they were rarely home and harry hoped that they would distract niall.

he was going to knock on louis' door, the portrait held carefully in his hands, when he heard crying from the bathroom right next to his bedroom door.

and of course. it had to be louis. and he wasn't even going to warn him this time.

he pulled the door open, and he was very surprised that it wasn't lock.

but the thing that hurt the worst was the way louis kneeled in front of the toilet, his forehead on the closed seat and an agonized look on his sweaty face.

harry's heart broke as he watched louis rip the blade off of his wrist in shock, pulling it back and clutching his wrist gently before looking at harry.

"harry," he whispered.

harry dropped the portrait on the ground and ran out the door, ignoring niall's yells after him when he sprinted out of the house and fell into a heap on the grass.

twenty-two

it was dark.

the kind of dark that when you opened your eyes, nothing would change. where you could only see your hand if you held it right to your face, the kind of dark that was eerie yet strangely comforting.

it helped with the fact that he could barely breathe, due to his spinning mind and heavy sobbing.

harry hoped that niall hadn't followed him all the way here.

he ran home. he ran and now his muscles were burning and there was mucus in his throat, but he didn't have time to get a drink.

it was very late when he had finally arrived home, but all he could think about was that he wanted to hide, and he wanted to scream and be *really* alone.

who knew the darkness under his own bed would be the solution.

the carpet beneath his elbows was starting to hurt, as was his neck because he was hunched over quite a bit in the small space.

harry had turned off all the lights and closed the blinds, making sure that he could see no light, then he had crawled under his bed, careful not to hit his head. and then he cried, he cried so hard that no matter how many times he wiped away his tears they would still keep coming, and he was hiccupping and choking but he couldn't even get a word out, if he wanted to.

and he was under there for about an hour or so, until even the crickets stopped chirping and he heard a car door slam from the driveway, which harry automatically assumed was his mum. so he hesitantly climbed out from underneath his small bad and stretched his aching muscles.

it was just as dark as before, and the only noise was his fan blowing softly and the sound of footsteps outside.

harry's eyes widened and his heart stopped when he realised that his mum was sleeping in her bed tonight.

she was already home.

and what scared him even more was the quiet tap on his window, and he let out a whimper, shooting away from the window and hiding behind the other side of his bed.

of course. right when his tears had finally dried he had to start crying again, but now it was because he was horrified and scared, and *somebody was outside his window.*

"harry? i know you're in there."

harry didn't know whether to sigh in relief or throw a brick.

but he walked over to the window, his eyes wide, and opened it.

the boy on the other side looked surprised, and his blue eyes shone incredibly pale and beautiful and his hair was incredibly messy and there were tear stains on his tan cheeks.

"i know it's one in the morning, but i couldn't take it," he sighed, biting his lip, and harry backed away from him, lowering his eyes to the ground and trying not to break down into tears.

"and i also know that you aren't going to forgive me, heck, you shouldn't, but i was hoping this would help." louis held up a light green book, the color of harry's eyes, and it was pretty much falling apart and there was sloppy handwriting on the front. "don't look at it now, look at it when i leave." but that sentence didn't make much sense when louis climbed through the window and landed on the floor next to harry.

"i want you to leave now," harry said quietly. "i wish you weren't even here. i wish you would just leave and never speak to me again."

the hurt was clear and painful on louis' face as he took a step back, his lip trembling.

"harry, you don't mean that. you always, you always.."

"i always forgive you. i know. but you," harry stopped speaking as a choked sob escaped louis' lips. he looked utterly miserable the minute harry had started speaking. and harry watched as his walls crumbled, as he broke down in front of the younger boy.

and although harry was so completely *done* with louis, he realised that louis would never be ugly. he could be in the worst situation, with tears streaming down his cheeks and his face crumpled and his eyes squeezed shut and red, but he still looked so freaking beautiful.

it was heartbreaking to watch as louis wrapped his arms around himself, taking shuddery breaths and looking everywhere but harry.

"i was trying harry," he breathed out, and he was so quiet that harry could barely hear him. "i tried but i couldn't do it. i told you i couldn't, but you said i could. you always believed in me even though i'm screwed up, when you shouldn't have." he paused, and harry pretended not to notice louis push his thumb angrily against his bandaged wrists. he was done with louis, which meant he could no longer help him. "i will never be good enough for someone as beautiful and nice as you, harry styles."

harry shook his head quickly in disagreement. "'m not beautiful."

louis ignored him, instead biting his wobbly lips and gently squeezing his eyes shut as another tear slid slowly past. harry was so tempted to reach over and wipe that tear away.

"harry, i thought you loved me."

i do! harry wanted to scream. but something was holding him back, making him bite his tongue and instead just cry silently along with louis.

"and i love you. i love how shy you are and i love that you smile at everything i say even if it's not funny."

harry closed his eyes, taking in louis' words that he had longed to hear for two years.

"how about i just say what i love about you? yeah, yeah that's a good idea."

it sounded like he was talking to himself.

"uhm.. i love your curly locks, they're quite charming."

harry couldn't help but smile a little when he said that.

"i love that i can make you talk, the way no one else can, and that when i'm in a room with you, you're the only person i see."

"i love how you never answer the door unless you don't have shoes or socks on."

harry lifted his head, his mouth about to fall open. "how did you know that?" he whispered.

"i love how you only like to eat cheerios for breakfast and how clean your room is and i love that you can never hold eye contact for long unless it's with me."

and as if to prove his point, louis caught harry's eye, with a shaky, teary smile.

it was painful to watch, to see such a happy, funny person break down in front of you.

and harry held his gaze, only flickering his eyes to examine louis' wonderful face, the face that he probably never see this close ever again.

"i love you," louis said simply. it wasn't quite or dramatic, he just stated it with his eyebrows raised and a determined look on his face. "i love you i love you i love you and you can do nothing about it, harry styles. harry edward styles."

"how do you know my middle name?"

louis just smirked knowingly, and it looked so good on him.

but harry couldn't get over the fact that louis loved him, and he had said it quite a bit. and he had barely spoken. he was so flustered and confused and frustrated. the minute something bad happened, louis would come back and do something like *this*.

except, this time, it felt different. louis was just apologising and harry was no longer begging him not to be mean.

and he was still waiting for when louis would start being mean again, when he would throw up his medicine in the toilet and then take razor to his wrist just enough times for harry to finally cave and do it himself.

and the thought made harry sad.

he gently took louis' wrist in his large hands, ignoring louis' gentle protests.

"harry, don't do this. i don't want to hurt you, please." his voice cracked harshly, making the ache in harry's heart so much worse.

but he softly unwrapped the white bandage, even though his stomach was churning at the sight of blood and then the jagged, fresh cuts that went through louis' wrists.

harry's shoulders shook as a strangled sound escaped his lips, and he didn't let himself close his eyes, even when louis told him to.

"harry, just close your eyes," louis said quietly.

harry was grateful that the older boy wasn't trying to take his wrist back.

and his eyes burned so bad with overflowing tears as he brought louis' wrist to his face, and gently placed his lips on the cuts. he closed his eyes tightly, kissing each and every one of the cuts with shaky lips and it was so bittersweet but he couldn't even freaking breathe.

he could feel louis shaking, he could hear his whimpers as he let his tears fall onto the open cuts, and he knew it hurt but so did seeing them so maybe it was even now.

"i hope it hurts," he breathed, before his shaking his head and meeting his teary eyes with louis. "no, i don't. i don't want it to hurt. i don't want you to hurt. i don't want you to hurt. i don't want you..."

"okay, harry," louis sighed, pulling his bare wrist away before wrapping his arms around the younger boy.

"i don't want you to hurt," harry whispered. his mind was blanking, he could feel the exhaustion and feelings take over his spinning mind, the familiar feeling that he hated.

"harry, i love you so much. don't cry, angel."

"i don't want you to hurt," harry repeated, because he feel like if he said anything else it wouldn't even make sense.

"angel, curly, harold, my harry. angel angel angel," was all louis said, and harry really liked the way louis rocked him, a gentle swinging that was so much less harsh than everything else that was happening.

he leaned over a little, because of their small height difference, and he put his head on louis' shoulder, taking uneven breaths through his lips.

you're done with louis.

the thought seemed so pointless and unreasonable now, as louis stood on his tiptoes to whisper sweet words in harry's ear, words that harry thought he would never hear.

but the thing that stuck out the most, as it was one in the morning and harry could barely keep his eyes open was, "go to sleep, love."

he felt half asleep when he finally landed in his bed, his eyes immediately closing as he leaned into the pillow. it felt so soft, especially since louis was his pillow.

twenty-three

harry woke up that saturday morning to the sound of crumpling paper.

it was quite an annoying noise, and he had no idea what it was coming from.

until he sat up in bed, looking around his clean room and his eyes landed on... louis.

he was hugging a piece of paper to his chest, a closed mouth smile on his face and his eyes closed. he looked blissful.

"louis?" harry asked, his voice still not clear as he just woke up. "what is that?"

louis' eyes shot open, and he quickly put the paper behind his back. "what are you talking about, harold?"

"what's on that paper?" harry asked softly, grabbing louis' hands gently and holding them with wide eyes.

louis sighed. "i love it, harry. i just looked at it now, and i love it so much."

harry raised an eyebrow, until realisation washed over his features. "the portrait."

louis smiled at him, pulling the slightly worn paper from behind his back and then harry was melting and he couldn't breathe because louis held the paper next to his face and matched their expressions. he showed the sunshine smile, on purpose.

yep. harry corrected his portrait for the millionth time, and it took him so long to make louis' sunshine smile correctly and perfectly, and now louis was here showing him that he actually did pretty good.

"does it look like me?" his voice was quiet and clear.

harry just nodded, ignoring his portrait that he had already seen so many times and instead staring at louis' curved eyebrows and crinkly eyes and rosy lips.

but then again, he had seen louis many times as well.

but he was still so beautiful.

"so you like it?" he asked nervously.

"no," louis shook his head, and harry pretended not to feel the pang in his chest.

"i love it," he grinned.

***

summer was a time when all of your social groups weren't as important anymore, when friends went separate way on vacations with their families or walks late at night when the air was warm, and the crickets were chirping. and summer jobs at the grocery store seemed to be the only thing that was taking up your time, and the only time you had friends was on social media and random days where you would hang out with some people at amusement parks or local restaurants.

and harry loved it.

the rest of the school year had gone by unbelievably fast, consisting of cheesy dates on friday nights and late night fights with louis, and a small birthday party where he received another book from louis and some gift cards and a phone case from his other best friends.

and the last day of school, after he had gotten dropped off by zayn, who was acting a bit suspicious, he dived into his bed and breathed in the smell of his pillow.

well, not really his pillow.

the day louis had slept in harry's bed, the older boy had come up with an odd idea where they would switch pillows for a while. harry, who loved his musky, wonderful smell, agreed happily.

and here he was, pushing his face into the white pillow that louis' head had touched hundreds of times and breathing in the smell deeply.

he honestly didn't know what louis and he were. they weren't boyfriends, but they're weren't just friends either.

truthfully, he wanted louis to ask him.

after sitting there for a minute or two, harry rose from his bed, closing his eyes and smiling at the warm breeze blowing through his open window. he ended up getting an a in all of his classes, except for his b in math. so his school year had ended well, and now he had all summer to spend not worrying about homework or teachers or people like stan lucas.

then he remembered how weird zayn was acting in the car after school, all goofy and jumpy. niall, louis, and liam were like that as well, but he just pushed it off because they were probably excited for the last day of school. it was louis' senior year, which meant he was done with high school, and that made harry sad.

it was in the middle of imagining next year, when he would walk through the hallways without louis and liam by his side anymore, and his heart was hurting. but then a loud noise sounded against the top of his window, like rocks, and he jumped back in horror when a pebble went through the open part and hit him right in the forehead.

"ow!" he yelped, cowering away and trying to dodge the flying pebbles. when they finally stopped, he stalked up to his window and looked across the lawn (his room was on the first floor) and it was empty. well, it was until louis, fists full of pebbles and a sunshine smile on his face, popped right in front of his face with tears of laughter in his eyes. "louis!" he cried, crossing his arms.

"hi angel," louis laughed casually, gently moving a pouting harry out of the way and climbing through the window.

when harry didn't speak, louis nudged his arm and made little whimpering noises. "harry," he said lightly.

harry kept looking down, and he wanted to rub his aching forehead but nope. louis was going to apologise.

louis grabbed his chin, forcing eye contact.

"harry."

he smiled slightly before brushing back harry's fringe, placing a light kiss on his lips. he breathed a long sigh and whispered, "i'm sorry."

"okay," harry breathed, eyes wide.

"me and the other lads have a surprise for you, harold." louis excitedly took harry's hand, helping him climb out the window before leading him around to the front of the house.

the younger boy jumped when he heard a loud car horn, but then he was smiling when he saw zayn, niall, and liam.

"c'mon, guys!" niall called over the booming music coming from the car, and harry looked at louis, confused.

"where are we going?"

"you'll see, curly."

and when louis raised his eyebrows, with a fond look and a gentle smile, harry realised that louis had been so nice to him lately. there was usually a time, about now, where louis would change moods and start saying really mean things to harry.

maybe the medicine was working.

***

"can you please tell me where we're going?" harry begged. "why do you all get to know?"

"we planned it. don't worry, we asked your mum if you could go," zayn turned around where he was sitting in the passenger seat to look at harry. "you'll love it i swear it."

harry sighed, closing his eyes and leaning back against the seat. "don't talk to me unless you tell me."

everyone was silent for a minute, until louis' light voice filled the car.

"harry, we're going to-"

"louis!" liam yelled, and harry opened his eyes, watching as liam slapped a hand over the older boy's mouth.

and he wasn't jealous that liam was touching louis' mouth. nope, not at all.

"don't tell him, we want to surprise him."

"but i want him to talk to me!" louis whined, ripping liam' hand off of his mouth and longingly staring at harry, who refused to open his mouth.

"he'll find out, lou!" niall piped in from where he was sitting behind the steering wheel. he had just got his driver's license and insisted on driving them all.

they were all quiet for a few minutes. harry slipped in his headphones, figuring that since he wouldn't be talking to anyone the rest of the trip, they wouldn't be talking to him. he played the song "summer fog" by the album leaf, and it felt like a perfect song to listen to on a car ride in the summer. he looked out the window, watching the trees and houses as they passed them by, and he felt so peaceful that he became unaware that his four other friends were still in the car.

just as he was closing his eyes, slouching against the seat and trying not to stick out his body to far as not to bump louis, he felt something poke his cheek.

his green eyes snapped open, and he pulled a headphone out of his ear, looking to see louis. he had his phone in his hand and a curious look on his face.

"what are you listening to?" he asked quietly.

harry didn't speak, because he couldn't. instead, he took the ear bud hanging by his side and handed it to louis, who took it and pushed it in his ear. he raised his eyebrows at the curly headed lad as the soft, instrumental music came through the speakers, before his expression turned relaxed and he nodded his head.

"i like this," he whispered, as if they couldn't be loud, because the rest of the car was silent

harry gave him a gentle smile, hesitantly laying his head on the window of the car and closing his eyes once more. and everything felt so peaceful although he had no idea where they were going but he was with his best friends and his favorite sunshine in the world, so it was okay.

when the car bumped a bit, and harry had no thoughts left in his mind, the younger boy adjusted so he was facing towards louis instead, and then he felt his head slightly lolling with the bumps. he tried to keep his head up against the soft leather of niall's car, but as he grew more tired he felt himself slipping until his head landed on louis' shoulder.

and then louis lifted his legs and laid them across harry's lap, and they were both asleep.

***

it was when he felt a pressure on his lips that he woke up.

he fluttered his eyes open, adjusting to the dim light of the car, and when his vision cleared he saw louis, their foreheads brushing and louis smirking goofily.

"you look pretty when you sleep," he whispered, his breath tickling harry's lips.

"oh," harry breathed, unable to say a word because louis was so close, and his heart was racing although he just woke up.

"how long have we been driving?" he heard zayn ask, and niall quickly answered tiredly.

"'bout four hours."

but all harry could focus on was louis, who grabbed his face and pulled their lips together, kissing him so unbelievably passionately and quickly that harry didn't even have time to process it before louis was pulling back, smiling again. "are you awake yet, harold?"

harry let out a little noise, a mix between a whimper and a squeak, and zayn laughed. "the boy can't even speak."

"we don't want any more pda in the car," liam said sternly, and harry watched as louis rolled his eyes.

"okay ma'am."

"well, we're here," zayn sighed. "harry, your suitcase is in the trunk if you're wondering. jay packed it."

harry nodded, and he was kinda flustered when he realized that louis' bum was on his lap.

"are you gonna get off harry, lou?" liam said in a teasing voice.

louis sighed, putting his hand on harry's thigh and pushing himself up.

harry let out a strangled noise, the pressure of louis' fingers on his inner thighs causing him to moan.

louis laughed, as if he did it on purpose, and harry blushed as all of his friends started teasing him.

"'s not my fault," he murmured, rubbing his legs were louis' hand had been

"okay, let's just go. we're staying here for a week, if you were wondering, harold," louis smiled.

harry lifted his head and looked around. "where are we anyway?"

"you'll see love."

***

salt was the first thing harry smelled when he stepped out of niall's cramped up car, and he breathed it in happily. it smelled wonderful, mixed with food and gas and the smells of the city.

it brought him back to family vacations with his mum and gemma. he remembered how they always let him choose the vacation spot, and he always chose the city. one time, when they still had money, they even flew to new york city, a dream of harry's, and it was one of the best times of his life. walking around all the people who each had different stories, different lives. some people had lives that could be in a novel, and others just plain and simple and easy.

the only part that was bad was how rude people could be. he remembered when some random middle aged women got mad at him for spilling his hot chocolate all over the sidewalk, and she started screaming at him, and he cried and gemma had to help him to the car and hold him while his mum told the woman off.

so he avoided ever spilling hot chocolate again.

"it smells good," was all he commented, and the other four boys nodded.

"your mum told us you would like it," zayn smiled.

"who's paying for it?" he asked shyly, wishing he could cover his mouth.

"my dad," niall laughed.

"and my mum," louis added.

"oh," harry nodded in understanding, saying a quiet thank you when liam handed him his suitcase. he wondered what his mum had packed for him. hopefully outfits that weren't too embarrassing.

when he checked his watch it read eight thirty, and he found himself yawning and looking around. it was dark, he finally noticed, and there were stars in the sky.

or were those.. lights?

harry found himself grinning when he saw a massive skyline, with city lights and alleys. he turned around and his eyes widened, and he stepped away from the group with a smile. he saw the sun setting.

on a beach.

"this is going to be so fun."

harry jumped when he realised louis had walked up beside him, dressed in the clothes he wore to school, and there was a smile on his face.

"why are you being so nice?" harry asked quietly, hoping louis wouldn't get mad.

louis rustled in his pocket coming up with a bottle of pills.

"they're working," he grinned.

twenty-four

harry looked at the bottle louis held in his hand. it was labeled *prozac,* an antidepressant drug that the younger boy had heard of before.

and he knew the side effects.

but louis didn't seem to be experiencing any of them. he looked happy and healthy.

and that made harry unbelievably happy.

"let's go walk around, yeah?" louis asked, shoving the bottle of pills back in his pocket before grabbing harry's hand.

harry blushed and nodded, letting louis tug him along into the small condo that the boys had parked next to. it was light blue, surrounded by grass and pebbles. it was beautiful, especially since there were no houses around it, just a few lone pine trees that didn't match the city that was miles away from them.

but it wasn't until he saw the tower and the ferris wheel when he finally realised where they were, a place he always wanted to go.

blackpool, england.

his thoughts were confirmed when he saw the mailbox with the address as louis and him passed.

niall, zayn, and liam were already inside, so it was just him and louis.

"it feels good out here, doesn't it?" louis stopped them next to a wooden swing hanging by two chains near the house. "perfect amount of breeze."

harry nodded, and he loved listening to louis' voice, especially when it was so soft and sweet.

"i know you don't like to talk, harry, but tell me a story," louis smiled, gently snaking his arm around the younger boy's waist.

harry's eyes widened, and he couldn't think of anything to say. "about what?" he finally asked.

"tell me about the first time you saw me."

and now harry really was frozen, because although he remembered the moment all too clear in his head, he did not want to say it out loud to louis.

"how about you go first?" he asked quietly, letting himself melt into louis' side as louis wrapped his arms around him.

"okay," louis said softly, resting his chin on the crown of harry's head, which made harry's cheeks flush a light shade of red, and he buried his face in louis' chest. "i thought you read the book."

"i did," harry whispered. "but i want to hear you say it."

a low hum of laughter escaped louis' closed lips and harry smiled a bit. they sat there, swinging gently and feeling the wind brush their flushed cheeks, until louis' soft, clear voice broke the silence.

"well, i don't remember it word for word, well, i do."

harry giggled, pushing his forehead impossibly further against louis' warm chest. never had he felt so relaxed in a situation like this, although there were still butterflies fluttering in his stomach and he was smiling so much.

"i first saw harry styles when he was a little freshie and i was all pumped for my junior year," louis began, and those familiar words were the exact ones harry had read over and over before he went to bed. "i had dropped off my little stepbrother niall, with his too-long brown hair and nerdy braces. and i was just about to drive off when i saw a boy."

harry was actually shaking, his breath caught in his throat and an odd feeling in his chest.

"niall seemed extremely protective over him, like he was some fragile doll. and i understood why, because he looked so small even though he was two inches taller than niall. his curls were flying all over the place in the wind, and i just wanted to touch them. there was a scared look on his face, and his skin was pale and.. perfect. and then, someone bumped into him and he looked absolutely mortified."

harry blushed, remembering that moment all too well.

"i knew right then, that that beautiful boy who stood too tall for his own good and wore worn out black high tops and all black clothes and looked so sensitive that just a little remark could make him cry, i knew that he was fragile. and i told myself to never come close enough to hurt him anymore, because why would you hurt a beautiful soul such as harry styles? i knew by the way he smiled so admiringly at zayn and niall and how much he tried to make everyone happy that a person like me would be way too harsh for someone like him."

the way he spoke, how he paused and made a few motions with his hands between his sentences, and the words themselves made harry's heart hurt so much, and he tried not to make a noise as a tear silently slipped down his cheek and onto louis' white t-shirt.

"but then," louis continued, and harry could imagine turning the page to the last chapter when he spoke his next words. "then i volunteered to wake the boy up, and he wasn't wearing anything! and darn if he didn't look so perfect, although i would never say that to his face," louis chuckled.

"and i started paying more attention to him, because the last two years i had completely forgot about him, i didn't want him to do anything where i was involved. when he was over, i was nowhere near him. but i started to notice the way he never met eyes with anyone, not even his best friends, who care about him so much it hurts. he rarely spoke unless he was spoken to, and even then he was so quiet, and he spoke so slowly. i loved watching his lips move that slow, and the way his eyes would flicker everywhere *but* the person."

harry realised after the third sentence that louis wasn't reciting it word for word anymore. the book was never finished after that.

"and he always forgot to tie his shoes and the way he was constantly touching his curls was *so annoying* and his eyes were so freaking green, so green. he was constantly staring at me with those wide green eyes, like all the time. and staring turned into talking and even though i was so annoyed and frustrated and i yelled at him all the time he was just so cute, and i kept making him cry and it hurt. but every time he smiled it was a beautiful wonderful lovely reward that i didn't even deserve. he would just smile and all my instincts not to hurt him would go away and i would just watch the nervous way his eyes sparkled and i could practically see his hands shaking."

"but he was always in my way, standing wherever i was, and he wanted *cheese pizza* for goodness sakes, and he was on his phone too much. he would always hog the bathroom when he was over, and he had these awful break downs half the time, and sometimes he would scream so loud so i would just shut up, and i wanted to punch something. and he may still obsess over the weirdest things, like how his room is always completely spotless and he only eats cheerios and he can't open the door unless his shoes are off and he needs a tutor in math because it doesn't make perfect sense. but you know what, those are the things i love most about him."

there was now a hot, bubbling moisture behind harry's eyelids as louis spoke, in an unbearably soft tone that was argued to be there at all, and he let out a broken whimper as tears began dribbling off his lashes and onto his cheeks.

"and although i may be way too much of a screw up for the boy to handle, he is perfect for me. he will always have flaws. but i will always love him."

harry loved it, he loved it and he felt so *loved* and it was so much different than anything he had experienced before, it was wonderful and perfect and yet so *hard.*

the younger boy felt another salty tear cascade down his cheek, leaving a burning trail behind it.

"and he's just got to keep his curly little head up."

harry burst into tears once again, the pressure and sadness of the past school year finally pushing on him, and he was so incredibly embarrassed and brokenly happy when louis lifted harry's head off of his chest and put his hands on either side of his face, his thumbs brushing off the tears that dripped off of harry's chin.

"keep it up, hazza," louis whispered, his fingers gripping so hard yet so soft against the skin of harry's cheeks, and his warm, minty breath brushing his lips and causing his skin to tingle. "keep your pretty little head up."

and for once, it wasn't the doctors or his mum's worried voice or his frustrated teachers or his bullies taunting voices going through his head. it was louis. just *louis louis louis.*

and just as louis' lips ghosted across his, a wonderful, numb feeling, a voice came from somewhere behind the younger boy.

"why aren't you guys coming inside?"

louis pulled back, just a little, and harry watched the way he closed his eyes and let out an annoyed sigh, as if he was trying to hold his temper. it was an odd thing to watch. the pills were working, harry was sure of it.

"guys."

harry turned around shakily, and he knew that his face was flushed with tears and he probably looked like crap, but nothing, *nothing,* could ruin how he felt right now.

niall was standing there, his blonde hair spiked unbelievably high on his head and an awkward yet worried look on his face.

"harry, mate, you okay?"

and harry could just feel louis' soft touch on his head, telling him to keep it up. so he nodded, a tiny smile flitting across his lips as he stood from the swing. "yeah, 'm good."

niall gave harry a look that said, *you are talking to me later,* before gesturing for them to come inside and then going through the screen door.

harry could feel louis' warm fingers lightly brushing his as they walked inside, their feet crunching on the gravel driveway.

***

it was ten o'clock by the time harry unpacked his bags (that his mum had packed exceptionally well) and brushed his teeth for exactly three minutes. now he was laying under his covers, his pajamas still on because he was afraid louis would walk in on him like that again.

zayn and harry were sharing a room, niall had his own, and liam and louis were sharing. harry was happy with the arrangement, but at the same time he was hoping he could be in louis' room. he loved watching the way louis breathed and slept and fluttered his eyelashes a bit.

you're creepy.

harry made an odd sound as the thought ran through his head, a mix between a giggle and a worried noise because what if louis *did* think he was creepy?

"you okay over there, harry?" zayn chuckled in the dark, and harry stared at the slight light from the clock as he responded.

"yeah, just thinking."

"about *louis?*" zayn said in a teasing voice, and harry had the urge to throw a pillow at him.

he was already feeling exhausted from the many questions his two best friends had asked him earlier, because one, he didn't talk that much, and two, he didn't want anyone else to know about what happened with louis. it was a moment that he wanted to keep to himself, forever.

he could still feel the burn in his eyes from crying, and he didn't know why he was so upset.

maybe it was because never in the world had anyone loved him like louis.

and it was still so hard to believe, although he kept replaying what the older boy said over and over in his head.

"no, not about *louis*," he lied, clutching louis' pillow tightly to his chest, and he lightly brushed his nose to it and breathed in the sweet smell.

"i know h. i know you're not."

twenty-five

it felt like it was over.

all the fighting, the crying, the shoving and arguing and mood swings. it felt like all that was done.

harry hadn't had a severe episode in forever.

he slept so well that first night in the small cabin the boys were sharing. the air condition was whirring softly at the edge of the room under the window, sending a cool breeze and making his face colder than the rest of his body, which was covered in a comforter with tiny whales all over it.

his dreams consisted of ferris wheels and swimming and so many fun things they could do on their vacation.

and he woke up extremely refreshed, his bleary eyes clearing quickly and only one yawn escaping his mouth.

"sleep good?" zayn asked, breaking the peaceful silence of the bright room. there was already sun cascading through the large windows of the room, casting shadows over the carpet and across both the boys' faces. zayn looked very awake as well, an excited, energized smile on his face.

"yeah, perfect," harry said quietly, brushing a curl behind his ear and cringing because he knew he was going to have a bad hair day.

"i have a beanie in my bag," zayn smiled knowingly as he looked at harry's unruly curls.

harry nodded thankfully, reaching over the bed and grabbing a pair of boxers and gym shorts he had put there the night before. he slipped them on under the blankets before climbing out of bed and placing his large bare feet on the ground.

"what's for breakfast?" he murmured, deciding on leaving his shirt off as they walked into the hallway. "anything good?"

"donuts."

and suddenly louis was at harry's side, wrapping a tan arm around him and squeezing him tightly. "chocolate ones."

harry tried not to look surprised, instead asked another question. "with the sprinkles?"

"with the sprinkles."

"how did you get here so fast?" zayn asked from where he was walking beside harry.

"i was listening the whole time, lads," louis smirked, tightening his hold around harry's bare waist.

"that's creepy," zayn murmured, and even if harry wanted to say something he couldn't because louis was gripping his hip with his small fingers and he felt hot all over. he couldn't help but notice the way louis leaned into him, and he stumbled a bit before catching his balance and continuing to walk.

when they finally arrived in the kitchen, niall and liam were sitting at the table, donuts in hand. it was a very nice kitchen, with dark wood floor and stainless steel appliances, along with a small island and a bar.

harry hesitantly picked up a chocolate donut from one of the open boxes, the one with the most rainbow sprinkles. they looked quite good.

"what are we doing today?" niall murmured through a mouthful of food and harry giggled as some of his donut fell out of his mouth.

"don't talk with your mouth full," liam said lightly, "and we were thinking of going skydiving."

harry spit out his food, his eyes growing impossibly wide as he looked around to see if the boys were kidding. louis was pointing at harry and laughing so hard that he was squeaking. "his face!" he cried.

when he finally calmed down, louis averted his eyes at the table due to the stares he was receiving. "it was cute," he mumbled.

harry blushed, wiping his mouth with a napkin and avoiding the intense look louis was sending him with his soft blue eyes.

"so are we actually going sky diving?" zayn finally broke the silence and harry flinched in surprise when he wrapped an arm around him.

"yep," niall nodded, and harry felt his heart race a million miles a minute. thinking of jumping out a helicopter, especially with louis near him, was terrifying.

"i'm scared of heights," he whispered, uncomfortable with all the eyes on him. he felt like he did whenever he walked through the hallways of school; insecure, nervous, and so freaking scared.

zayn mumbled a, "you don't have to do it, h," just as louis shot up out of his seat.

harry's breath caught in surprise when louis wrapped his arms around him, lifting him out of his seat and swinging harry around. "oh harry!" he cried.

harry was so confused yet he felt so wonderful because louis was hugging the crap out of him and burying his face in his neck and it felt nice to not have his feet touch the ground.

"it's okay harold, i'll jump with you and we can hold hands and it'll be okay because you're an angel and angels can fly!"

the younger boy absolutely melted at that, and he decided to just smile this goofy smile that probably made him look ridiculous, but he didn't care. his arms were still at his sides while louis, well, held him and it was so lovely until niall had to go and ruin it by clearing his throat loudly.

louis put him down gently, so that his bare feet didn't make a sound against the wood floor. "you still scared?" he said quietly, and his face was so close to harry's that he could feel louis' warm breath that smelled like honey.

harry's lip quivered a bit because he was so touched by what louis was saying but he didn't think he could jump out of helicopter so far from the ground. what if his parachute broke? what if it didn't even pop out? so he nodded, and he was blushing because he was embarrassed, but louis gave him this soft look through his wonderfully thick eyelashes and his lips were turned into this little grin.

"why're you smiling?" harry felt an ache in his chest as a tear slipped down his cheek, because he was so scared of heights.

"you're so cool, angel," louis breathed, attacking harry in another hug, and the younger boy relaxed a bit, even though louis was touching his bare skin because he had yet to put a shirt on.

"*guys we're right here!*"

harry never thought he would be annoyed with that irish accent, but it was really getting on his nerves and he wanted to punch something but that would hurt him and that wouldn't be good.

so he just pulled away from louis and closed his eyes so they wouldn't narrow at the blonde boy sitting at the counter, his third donut in his hand.

but louis let him have it.

"so what if you're here, neil?! no one gives a crap! just go stick your dick up a pole and leave us alone! harold is scared and all you can do is complain about our festivities!"

festivities? stick your dick up a pole?

harry held in a laugh, biting his trembling lip and squeezing his eyes shut. because louis was so funny, he was so funny, and he was still yelling odd sentences at the irish boy who was now flinching with every time louis said something that involved getting hurt.

when louis finally finished his rant, liam let out a low whistle with his eyes wide.

"wow, lou, haven't seen you like that in a while. it's kinda nice."

and that's when harry realised that although louis was saying funny things, he actually looked *mad,* with a large frown on his face and his eyebrows furrowed angrily.

"i'm tired of this crap," he sighed, and harry cringed when he kicked a nearby chair before storming away, his hands clenched in fists and his pink socks making a slight noise on the hard floor.

liam got out of his chair to follow him, but niall grabbed his arm and told him to stop.

so harry decided to take initiative for once, so he brushed his fringe out of his eyes before hesitantly following after the older boy, despite the other's protests. as he walked down the hallway, he thought about what he was going to say, but nothing came to him, so he decided to just wing it.

well, that was, until he heard a loud noise in the bathroom next to him.

it sounded like a rattling noise.

the door was barely open, a tiny crack available, which harry was extremely surprised about.

he carefully looked through the opening and held in a gasp at what he saw.

louis had about six pills in his hand and harry was sure those pills were for his bpd. but he was only supposed to take two a day.

what was worse was the blood on louis' wrists. the dark red blood that was smeared across his wrists, almost covering the fresh cuts on his skin.

harry's lip was trembling, so bad and he could feel fat, hot tears on his face, and it stung really bad, but he was too focused on louis as he stuffed the pills in his mouth, along with a gulp from a cup of water he was holding. he looked miserable.

it wasn't until harry's back was pressed against his closed bedroom door that he finally let out a choked sob, sliding down the door until his bum landed hardly on the carpeted floor, and he tangled his fingers in his curls, tugging tightly so it hurt.

***

"harry! get ready, we're leaving in twenty minutes!"

harry's head hurt when he heard zayn yelling, and he could tell that he was walking towards their room. so he wiped quickly under his watery eyes before grabbing some clothes and running into the bathroom, before zayn could see him.

"okay," he responded in a shaky voice, looking at his green eyes in the mirror. thankfully, they weren't too bloodshot, just a bit red, and his hair looked surprisingly good. harry could hear zayn rustling in the room, getting ready.

so he put on the shirt he had ripped out of his bag on. it was black, and so were the jeans.

great, harry thought, as he slipped on the clothes over his long legs and lanky torso. *i look like the old me.*

and this thought continued when he realised that he left his boots at home, so he was left with his black high tops. so he just put them on wordlessly and followed his laughing friends to the car.

well except for louis, who was also silent as he followed behind the group, a few feet away from harry.

harry pretended not to notice the bandages that were slightly hidden from his bracelets.

twenty-six

"it's so loud!" niall yelled.

it was quite loud.

they were on the helicopter, way high up in the air. after five hours of training, five long hours in which an instructor told them exactly how to do everything, they were finally on the helicopter. harry felt like he was about to hurl, he really did. the sound of the helicopter's wings spinning was incredibly loud, causing harry's ears to pound. his stomach dropped every time he looked at the ground, which was so far away. louis was holding his hand. but louis' hand was sweaty, and it was shaking.

overall, louis looked so excited yet miserable. his eyes were bloodshot, his whole body was shaking.

and every time harry looked at him, he flashed back to louis downing all those pills, crying as he gulped down the water.

but that's not what they were here for. they were here to jump off the dreaded helicopter and pop up their parachutes. they were here to have fun.

so harry took a deep breath, squeezing louis' hand tighter and trying not to burst into tears. doing this just added to his stress. any minute the helicopter could break, he could fall off the edge, he could...

"harry! you ready!?" liam shouted over the pounding wings, a crazy big grin on his face. he looked ready to go, as he was constantly looking over the edge and letting out whoops, pumping his fist in the air.

"yeah," harry lied, a fake smile on his face.

"you wanna jump here!?" the instructor yelled, squinting his eyes against the wind blowing against all of them. they all nodded. well, except for harry. he just held in a gag and grabbed the pole near him so tightly his knuckles were white.

 and then they were all strapping their parachutes on, the tightening of belts and velcro sounding throughout the small helicopter. harry was aware of louis' eyes on him as they all prepared to jump. his blue eyes looked so bright blue, so bright blue just like the sky and his hair was flying everywhere, blowing in his eyes and across his forehead.

overall, he looked so freaking beautiful but that didn't matter, because he had just betrayed harry, *again,* and even though he looked beautiful he also looked so sick, like the motion and noise was finally getting to him.

the instructor claimed he was going to jump last, and just that made harry's heart tremor in his chest. he was *going* to jump, whether he wanted to or not, and the regret for even letting the other boys talk him into this grew larger.

"i'll go first!" niall yelled, his eyes gleaming with excitement, his blonde hair flying up so you could see the brown roots underneath. "and i want zayn to go with me."

zayn looked a less excited, even a bit fearful. but, he listened intently as the person told them the instructions for the hundredth time, demonstrating how to open their parachutes and what positions they needed to go in.

and a few minutes later, after tons of hollers and screeching, harry's two best friends hopped off the helicopter, squawks of surprise escaping their lips before disappearing into the cool air of the sky. another instructor followed behind them and harry could barely see them link hands before they practically vanished.

"louis?" liam looked at the oldest boy hopefully, biting his lips and clinging to the straps on his shoulders. "you wanna jump with me?"

louis looked torn. "i think i wanna go with harry."

"you can all three go together, you know," the instructor pointed out, gesturing his hands at the three of them before motioning into the bright sky.

harry's eyes widened. this was it. he was going to jump. he, harry styles, was about to dive, *into the sky.*

he was numb, he knew it because he could see louis and liam grabbing his hands, louis on his right and liam on his left, and they were leading him across the small area of the helicopter towards the edge, and he could see the instructor yelling what to do again, but he couldn't hear it. his legs were shaking, and he knew his knees were about to give out.

luckily, right when they did, the boys were off the edge.

harry felt his stomach drop, like a rock had been thrown into it and he gulped thickly as a strangled scream threatened to escape his dry lips. the clouds, they were so close, he was practically *in* them, and liam had let go of his hand and decided to go freestyle, doing crazy flips in the air that looked so scary but so cool. louis was still holding onto him. in fact, his arms were all the way around him, but he felt weightless. their hair was going straight up, their legs flying up behind them. harry couldn't see zayn or niall, as they had jumped a couple of minutes ago.

basically, looking at the sky around him, at the random clouds and smelling the fresh air and feeling the pressure popping his ears... it made him forget about everything. it was all he could focus on, was the fact that he was in the sky that he always looked at when he was walking on the sidewalk, the sky that held the moon he stared at every night.

and so he finally screamed, feeling adrenaline rush through his veins and his head and his freaking *heart.* it was a high pitched, excited scream, unlike the one's he let out when he was upset. he was just so buzzed, nothing could touch him, at least until his feet touched the ground.

but louis was still holding onto him, laughing into his ear with his goggles pressing against harry's temple, and he was warmer than everything else around them and it was so exhilarating.

he felt amazing.

and then liam let his parachute up, so louis and harry followed suit, which meant they had to let go of each other. and when the colored fabric finally shot into the air, their pace slowed immensely, the wind not near as rough against their faces, and it was suddenly peaceful and so much warmer than it was up there in the helicopter.

harry closed his eyes, because he was literally floating, his arms held out and his legs hanging weightlessly. it was like staying still underwater in a pool, except he could breathe.

the smell of blackpool suddenly became much more prominent, and he scrunched up his nose, because he never realised that pollution was that bad until he left it for a while and came back.

but harry closed his eyes, feeling his eyelashes brush his cheekbones and taking deep breaths through his nose, until his feet touched the ground.

the procedures on how to land were flashing through his mind, and he successfully did it, and he was very proud of himself. most newbies preferred to have an instructor to be harnessed to them, and he just didn't like touching very many people. there were a few exceptions.

and now here he was, his feet on the parking lot of "sky zone." liam was already there, screaming profanities and incoherent words while shaking his head like a crazy person.

"he looks excited," harry mumbled to himself, just as louis did a not-so-smooth landing, his feet dragging harshly against the concrete and his eyes widened with fear.

his eyes were now more bloodshot than ever, making it obvious that he did, in fact, open his eyes the whole time.

but now that the adrenaline was wearing off, harry was brought back to reality. and that reality involved not speaking to louis, at least until he apologised for overdosing on his pills.

so he followed the group that had finally all landed into the building, signing their name on the "board of names" before thanking each employee. harry was actually kind of jealous. their jobs seemed so fun.

all they really talked about was how they felt when they were skydiving, until the conversation was turned on harry.

it was niall.

"so, h, how's that for our first vacation activity for ya? did ye have fun?"

harry smiled at his blonde friend, because he was showing his crooked goofy smile and his sparkling happy eyes, which were impossible *not* to smile at.

"more fun than i've had in ages," he admitted.

well, except for your late night phone calls with louis, those are pretty fun too, his thoughts interrupted him, and he quickly shook them away and tried to focus his attention on niall, who was now rambling on about what they were going to do next.

"how about we let..." liam interrupted, looking at the group through his rearview mirror, "louis choose."

louis, for the first time, looked uncomfortable in the center of attention. he squirmed from where he was sitting in the left window seat, since zayn had called shotgun.

and the boys waited in silence as louis contemplated what he was going to say, and harry's heart couldn't help but *feel* a little because louis did this tiny little smile, his blue eyes crinkling and his fringe brushing his eyelashes.

"movie night."

***

they found themselves slouched on the couch, niall and zayn sharing the big armchair and louis and liam taking up the whole couch. so harry opted to just sit crisscross on the soft white carpet. his back leaned against the couch and his eyes trained on the screen.

they had all taken showers, except for niall, who claimed he didn't want to "wash the sky off of his body."

21 jump street was in the dvd player, a movie all the boys had watched except for harry.

he actually didn't want to watch it. he *wanted* to brush his teeth and take off all his clothes and climb into his comfy warm bed and just close his eyes that were struggling to stay open even though the movie hadn't even started. but he didn't want to be a party pooper, so he just slipped on a white shirt and some black gym shorts after combing carefully through his damp curls.

and he didn't want to talk to louis. he didn't want to watch as louis pretended to be fine when really he wasn't. he didn't want to hear louis' musical laugh or look at his short legs or his wonderful thighs or his messy, wet brown hair.

he told himself to keep his eyes on the movie the whole time. he prayed that he wouldn't fall asleep, because he just knew that louis would carry him to bed, and he needed to brush his teeth.

harry was interrupted from his thoughts when a pack of twizzlers came sailing his way, hitting his lap and settling in-between his legs.

"ow," he murmured, and he knew it was from liam because liam was throwing packs of candy at everyone.

harry flinched when louis reached over and pulled a twizzler out of his bag, placing it between his rosy lips before leaning back into the brown couch.

the only sound was chewing and boxes opening when the movie started.

harry saw the movie, but he didn't hear it or get into it because louis' laugh was so close to his ears, so close and there was nothing he could do about it but sit and pretend to watch the movie that apparently was funny because all his mates were laughing.

at the point in the movie where channing tatum was doing weird things with his tongue, harry felt somebody nudge his shoulder. he lifted his head with wide eyes, and he felt a burn in his heart when he saw louis' blue eyes, glowing against the bright light of the television screen.

"harold, it's a little bit uncomfortable there, innit?"

harry wanted to nod, to climb onto the couch where louis was gesturing and cuddle into his side and smell louis' honey smell, but he didn't.

"no, i'm fine," he brushed louis off, feeling his lip tremble as he looked back at the screen. "'m fine."

it wasn't until he could feel tears as hot as summer building up in his eyes that he excused himself, saying that he wanted to sleep, which wasn't false.

and the boys mumbled their goodnights.

harry made his way through the dark hallway into the bathroom, brushing his teeth and splashing some water on his face before stumbling to his bed and climbing in.

the covers were so warm once he sat there for a while.

and he was almost asleep, almost, and he could feel the beginning of a dream entering his mind when he felt somebody climb into his bed.

and he smelled like honey.

twenty-seven

love.

it's probably the most unpredictable thing of all. no matter how hard you think, or how much you try to change things, things will go differently than planned. the person you trust the most will also break you the most. the person who kisses you until you can barely breathe can also shove you and treat you like a punching bag. it's all about fate.

and that's why, when harry woke up and nobody was in his bed, he wasn't very surprised.

he yawned quietly, squeezing his eyes shut and stretching his arms above his head.

but when he looked down, he jumped.

louis was laying there, his mouth hanging open and his eyes closed. soft, gentle breaths were escaping his rosy lips and disappearing into the cool air of zayn and harry's room. he was dressed in the sweatshirt harry had given him a long time ago and a pair of blue boxer shorts.

"are you surprised?"

harry whipped around in bed, a few of his curls falling in his face and in his eyes as he looked at zayn, who was looking at harry knowingly.

"what do you mean, am i surprised?" harry blinked and rubbed the back of his neck, still not fully awake. "there's nothing i would be surprised about."

zayn shrugged. "you do know louis was sleeping with you at first." he paused, gauging harry's reaction. "but he woke me up at like midnight because he was..uhm..."

harry sighed when zayn stopped his sentence, as if he was unsure if he should say it or not.

"what? what was he doing?"

"he was kinda crying. and then he just like climbed out of your bed and just like settled there on the floor."

harry frowned, turning around and looking at louis, at his wonderful tan legs and long black eyelashes. he was crying?

and he blocked out what zayn was saying to him, and his mind. he just climbed off his bed and sat crisscross right next to the sleeping boy, hesitantly touching his cheek. it was soft, so soft and of course it was because louis was perfect, he was always so perfect.

"what are you doing?" zayn called from where he was standing from his bed.

"nothing," harry murmured. he continued to run his long fingers over louis features, just like he did with his lock screen. he touched his small, round nose and his soft, thick hair. his heart ached as he looked at such a beautiful person who had such horrible things happen to them.

he was innocent now. his eyes were not harsh, his eyebrows relaxed, and his hands unclenched on his stomach.

suddenly his eyes were opening, just as zayn said, "stop acting creepy."

harry would never get tired of the vibrant blue color of louis' eyes, nor would he get tired of louis' smile that he was showing right now.

"why hello harry." his voice was rough and tired and *so freaking beautiful.* "why are you staring at me on this lovely morning?" he sat up, pulling his sweatshirt down a bit and running a hand through his chaotic hair.

harry blushed, his heart beating really fast. "i wasn't staring at you," he murmured. "simply checking to see if you were still breathing, is all."

"mhm," zayn said, and harry glared at him. he was now standing at the door, watching the pair with an amused expression on his face. "sure you were, harold."

"don't call him that!" louis shot, making both zayn and harry jump in surprise, because his voice got so much louder.

harry looked at louis curiously, watching the way his eyes burned with something he couldn't interpret, and he was glaring at zayn, who looked completely confused.

"why can't i call him that?"

"why do you have to know? just don't freaking call him that." then he turned to look at harry. "good morning harold."

and harry smiled really widely, even his bottom teeth were showing and he felt kind of happy. "morning lou."

"okay, this is disgusting. i'm going to make some breakfast before liam and niall wake up," zayn sighed, running his hand over his face before shutting the door quite loudly behind him.

"he thinks we're disgusting!" louis exclaimed, raising his eyebrows and looking at harry. "zayn malik thinks we're disgusting!"

harry giggled, looking at the ground and biting his lip.

"harold, how about we go out today, just you and me?"

the question was so tempting, so tempting and his heart said yes but his head said no. so he didn't respond at all, just stared at his hands that were laying in his lap. his heart was beating incredibly fast and he felt so horrible. he could hear louis' breath catch, obviously picking up what harry was saying.

"are you mad at me or something, angel?"

the younger boy nodded, squeezing his eyes shut and feeling those awful emotions beginning to enter his mind, those emotions that he thought had gone away forever.

"what did i do?" louis stood up, his voice rising. they were both entering their first stages, louis' was anger and harry's was just utter exhaustion and sadness. it was an odd combination.

"you," harry began, and he stopped when louis interrupted him.

"i what? you act like i'm supposed to just be perfect, like all the freaking time harry! i fix one problem, and then you expect me to fix another! am i just some big *problem* to you!?"

harry' heart sank when he realised that louis was right. he was constantly, *constantly* expecting for louis to be perfect, and he got mad at him for his mistakes. but it hurt, it hurt so much when louis pushed the blade against his beautiful soft skin, or when he downed all those pills.

"you're not a problem to me. i just, i don't like when you hurt," harry whispered, and just as louis had begun to yell back at him, his temper showing, he placed his hands over his ears so he couldn't hear any of it. when he finally looked up at louis, his eyes had softened and his mouth just hung open, midsentence.

how was louis tomlinson so lovely?

and they sat there, looking at each other. the only noise was the air conditioner and the faint laughs of their mates in the kitchen. obviously they could have fun without the dysfunctional pair. harry was happy for them but at the same time he was sorry for himself which was so *selfish*. but he wished that for one day, his asperger's would just disappear and louis' wrists would just be clean again.

no, harry shook his head to himself. *his scars are beautiful. it's part of who he is, whether it's a bad memory or not.*

louis finally took a shaky breath, placing a hand on his hip and glancing to the side, squeezing his eyes shut as if contemplating what to say. "harry," he said in a trembling voice, "i don't know if i can do this anymore."

"do what?" harry asked, scarily quiet but that's because he was *so freaking scared.*

"this," louis gestured between the two of them, "us."

harry suddenly felt as if he couldn't breathe, because hearing it come out of louis' voice was so different, so final. he jumped up, hot tears beginning to build up in his eyes and drip down his face. "no, no, no louis no. no no no we can't be done. no louis no louis louis louis louis," he repeated, his whole body was shaking, and that familiar feeling was taking over him. "louis louis louis," he whispered, the ache in his chest growing with every breath because really he *couldn't* breathe.

louis reached out to touch harry's arm. "i'm sorry harry, i still care about you but it won't work. just please don't get too upset about it, angel."

"don't call me angel," harry breathed, shuddering breaths escaping his lips. "don't don't *don't*!"

and just as louis had begun to cry as well, zayn burst through the door, niall and liam trailing behind him with worried looks on their faces.

"what the," zayn began, before mumbling a string cuss words. "louis what did you do?" he rushed towards harry and cradled him in his arms, rocking the boy back and forth as he broke down.

niall pulled louis out of the room, looking incredibly angry. liam followed the other two out, shutting the door behind him and leaving zayn and harry.

"don't think about him, harry, he doesn't matter," zayn whispered, squeezing him tight, and harry just numbly nodded, closing his eyes and willing himself to sleep because he couldn't handle this anymore.

he finally, *finally* did.

***

the rest of the vacation was simply horrible for harry.

they went to the beach, but he was too distracted and sad and tired to enjoy it. he just sat in the sand, running his fingers through the soft white grains carefully, contemplating on what his sandcastle would look like.

he finally constructed a two story house, with tiny little windows and little tables and beds inside and a door. he felt a bit of pride as he stared at it, and niall, zayn, and liam cheered for him.

he pretended not to notice louis, sitting a few feet away with an unreadable expression on his face.

harry was so upset on the day before they left, that the boys all went to do something without him, while he stayed home, watching dumb movies that the renter of the house had kept in the cabinets. most of them reeked of cheesiness, one of harry's least favorite things.

it just kinda hurt a little how every single romance movie the couple ended up happily together.

he was busy drowning his sorrows in some gummy bears his mum had packed him when the phone rang.

"hello?" he asked hesitantly, biting the head off one of the blue ones quite angrily. it was left beheaded, just a little bear with tiny arms and stubby legs, with a bite mark the shape of harry's tooth on its neck. harry chuckled a bit. gummy bears were so fun.

"hi, this is the police. there has been suspicious movement outside your premises, so we recommend you hide somewhere immediately."

harry's heart stopped, until a string of laughter bubbled through the phone and into harry's ear painfully. he pulled it back, stuffing a handful of gummy bears in his mouth to keep him from groaning in frustration.

"niall, you're not funny," he mumbled through a mouthful of food.

"yes, he is," harry hear zayn say over the phone, and he couldn't help but smile a bit. he stared ahead at the muted television, at the couple making out intensely on the bed that just *happened* to be covered in rose petals even though it was a cheap hotel.

"i think i am going to go out," harry declared, deciding that if his friends were going to have fun, then so was he.

little did he know that he would end up in an old coffee shop, talking out his problems with two nice women with bright smiles and care in their eyes.

"he has borderline personality disorder," harry explained, watching the reels in the other girl's minds moving.

girls thought about things so much.

"and what's his name?" the one named heather asked curiously, brushing a few red strands out of her hair. she looked about twenty or thirty, young enough to be considered *young* but old enough to not be considered a reckless teenager who knew nothing.

"louis," harry said quietly, just the name causing his chest to hurt a bit.

"tell us everything, we have time," bethany grinned, ruffling the younger boy's curls, who blushed a bit and smiled at the circle table they were sitting at. it had little coffee cups all over it, and above it words written in a beautiful font but also in a different language.

so harry told them everything.

and finally, someone listened, although they were two random people he had just met in a coffee shop and happened to be so lovely.

someone listened.

they didn't even flinch when harry showed them the fresh cut marks on his pale wrists.

twenty-eight

the rest of the summer went by slow.

the boys never noticed the tension between louis and harry, either that or they didn't say anything. that was perfectly fine with harry, and when they dropped him off at his house a week later, he went inside without so much as wave.

and since then, harry spent his days going out. every morning he would eat his bowl of cheerios and put on his black high tops and shorts, along with a random shirt he pulled from his drawers. then, he would quietly tiptoe into his mum' room and kiss her cheek, watching her sleep for a few seconds, at the worry lines between her forehead and the soft curve of her lips. he missed her terribly.

and after he did that, he would run a comb through his curls and put on some sunglasses to cover the bags under his eyes. he looked into his smeared mirror, standing in his bathroom that was cluttered for the first time since he could remember anything. as the days passed on, everything around him grew messier, as he didn't have the energy to pick up after himself anymore.

and today, the second day before summer ended, harry was out on his driveway, feeling the warm sun seep into his tan skin. after going outside every day, he went from being a pale ghost to an extremely tan surfer who spent their days on the beach.

which was partly true. although there was an ocean for miles away from where harry lived, there was a lake with light sand and partially clean water. today, he decided, he was going to sit out at least one more time before he entered through those awful double doors that were school.

he was wearing the swimsuit that louis had never gotten back from him, the green one he wore when they went to the pool his mum owned. he actually liked how it looked on him, although a bit small. his light almost-blonde hair was longer now, curling down to his neck, although whenever his mum saw it she begged him to cut it. he liked it though, it was different.

he never thought he would like different. never. but ever since his life took an unexpected turn and he found himself crying every night, he knew he needed a change. he was already slowly trying to forget louis. not altogether, slowly.

one way he did that was throwing his pillow in the trash can outside and buying himself a new one. and every time he ever had a thought about louis, he would write it down and then burn the paper he wrote it on. he deleted every picture except for the one he took two years ago, because he could never change his lock screen, no matter what happened.

and here he was, his shoes echoing off the hot sidewalk and into the humid air. there was sweat forming under harry's eyes as he walked, looking straight ahead and swinging his arms slightly. he could hear kids laughing somewhere near him, probably riding their bikes or playing tag or something. he wished he was like them; carefree, young, normal.

but instead, he was seventeen years old and he was too messed up to even handle emotional situations correctly. it seemed as if his friends had forgotten about him, but he knew deep down that was his fault. they texted and called him all the time, asking what was wrong and if he wanted to hang out. but he always declined. he even pretended he wasn't home when they came knocking on his door and yelling for him to open up. it took a lot of self-control, but he did it, and when they left he distracted himself by watching cartoons and trying not to cry.

as all the depressing thoughts of this summer flooded his mind, he could feel his wrist itching behind the rubber bracelets that were sliding up and down as he moved his arms. the urge was still there, even though he had only done it once. it hurt, it really did, but it was the best way to distract himself, and also he was just doing what he told louis. louis was still cutting; he saw it himself.

harry could feel the wind starting to pick it up, blowing a few stray leaves around him and it felt nice on his sweaty face. he stopped and closed his eyes, letting the breeze tickle his face and wrap around strands of his hair before releasing it.

he didn't realise he had been standing there that long until he felt a droplet on his nose, and he snapped out of his trance. he lifted his head and looked up at the sky, which was now an angry shade of grey. the clouds were right above his head, and he flinched when another droplet hit him right between the eyes.

part of him wanted to walk back to his house, to sit at his seat by the window and press his nose to the glass, watching it fog up and then get quickly pounded by the rain. but another part of him wanted to continue his walk to the beach, which he knew was going to be empty if he did go there.

he decided on the latter, and with that, he shook his curls out and stepped forward, feeling a shiver run across his spine as the temperature dropped drastically. he could see goose bumps running up his arms, and he tried his best to rub them away.

he was soaked in water by the time he reached the lake, his converse sinking into the damp sand. he was right; nobody was there except for a few stray pigeons that were waddling along the shore. so he sat criss cross on the sand, feeling moistness against his swimsuit.

he had been sitting there, contemplating whether or not he wanted to go for a swim and wondering if he was crying or not, when his phone went off. he hesitantly took it out, shielding it as best as he could from the rain and placing it against his ear.

"hullo?" he mumbled, and it was kind of hard to hear the response because of the rain.

"harry? where are you? you and me and zayn are hanging, i don't care what you say."

"i don't know," was all he could think of to say, because he didn't *want* to hang out with zayn and niall.

niall sighed. "harry, we haven't seen you in ages. we miss you. louis misses you."

harry felt his heart stop for a second, and his breath caught in his throat. he didn't want to think about whether what niall was saying was true. he didn't want to think about anything. he just wanted to stay here on the beach and cry in the rain and bite his fingernails and try not to break down.

"harry," niall's voice softened, "what happened? between you and louis, i mean?"

harry didn't respond, just bit his lip and squeezed his eyes shut, letting a tear leak from his eyes as the scene he had hid from his mind came back, bringing back the hollow in his heart that he had spent all summer trying to fix. now he had to start all over. and with that, he hung up the phone and pulled his knees to his chest, rocking back and forth and burying his face against the wet skin of his legs, feeling rain pound against the back of neck.

maybe, just maybe niall was looking for him, because knowing niall he was worried, and harry hoped he wouldn't find him. he just wanted to alone. he let out a choked sob, louis' glowing blue eyes entering his head and causing his heart to throb. he could feel his body shaking. was he cold?

he couldn't tell.

he lifted his forehead off of knees, looking with shining eyes at the lake, which was now splashing with large waves that covered the sounds of his gasping breaths he took through his wet lips. maybe if he just laid here then the world around him would forget. forget that he was alive.

but then again, wasn't that already happening? niall and zayn's calls were declining, louis hadn't spoken to him for two months, and his mum hadn't said anything about his trips to unknown places. he bit his lip as another sob shook his shoulders, and his tears tasted like rainwater and salt.

he finally stood on shaky legs, walking towards the shore of the lake just as white lightning flashed through the sky, echoed by a loud boom of thunder. he didn't care that he was sitting in the water; lightning could hurt him if it wanted.

he didn't care.

he laid down, the lake water reaching his waist and his back on the damp sand. he fell asleep to the sound of thunder shaking the once-peaceful skies.

***

"harry!"

it was a familiar, yet distant sound. it was a wonderful, yet awful sound. bittersweet.

"harry, where are you!?"

the voice this time was niall's, and harry's eyes shot open.

he was cold, so cold. his legs were numb and.. wet?

he sat up quickly, a lump in his throat as he looked around. everything looked wet. he was still at the beach, and he could hear dripping as droplets fell of surfaces and onto the ground. he was now sitting in water up to his chest.

what happened?

"angel!"

harry felt something, he felt it all the way to the bottom of his ribs. and he was so cold.

it's too cold outside, for angels to fly.

"do you see him anywhere?"

harry wanted to run away, to hide somewhere so his friends would never find him, and he could stay cold and numb for the rest of his life.

but he was glued to the spot, in the same position, even when he was the one person who broke him the most running down the beach in a big blue sweatshirt and shorts. his hair was frazzled, half wet and half dry. his eyes were red and puffy, yet harry could still see pale blue, bluer than the lake he was sitting in.

but mostly, harry noticed how skinny he was. his legs looked so much smaller, his arms like sticks hanging at his sides.

but he was still proper beautiful.

harry looked away from him, closing his eyes and wrapping his arms around himself. the sky was darker now, the sun not beating down as hard on his skin that was now a bit red.

he could hear footsteps growing closer to him, but he still sat there, his eyes gently closed as he rocked to the rhythm of the waves. he pretended not to feel louis' arm brush his when he sat down next to him. it took quite a bit of self-control not to take a deep breath through his nose, to smell that scent of honey and laundry that he had missed so much.

"what are you doing with yourself, harry?" louis finally sighed from beside him, and harry pushed his knees against his eyes, and he could see black and yellow and it stung.

another heaving sigh escaped louis' lips, quickly disappearing into the air and blending in with the waves on the lake. he jumped a bit as louis told niall to head on home, that he could handle this.

harry was surprised that he listened.

"harry, can you please speak for me?"

harry shook his head, the wet curls brushing against his neck, tickling him.

he froze when louis put an arm around him. he wasn't speaking, but he hoped his big shoulder shrug sent the signal that he wanted louis to stop touching him.

"harry, i-i didn't mean what i said at blackpool. i didn't mean it."

silence.

"it's just that i feel like to be with you i have to be perfect. but you know, i'm not actually. i have cuts on my wrists and i am addicted to my bpd medicine-"

he stopped when harry stuck his hand in the air, letting his bracelets slide down his arm to brush his elbow.

louis' reaction was... kinda heartbreaking.

first he gasped and harry made himself lift his head to look at louis' face.

he was biting his lip, his eyes closed tightly, and he was looking away. harry could physically see louis trembling, and he lowered his wrist.

"this is all my freaking fault," louis breathed out, his voice choked and thick with emotion.

harry could feel himself start to cry, he could feel the lump in his throat and the familiar hot moisture behind his eyes.

and just as a sob shook his shoulders, he felt a pressure under his chin, lifting his head up. louis was looking at him, his eyes watery and his lips shaky.

"harry," he paused. "angel. i told you, i told you to keep your head up. no matter what, keep that curly, wonderful head up and never forget to show me your smile."

harry didn't think he could take anymore. he was cold and shivering and his head was clouded, and he could barely see anything through his tears.

louis finally noticed the goose bumps on harry's arms, but when he did he ripped his blue sweatshirt with a footie logo on it and first lifted up harry's arms for him and then pulled it over his head. harry felt like he was a kid again, when his mum would help him get dressed and was so gentle with him.

harry couldn't help but close his eyes and melt into the heat, especially when louis wrapped his arms around him.

"harry.." louis said hesitantly, "if i explain everything later..." he trailed off, squeezing harry tighter, and harry just listened numbly.

"then can i kiss you?"

harry didn't nod, nor did he shake his head. he just opened his eyes wide as louis lifted his head, gently running his fingertips across harry's jawline.

his lips were so soft, so warm and plush like a pillow and warm honey and soft like a blanket. and he smelled like newly washed towels and it was wonderful.

but harry was so confused, and although he was kissing louis his mind was somewhere else.

he still felt cold.

twenty-nine

coffee.

it slid down his throat, sending warmth through his whole body.

it tasted like hazelnut, with caramel and vanilla and it was warm.

harry wanted to stay in this coffee shop around the corner of his house forever. it was quiet, everybody around listening to music while reading big college books. he felt young, and small. this was known as a place to study for uni students who lived in the campus nearby.

but here he was, wrapped in a light blue sweater that was a bit too big for him, but it was soft. his worn brown boots were back, fit snug around his feet with his black jeans tucked into them. he could practically smell the season. cinnamon, pine trees, and candy canes. he could see his friends, he could see them at the table right next to him, talking. louis was sipping peppermint tea, holding onto his cup with only his fingers sticking out from underneath his snowman jumper.

niall had invited them all here, despite the fact it was snowing quite hard, covering what was left of green grass and paved streets. now it was just a blanket of white.

harry liked to be at his own table, sitting at a cushiony green chair with a few names engraved on the wooden armrests. his hands went from being completely numb and red to warm as he held them over the steam of his coffee. he couldn't help but smile as ed sheeran blasted through his ear buds, covering the sounds of clinking dishes and quiet murmurs.

christmas was harry's favorite season. he loved the winter; he loved the cold that nipped at his nose and ears the minute he walked outside. he loved putting up a tree that his mum and him had found on discount at the tree farm. he loved hanging rainbow and white lights throughout their house, saving the best ones for his small bedroom.

and he loved watching all the people around him change their clothing apparel, watching their spirits heighten from all of the christmas cheer going around. it made somewhere deep in him feel warm, although the rest of his him was still so cold.

his junior year was, in one word, tiring. niall, him, and zayn were the only ones that still went to school, and they were all so busy with their classes and homework that they barely had time to talk anymore. but now, it was christmas holiday, and harry was so thankful for the break. this whole year was going by awfully slow and just.. sad.

yeah, louis would kiss him almost every day, he would meet harry at the bus stop and give him a goodbye kiss.

but harry just felt so numb. at least he felt numb to louis. his heart wasn't in it, he didn't feel so utterly in love that he could sing anymore, he didn't blush like crazy whenever louis touched him. it was perhaps more painful though, to get something that you've wanted forever but not to let yourself enjoy it.

he liked to call it a shield. a shield from hurt.

but that's not what he was thinking about. no, he was enjoying his drink and closing his eyes under the dim lights of the cafe. it felt nice, although the santa hat that was nestled in his curls was a bit itchy and smelled like the box he dug it up from.

he licked his warm lips, opening his eyes so he could see his four friends. they were laughing about something liam was saying, at least everybody but louis was. he was staring out the small window on the walls that were painted a soft shade of brown, and outside were small snowflakes falling to the ground. so harry watched louis watch snow, and it was a bit endearing.

his blue eyes were sparkling and harry didn't know if it was with tears or the reflection of light. his lips were moist and a dark rose color due to his peppermint tea, and his cheeks were flushed pink. harry liked the way the tips of his hair curled at the ends, getting lighter from his roots to his tips. he also liked his bangs, his shaggy bangs that sometimes brushed his eyelashes and made louis blink in this wonderful way.

harry almost fell out of his chair when he realised what he was thinking. he was doing exactly what he had been trying to stop this whole time; he was thinking about louis in a fond way.

no. no fond.

so he instead thought, all my friends are pretty, all of their hair is wonderful, and they all make my heart feel this way. louis isn't anything more than a friend.

there. that's better.

he nodded slightly, to the beat of his music, and he tapped his boot along as well.

he felt as if they were in there forever, and he started to feel a bit suffocated and restless from sitting for so long.

the sad thing was, nobody except louis noticed when harry got up and walked out, wrapping a coat around his shoulders tightly. but louis didn't count. the curious, worried look in his eyes didn't count. nope.

harry could barely hear the bell ding as he walked out the door because of the music blasting through his ear buds. he was immediately greeted with the cold, like a wall, and he scrunched up his nose. the streets were empty, and dark as it was nine o'clock at night and it was snowing buckets.

you could say that harry felt more alive than ever as he trudged through snow up to his knees covering what used to be sidewalks, and his nose was numb. he did, really.

he walked until he could no more, or at least until he came onto streets where there were no longer streetlamps and he was blanketed by darkness, so thick you could almost touch it. he could hear footsteps behind him and in front of him and all around him and he would be lying if he said he wasn't scared.

so he held his breath, causing the puffs of air that looked like smoke to cease, and he flinched when he heard his name.

"harry."

a soft, raspy, musical voice. a voice that caused harry's heart to flutter, although he willed it not to.

"harry why are you out here?"

harry couldn't see him.

he could hear him though, and it was like a dull ache in his chest to listen to his voice.

"it's so cold."

maybe if he stood here, silently, then he would go away. it was so painful right now, not being able to see him, because the rest of his senses were heightened. when louis touched his shoulder, he felt it so much more. when louis murmured, "angel," it sounded like someone was announcing it over the intercom, blasting in his ears even though it was just above a whisper.

harry was shaking, maybe it was because of the cold, but he didn't know because there was still an awful fear in his chest, and he didn't know why.

"harry are you okay?"

harry was still looking down, and he could see louis' knees, but he couldn't see his feet because of the snow. the snow was reaching way above their ankles.

and it was cold.

harry didn't know what happened after that. he could feel the blood rushing through his head as it happened. but louis was gone, and maybe he screamed but harry couldn't remember.

he was just so cold.

and louis was gone, he was gone. his soft, worried voice was gone and there was a ghost of a hand on his shoulder, a lingering warmth that tingled whenever he touched it. he stared at it for a second. he could practically see louis' short fingers gripping onto his coat sleeve gently.

or were there hands actually there? he didn't want to think about it, either way he couldn't move because his legs were now knee deep in snow and his jeans were soaked and his feet were long past numb. when he lifted his head, he couldn't see much but an outline of a face, but it wasn't louis' or niall's or zayn's or liam's. and that scared him, that made that fear in his heart grow even bigger and he wanted to scream but his lips felt frozen, numb. there were snowflakes on them, and he knew they were practically blue now.

he blinked some of the soft snow out of his eyes, though it came right back as the snow fell, harder.

"what is a kid like you doing out in a blizzard two nights before christmas?"

harry willed himself to shrug, but it didn't happen. maybe he was completely numb now.

he was really cold.

"come with me."

no.

he could see the man take his hand, could feel some warmth from his black gloves that covered his fingers. his feet dragged behind him, and they were walking so slow, it felt like they were going in tiny circles. it frustrated harry immensely, but his mind was so clouded he couldn't think straight.

before he knew it he was stepping into a building, but it didn't get much warmer. he could still see his breath, watching it dissolve in the bitterly cold air.

"i can make you warm, love."

his voice was eerie, and too warm and harry didn't like it. he didn't like that the man called him love although they didn't know each other.

"what's your name?"

harry didn't respond, just stared straight ahead and let the man drag him through the cold, empty room. there was a couch, with ripped holes in it and it was dark so he couldn't tell what color it was. there were also some dirty dishes in a sink, and he could hear sirens too. they were distant, fading as they entered into a bedroom with a mattress with blue flowers on it sprawled on the stained carpet.

it smelled like smoke and alcohol, and it reminded harry of how his dad used to smell when he came home, when he was about six.

he shivered.

the man with piercing green eyes laid him on the mattress and harry could feel his santa hat slide off and some of the snow was melting in his hair and it was so cold.

first his boots came off, and harry had the urge to grab them, to cuddle them to his chest. they were his boots, his favorite ones. all of his friends had even signed the bottoms.

his pants were wet, sticking to his legs as the man attempted to pull them off. his eyes were asking for his help, but there was this disgusting smirk on his face that made harry's stomach churn.

harry could feel tears streaming down his cheeks, warming his icy skin as the man finished removing his clothes and undergarments. he felt bare and numb and cold and scared and the sirens were getting louder and they were strangely comforting.

he would say that the man pushing his fingers between his legs and rubbing him was awful, but he couldn't feel it. until blood started to rush through his body a little more, then it stung. it stung a lot.

the man was mouthing at his neck, it felt disgusting and spitty, and it also stung. harry didn't move with the man, he just cried as he felt rough pressure against his lips and nails against his hips. he saw blood too, and even that felt cold.

he was so cold.

the mattress was now stained, and it could match everything else around it. harry wanted to run away, he wanted to hide, but he still couldn't bring himself to move, even when the man gave him one more kiss on his cold lips and rose, naked and flustered, and harry closed his eyes.

louis' hands were much gentler when he finally picked harry up off the mattress.

louis was warm.

thirty

cold.

it was so cold.

maybe, if he kept his eyes closed, it would go away. these dreams.

his arms were so real. warm.

he blinked the falling snow out of his eyelashes, causing icy water to slide down his numb, stinging cheeks.

louis was really there.

"it was just a dream."

his voice.

"you passed out, harry."

harry was shaking, he was shaking really hard in louis' arms and he needed a blanket.

"can you speak for me, angel?"

harry still felt the lingering warmth on his shoulder from when louis touched him earlier.

but it was so hazy, and he wondered what was even real.

he could remember laying down in the snow, spreading his arms out really wide and letting the white snowflakes land on him gently, one by one.

louis screamed, he remembered that too.

and his dad was there, with his green eyes and he tried to kiss him and hurt him.

"where's my dad?" harry whispered, closing his eyes with every step louis took in the dark, towards a streetlamp that was barely visible through the heavy snow. "why did he hurt me?"

louis' eyes softened, glowing pale blue in the dark blizzard, and his lips were pale, and he was shivering.

"you fell asleep. and i tried to wake you up and i screamed your name but you were just crying and i didn't," he trailed off, looking into the distance as a tear rolled down his cheek. "i didn't know what to do and i was so worried about you, angel."

harry didn't know what to say, because he could remember clearly walking into that cold house and laying on the flower mattress that... that still lived in his attic.

maybe it was a dream.

his mind was too frozen to bear a sensible thought, so he instead laid his head against louis' chest, feeling the slick material of his coat underneath his cheek and his head bobbed up and down with every crunching, slow step louis took through the knee deep snow.

he could almost fall asleep, except for the fact that he felt like he had hypothermia and his toes were long past numb.

"why did you come out here, hazza?"

hazza.

"i was tired of sitting," harry murmured, feeling his eyes droop a little with the gentle rhythm he was bouncing in. "so i went out for a stroll."

"in the middle of a blizzard, two days before christmas?" louis chuckled a bit. "harold, you amuse me with things like this. you're so cute, and innocent, and you freaking scared me to death because you just fell backwards and i didn't know if you were breathing and you looked so miserable, but you weren't moving and i-"

harry had no idea what to say when louis began to cry, silently and he looked so.. scared.

"you're so small." as if to prove his point, he squeezed harry tightly in his arms, and harry just scrunched up a little bit, snuggling his head impossibly farther into louis' chest. "my pretty paper doll."

and when louis squeezed him again, placing a shaky, yet warm kiss on harry's cold forehead, harry felt his heart feel that way again, he felt love. a soft flutter that even the most self-control in the world couldn't stop. he loved louis. he loved him even though he didn't want to, he really didn't.

okay, maybe a little.

harry realised that louis was carrying him back to the coffee shop, and niall's car was still parked there, now covered in white snow up to the door handles. harry let louis open the passenger door and lay him down, before rushing to the driver's side and turning the key.

the heat that blasted through the vents was wonderful, it really was, but harry was wondering why they didn't go into the coffee shop.

it seemed as if louis read his mind. "the door is blocked with snow, angel."

harry nodded numbly, feeling his toes and hands tingle as blood began to rush through them. he flinched when louis leaned over and started pulling his clothes off, and it reminded him of his dream.

"harry, it's okay," louis murmured. "your wet clothes are making you colder, breathe." harry let out a breath, letting louis unzip his blue coat.

then his wet shirt was coming off and his chest was bare, and louis' hot hands were on his skin and he suddenly couldn't breathe. his skin was hot, his fingers leaving a burning trail in their path as louis' tiny hands slowly slid down across his stomach and he squeezed his hipbones gently.

harry felt lust burning in his heart, matching with the heat of the car.

and he didn't even tell himself to stop when he leaned over and pressed a bruising kiss to louis' lips, erasing any memories of his father and the mattress with flowers and the smell of alcohol. because now all he could smell was clean laundry and honey and that boy and sweat smell that he loved.

he breathed in through his nose deeply as louis kissed him back, with the same amount of passion and lust and harry could practically see the car windows fogging up.

their lips molded together perfectly, moving in a little dance as their hands flitted across each other's faces and hair and arms, as if memorizing every part of each other.

i miss this, harry thought with a dull ache in his chest. *i missed sunshine. sunshine.*

"'m sorry," louis whispered as they parted for a few seconds, catching their breaths.

harry could feel every part of his body getting warmer and it kind of hurt but he was too focused on louis' eyes, on how they reflected the gently falling snow, pale blue with little speckles of white. his eyes were wide, as if he was surprised, and there was this tiny little smile on his lips, heavy, shaky breaths escaping into the warm air of the car.

"i don't know what i was thinking when i said that, i was just so overwhelmed and then i was scared you hated me. i thought that you had moved on, and maybe you have, but i still love you, like so much, really, more than life."

harry just kept his steady gaze on louis' face, which was flushed from the cold it was exposed to earlier, either that or a blush.

and then green met blue again, and they kissed, they kissed until their lungs were burning and harry felt a pang somewhere at the bottom of his ribs, maybe it was because he loved it but it felt like someone was pushing on his stomach and he could just *feel* something.

louis pulled back, breathless, examining harry's face with his eyebrows pulled together.

"i love you, okay?"

harry smiled, nudging his forehead into louis' slightly and averting his eyes to his hands.

"okay."

there was a long pause, when all you could hear was kissing and it was wonderful but harry could make out somewhere in the mix louis saying, "be my boyfriend?"

and he just kinda nodded, but really he was smiling too much to say anything.

thirty-one

kissing.

a wonderful thing, a wonderful, heart fluttering thing.

harry's eyes were closed, his eyelashes brushing louis' cheekbones and his fingers ghosting across louis' wrist as he kissed him. he kissed him hard, he memorized the way louis cradled his jaw and face, the way he bit his bottom lip gently and fluttered his eyes open and closed from time to time.

the car was so unbelievably hot now, the heated seats now burning harry's legs and the warm air from the vents causing sweat to form across his nose and under his eyes.

and, of course, the way louis was pulling harry onto his lap was pretty hot too.

harry could sometimes see, when his eyes were open and louis was just kinda pushing his forehead into his neck, he could see the shadows from the lit up cafe running across the windshield of the car and over their bodies. he wasn't shivering anymore; but there were still goose bumps running down his skin.

he shuddered and his breath caught when louis started to tug on his hair, curling his fingers around the brown tendrils and yanking gently. harry went along with it, squeezing louis' wrists tighter and trying not to kiss him too hard. he didn't have any experience with anyone besides louis, and he was scared he was doing something wrong.

"angel." louis' voice was a raspy whisper, raw with emotion, "angel i love you."

and harry knew he loved him back, he knew, just by the way he shivered again when louis blue eyes stared into his jade ones.

but he couldn't bring himself to say it.

so he just nodded, a quick, hurried nod before grabbing louis behind the neck, pushing their lips together in a bruising kiss and he was so nervous but so excited and it was really quite nice.

then the sound of rushed breaths filled the air, along with harry's whimpers when louis' hot fingers brushed across his bare hipbone. harry was a wreck, just louis' soft touch causing him to fall apart.

and harry kissed him with as much passion as he could muster. he squeezed his eyes shut tightly, pushing his forehead against louis' and removing his tight hold on louis' wrist. he placed one hand on his hip and the other against his soft, warm tummy that he just loved so much.

harry felt a flush throughout his whole body when louis slipped two fingers under the waistband of his boxers, and he grabbed his hand.

louis looked up, eyes hooded, and eyebrows pulled together. "what?"

"'m not ready," he shook his head. he could feel tears of embarrassment flow to his eyes as louis slowly removed his hand. "'m just not ready."

louis took a sharp intake of breath when he saw that harry was crying. "harry," he whispered, reaching out and thumbing away his hot, stinging tears. "harry love it's okay. it's okay." his voice was unbelievably soft, reminding harry of pillows and fuzzy blankets and honey. "it's so okay."

harry took a shaky breath, resting his wary eyes on louis' gentle face, on his curved nose and thin rosy lips and long eyelashes. "'m not ready."

"i know," louis said quietly, snaking his arms around harry's waist and pulling him to his chest. harry kept his eyes open, staring ahead as he laid his cheek against louis' torso. he could feel louis' steady heartbeat through his purple sweatshirt, and it was soothing, it was soothing and unique and *louis*.

so harry listened, focusing his eyes on the dark backseat of the car, and out the window he could see white snow falling down rapidly, so thick that you couldn't even see the next car in the parking lot. and his head rose as louis' chest did, with his soft, calming breaths as he whispered comforting words into his hair.

"louis," harry finally whispered, and he felt like a little kid who was scared of the dark, tiny and quiet. "louis louis louis."

"harry."

the wind was howling outside, causing snow to brush roughly against the window in sweeping movements. but it still felt so quiet in the car, the sound of the air coming from the vents muffling it.

"louis louis louis louis."

louis chuckled. "harry."

harry smiled a bit, snuggling his cheek even further against louis soft sweatshirt. "louis louis louis."

"harry harry harry."

"louis."

"harry."

when he laughed it made his chest bump up and down, and harry giggled, sticking his fingers underneath louis' sweater and squeezing his sides. "louis louis louis louis louis."

louis turned harry around on his lap, like he was the lightest person in the world even though harry was taller than him. and he grabbed the sides of his face, staring into his eyes while brushing his curls behind his ears.

"harreh." he titled his head, a smirk playing on his lips as he stared at harry, he stared at him like he was the only person in the world. "cute bum."

harry blushed, just a tiny bit, but he was too busy admiring the way louis' eyelashes casted a shadow on his face to focus on that.

and just as louis kissed his nose, in this endearing way that kinda made harry want to squeal, a loud, screeching ringtone broke the comfortable silence.

it was *actually* screeching. like dying birds or screaming women. harry cringed, watching warily as louis pulled his phone out of his pocket. "niall," he explained, and harry nodded in understanding.

"yellow."

yellow.

harry could hear niall's worried yell through the phone. "*where are you guys?!*"

harry watched the way louis yanked the phone away from his ear. "we're in your car. door was blocked by the snow and all," he sighed, but he was still holding harry's hand.

"sure. i'll tell him. okay. bye."

louis let out another heaving sigh as he shoved his phone back into his pocket. "niall wants me to tell you to never run off like that again."

"ugh," harry murmured. "he doesn't know anything."

"no," louis argued. "no, i agree with him. harry, you scared me -all of us- to death. i seriously thought you weren't okay when you just passed out in the snow. "

harry looked down, picking at his fingernails. he didn't like getting scolded.

there was silence for a minute or two, both of them consumed in their own thoughts, until louis spoke again.

"what were you dreaming about?"

harry felt his heart stop for a second, the dream slamming back into his mind like a car crashing. he thought that he had pushed that out of his mind forever.

because, no. he couldn't let those dreams, those visions, come back. no.

he could remember having them every night, when he was just in primary school and the events of what happened with his father were still fresh, and whenever someone brought it up it was like a million knives twisting into his chest.

"i," harry said, his lips shaking as he struggled to get the words out, "i, i."

"harry," louis breathed, and he kind of frowned when harry scrambled off of his lap and onto his own seat again. "harry what is it?"

it was a dream, not memory.

he always told himself that, and he thought that maybe if he said it enough he would convince himself and it would be okay, and his dad wouldn't have existed.

not a memory.

he was shaking now, the memory - the *dream*- flashing through his mind. he could remember his dad hoisting his thighs over his shoulders and rubbing him roughly. he remembered so freaking well, and he hated it so, so much.

he didn't realise he was whimpering, or crying, until louis let out a worried noise. he closed his eyes, and he could feel louis' hands under his armpits as he lifted him up, like a kitten, and laid him gently across his lap. harry was shaking so much, his hands unable to hold anything but a weak grasp onto the hem of louis' shirt.

"it was a dream," he whispered, squeezing his eyes shut and letting the hot, bubbling moisture that was building up behind his eyes finally escape. "a dream, it was a dream, a dream a dream adreamadreamadream."

louis massaged his curls, the tips of his fingers pushing against harry's scalp gently. "baby, angel, baby it's okay."

baby.

"baby. my baby boy."

harry was kind of numb. he could smell his dad's sweat; it reminded him of when they went to soccer games together and the air was hot and humid.

"baby." harry shivered as his dad pulled his pants off, tugging them down his short, skinny legs. his knees were knobby, and his skin was littered with scars that he had received from attempting to play many sports his father forced him to do.

"i love you. i love you so much harry."

harry didn't nod, he just cried when his dad stuck one of his fingers between his legs, dry and so freaking painful.

"ow, ow ow ow," he whimpered, sweat forming under his arms and tears leaking out of his eyes. "ow, daddy, ow, ow ow."

"it's okay, baby."

harry let out a strangled whimper, thrashing out of louis' grasp and back onto his seat once again. "no, daddy, no don't!" he exclaimed, hugging himself and closing his legs tightly together.

"harry!" louis shouted, attempting to touch the younger boy but harry pushed him away.

"daddy, stop, i don't want to!"

"daddy," louis mumbled in realisation. harry could see through his tear filled eyes his angry expression, his quivering lip as he stared at the fragile boy.

"harry, harry it's louis. angel, you're an angel, it's louis, louis, louis louis louis."

harry stopped thrashing when louis hugged him, letting himself go limp in louis' arms. it *was* louis. he smelled like honey and soap like always, and his voice was still soft, and he was still sunshine.

he felt so vulnerable, so vulnerable when all of his thoughts were jumbled, and he was confused between his dreams and reality.

but maybe, maybe if something would distract him then his mind wouldn't even think at all.

so he lifted his head, looking louis in the eyes, watching the way they sparkled with tears just like his. and he kissed him, tasting the sweetness on his lips and trying to make his heart feel good again.

and yeah, his past still came back and hit him hard in the heart, but he knew that nothing in the world could get better than this. louis was kissing him tenderly, threading their fingers together and causing harry to melt a bit.

"go to sleep," louis murmured against his lips. "we're gonna be snowed in all night."

as if to emphasize his point, louis touched one of his hands to the cold, wet window before placing it on harry's burning skin.

harry lived for the way louis smiled at him as he squirmed, as if he was some adorable puppy.

"cold, innit?"

harry nodded, snuggling into louis and soaking in his warmth.

"yeah," he mumbled.

"g'night, angel."

harry closed his eyes, taking what was left of the light and shutting it out.

"night, louis louis louis."

thirty-two

car trips.

harry had always loved them. he loved laying his head against the cool glass of the moving car, sometimes having to hold himself when they went over a bumpy area. he loved watching the trees and buildings and fields zoom by in a blur, colors blending together like wet paint.

he remembered when he was only eight and his mum and sister took him to the airport. they were planning on going to disney world, and that was all the way in america, and harry was so excited. but the plane ride wasn't his favorite part of getting there. he just loved driving to the airport, which was about two hours away from where his home was.

gemma had packed his suitcase for him, remembering to pack his little box of cheerios that he was planning on eating on the plane for breakfast. they were rushing too much to eat breakfast at home. well, gemma and his mum were rushing. harry just stood in the bathroom, combing each curl of his carefully, making sure there were no tangles. he styled it in a perfect fringe across his pale forehead, staring at his jade eyes in the mirror. his lips were dark pink, and he had a few light freckles running across his nose if you looked close enough.

"harry, c'mon babe! we gotta go!"

it was gemma, harry could tell by her accent and the sweet tone in her voice. he knew that she got stressed out sometimes, because mum said that teenagers were "unbalanced." so he listened to her, slipping on his small pair of high tops and some cargo shorts. then, he put on a blue polo his mum had bought him.

"coming!" he responded in his small, eight year old voice. and then he stumbled his way to the car, clutching his power ranger in one hand and his ipod shuffle in the other.

when they finally settled in the small car, harry tried to ignore the missing space in the passenger seat. instead, he pushed his headphones into his ears, playing his classical music that gemma had download for him. then, he watched the scenery as his mum pulled out of the garage and onto the streets of his neighborhood.

and they were off and harry loved every second of it.

and now, here he was, sitting in a car. but it wasn't moving, and his mum and gemma weren't there, and his headphones weren't in.

but he still loved it so, so much.

the sun was coming up and causing the snow on the ground to sparkle, indicating that it was, in fact, morning.

harry took a deep breath, holding in a yawn and stretching his arms above his head. his back kind of hurt from the uncomfortable seats of niall's car, but that was okay. he could still see louis sleeping in the driver's seat, his lips parted, and there was a bit of sweat on his face.

harry reached over and turned off the heat, because it was quite hot in there, despite the weather outside.

"louis," he whispered hesitantly, touching louis' cheek with his pointer finger and quickly shooting it back to his lap. "louis, wake up."

he giggled when louis' eyes shot open, revealing pale blue that shined so pretty in the morning sun that was beaming through the windshield of the car.

he looked quickly to his side, and his expression relaxed when he saw harry's amused face. "oh," he sighed, before pausing and blushing a bit. "'s not funny, harold. don't you laugh at me."

harry giggled, looking at his hands, and he didn't know what to say.

"don't smile," louis said in a teasing voice, poking harry's nose and adjusting some of the curls on his forehead.

harry bit his lip, trying so freaking hard, but he couldn't help but let his lips spread into a huge grin. louis just did this little smile as he looked at harry, his eyes crinkled up and his lips closed.

and god if he didn't look freaking beautiful.

***

they found themselves on the floor of harry's room, sitting criss cross. the snowplows had come through that morning, moving all the snow so people could at least drive home. stores were closed because the blizzard was still going on and harry was extremely excited.

because who didn't like snow days?

"do you keep all your special stuff under your bed?" louis asked curiously, watching harry draw something on his large sketchbook that was sitting in front of him on the floor. "or like, in your closet or something?"

harry lifted his head and averted his eyes away from his drawing. "under my bed," he replied.

"oh," louis said, nodding. "what kind of special stuff do you keep under there?"

harry added some more snowflakes. he was sketching a picture of niall's car, outside the cafe. because he drew every place where a special moment happened. he had drawn outside his window, where louis had stood so long ago, and he drew niall's room and the hallway outside, and even his room in blackpool, even though the moment wasn't very pleasant.

"i keep my drawings, and pictures, and just stuff i collected over the years," harry finally responded to louis, who was gazing at him carefully. "don't ever look at it though."

"well," louis paused, moving his butt towards harry's bed. "we should change that."

"no," harry shook his head. "scary things might be under there."

he was half kidding.

louis just rolled his eyes, laughing. "you'll never know, unless you look."

harry sighed, continuing to sketch and ignoring louis.

louis let out another laugh, ruffling harry's curls before falling onto his stomach. he army crawled himself under the bed so only his legs were sticking out. it took all of harry's self-control to keep his eyes on the tree he was currently drawing.

when he finally couldn't take it anymore, listening to louis' incoherent mumbles coming from underneath the bed, and some of his squeals, he averted his eyes and forced them to look at louis' fuzzy black boots that were on his feet.

don't look at his bum.

louis let out a grunt as he scooted back out into the light, shaking his hair out and brushing some of it out of his blue eyes. "what's this?" he asked and harry looked at what he was holding.

"you found it!" harry exclaimed, a big grin breaking out on his face. "i looked for that for ages!"

"i love how loud you are now," louis said quietly, and just as harry said, "what?" louis continued to talk. "i love polaroid cameras."

"me too." harry brushed off what louis said earlier.

he stared at louis as louis stared at the camera, and he went back to his drawing as louis stood up, looking through the lens and taking random pictures, letting out little noises of approval as he stared at the photo in his hand.

he smiled a bit, adding a few leaves to the tree, as louis snorted. "angel, angel c'mere," he laughed, waving his hand quickly, and harry slowly stood up on his long legs and walked over.

"what?" he asked shakily, because his heart was still racing because *angel.*

"i took a picture of the picture of gemma and your mum you have on your wall, but i'm too short to take it straight on and it's kinda angled up and it makes their chins," he paused, shoving the camera in front of harry's eyes, "like this."

harry burst into laughter. gemma looked like her chin was double the size of the rest of her head, and so did his mum.

"it's all because i'm much too short," louis said in a fake-sad voice.

harry looked down at him. he was a couple inches shorter, his head reached harry's nose. "doesn't seem like it," he said simply.

"yeah," louis said softly, staring into harry's eyes. "it seems like it should be like this."

he took his fuzzy boots and placed them on harry's, causing him to rise a few inches. now they were almost eye to eye, although louis was a bit taller.

"a feather," harry giggled. "a feather is how light you are. a feather has landed on my toes."

there was a playful glint in louis' eyes as he stomped on harry's toes. "am not! i'm not a feather!"

"okay," harry whispered, his voice lowering as louis moved his face closer to his. he could feel louis' warm, peppermint breath on his face.

harry had made them both hot chocolate with candy canes when they arrived, but they had brushed their teeth first. and he was thanking himself for that now.

and just as harry had tilted his head, ready to kiss the irresistible blue eyed boy with a beanie over his fringe, louis was gone, and a camera was in his face.

snap!

he pouted as the picture printed out, choosing not to look at it to save himself from the embarrassment.

but louis just looked at it for a second, a small little smile on his face. he shook his head. "you're so beautiful."

harry snatched the camera out of his hand. "stop it," he whined, but then he got an idea. he just needed some sunshine.

so he smiled really wide, because he knew that's how he would get louis' sunshine smile.

and it worked. louis looked at him, a bit confused for a second, but then he smiled back, the crinkles by his eyes much more prominent and his teeth were all showing, and he just looked like sparkles.

like sunshine.

harry lifted the camera and snapped it perfectly, waiting impatiently for it to print. and when it did, his heart kinda just swelled.

he was caught off guard when louis pulled the camera away and threw it on the bed, then grabbed harry around the waist and bent him so his curls were hovering over the floor.

"angel."

and then harry was consumed with peppermint and honey and *love* and louis' lips were pushing against his roughly but gently at the same time, moving slow and then fast. harry kissed back, letting louis hold his weight above the ground, at least until he pulled them both up swiftly, still kissing him.

this kiss.... this was different. harry had never been kissed like this before. because louis' hands were everywhere now, and his lips were moving with so much purpose. this was a movie star kiss, the one where everyone in the crowd feels it too, a kiss that sent goose bumps all over harry's body. this was a kiss that deserved to be talked about.

and when they pulled back for air, harry just stared at that wonderful boy with those dreamy blue eyes with wonder in his own, and his bruised lips still felt like they were being kissed.

"whoa," he whispered, lifting his fingers up touching his lips.

louis let out a breathless laugh. "angel, i didn't know you could do that."

that was all you, louis tomlinson, harry wanted to say, but he just looked at louis through hooded eyes and tried to figure out how someone so beautiful could like someone like him.

louis grabbed his hand, holding it up against his lips gently and closing his eyes. "i love you." then he leaned it and placed another kiss on his lips, a much more gentle, simple kiss.

and yeah, harry wasn't ready for anything to extreme, but that was okay. because this, *this,* being able to touch louis and see his smile and feel his warm, soft lips, was enough. he hoped the love radiating off of him wasn't too obvious.

and when they were finally finished taking pictures, they went out and made a lopsided snowman before sitting on harry's old beat up couch in front of a lopsided tree drinking tea and making up song lyrics to a lopsided song.

and it was so, so wonderful.

thirty-three

birthdays.

harry considered birthdays the most important holiday of the year. it was the day that a person was born, the day a soul came into the world and that person would fall in love and get married and they would get a job and create a life of themselves. and it all started on *one certain day.*

so that's why harry was extremely excited for christmas eve, which also happened to be louis tomlinson's birthday.

harry had started to contemplate the possibilities of presents and parties after he had gotten off the phone with louis. they had talked about louis big news for hours on end. a college had offered him a scholarship for football. it was louis' dream and harry had never been so happy for him.

at first, he had gotten out his laptop and opened an empty document, ready to write down tons of great ideas for louis. but his mind went blank, and he was tempted to call louis and just ask him what he wanted.

no. then it wouldn't be a surprise.

and so now, here he was, laying on his bed, closing his eyes and munching on some gummy bears, searching through his cluttered mind for something to give louis tomlinson.

louis tomlinson.

harry was still trying to figure out everything about him. he knew that louis had a bad temper, which he was already trying to avoid. he knew that louis liked to eat desert for breakfast, and he slept on the left side of the bed. he knew his favorite color was red and he was obsessed with reading and writing, although he didn't tell anybody. he knew that he loved the smell of gasoline and burning fires and pine trees. he knew that he was a great footie player and he was the easiest person to talk to in the world.

and he had a nice bum.

but, none of those things could come even close to what harry wanted for louis. he wanted louis' present to be the present of all presents, so that everyone who saw it would be jealous that they didn't think of it. he wanted nobody else to be *able* to give louis this present.

and just as he was researching puppies who knew how to play kickarse footie, an idea popped in his head.

scary. it was a scary, stomach churning idea. harry could feel his heart racing just thinking about it.

it didn't help that it was midnight and his imagination could run utterly wild. so he just put the idea on his notes, careful to make sure it was private so nobody could see it, and he shut it with a rushed breath. he didn't realise he was blushing until he touched his cheeks and felt them burning.

go to bed, he told himself, trying to calm his mind and keep himself from squirming there on his bed.

so he pushed his headphones in his ears, turning it to a song that would distract him from his, interesting, mind.

***

harry felt as if the night before christmas eve was one of the busiest of the whole year. everybody was preparing for the wild parties, buying last minute gifts and trying to find a faster way to wrap them.

but harry wasn't worried about that. his present required mental preparation, along with lots of soap.

"harry, i would go to bed! you're going to be up quite late tomorrow!"

his mum was right. it was eleven o'clock, and here he was, in the shower, scrubbing every crevice of his small, frail body. well, except for his tummy. he *hated* his tummy. louis' was cute, but his was just... gross.

you're not ready! his mind was screaming.

but his heart...

he took a shaky breath, letting the warm water shower against his bare back and run down behind his thighs and onto the white shower floor.

he knew he was going to take another shower tomorrow, just in case, but he was determined to smell good. he pumped a mountain of shampoo on his hand and plopped it onto his curls that were a bit straight due to the water. then he scrubbed it unbelievably hard, although his scalp was starting to hurt, and then he re-washed all of his body just in case.

when he stepped out, the mirror was completely fogged up. he reached his large hand out, wiping away the blurriness to reveal himself. his hair was hanging to his neck now, the curls deflated. he saw light green, almost blue, and his eyebrows were dark. his lips were moist and red, almost matching his cheeks that were flushed from the hot water. he was already cold, the winter air still not blocked from the heat that was turned on in the house.

he wrapped a blue towel around his hips, before stepping out of the bathroom and into the cool air of his room.

he dried himself off quickly, hung the towel up, and slipped into the bed. he shivered as the cold sheet brushed his bare skin, but after a while, his body heat took over and he was warm.

he fell asleep to a million scenes flashing through his head, and his heart pounding.

***

harry was *not* the one that changed louis' ringtone.

it used to be the dog barking, because it made him laugh and it reminded him of louis a bit.

but now, it was louis saying, "it's louis louis louis. answer. answer. answer. answer."

harry giggled when he heard it, even though he had just woken up and it was only five thirty in the morning.

"hullo?" he mumbled into the phone, his lips barely opening as he was too tired to do that. that required too much effort.

"harry, guess what day it is?"

harry' eyes widened, and he shot up in bed. louis' birthday. it was today. he had to get ready.

he could hear louis' rushed, eager chuckles over the phone as he waited for harry to respond.

"happy birthday," harry said softly, holding his phone between his shoulder and his ear as he wrapped his arms around himself. "and happy christmas." harry looked out the window, and it was still dark outside, the snow glowing white as it fell to the ground.

"christmas is tomorrow, angel," louis said gently. "but thank you. i'm nineteen now."

"i know," harry whispered.

"what's wrong, harold?"

harry bit his lip, hiding a smile. there was mix of terror and excitement in his heart.

"nothing."

"louis doesn't believe you." his voice was suspicious, and kind and worried and harry loved his *so freaking much.*

"no, 'm just thinking about your present."

you could practically hear louis smiling over the phone.

"'m so excited to see you, harry. just seeing your curly little head is enough of a present for me."

"sunshine," was all harry whispered before they hung up.

and then he was distracted by his mum rushing into his room and throwing outfits at him. he didn't have the heart to tell her that he already had one that he picked out with zayn and niall.

so he let her put up shirts against him and fluff his curls, and he tried on some really tight jeans that she said were "in" now. the funny thing was, she picked the outfit that harry was planning on wearing in the first place.

it was a soft, fuzzy green sweater that matched his eyes, and some dark black skinnies along with his boots.

he pushed his curly fringe across his pale forehead, blinking his eyes a little to see himself better in his full length mirror.

harry could hear zayn and niall come in his house, he could hear niall's loud laugh and zayn's low, raspy voice all the way from his bathroom. he ignored it, biting his lip and watching the color appear.

"harry, your friends are here!" anne called, and harry took a shaky breath, pulling his sweater a little farther down his arms and grabbing the sleeves with his fingers.

"coming!" he called out, ignoring the crack in his voice.

he took one more look at his hair in the mirror, at the little tendrils that he could never manage, and smiled. one of his favorite qualities about himself was his teeth.

"h, get your bloody arse in this living room right now!" he heard niall call, which resulted in a fit of laughter from the whole group.

harry took small steps with his boots, ignoring the ache that he felt all the way to the bottom of his ribs and the nervous flutter of his heart.

"hi," he murmured, before he was trampled and pulled into a big bear hug by his best friends.

"harry, you excited for lou's birthday?" zayn said quietly into his ear, and harry nodded, before niall kissed his cheek and gave him a warm smile.

"louis would not stop trying to fix himself up in the mirror, mate. it was embarrassing. and who doesn't despise second-hand embarrassment?" to emphasise his point, niall looked into the sky and pretended to wipe sweat off of his forehead.

harry cracked a smile, already feeling a little better now that his friends were here.

"you boys better get going, but first let me get a photo," anne smiled, and harry let out a little gasp when he realised she stole his polaroid camera.

"mum, you took it," he accused, ruffling her hair a bit.

she just rolled her eyes, motioning for the three boys to stand in front of their small tree and yelled, "cheese!"

harry smiled, as wide as he possibly could, imagining louis to make himself smile bigger.

finally, after anne was holding about twenty photos in her hand, she shooed them out the door and gave harry a quick kiss. "have fun!" she called after them as they sprinted to the warmth of zayn's car.

harry rubbed his arms quickly to create friction. "'s cold," he murmured, shaking the snowflakes out of his curls and watching zayn try to get some of the snow off the windshield.

"it's dangerous is what it is," zayn mumbled.

"let's go!" niall groaned, leaning back in his heated seat and putting on his ray bans, which harry didn't understand because it was dark outside and there was no sun in the sky. but he just shrugged, putting some mint gum in his mouth and listening to the christmas music play softly through zayn's radio.

after about three minutes, they were pulling into louis' drive, his long, long drive. they had scraped off their whole driveway, surprisingly, so it was smooth but harry's stomach felt like he was on a roller coaster.

"we're here!" niall screeched, throwing open the door the minute zayn pulled to a stop.

"yes, we are," harry whispered, squeezing his eyes shut for a few seconds and taking a deep breath.

they ran through the cold, tightening their coats around their shoulders and shielding their selves from the falling snow until they finally stepped into louis and niall's house.

"we're back! we come bearing harry!" zayn yelled and harry blushed when louis finally arrived.

he looked... wonderful. he was wearing a white jumper that matched his eyes and his legs looked so short and cute in his red skinny jeans and he had on blue toms and his hair was pushed across his forehead and he had a santa hat on and he looked like sunshine.

harry shifted from leg to leg, nervous to meet eyes with louis. but when louis finally just said, "hi angel," all casual and that, harry wanted to rip his heart out and feed it to some hungry birds.

he took a deep breath, gazing at louis for real and making eye contact.

"hi louis," he responded, and then he was smiling because louis slid towards him on his little blue toms and picked him up around the waist, spinning the two around like they were the only ones there. harry let laughter bubble out of his lips for a few seconds before louis captured harry's lips with his own.

he tasted like cinnamon.

harry could feel zayn and niall's eyes on them for a few seconds, but he just kissed his louis back and breathed in all the sunshine.

"happy birthday," harry said softly against louis' warm lips.

"happy christmas," louis hummed in response.

***

they found themselves at the dining room table, sitting with jay and bobby and also liam who had joined in.

"so, louis," jay began, taking a bite of her ham before continuing, "what's the one thing you want for your birthday?"

"mum, that's a hard question," louis said in that loud voice of his, "but i'm gonna have to say that i want a hug from you."

the table burst into laughter. well, except for harry, who was sitting nervously with his hands in his lap and his eyes averted to his food.

he felt someone nudge him, and he realised it was louis' knee.

he lifted his head, meeting louis' worried eyes. "you okay?" he whispered, almost inaudible.

harry nodded.

when dinner was finally over, niall proclaimed that the two boys needed alone time together, which harry was grateful for but at the same time he wanted to die.

"so, harold, what did you get me for my birthday?" louis asked hesitantly, eyeing harry's empty hands.

harry could feel his legs shaking.

"it's me. you can have me."

louis' eyes widened. "harry, you don't have to-"

harry interrupted him. "i want to." he meant it.

louis rushed towards him, cradling his face and staring at him for a second before kissing him gently.

when they pulled back, harry spoke.

"wrapped it myself."

thirty-four

louis mouth kind of just opened, as he stood back and stared at harry.

he looked kind of perfect, standing there with his sweater and harry could see his hands shaking.

"you wrapped it," he stuttered, running a trembling hand across harry's jawline, "you wrapped it your, yourself."

harry blushed and nodded, biting his lip and feeling his heart jump at the thought of what he was implying.

"cake!" somebody, probably jay, called from the kitchen. louis didn't move his eyes, just yelled "okay!" and continued to stare at the curly-headed boy who was squirming under louis' heavy gaze.

"we should probably go get some cake," he said softly, shaking his head before grabbing harry's hand. "it's my favorite. red velvet." then he smiled, squeezing harry's hand as they walked into the large kitchen. niall was already sitting next to zayn, a fork in hand and a smile on his face as he watched jay push the candles into the big cake that was covered in cream cheese icing.

"louis!" liam exclaimed and harry noticed that he was eyeing their hands.

"hey li, you gonna sing me an impressive happy birthday?" louis joked, leading harry to sit down at the table in front of his cake. "or am i gonna have to sing it to myself?"

while liam laughed, harry shook his head quickly. "no, no you don't have to sing it to yourself," he said quietly, smiling shyly when louis poked his cheek and let out a little noise.

"you're so cute, angel," he murmured in harry's ear.

"hey!" bobby clapped his hands in front of everyone, standing up out of his chair. "let's start the song!"

harry looked at the now-lit candles, watching the way they flickered around and cast a glow around the dim lighting of the room. he couldn't help but smile as he watched the excited look on louis' face as they started the song. harry sang it quietly, gazing at louis' face the whole time.

"happy birthday dear louis, happy birthday to you," he finished, his voice ending in a fond whisper. he couldn't help but admire louis' lips as he blew out the candles, his eyes squeezed shut and his hands grasping the edges of the table as he leaned over the cake.

"what'd you wish for?" niall asked loudly, looking expectantly at louis.

"i wished for this to be the best birthday ever, which i'm sure it will."

harry pretended not to notice the way louis' eyes lingered on his face as he looked around the table.

"now, time for cake!" jay smiled, before slicing the cake up into pieces and placing them on plates. "louis gets to pick the first piece, because it's his nineteenth birthday today."

there was silence for a few moments, and they all watched as jay gave louis a watery smile and handed him the cake he pointed at.

"mum, don't cry!" louis laughed, smiling widely at her as he wiped away her tears. "'m not even twenty yet, it's okay!"

harry giggled, gently cutting a small bite sized piece off of his cake and stabbing it with his fork. he went over what could happen tonight in his head, feeling butterflies in his stomach at just the thought.

and then he just listened carefully as jay talked and talked about stories from louis' childhood.

harry's favorite one was the one about the time he fell asleep reading and his glasses left an imprint on his face.

***

"so, mum, me and harry decided that we wanted to go out tonight, to celebrate ourselves for our birthday. is that okay?"

jay gave louis a wary look. "and how exactly are you going to 'celebrate'?" she put quotes in the air with her fingers.

"maybe drive around, look at christmas lights, go to this hotel with this really nice pool, sleep there. *just sleep*." he emphasized.

harry blushed as jay looked back and forth between the two of them. "right," she murmured, rolling her eyes. "fine, go, but make sure to text me tomorrow so i know you're alright."

"okay," louis responded, and just as he was opening the door, jay pulled him into a tight hug.

"happy birthday, louis. don't do anything stupid, please." she kissed his cheek, although she had to stand on her tiptoes to reach. "i love you."

"love you too, mum," louis said gently, kissing her back before leading himself and harry out the door.

they were greeted with a wall of freezing air. harry literally fell backwards when he came outside.

"whoa there, harold, no need to slip," louis chuckled, grabbing him under the arms and helping him catch his balance. "it's not even that icy."

harry rolled his eyes, gesturing to the wonderland around them. snow was falling everywhere, making it hard to see very far, but you could make out some blurry lights through the blanket of white.

"right," he murmured, letting louis link their arms and rush them through the thick layer of snow to his car.

when the cold car finally heated up, harry let his head relax against the seat, letting himself close his eyes as louis drove them around doncaster. it was wonderful; sitting in silence with louis always was.

harry opened his eyes after he heard a little chuckle from the boy sitting in the seat on his right. his hands were relaxed on the steering wheel, turning it lazy and slowly as he cruised through the neighborhood. his hair was kind of wet due to the snow that had melted in it, even under his santa hat.

"what's so funny?" harry asked quietly, his eyes widening as he looked at the world around him.

"you're just being all quiet and that, like always, but you're not looking at the lights."

"i am now."

he leaned his forehead against the cool glass of the car, feeling a smile on his lips as he stared at all the rainbow lights surrounding them, reflecting a pretty glow off the snow. it was quite dark outside and harry could see shadows of people inside their houses, partying, and he knew that they would probably be like that all night.

what made him really smile was what louis said when they passed a particularly decorative house, and he pointed at the lit up angels. "look at the angels, angel. you wanna know something about that?"

harry just nodded, listening to the hum of louis' voice as he thought about what he was going to say.

"you're more beautiful than all of those angels. you're the prettiest angel, harry."

harry pressed his cheek up against the glass, hoping to cool his burning cheeks, but it didn't work. he could feel his heart melt as he listened to louis' words, the words he spoke in such a quiet voice. louis reached over and placed a hand in his curls, tangling his fingers in the strands and gently tugging. harry closed his eyes immediately, nudging his head against louis' hand like a kitten.

"are you getting tired?" louis asked softly and harry quickly shook his head.

"no, that just feels good," he mumbled.

louis smiled, and there were all these rainbow colors on his face because of the lights and his eyes were kind of glowing and his santa hat was falling off of his head and his eyes were hooded and harry never thought anybody could be so perfect, so beautiful.

they drove in silence for the rest of time, listening to the christmas music play from louis' car radio, and watching all of the lights and the occasional car pass on the paved roads. harry felt as if he should be tired; it was eleven, but he was so wide awake.

finally, louis pulled into a hotel that harry had never seen before, but it looked quite nice. it was also decorated with christmas lights, except they were just red and green. he cringed when louis opened his door for him, feeling goose bumps rise on his arms the minute the cold air hit his warm body. they sprinted to the hotel, pushing themselves through the door, causing a little bell to go off. it smelled like coffee and disinfectant; a smell harry was surprised to enjoy. he could see a pair of vending machines in a room with a little table and a coffee machine. there were chairs in the lobby, along with only about three people sitting in them.

two of the people were a girl and a boy, kissing deeply as they leaned over their chairs. harry tried his best to tear his eyes away from them, but it was almost impossible.

so he stood awkwardly as louis checked the two boys in, clasping his large hands behind his back and crossing his long, skinny legs.

louis wrapped a warm, soft arm around his waist, walking them to the elevator and only looking at harry when the doors shut.

"that was intense, huh?" he breathed, and harry laughed.

but then louis changed his whole demeanor. his eyes softened as he ran them over harry's lanky body, and a hesitant smile ghosted across his lips. "are you sure you're ready, angel?" he asked gently.

harry paused for a moment, searching for a sign that he wasn't ready. and yeah, a few images of his dad flashed through his mind, but he quickly blocked them out, nodding eagerly and causing his curls to bounce.

"okay, tell me to stop and i will," louis said, just as the door of the elevator opened with a ding.

harry could feel himself blushing, and his whole body was just really hot, and it was an odd, unusual feeling that he had never felt before.

he was caught off guard when louis pressed him against the wall, whispered, "i've never done this before either," and kissed him roughly.

harry could feel tingles all the way to his toe because of the way louis was kissing him. their lips were moving together slow and then fast, and louis' hand was under his sweater, cool against his burning skin. louis was holding him unbelievably hard against the wall, lifting his hips up with his hands and causing harry's boots to linger above the ground.

harry didn't realise they were against the door of their own room until louis fumbled with the key and after several attempts to put it in the lock with shaking hands, he opened it. it was long before the door was shut, and louis was tossing harry onto the bed with a laugh. harry burst into a fit of giggles, rolling on the soft hotel mattress, and louis chuckled as he pulled his shirt off.

"now let's get your shirt off silly," louis laughed fondly, and harry squirmed when louis' cold fingers touched his skin, trying to get his shirt off.

"stop, that tickles!" he screeched, grabbing louis' hands and louis laughed harder, snorts escaping his nose as he tried to pull harry's shirt off.

"harry, you're gonna have to deal," he gasped, pushing his forehead into harry's side in defeat. "c'mon, it's not that hard."

harry snickered as he took his green sweater off, throwing it onto the purple carpet of the hotel room. the heat was turned up obviously high; he was starting to sweat.

"you're so pretty, harry," louis said softly, running his hands up and down harry's arms.

then it was silent, unbelievably quiet as louis leaned in quickly, capturing harry's lips in a deep kiss. harry could taste the red velvet on his lips, and he breathed in deeply through his nose, the smile fading from his lips as he got distracted.

it wasn't long before the both pulled their skinnies off their legs, throwing them on the floor, next to their shirts. harry tried to ignore the racing of his heart as he saw louis examine him, run his eyes over his body that was completely naked except for his boxers.

there was blood rushing between his legs, causing him to squirm uncomfortably, especially when louis ran his finger along the outline of him in the boxers.

"off," he said in a rushed breath, pushing his face into harry's neck and pulling his boxers down.

harry felt goose bumps cover his entire body as he was completely exposed now, and then louis followed after. then, louis gently ran his hands up and down his arms first, then across his chest and tummy, and then over his sensitive member and harry let out a little whimper.

"angel," he whispered, before grabbing harry's hand and placing it between his legs.

harry didn't know what to do with his hand. he opted on first squeezing, which caused louis to let out a yell, sweat forming under his eyes that were glowing in the dark of the hotel room.

"i don't care how you do it, it's you and i love everything that you do," he breathed, caressing harry's cheek.

"i'm scared," harry whispered honestly, not as afraid when he was in the dark.

"so am i, and it's okay. it's okay, harry."

they kissed lazily for a few minutes, just letting themselves feel every inch of each other. harry rubbed his hands across louis' hipbones, memorizing the shape and then he touched between his legs, pinching and squeezing and louis was falling apart beneath his hands and he didn't even realise what he was doing.

harry's eyes widened when louis quickly leaned over and pulled a bottle of some type of gel thing from his little bag he carried with himself everywhere. he claimed that it wasn't a purse but harry thought otherwise.

"what is that?" he asked innocently, hugging himself as he watched louis pop open the cap and squeeze some of it onto his fingers.

"lube," louis chuckled. "it's lube, baby."

"oh."

louis kissed all over his face, his nose, his forehead, his cheeks, his lips. and then he whispered a few comforting words.

"this is gonna hurt, but trust me, i know what i'm doing. i did a little, research."

harry couldn't help but giggle a bit, but his breath caught quickly when he felt the cool liquid touch his rim.

he grabbed louis' hair, tugging and pulling as the sensation took over.

"ow, ow, ow," he whimpered, and there were tears in his eyes as he felt a tearing.

"i know, i know it hurts, but it'll feel good, trust me angel, it will."

harry nodded, biting his lip and letting little squeaks escape his mouth as louis pushed his fingers in further, and then he was pushing in too and it was *so freaking painful,* but it also felt amazing. harry shuddered and let out a tiny squeak when louis crooked his finger, brushing his prostate.

"do that again," he pleaded, gripping anywhere he could and squeezing his eyes shut. "do it again, that feels so good."

he felt louis' finger the sensitive spot again, sending a shiver throughout his whole body. "put a third, a third one," he hiccupped.

louis kissed him gently, before inserting his third finger. it was a stretch, and very painful, but it also was wonderful and harry was falling apart just from louis' fingers.

he felt empty when louis pulled out, and he let out whimpers of protest until he noticed louis rubbing the lube all over himself. "let me do it," he murmured, wanting to feel louis against his skin again. he rubbed the lube on gently, careful in case he hurt louis. louis seemed to be a wreck just by harry's slight, sensitive touch, especially when his fingers brushed the sensitive head and it leaked precum.

harry's stomach churned with an odd, warm feeling when louis hoisted harry's legs over his shoulders, kissing the inside of each of his thighs, and then laid him back down.

before harry knew it louis was pushing into him, linking them in this way that harry knew was special. he was shaking, pressing frantic kisses to louis lips to distract himself from the bittersweet pain.

"i love you," he whispered, clutching louis' hips and pushing his sweaty forehead against louis' feathery hair.

"i, i love you too," louis murmured. "so much."

then louis was thrusting into him, kissing him roughly the whole time and harry could just hear two words, the whole time louis was rubbing and kissing him senseless and his knees were far past weak.

soul mates.

he finally came to the sound of louis' heavy breaths. and so did louis, and when he pulled out he felt so empty and lonely. so he decided to hug louis, as tight as he could, and he was a wreck but that didn't matter. it was christmas eve and it was snowing but together they were so warm.

"happy birthday."

thirty-five

the first thing harry smelled when he woke up was tea.

he scrunched up his nose, squeezing his eyes shut and blinking them before adjusting to the light.

where am i? he thought.

he glanced around him, seeing an unfamiliar lamp and a window with white curtains that looked out onto a parking lot covered with a thick layer of snow. it wasn't until he saw louis, in a small room that looked to be a kitchen attached to the bedroom, wearing a big fluffy sweater and pajama pants, that he realised they were in the hotel. harry could vaguely remember louis bringing the outfit in the small bag he always wore over his shoulders. the pants had little snowmen over them, with big black eyes and orange carrot noses.

louis didn't seem to notice that the younger boy had woken up, as he crossed his ankles and stared out the window of the hotel, his elbows bent as he hunched over and took a sip of his steaming tea. his eyes were bleary from sleep, making his eyes just look dark and smoldering, which harry absolutely loved. his pants were a bit too big for him, and he was using the sleeves of his sweater to shield his hands from the heat of his mug. it was a blue mug with the hotel's logo on it.

harry probably laid there for about two minutes, his cheek pressed against the pillow and his curls splayed everywhere as he kept a steady, lazy gaze on louis. he liked to watch the way louis brushed his fringe out of his eyes, even though it just flopped back in the same place it was before. he loved seeing him lick his lips after he took a sip of his tea, his adam's apple bobbing whenever he took big gulps.

right as louis turned his head, harry closed his eyes quickly, making his breaths slow to look like he was sleeping. he could hear louis' bare feet across the tile floor of the kitchen until he reached the bedroom, which had purple carpet. harry had to hold back a smile whenever louis sat on the edge of the bed, causing it the mattress to sink to the side a bit, and then louis brushed a few curls behind his ears and ran his fingers across the boy's cheek.

"harry," he whispered lightly. "harry, time to get up. louis made you tea."

harry pretended to wake up, stretching his arms and doing the same thing he usual did. "okay," he yawned, rubbing his eyes and hesitating before throwing the covers off of his body.

"i need clothes," harry said.

louis chuckled. "that you are right, harold."

harry blushed, pulling the blankets back over himself while louis pulled some more clothes out of his bag. "they're mine, so they may be a bit too small, but i didn't feel like stopping at your house."

harry nodded. "it's okay."

louis went back into the kitchen, leaving harry to change. harry quickly pulled on the blue pair of boxers and his other pajama pants. these didn't have snowman; they had christmas trees with cute little rainbow ornaments. harry immediately loved them, especially because they were extra soft and felt really nice against his legs.

he made sure louis wasn't looking before looking in the mirror that was hanging over the desk. it was quite big, with fancy trim around it.

what he was inside, though, was breathtaking. his face was glowing, this odd glow that he had never seen before, his lips were still a bit swollen and dark red. his eyes were blurry and light, and he could just feel himself smiling. you could tell just by the haze around him, the relaxed and happy aura that something happened. it was like someone had written **i just had sex** on his head.

he laughed, adjusting his curls and trying not to make it too obvious that he was disgustingly happy. then he took a deep breath, bringing back his usual presence; shy and reserved. the way he liked it.

"i like these," he said quietly, walking into the other room and touching louis' elbow with his hand, gently nudging his forehead into louis' back between his shoulder blades. he was extremely sore, and every time he walked he held in a wince. but he just braved it out, deciding not to let louis worry about him.

"i thought you would," louis said gently, putting the cup he was preparing for the curly headed boy, the way he knew harry liked it, and turning around. harry's heart fluttered when louis wrapped his soft sweater arms around his waist, pulling their hips together softly before capturing their lips in a small, patient kiss.

"let's brush our teeth, then you can drink your tea," louis smiled, and harry frowned.

"i didn't bring a toothbrush."

louis smirked. "just use mine. it's the same as kissing me, you know."

harry at first was a bit disgusted, but the more he thought about it, he knew louis was right. so he nodded, following louis when he got his toothbrush out and led them into the small bathroom. there was a small toilet and a tiny mirror, reflecting harry's pale face and louis' tan one. harry liked the way it looked when louis kissed his cheek and he could see it. he could see the way louis' eyes fluttered shut for a second and he let his lips linger there, and you could see he was smiling.

they brushed their teeth hastily, rinsing with the surprisingly cold water from the hotel sink. harry loved the minty taste left on his tongue afterwards, and he practically skipped back to his tea that was probably cool enough to drink by now. unlike louis, he liked drinking his tea when it was lukewarm, not steaming hot.

"we need to go back to my mum's soon. she wants to open presents. you know she invited anne over, right?"

harry's eyes widened. "our mum's are friends?"

louis laughed. "of course, angel."

***

harry had always loved the smell of louis' house. not as much as the smell of louis, but close. their house smelled like cinnamon and candles and warmth, although it's high ceilings and large windows. whenever niall had him and zayn over, harry loved how warm it felt.

he especially loved it when him and louis finally stumbled out of the snow and into their house. harry could hear the sound of people laughing and talking from the living room, and he smiled when he heard his mum's laughter above all of the rest, loud and musical and wonderful.

"you ready?" louis asked nervously and harry was surprised because louis was *never* nervous.

"'course," harry murmured, pushing himself into louis' side and letting louis grab his hand. "let's go. i want you to get your present."

louis stopped in his tracks. "you already gave me my present," he said.

harry blushed just at that, his hand suddenly starting to sweat in louis'.

"that was the big one. but i had to get you a little one too."

louis rolled his eyes. "harry! you're making me look bad!"

harry giggled. "you'll never look bad."

louis just sighed, pulling harry to him by his waist and dragging them into the crowded living room. zayn was sitting there on the loveseat by himself, watching with a laugh as niall ripped open his present with his teeth, and it reminded harry of a dog.

"what is this crap!" niall yelled into the air, pulling out a football and holding it before his eyes. it was a really expensive one that harry knew niall had always wanted.

"zayn you little," niall continued, an impossible large smile growing on his face, and zayn gave a scared smile. harry couldn't help but laugh fondly as niall attacked the other boy in a hug, his limbs flailing in the air as he leaped in the air into the loveseat.

harry's smile faltered when he felt louis' gaze on his face. his eyes were soft, soft and pale blue, and the look he was giving him was so intense and it made harry feel so warm but also nervous and he shuffled his feet a bit.

harry could see his mum watching the two of them, a curious look in her eyes.

he loves me, was the only thing going through harry's mind as he stared right back at louis.

they stood there for a minute before harry decided to sit by his mum on the couch, giving her a big hug before snuggling into louis who sat right next to them.

he kind of went into a trance, staring out the window at the snow that was still ceasing to stop, and biting his chapped lips. he watched the smoke in the distance, probably coming from a chimney connected to a fireplace that some random, happy family was sitting next to, unwrapping presents just like them. harry wondered if they also had laid out cookies for santa, even though he wasn't real. he wondered if they had two boys with borderline personality disorder and asperger's, and a blonde boy who acted like a child and dyed his hair blonde.

probably not.

harry smiled, looking at the trees now, that were just branches, and he could see a snowman right behind it, and he knew it was zayn and niall's because of the stick sticking out between the legs he didn't have. he kind of wished he could've been there when they made it. he loved snowmen.

"i want to make a snowman," he said, interrupting the conversations they were having amongst themselves as jay opened her presents.

they all were silent, and harry' heart felt weird when he realised that he did, in fact, have that effect on people. because of his lack of speaking, when he did speak, everybody would listen.

he loved it and loathed it at the same time.

they all looked at him for a second, until louis finally broke the silence.

"okay, angel. we'll build a snowman." he paused for a second. "but after we open presents."

harry frowned. "i want to make one now," he pouted.

harry expected louis to get upset, but he just laughed, patting harry's pale cheek with his warm hands.

"okay."

***

they found themselves outside, harry wearing a coat much too big for him, and louis' was even *more* too big for him. there pants made them look extremely fat, and harry had a scarf wrapped around his face so only his eyes could be seen. the cold was already causing his feet to go numb, although he was wearing boots.

"let's go!" louis screamed, and harry smiled when niall and zayn ran out, just as puffy as the other two were. they all burst out laughing when liam came out wearing hot pink with a purple scarf.

they went to work, piling snow into a small ball at first, and then rolling it all over the snow-covered ground. harry pretended not to notice the way louis only used one hand to push the ball and with his other gloved hand he pushed harry's waist, as if helping him along. it actually did help, because it hurt for harry to walk.

when their snowball was finally as tall as harry, they moved onto the next ball. harry spent his time rolling snow wondering how in the heck they were gonna get the next one on there, but he decided to face that obstacle when they came to it.

niall let out a squeal when zayn pushed him instead of the snowball, and it was one of the most girly squeals harry had ever heard. he giggled, rolling his eyes at his best friends as they wrestled it out on the ground. it wasn't long before they were both buried in snow, only their pink noses sticking out.

"we're supposed to be making a huge snowman!" liam complained, punching a hole in the slightly smaller ball he was holding up. he was smiling though, the crinkles by his eyes more prominent than ever.

but really, harry couldn't keep his eyes off of louis, who was sitting criss cross in the snow and preparing the small head they were going to put on the huge body. he looked as if he was in deep concentration; his eyebrows were furrowed as he tried to shape it into the perfect ball. harry watched as he smoothed the sides, turning it over every once in a while, and brushing those sides off as well. his pale blue eyes were sparkling from the sunlight reflecting off the snow, and his cheeks were flushed.

harry slowly walked towards him, pocketing the carrot and two buttons that jay had given him before they even went outside. apparently, he should do the honors because anne had told her all about his artistic abilities. harry had just blushed, taking the objects and giving louis' mum a soft smile that was slightly embarrassed. what if she had seen the drawing he made for louis?

louis looked up when he heard harry's boots crunching in the snow, which overlapped the sounds of niall, zayn, and liam's screams. they were taking turns head-butting the ball, making huge head shaped holes in it, ruining all the work they had done.

"angel, c'mere, i had this idea when i was making this head."

harry walked a bit faster, ignoring the ache in his bum.

"what's your idea?" he asked quietly, shaking the snowflakes out of his hair.

"i never said i was going to tell you; i'll tell you later."

"then why'd you tell me to come here?" harry raised his eyebrows, but he didn't feel it.

"because i wanted you to sit by me," louis said shyly, turning his attention back to the head. despite all of his touching up, harry could see a few major lumps in his creation. but when he reached his hand over to fix it, louis slapped it away with a yell.

"no! you're going to ruin it! it's almost perfect!"

harry laughed, putting his hands in his lap. he was sure that they were past red by now, and it was going to hurt like heck warming them up.

"done!" harry heard from a few feet away, and he looked to see niall, zayn, and liam putting the second ball on with a final grunt. it was covered in holes but harry thought it looked perfect.

"time for the head," he whispered to louis, standing up and brushing some of the snow off of his pants.

louis sighed, kissing the top with his dark red lips before lifting it up. he was cradling it tightly to his chest, as if he any touch would ruin it. that is, until he held it in front of harry's face, so the cold water dripped onto his nose.

"you have to kiss it too."

harry looked at louis from around the ball for a second. "what?"

"good luck. so it doesn't crush through the whole snowman."

harry foolishly kissed it, feeling his lips tingle.

they walked towards the huge snowman, which was now the size of two niall's.

"how are we going to get that up there?" liam said, exasperated as he flicked some sweat off of his forehead, although it caused snow to fall in his eyes.

"i can get on harry's shoulders," zayn offered.

"no!" louis protested immediately, glaring at the younger boy. "no, you will not. i will."

harry held in a laugh.

soon, louis was sitting on harry's shoulders, and harry pretended that the way louis squeezed his thighs together tightly didn't affect him. nope. not at all.

"i. can't. reach," louis whined, and harry strained as louis reached over the huge snowman and tried to put the head on perfectly.

it took a few more minutes until louis was satisfied with its position. and harry opted on just falling backwards into the knee deep snow instead of letting louis off another way. louis screamed bloody murder into the sky, and it echoed.

"now i have to put the features on," harry mumbled, pulling the carrot out of his pocket and rolling it around between his nubby, gloved fingers.

louis sighed. "i'll hold you."

harry eyed louis' height, before shrugging his shoulders and getting on louis.

and the snowman looked to be perfect when it was done. at least, harry thought so.

"harry, there's something missing."

harry gasped when louis pushed him hardly into the snow, causing his heart to race uncontrollably.

"what was that for?" he choked out, watching as niall shoved louis back.

"you have to make a snow angel, angel."

***

while harry was busy warming up on the couch of louis' living room, drinking hot chocolate, he was staring at the picture jay had taken of the five boys in front of the snowman on his camera.

they were finishing up opening presents. louis almost cried when he realised that harry had given him a drawing of both of them, together in the car.

and louis gave harry a promise ring. it was wrapped in birthday wrapping, with a card with the words *to angel* written in louis' messy scrawl.

and harry fell in love with him all over again.

thirty-six

"i love your feet. they're warm."

harry smiled, wiggling his toes from underneath his fuzzy, thick white socks.

"what are your new year's resolutions?"

harry thought for a second, watching the newscaster with blonde hair on the television, clutching a coat around her body and pointing excitedly at the clock. there was about an hour left.

"to accept you, no matter how many mistakes you make," harry responded, looking straight into those twinkly, captivating eyes.

"well," louis responded. "mine is to never get off this medication, because it works so freaking well." he paused, before reaching out and grabbing a stray curl between his thumb and his pointer finger, placing it back in its place before running his hands through all of harry's hair. "and another one is to make sure that you are absolutely speechless when i'm done kissing you, because i love that. i love how affected you are by me."

harry blushed. "you're affected by me too," he defended weakly.

and harry thought that maybe, just maybe, that might've been true, by the way louis bit his lip when harry's voice cracked and his eyes were glossy, and he looked so *needy*.

"i most definitely am," louis whispered, looking a bit flustered.

they both stopped talking and turned their attention to the rest of their company, who were sitting on the couch laughing. louis and harry were both laying on the floor (or each other), waiting for 2011 to finally arrive.

"no! she's only a friend!" niall was saying, but at the same time he was chewing on his crisps and laughing.

"you tied her shoe for her in the middle of class! you're whipped!" zayn declared, leaning back into the couch.

"i didn't want her to trip," niall protested weakly.

harry laughed, snuggling his feet between louis' legs to keep them warm. there was still snow falling, not as harshly as it had a few days ago, but it was still quite deep. harry watched the trees sway in the howling winds that came with december weather. harry loved the idea of being safe inside, warm and listening to the laughter as they anxiously waited for the year to be over.

he felt extremely peaceful. the blue blanket they were laying on was soft, almost as soft as the pajama pants harry was wearing. the volume on the television was just right, so that if you listened for it you could hear it, but it wasn't distracting. louis was laying on his back, holding harry's foot in his hand and massaging it slightly, and at the same time fluttering his eyes shut and open as he stared at the ceiling above him. he looked tired, especially when he let out a kitten-like yawn and harry loved the way his nose crinkled up and all of his body tensed for a second.

there was about thirty minutes left, giving zayn and niall plenty of time to do their arm wrestling while jay and anne gossiped about people harry had never heard of.

so, instead, he balanced on his elbow and pushed the side of his head into his hand, his neck too tired to do it on its own. he held a lazy gaze on louis, on his long coal eyelashes and legs that looked incredibly short in his onesie pants.

"'m cold," he mumbled out randomly, but the buzz of talking around them ceased to stop.

harry looked around for a blanket, but it looked as if jay was taking most of them. apparently, she got cold quite easily.

so, he pulled his feet away from louis' hand, despite his quiet murmurs of protest. then he crawled towards the older, yet smaller boy. louis didn't seem to mind when harry hooked a leg around louis' waist, the way he used to do when his mum was cold. he wrapped his left arm around him and the other he fisted into louis' chest. then, he snuggled his face into louis' warm neck, breathing in the smell of honey.

"'s that better?" he asked quietly, ignoring the teasing from niall and zayn.

"get a room!" niall called, which resulted in a slap on the arm from jay.

harry fluttered his eyelashes, listening to louis' steady breaths. his heart kind of melted when louis pressed a feather-like kiss to his hair, whispering incoherent things, and harry giggled a bit at the coolness on his head.

"i'm hungry," louis sighed, and harry rolled his eyes.

"then get food."

"i don't wanna move. you're warm and i like your curls and you smell good," louis said.

harry felt like he was supposed to laugh, but it just made his breath catch. and that sentence, *that one sentence*, caused him to feel something, he could feel it so much. he was brought back to louis' birthday, when louis placed shaky touches to his skin and kissed him hotly and loved him and *made love to him*, and it was all about him and for some reason that made him so happy but it felt like a dream and he just loved louis so much.

"i love you," harry breathed, his voice cracking a bit and there was an ache in his chest as he said it but louis could tell something was different, and he shot up, causing the hood of his onesie to slide off of his head.

"what?"

harry suddenly wasn't aware of everyone around him, except for louis and it was just *louis* with the blue eyes that mesmerized him and confused him and *louis* with the awful mood swings, *louis* who's hair always looked like a movie star's and louis who still had one outfit to his name. louis whose skin was soft like soap and louis who set of fireworks in his tummy the minute they touched.

"i love you," was all harry could say, shyly, and louis cocked his head at the younger boy, but he seemed to know that harry was thinking and when harry was thinking there wasn't much you could do about it except let him. so he nodded, and harry watched him smiling, this pleased, flattered, and happy smile, before he whispered, "okay. i love you too, baby."

harry nodded again, laying back down and pushing even further into louis' body, trying to get as warm as possible. he could hear zayn and niall discussing which news reporter was uglier, the boy or the girl. harry, personally, thought it was the girl, but he wasn't going to get involved.

he just needed to wait for 2010 to be done with, finished. and this was the perfect way to wait, not boring at all, no.

***

"twenty seconds!" niall screeched, causing harry to jolt from his half-trance. louis was sound asleep, gentle breaths escaping his open lips.

"get up," harry said quietly, clutching louis' shoulder, and louis' eyes snapped open.

"it's new year's?!" his voice was slurred from sleep.

harry was unable to respond.

because louis was kissing him, and niall was dying from laughter as he struggled to finish counting down until new year's. but harry didn't focus on that.

he was too busy focusing on all the other, wonderful things.

first, louis was kissing him, definitely longer than twenty seconds because there was cheering now, and the floor was literally shaking from his friends' jumping.

two, louis tasted like hot chocolate and his lips were so incredibly warm and gentle because of his tiredness.

three, he loved louis.

so he kissed him back passionately, letting louis tug them to a sitting position and tangling his fingers in the younger boy's curls. and there were these butterflies fluttering in harry's tummy and his heart was soaring.

and as louis kissed him, all the events of this year -last year- flashed through harry's mind. he thought about that whole summer, how he was so lonely, and he thought he was fine. but as school went on, he realised that he missed louis and then he passed out in the snow and his dad came back and it was awful, but louis was *there for him.*

everyone was catcalling and harry realised that their parents were still in the room and he pulled back, breathless.

and heck if louis didn't look like sunshine.

his eyes were sparkling, his lips wet and a bit chapped and his nose was just perfect like always and harry loved his nose *so much*.

"happy new year's," louis whispered, almost inaudible over the laughing coming from their families.

"you too," was all harry could choke out because he was having so many emotions at once and it was wonderful, but he also felt kind of overwhelmed.

he was so overwhelmed, in fact, that he started crying.

"harry!" louis cried, pulling him into this really tight hug that made harry want to cry harder. "angel, baby, what's wrong?!"

"i'm," harry began, but his voice was so strained that he had to stop for a second. "i, feel, feelings."

louis furrowed his brows. "what d'you mean, my lovely curly?"

harry let out a watery laugh. "i'm not sad. i just can't take all these emotions at once, i guess," he admitted.

louis chuckled fondly. "louis loves you, okay? he loves you, more than anything, more than life."

harry jumped in surprised when he felt arms wrap around him from behind.

"oh, baby, it's new year's!"

it was anne.

"are you excited? it's a fresh start!"

harry smiled, nodding in agreement and craning his neck to place a soft kiss on anne's cheek.

"i know mum, it's great."

"now you should be going to bed. it's past your bedtime."

louis met eyes with harry. "let's go, sweets. we don't any sleepy kitten harry, do we?" his smile was like sparkles.

"no, no we don't," harry responded sheepishly, letting louis pull the two to their feet.

louis led them to his room, after niall, zayn, and liam gave both of them an odd goodnight, which consisted of dirty comments that were too quiet for the girls to hear.

harry let out a relaxed sigh when they finally entered, savoring the silence, except for the heater by his window, which was glowing red in the dark room. they walked in quietly, louis holding harry's fingers loosely, almost as if he was too tired to do it properly.

they quickly went into the attached bathroom, brushing their teeth, going to the restroom, kissing lazily in-between.

"did you have a good year?" louis asked quietly, pushing harry gently by the waist back into his room. "any regrets?"

harry had to think about that for a little, but he found himself nodding slowly and meeting eyes with louis in the dark. "yeah, i do, but i did have a good year."

"what was your favorite part?"

harry looked away, a sheepish grin on his face. "your birthday."

louis seemed taken aback. "really?" he was smiling, this soft, nervous, tentative smile.

"yeah."

"it's 2011 now, bloody crazy."

harry nodded, leaning forward and kissing louis deeply.

louis cradled harry's face in his hand, but his touch was so gentle it was like he was holding fragile glass and harry loved him because of that.

they finally found themselves in louis' bed, the blankets pulled up to their chins, and harry no longer felt somewhat chilly when he snuggled as close as tightly as possible. he felt wonderful.

"happy new year's, angel," louis whispered, massaging his curls a bit.

"happy new year's."

thirty-seven

who knew 2011 would be the year that everything changed?

harry, who was still just a plain junior that still hated school, certainly didn't.

"do you miss him?"

harry would find himself nodding blankly, unable to pull his stare away from the wall of their newly remodeled lunchroom.

it smelled of disinfectant and frozen food. he wanted to get out, he wanted to jump into louis' car that was currently moving farther and farther away from their home, towards doncaster. and he wanted to kiss him and beg him not to, but he couldn't take louis' dream away from him.

it felt as if new year's was a million years away. harry could recall these really nice nights with louis, where they would go out and feed each other and cuddle on the couch and whenever louis was gone harry was just an utter mess and he was always looking at the door, asking if louis was there every noise he heard.

but, it was one of those times where louis sat him down, kissing him so hard it hurt and harry could tell something was wrong and there was this ache in his throat although he didn't even know what louis was upset about.

"i'm gonna miss my angel so, so much," louis had said.

and harry had given him a confused look, furrowing his brows and looking up at him. louis' pale blue eyes were sparkling with tears, a sight that caused harry to feel an ache all the way to the bottom of his ribs.

"what do you mean?" harry adjusted his position on the couch, feeling his throat beginning to hurt. "you're right here. why are you going to miss me?"

he thought it was a logical question. why would his louis leave? they were so *together,* everywhere they went.

louis had gulped loudly, his lips trembling as he squeezed his eyes shut. "we can skype, okay baby? we can skype, and you can still see my face and maybe those green eyes that i love will be just as vibrant on my camera, i heard macbook's cameras are pretty good. and i'll even blow you kiss-" he cut himself off, a shudder going through his body, and it seemed that if he tried to talk all that came out was a whimper.

harry could feel his head clouding, a sensation he hadn't experienced in a while, and he certainly hadn't missed it.

and louis had pulled him into this bone crushing hug and harry could feel himself going numb, but he hugged back just as hard, hugging his louis with everything he had, and he pushed his head into louis' warm chest. he had on this really soft sweatshirt and it smelled just like him, like boy and sweat and honey and cologne and harry just wanted to breathe it in forever.

"where are you going?" harry had whispered, putting his hands on louis' waist and squeezing his sides.

"'m going off to uni. 'm gonna be a football player, 'member?"

harry imagined louis in his uniform, a big black number on his back and his hair sweaty and pushed back and he was living his dream and he was so *proud* of louis.

but right now he really couldn't breathe again. louis whispered comforting things to him as he started to breathe harder, trying to get air into his lungs but he couldn't see through his eyes because they were blurred with tears. and they stung his cheeks, except for when louis wiped them away with his soft fingers.

"don't leave, don't don't don't don't don't," he struggled to get out, shoving louis' arms away from him and trying to get comfort, a sob shaking his shoulders, and he couldn't even close his mouth as strangled whimpers escaped his lips. he squeezed his eyes shut, wrapping his arms around his legs and rocking back and forth on the couch and louis was touching him but he wanted him to stop.

"it's only for a couple years, angel, calm down, it's okay." louis grabbed his wrists gently, moving them so harry wasn't holding himself. then, he picked up harry and pulled him on his lap, letting harry fist against his shirt and cry but he was shaking so freaking bad, making louis cry too.

"don't don't don't don't," harry rushed out, and louis just held him, he held him so tightly and it made him want to cry even harder.

but all louis had said, that last week before he left, was "i love you, my baby angel."

and they spent the whole week trying to make the time go by utterly slow, staying up all night even though harry had a test the next day and he was so worn out from crying.

the first day was the easiest to get through. the end of the week, saturday, seemed a million years away, even though it wasn't.

but harry and louis pretended it was.

they first went to that old amusement park they had a while back, and they rode that roller coaster and harry kissed him again except this time it was more of a rushed, urgent kiss rather than a patient, nervous one.

then louis took them back to harry's flat, which was empty. anne was on a date with the same guy she had been dating for a couple months now and harry was happy for her, but he wasn't happy for himself and louis was what he was focused on at the time.

their kisses were so desperate and needy and harry could feel his heart breaking as he kissed him with everything he had. and they had kissed until their lips were sore, and then they made love on harry's bed and it was wonderful but although they had only done it twice harry felt like he would miss it so much.

harry fell asleep in louis' arms for the second time that week.

and then, on wednesday, after school louis took harry to an empty part of their town, where houses were few and far between and the streets were gravel. he parked next to the lake, although it got sand on his tires, then he tugged harry out of the car and picked him up, throwing him over his shoulder.

"put me down!" harry had yelled, happiness filling his mind for a second as louis ran them both across the sand, until he grew too tired and opted on just throwing harry into the cold water, as it was only january. harry could feel water beginning to pull his sweatshirt and skinnies down, but louis wasn't hesitant to take them off for him. then he took his clothes off until they were both shivering in the lake, all of their clothes drying in the cold weather on the sand. harry felt warm all over, though, when louis grabbed behind his thighs and hoisted his legs up, wrapping them around his curvy waist. harry shivered when he felt louis touch him underwater, this odd but numbing feeling. louis was laughing so hard, though, when harry squeezed his sides.

"that tickles!" he screeched and harry raised his eyebrow with a soft smile.

"but i always do that?"

"my senses are heightened," louis explained, snickering.

harry had laughed, really hard, especially when louis began to tell him stories, still holding him around his waist under the water. harry had to look down at him, his curls hanging down and dripping in front of louis' face. louis' lips were trembling, but his eyes were sparked with excitement and adrenaline.

harry didn't know what had come over him when he leaned down just a little bit, capturing louis' lips in a breathtaking kiss, and harry would never, *ever*, get tired of the feeling of kissing louis. his lips were so soft and there was numbing electricity shooting through his body. every time louis reached up and cupped his cheek it burned his cold skin. it was a heated, aching kiss and harry never wanted to *stop* kissing him.

then louis finally let him go, twirling them around in circles in the water, breathless laughs escaping their lips.

after a while, they just sat there, staring at each other. the only noise was their hair dripping into the lake, and harry stared at louis for a good minute, before a soft smile broke his cheeks and he crossed his ankles under the water. how, how did he get so freaking lucky?

louis clumsily trundled towards him, shaking his head and poking his cheeks. "you're silly, harold."

harry shivered, moving the cold water of the lake around with his hands. "i am?"

"yes. and i love you so much. i love you i love you!" louis sang into the sky, a foolish grin on his face as he tilted his head to look up. "i love you i love you!"

harry just blushed.

and then, on friday, they spent the whole day talking about the things they loved most about each other, and they were crying, harry was bawling like a baby and he probably looked utterly miserable but that's because he was.

he finally understood what lovesick meant.

but then, friday became saturday and sad smiles turned into kisses that tasted like their tears and hugs that lasted a billion years.

harry actually fell to his knees on the sidewalk when louis' car disappeared, and he wasn't really there when zayn picked him up off the pavement and carried him to his bed, rocking him until he fell asleep.

and now, it was monday and harry's eyes were swollen from crying because he couldn't handle this, he wasn't that strong. niall had already flushed all of his razors, and he was so tempted to go the store and buy some more blades. never had his wrist itched more, and his heart felt like somebody had torn it.

the only time that he felt somewhat functional was him and louis' nightly phone calls. well, for him it was night. for louis is was in the afternoon, on his lunch break. his voice sounded so far away on the phone and harry just wanted to grab it and squeeze it in his fist and find some way to play it over and over on tape. every crack in his voice harry had memorized already, he could just see louis' face when he explained his exciting life at uni.

and yeah, harry knew louis missed him by the way he whispered i love you when they finally had to hang up, but then he had something nice to go back to afterwards. harry just had to go to school. niall and zayn were already distracted with their own problems; it wasn't their fault, it's just the way it was, and harry understood that.

and here he was, sitting at the lunch table, the only thing on his mind was sunshine and every time he thought about their kiss he saw stars and he just kind of hurt all over.

"harry, harry snap out of it."

he could just remember when him and louis had a pillow fight. he loved how when louis hit his head he immediately apologises profusely, cradling harry in his arms even though harry was giggling against his chest, because he was ridiculous.

"harry!" louis had cried. "baby, i hurt you! louis is sorry, he's so sorry!"

harry's stomach was actually hurting from laughing when louis kissed it better before hitting *himself* in the head with the pillow.

"i'm gonna miss you much," louis murmured into his hair when they had finally laid down, both breathing heavily and sweating a bit.

"bunches," harry had replied.

"harry edward freaking styles, look at me right now!"

he also remembered when louis burned their macaroni cheese dinner, and when harry called him silly, he just replied, "i'm in love with you, do you think that's silly, sassy pants?"

before harry could respond, louis picked him up and spanked him on the bum. "bad!" he teased.

harry's heart was racing, a lot. yeah.

he cringed when he felt something hit him upside the head. it was zayn's hand.

"harry!" he said, frustrated.

harry looked up at him, a bit dazed and sad from what was going through his mind.

"yeah?" he whispered.

"what're you thinking 'bout, h? you just spilled your drink everywhere."

harry frowned when he realised that his mountain dew was tipped over, a pile of napkins laying on some of it, but his peanut butter and jelly was soggy and inedible now.

"i'm thinking about.."

"louis?"

"yeah."

thirty-eight

the room smelled like hamburgers.

he hated it. he hated that it smelled so bad and he hated everything, and he wanted to just cry.

was it the fact that the lights of this fast food restaurant shone so brightly it caused his head to throb? maybe, but now he was sitting on a hard stool and his phone was floating, taunting him in his glass of coke. he grimaced at it, pushing it away despite the confused glances he got sent his way by nearby strangers. he felt disgusting, he felt so gross and his chest felt like there were knives stabbing in it.

"no, no no no no," he whispered, rubbing the back of his neck and squeezing his eyes shut, trying to remember why he was happy before this. why was he ever happy?

harry was hurting, he was hurting so bad and the one person in the world he cared about the most was the cause.

his giggle, his wonderful musical laugh, it was so clear over his phone. but it wasn't caused by him. it was caused by louis' new friend, the friend with smoky brown eyes and plush pink lips. the friend that added harry on facebook the minute louis had told him about harry.

his name was mitchell. he had this shaggy black hair that harry could never sculpt his wild curls into and these brown eyes that harry could never compete with. his eyelashes were a mile long; harry could just imagine louis staring at them, admiring them without a single lingering thought of harry, not even in the back of his mind.

it had been four months since harry had seen louis in person, but it felt as if had been a lifetime. harry found himself crying just when he saw a pair of vans in his closet or even the sun.

the skype calls used to be every night, and louis would tease him across the screen, his blue eyes sparkling despite the grittiness of the screen and the darkness of his dorm room. there was so much fond in his eyes, so much love and care and harry would feel his heart just swell every time he saw that bright smile that was reserved just for him. he would squirm under the laptop on his thighs, feeling his hand ache for louis'.

that ache in his heart was always there. it was a constant reminder that louis was gone at uni, having a laugh with his new friends and winning every football game he played. but soon, that ache in his heart was everywhere, it was in his stomach, especially.

he was beginning to believe that this was all his fault. he was the reason that louis was beginning to forget about him. it was his fault that he was so heartbroken about all of this in the first place.

he should've known the first day he saw louis, when he was the danger that was buried deep beneath his pale blue eyes, that he was going to get hurt. he was going to get rejected, louis was going to leave and take part of harry with him. he took his laugh with him, he took harry's laugh and his self-confidence and his heart.

harry stood up, feeling his eyes flutter shut for a moment as his tiredness swept over him. he hadn't had a proper night's sleep since louis left. his pillow still smelled so painfully like louis, and it shouldn't have *been* painful because louis said that they were still together, that he still loved harry.

harry believed him, but that was when louis was so kind and good to him, when louis grabbed his hand when they were walking and when he kissed him until he was breathless. when louis traced nonsensical patterns on his back when they would lay in harry's bed when he got home from school.

"i love you," louis would whisper randomly, cupping harry's cheek with his small hands and staring into his eyes, a little smile on his lips. he looked so freaking beautiful then; his jawline perfect and his eyelashes brushing lightly against his cheeks when he blinked.

he reached for his phone in his coke, which was room temperature now, and sadly dropped it in the trashcan. he could feel a bit of regret as he looked at it's sad, broken figure in the rubbish can surrounded by half eaten burgers and leftover french fries and napkins covered with ketchup.

this was his fault too. everything was his fault. his mum wasn't happy anymore and that was his fault because he scared the one chance she thought she had away just because he liked boys. harry could see the hurt in her eyes when ross spoke, glaring at harry the whole time he was telling anne to choose between the two.

"it's me or the faggot," was what he said, and anne looked ready to slap him but at the same time like she wanted to kiss his words away. harry could read it, in her eyes that looked so much like his.

she finally told him to leave but harry did notice when she left a lingering touch on his shoulder, as if to say he could come back some other time. when she finally shut the door behind the man harry decided he hated, she couldn't even look at harry. she just shook her head, her lip trembling before she stormed to her room, sobs escaping her mouth.

harry was in the same position. he slid down the wall, his shoulders shaking with silent sobs. why did he have to be such a screw-up? why did he have to be gay and why did he have to be so sensitive about everything? now his mum was hurt, and it was all because of him and his skin was crawling because he felt so freaking disgusting.

who knew that in four months harry would think of himself as a fat ugly mess of a person? his curls were outgrown again, but this time he didn't style them, just let them hang in curly strands in his face.

those past four months, everything was going wrong. louis was beginning to drift away from him, well, not drift. he was already gone. he ripped harry's heart out and used it on someone who deserved it. mitchell. harry wanted to hurt mitchell, but at the same time he was glad that louis found someone that was good enough for him. louis never said that him and mitchell were dating but harry could tell by the way mitchell touched louis' shoulder when he sometimes visited their skype calls. it was beyond awkward, watching another boy flirt with harry's boyfriend right in front of his eyes. but the worst part was that louis flirted back, fluttering his eyelashes and laughing incredibly hard at everything mitchell said.

harry knew it was bad when he whispered, "i knew you would leave me," but louis was too distracted with texting mitchell that he didn't respond. that was the day harry had an anxiety attack, slamming his laptop shut and trying to steady his breaths. but now, there wasn't anyone to comfort him, to hold him. louis was a million miles away and his mum was still locked up in her room, almost depressed as he was. so he comforted himself, rocking back and forth on his mattress and taking large, shuddery breaths through his lungs, and he just.. he hated himself.

harry never thought he would hate himself. he sometimes disliked himself, and there were many features that he just didn't like, like his tummy and nose hips and thighs and feet. but now, it wasn't just physical. he loathed himself, he loathed himself even more every day when niall and zayn began to ignore him as well. they always refrained to tell him about parties now, and they even had sleepovers without him. harry would be lying if he said that didn't hurt.

harry shoved his hands in his pockets as he walked outside. it was the last day of may, which meant the end of school was coming impossibly quickly. harry looked forward to it, a lot.

his long legs carried him across the parking lot. he hated his legs. he hated that everywhere he went he tripped over his own feet. he hated that when that happened louis used to always chuckle and balance him, touching his elbow gently. then he would lift his chin with his short fingers and kiss him senseless, and he tasted like honey. but now he was alone, and his mum hadn't even checked to see where he went. niall and zayn hadn't either.

harry grimaced as a car zoomed by through the drive thru, causing water from the earlier rain to splash on him. it caused his white shirt to stick to his tummy, his fat bulbous tummy that he was growing to hate more and more as the days went on. louis never called him beautiful anymore; not even when they were somewhat okay. harry would sometimes go shirtless on the camera and louis' expression wouldn't change and harry could practically feel him hiding his disgust.

but louis, louis. he always looked like an angel, like some god had carved him up in the clouds and dropped him from the sky, putting sparkles of gold throughout all of his body.

harry hated himself for being jealous.

he pinched some of the fat on his hips, feeling tears prickle his eyes. no, he wasn't going to break down here. no. that was reserved for his room.

he ran to his car, using his shaky hands to put the keys in the ignition before driving away from this awful restaurant that he came to for no reason at all. the bare trees whizzed past him as he drove farther and farther away, biting his lip to conceal the whimpers that were trying to escape. he knew that the more he drove, the more he focused on the road, that he would control himself from breaking down.

harry remembered when louis actually cared about him. he remembered the believability and sincerity in louis' tone when he told harry that he loved him. and now harry was wondering what he did wrong that made louis, and everybody else, hate him so much.

harry felt his heart beating unbelievably fast in his chest as he let the memories of louis consume him, playing like a movie in his mind.

he was sobbing uncontrollably by the time he stopped in front of his house, and he ran inside to his bedroom as hastily as he could. then, harry slammed the door shut with a whimper, banging his fist and then his head against it. his room smelled like laundry detergent and deodorant and it was so unbelievably overwhelming and harry just wanted to hide himself in his closet.

but first, he forced himself to go to the restroom. he had needed to go for a while, but he had been putting it off. but right after harry relieved himself, he let all of his pants drop, pooling around his legs. there was a small metal scale that his mum had used sometimes, even used on harry when he was quite little and only weighed forty five pounds.

he felt his stomach churn as he first shook the fabric of his black jeans off of his ankles before stepping onto the cold metal of the scale. the numbers moved around for a while and harry sucked his stomach in as if that would help. he didn't know when this insecurity started; all he knew was that he shouldn't have eaten such fatty foods before. that's probably why louis spent so little time on his tummy, why he was always just kissing his lips and avoiding any area near his fat hips.

the number finally showed up, and it was freaking high and harry never knew that he would cry over something as little as this but here he was, staring at the numbers that went away after a while and letting tears drip down his cheeks and onto the floor.

he didn't even let himself look in the mirror, and he especially didn't look at the picture he had tucked in the frame of him and louis.

he was falling apart, now that louis was gone. louis was with mitchell now, just the way things should be.

thirty-nine

harry really loved rainy days.

it was raining today, quite hard and it swept against the windows roughly.

harry could hear a steady rumble of thunder, as if it was background music for the pounding rain. he wrapped a blanket around his shoulders, the cool air of outside causing it to be cold inside too. his mum wasn't home; she never was anymore. harry could only assume she was working, or maybe shopping. he had a tugging feeling that she was still seeing ross, but that was her right and none of harry's business.

well, it used to be his business until his mum shut him out.

harry was sitting on the couch, the telly muted in front of him on a random cartoon. he was holding a cuppa in his hands, letting the warmth from the tea seep into his skin. it seemed that harry only would drink these days; when he ate it wasn't much.

louis and he had skyped again, and he decided he wasn't going to take his shirt off. louis called him angel again, but it was half-hearted and kind of... kind of like he said it as a habit. harry knew that louis thought that he was fat, he knew.

harry gulped some tea, feeling the hot liquid cause a warmth in his chest to spread throughout his body. the house smelled of laundry detergent; harry had swept and cleaned the whole thing before doing all of the laundry.

harry tried not to let his mind wander to places he didn't want it to go, but it was quite hard when he had nothing to do as it was a friday night and zayn and niall were going out somewhere. his heart ached every time he thought about the fact that they ignored him now; but he knew he was a nuisance. they didn't want him around. who would want a fat, ugly, sensitive person hanging around all the time? harry knew that his friends didn't like his obsessive compulsive disorder or anxiety issues that came with his asperger's.

harry didn't realise he was crying until a tear splashed into his hot tea, causing the surface to ripple a bit. he brought his fingertips under his eyes, feeling the hot stinging moisture that signaled that he was, in fact, crying. he blinked his eyes quickly, taking a thick gulp and trying to numb the ache in his chest by *not thinking.*

but there was this person that was always at least in the corner of his cluttered mind. the last time harry saw him he was wearing these glasses that framed his wonderful blue eyes perfectly. his lips looked dark red on the camera and his eyelids were tainted a light lilac color, probably from lack of sleep. his nose was just as perfect as always, and his eyelashes just looked so incredibly long.

"are we still okay?" louis had asked him, brushing his fringe skillfully across his pale forehead with his eyebrows furrowed.

"yeah," harry whispered back, gripping the sides of his laptop incredibly tight, and it took everything in him not to shut the lid of his laptop. so he bit his lip hardly, until it drew blood. louis didn't seem to notice that he was upset, either that or he didn't care.

"i was thinking of coming down to visit sometime," louis had continued, leaning closer to the camera.

"yeah," harry said again.

"and maybe i could bring mitchell. i kind of want you to meet him."

"yeah."

the worse part of the skype call was that louis had logged out before harry had the chance to do their routine "blow a kiss to the camera." he sat there, frozen with his fingers still on his lips, and he was blushing and he hoped louis didn't see him beginning to do it.

that night, he read the book louis had wrote him, and then he had to hold himself to together, to keep from falling apart.

the rain was starting to pour harder, the thunder shaking the house. harry gripped his mug tighter in his hands, causing his knuckles to go white. he was holding it so tight, in fact, that it caused his hand to slide forward and the tea spilled all over his body.

harry jumped up with a yelp, feeling the hot tea burn his skin painfully. he ripped his shirt off, hopping around a bit as rushed breaths escaped his lips. no, why did he spill it? no, this wouldn't do. now his shirt was all dirty, and he was shirtless, and he didn't want to look at his tummy.

he burst into tears, throwing his mug onto the glass coffee table, causing it to shatter loudly. he covered his ears, squeezing his eyes shut. then he felt glass hit his shin sharply. he let out a scream, all of his stress escaping the way it used to: his mouth.

harry was so scared, he was scared of falling apart and he knew that he was tired of being tied together so loosely and tentatively, as if one wrong move would cause him to break.

but here he was, literally trying not to walk over broken glass and letting out all of his emotions, screaming loudly, but it was quite muffled because of the thunder and rain and wind. he hoped that his mum would never come home, because he would be ashamed for her to see him like this.

"this won't work," harry breathed. "this won't this won't this won't work no no no no."

then his new phone he bought himself was ringing, and he screamed again, because *wow* this was so hard and *why were there so many noises at once?*

he felt as if the word 'why' should be his mantra. why was he so disgusting? why did louis want to freaking introduce him to mitchell? why was he bleeding and why was he using the broken glass to open his healing cuts?

harry let out a sob that shook his shoulders, falling roughly on his bum, ignoring the sharp pain that went up his back. his hand was bleeding now; harry didn't realise that he was grabbing a piece of broken glass from his mug. he held it tighter, cringing as the sharp edges sliced into his skin and caused blood to run down his hand. he looked a mess; his wrists were awful bloody and so were his hands and he was crying, there were tear tracks on his cheeks.

he froze when he heard the door open, and it slammed roughly.

he opened his mouth to whisper his mum's name, but nothing came out but a broken whimper.

"harry! harry are you here? it's bloody awful out there!"

that voice. it was so... clear. and loud and painful to hear and harry hated the way his heart stopped in his chest at the hoarse tone of that voice and he was going to be in such a predicament when louis saw him.

he dropped the shard of glass he was holding, before running through his house and room until he slid into his bathroom.

"harry?"

his voice echoed through the empty house, and it sent chills through harry's body.

harry perched himself on the toilet after locking the bathroom door. he was shivering, and his wrist was bleeding badly. he grabbed the hand towel hanging nearby and wrapped it around his left wrist, squeezing tightly as tears slipped past his eyes.

"harry, what the heck happened out here?"

louis must've gone into the living room.

harry held his breath, hoping louis wouldn't come into his room and see the light under the bathroom door.

"anne? is anybody here?"

harry let a sob escape his lips. god, he missed that voice so freaking much. his heart ached as he let louis' beautiful voice echo through his ears.

his legs were starting to ache from squatting on the closed toilet seat. his eyes widened when he felt his nose tickle, signaling a sneeze.

harry could hear louis' footsteps coming closer, and he knew louis was wearing his vans.

then he sneezed, betraying himself.

"harry, are you in there?" louis' voice was sad, nervous. curious.

"no," harry whimpered.

"harry," louis breathed, and harry could hear him lay his forehead against the door. "harry what's wrong? open the door please."

harry bit his lip hardly, squeezing his eyes tightly to try and block his tears. he couldn't let louis in. no, that would be wrong. he didn't want to see louis, to feel his heat so close and on his skin. he could practically see louis' soft red lips, so easy to kiss, yet so hard to at the same time. he didn't want louis' soft skin against his or his pale blue eyes staring straight into his green ones. louis was bad, he was with mitchell, no matter how kind his voice sounded now.

so he stayed on the toilet, pushing his face into his knees. his hand was still wrapped around his skin; it stung. the bathroom was warm due to the hot air blowing through the air vent on the floor.

"harry, please," louis begged.

"go away!" harry shouted, and he could hear his heartbeat in his ears.

"why are you mad at me?"

harry's lip was trembling and his voice was shaky as he tried to speak. "'m not," he lied.

louis sighed. "harry, let me in. i want to see you. i actually wanted to surprise you, but you don't seem as happy to see me as i am to see you."

harry rose from the toilet, taking a shaky breath before unlocking the door. before louis could walk in, he turned around and laid his head against the back wall, holding his hands by his stomach so louis couldn't see him. it was bad enough that he wasn't wearing a shirt and his sweatpants were extremely baggy on him.

"harry, turn around."

"don't tell me what to do," harry responded weakly. his wrist was going numb from squeezing it so hard.

harry froze when he felt louis' short arms snake around his waist, his fingertips laying against harry's hips gently. his breath was caught in his throat and he felt as if there was a rock in his stomach.

"angel what's wrong?"

harry didn't respond, just tried to even his breathing. louis was so warm against him and his nose was nuzzled into his back.

"i don't understand why you're mad." louis' voice cracked.

"go away," harry said coolly, finally able to speak. "leave me alone and don't touch me." his voice was harsh, there was a hardness to it that even he had barely heard.

he couldn't recognize himself.

louis flinched away from him but harry didn't turn around to see his expression. though he did hear louis crying, but he pretended not to.

"you're so freaking stupid," louis spit. "i come here to surprise you and i try to be nice and you're just acting all dramatic and crap. you make me sick, harry."

his voice was getting louder with every word, with every shaky breath and gasp that escaped harry's trembling lips.

"and i hope you know that i'm getting really tired of you. i actually know someone who is a lot more normal than you. someone who doesn't burst into tears every single breath they take. and he kisses better than you too."

that was all it took for harry to break.

he turned around and crumpled to the floor, biting his lip but unable to control his sobs. his heart was literally aching, a throb in his chest that he had never felt so strongly before. louis was glaring down at him and harry wished he could read some sort of regret or guilt in his eyes, but all he saw was anger and distaste.

"am i that disgusting to you? is my disease that annoying to you?" harry said brokenly. "i thought you loved me."

"no i freaking hate you, and i stopped taking my medicine when i left just because you had to leave me."

"but you left-" harry began, already numb from the harsh blows from louis.

"just, just shut up, okay?"

harry gulped thickly, feeling his head spinning and he was dizzy, and his hands were shaking. he let out a scream, banging his fists on the ground despite the pain that shot up his arms and the stinging of his bleeding cuts.

"you're so freaking weird," louis shook his head, turning around and slamming the bathroom door behind him.

harry grabbed his tummy, as if holding himself together.

he couldn't fall asleep this time.

forty

harry didn't know why his wrists still itched even when they were cut open, bleeding. the damage was already done, but he still wanted to feel more pain. he wanted to feel more pain when louis stalked out of the room, but the thing was, he didn't hear the front door open and shut. maybe it was because of the storm raging outside.

harry wanted to hurt. he wanted to hurt to distract him from the awful, horrible pain in his chest. louis' words felt like knives literally stabbing into him, piercing his skin and thin layer of armor that he was in the middle of constructing. it pierced him all the way to the bone, and now he was bleeding out because of it.

harry took a deep breath, scratching his nails across the open gashes in his wrists and fingers. he was shivering, either because of the pain or because, every time he had an anxiety attack, he would feel hot and cold at the same time.

it stung. yeah, it stung a lot. but it wasn't enough. he was still suffering so much on the inside, and this pain wasn't even close to what he needed to feel.

he rammed his fist into the wall next to him suddenly, and it was agonizing. but it felt good.

so he punched the wall, over and over and over until he felt a loud voice right before a boom of thunder.

"stop! crap harry oh my god crap harry stop! please!"

harry didn't stop though, he punched and punched until he felt like his knuckles were broken; they were literally numb.

he kept doing it, and he was thrashing when fingers wrapped around his forearms and tried to control his hands. he let out a scream as he was pulled away from the wall and dragged to his bedroom.

"no!" harry cried. "let go of me, let, go, of me! i hate you!"

"baby it's okay, just lay down, calm down, sleep," louis said lowly, reaching out and pushing his fingers through harry's sweaty curls, tugging slightly. normally, it would be comforting, but the smell of honey was overwhelming harry. louis was sweating too;

his breathing was so heavy, and his eyes were rimmed red. harry pushed away any thought of *beautiful* and decided that louis was ugly. louis was so freaking ugly. he smelled like this awful boy sweat smell and laundry detergent, which made him nauseated, and his blue eyes caused chills to go down his spine.

"i'm not gonna sleep!" harry yelled, elbowing louis as hard as he could in the stomach, that tummy that he knew every inch of. louis reached for him with the hands harry had memorized, with the tan arms harry had fell asleep in. "don't touch me! please, please don't touch me," harry hiccupped, his tone changing from angry to pleading. "please, louis, no."

"i'm sorry."

harry glared at him, scrambling to the other side of his bed so he almost fell off. "no, no you're not. you're not sorry, if you were sorry you wouldn't have, you wouldn't have cheated on me, cheated, you cheated on me, you cheated on me, you cheated on me."

"harry i-"

"you. cheated. on. me."

"harry! let me explain!" there was some sort of regret in louis' watery blue eyes as he gazed at harry. "i di-"

"please, just get out!" harry yelled, exasperated.

"let me see your wrist," louis said softly. "you can hate me all you want, but please, please let me see your wrist. i know i don't deserve to even look at you right now but please. for me."

"why would i do anything for you?" harry spit, his throat aching as the words came out of his mouth. "you've done nothing for me."

"c'mere," louis breathed, and harry fought the instinct to crawl into his arms, to let the warmth seep into his body.

louis sighed. "i didn't cheat on you. i was lying to see if you would be jealous. but i regret it so much now."

harry glared at him, tears forming in his eyes at the searing pain in his hand and wrists. "you're lying," he said coldly.

"please just come to the bathroom with me? we don't want you getting an infection. for all we know you broke your hand."

harry wished he could just lay in his bed forever, but louis was right. so he grumbled and stood up, flinching and shouldering louis away whenever louis tried to put a hand on his shoulder.

"you're a jerk," harry whispered, licking his lips and sitting on the closed toilet seat. "a jerk and if my hand weren't hurt i wouldn't be letting you touch me."

"i know," louis said shakily. "but i love you too much to see you hurting like this."

"you're the reason i'm hurting in the first place!" harry said loudly, and louis flinched, a sad emotion flashing across his eyes. "louis you can't just blame every insult you throw at me on the medicine!"

louis didn't respond for a moment, just opened the cabinet above the sink and pulled out a bottle of advil.

"take some of this, we're going to the hospital," he said quietly.

harry snatched the bottle out of his hand and popped the cap off. but he didn't pour any into his hand, just sat there staring. he decided he wasn't going to talk to louis.

"harry, do you remember when i told you i lash out at people i have problems with?"

silence.

"i was just afraid you didn't love me anymore. to be honest, mitchell's straight, if he's who you're thinking of. we never kissed. i would never betray you like that."

louis looked at the ground. "harry?" he asked nervously.

harry wanted to respond, but he couldn't. maybe louis was suffering on the inside too.

louis sighed deeply and turned to walk out of the restroom.

"wait!"

louis turned around.

"where are you going?" harry asked quietly, shyly. tentative.

louis didn't say anything, but he was crying as he walked out of the restroom.

harry paused for a second before following him. "louis, i don't want you to leave." he played with his fingers for a moment.

"i was getting you a glass of water, angel." his voice cracked when he said the word, and he looked away. "so you can take your advil."

"oh," harry whispered. "why are you being so nice to me?"

louis' face fell. "crap, harry. i just, harry." he ran a hand over his face. "you have no idea how much i hate myself right now," he groaned behind his hands. "harry, god, harry."

harry realised that if you said his name enough it would start to sound weird.

he watched louis' hair flop back into place after he brushed it out of his eyes. it was light brown, feathery. harry could tell louis hadn't got a hair cut in a while by the way the ends by his neck curled up a bit and his bangs brushed his eyelashes.

harry didn't know he was beginning to drift into sleep, even though he was standing straight up, until louis returned from where he went to the kitchen with a glass of water in his hand.

louis gently took the advil bottle out of harry's hand and unscrewed the cap, pouring two of the pills into his hands and wrapping his fingers around then for a second before holding it out to harry. "here you go, ang-" he cut himself off, grunting as if it was just a cough. "harry." he blushed. "sorry."

harry was blushing too, but he didn't tell louis it was okay because he was still angry at him.

louis looked away when harry took the advil, as if it would invade harry's privacy in some odd way.

"let's go to the hospital," louis said quietly.

***

ever since harry's mum had cried in the hospital, harry had hated them. it was the place where harry found out he wasn't normal. it was the place where people knew too much, where people were always breaking bad news to nervous families.

he was actually quivering, still holding the towel around his right wrist with his good hand, the one that wasn't able to be moved after he had punched a wall.

they were in the emergency room, and there were worried voice of others surrounding harry and suffocating him. after louis had checked them in with the receptionist, they sat down in chairs that harry felt so incredibly big in. he could practically feel the narrow arm rests squeezing his sides, and he hunched over, so he didn't look so tall and lengthy. louis had pulled out a white shirt for harry to wear and harry knew it made him look paler than he already was.

"harold styles?"

harry turned to give a playful glare at louis, a smile beginning to form on his lips, but he quickly corrected himself. he pretended not to see the hope in louis' eyes. so what if louis called him harold? that meant nothing to harry, not after what louis had said.

harry was tapping his foot and rubbing his thighs, waiting as patiently as possible, when louis grabbed his knee gently.

"stop," he said in a strained voice. "you're killing me."

harry raised an eyebrow.

"you're so *freaking* attractive, you're unbelievably sexy, harry, god, so please stop."

harry felt a surge of blood rush to his cheeks at louis' words.

"and i love how innocent you are, how sensitive and wonderfully amusing you are." louis' lips barely brushed harry's ear as he whispered those words. the thing was, that was the exact opposite of what louis said earlier.

harry jumped when louis grabbed his hair. "harry, crap, i don't think your sensitivity is bad at all. i just love it so much."

harry had no idea what to say, and thankfully the nurse came into the waiting room and called harry's (full) name.

harry would have been embarrassed by his tear stained cheeks and puffy eyes, but his heart was beating too fast for him to think.

the nurse, who harry saw on her name tag was named breigh, looked at harry's wrist for a few seconds before her eyes widened.

"what happened?" she asked, obviously trying to sound neutral and nonjudgmental.

harry froze. what was he supposed to say- i fell on the ground and razors came up and sliced my wrist?

louis saved him, touching harry's elbow and leading him slightly down the hall as he responded. "he fell on broken glass because i dropped a glass of water," he lied easily. harry wondered if he should be worried how smooth that was.

breigh nodded, her bangs hanging out of her ponytail and brushing across her jaw. harry thought she was beautiful.

she led them into a room with a bed laying down and a seat in the corner. there was a television and posters of the human body and flowers all over the walls. it made harry feel nauseated. his head was starting to get dizzy; probably from the blood loss.

"the doctor will be here to see you in a couple minutes. if you need anything push the red button and the green button turns the telly. any questions?"

harry shook his head politely, casting his eyes to the white sheet he was laying on. his eyes were stinging with tears; he hoped she didn't notice.

the room was silent after breigh left and harry couldn't bring himself to turn the telly on.

"how are you feeling?" louis asked hesitantly, sitting himself down and fixing the cuffs of his jeans.

"fine," harry shrugged, avoiding eyes with the older boy.

"i hope your hand will be okay," he said softly.

harry didn't respond, he didn't speak until the doctor came in.

forty-one

broken.

that was a word that could describe many parts of harry's body.

it could describe his bloody, swollen hands. the doctor had x-rayed them, and come to the sad conclusion that his hand, was in fact, broken. all harry could think about was *how the heck am i going to pay for this?*

his heart was broken also. he could feel the dull throb in his chest as he watched louis discuss with the doctor how to take care of his hand that had been wrapped in a yellow cast. he watched how engaging louis was with his eyes and how he was constantly blinking his hair out of his eyes and how he used so much hand gestures when he spoke, with his beautiful modulated and singsong voice. harry kept telling himself that he didn't love louis, he *couldn't* love louis.

"rest always helps, give him the medicine i prescribed every two hours. does he have a parent that can take care of him?"

harry shook his head. yeah, his mum was there, but...

she wasn't.

"okay then-louis is it?" louis nodded. "okay, just make sure you follow all the instructions and when he showers he needs to put a plastic bag over his cast. also, change the bandages on his wrists every time they start to get dirty, and when you do rinse it with soap and warm water, then rub some of the cream i gave you on it. the nurse will hand you some bandages to use on your way out. any questions?"

louis looked slightly overwhelmed, and he let out a breath as he responded. "nope, i'm fine. thank you so much for helping him, you have no idea how much that means to me."

harry didn't realise he was blushing until he rested his fingers on his cheeks and they were hot.

"okay, nice to meet you louis." he shook hands with louis, before walking over to harry, who was flustered. "harry, you've been wonderful. i hope your hand feels better soon, i'll see you in six weeks to see if you're cast is ready to come off." he shook harry's hand too, a firm tight handshake that was quite awkward since the hand harry usually used was wrapped in a yellow cast.

"thanks," louis said again, as the doctor exited and right after a nurse came in to escort them to the front.

"do you have insurance?" the nurse at the front asked, her hands poised over a keyboard.

harry blinked, unsure what to respond. and louis saved him again, fishing his wallet out of his pocket and pulling out a card. "yes," he said softly.

"thank you," she smiled politely. "the co-pay is twenty-eight pounds."

harry opened his mouth to protests as louis handed his own money over. "louis!" he whispered loudly, nudging his arm. "i can't believe you!"

they were walking out of the hospital when louis finally responded. "i can't believe you have a cast on your hand. this is all my fault."

harry shook his head. "you can't just get away with paying that much money!" he said tightly.

"my baby. he has a cast on his wonderful hand. i love your hands. they're so big, and now one of them has this ugly-" he paused when harry frowned at his cast, "not-as-beautiful cast on it."

"don't call me that. i'm not your baby," harry huffed.

"the least i could do is pay for your visit," louis said, his voice thick and strangled.

"but i thought you hated me?" harry spit, his anger from earlier coming back to him. he was so freaking mad, no matter how many kind things louis said to him. when louis opened his mouth to respond, harry shook his head.

they walked in silence to louis' car. harry plopped angrily into the passenger seat, crossing his arms and leaning as far away from louis as he could.

"harry, please don't be like this."

harry bit his lip to keep from screaming. *be like this?!* for some reason, that sentence made him feel like louis thought of him as some annoying brat that he had to deal with.

"i don't like when we fight."

there is no we, harry thought.

"please talk to me. please, i can't stand this."

harry stood his ground. he was actually proud of his self-control the whole ride home. louis had begged him to talk a few more times, until he gave up with a sad sigh. harry felt as if he should be guilty, but he wasn't.

louis was full on sobbing by the time they walked into his house, where they found niall and zayn sweeping up the mess that harry had made in the living room. harry resisted the urge to hug both of them, and instead crossed his arms and asked shakily, "what are you doing here?

niall pointed at louis, sympathy in his eyes. "this guy sent us over here to clean up."

harry didn't even turn to look at louis, all he had to do was listen to know that he was crying. you could tell he was trying to keep it in by the way he was hiccupping and the brittle tone of his voice when he asked harry to talk to him.

"why is he crying so hard?" zayn asked softly.

"i won't talk to him," harry replied flatly, choosing not to be kind to either of his "best friends" either.

"god, he really wants you to talk to him," zayn remarked.

harry shrugged, storming past all three boys and slamming his bedroom door behind him. his room was cooler than the rest of the house, due to the fan he forgot to turn off. he sat down on his bed, lightly rubbing his fingertips across his cast. he couldn't feel anything, and he hated that. it was like a wall keeping him from slashing his wrists again. his lip trembled as he continued to stare at the fiberglass, his eyes starting to water from lack of blinking. he could smell disinfectant, probably because zayn and niall cleaned it all up. he could see the wet sink and newly polished mirror from his bed.

harry decided to lay down, carefully elevating his hand on a pillow and closing his eyes. the sound of the fan thankfully overlapped the sounds of louis, zayn, and niall. to be completely honest, every single one of them frustrated him to the point of screaming.

harry was happy that the medicine he was given at the hospital hadn't worn off yet, so his whole arm was just numb. he awkwardly lifted his blankets with his left hand, doing his best to snuggle under the covers, even though he was still fully dressed in his converse, skinnies, and white shirt.

he blew the curls off of his forehead, although they just flopped back when he stopped letting out a breath. the curtains in his room were shut, causing it to be quite dark and peaceful. if he could just forget that louis and his friends were in the other room then maybe he could get some sleep.

and he did. his breaths finally evened, and his heartbeat went to a normal sleep as he fell into a tired sleep.

***

"no, don't wake him up! let him sleep!"

the whisper was rushed, worried. harry could recognize it anywhere.

he didn't open his eyes, and he hoped they didn't notice the difference in his breathing.

"he's gotta wake up sometime. he probably hasn't eaten all day."

"but he looks so.. peaceful. love seeing him like that."

harry prayed that they wouldn't see the red dusting his cheeks.

he froze when a hand reached out and brushed his jaw, a gentle, feather-like touch. those fingers were so soft. it brought harry back to when they were in the hotel on christmas eve, celebrating louis' birthday. he remembered the way louis touched him so gently, as if he was a china doll he was scared to break. he remembered louis kissing up the hair line on his tummy and nuzzling his nose on each of his hips. he recalled louis kissing on the inside of each of his thighs before grabbing harry in his hands and rubbing him softly.

it make something churn deep in harry's stomach, and his eyes snapped open. he saw liam and louis.

liam's warm brown eyes and furrowed eyebrows were enough to make harry burst into tears. he bit his shaking lip, the memory of louis' birthday affecting him way too much. "hi liam," harry said in a small voice.

"hi harry," liam responded warmly, brushing some of harry's curls out of his face. harry could tell it bothered louis by the way his eyes flickered around the room angrily, but he didn't say anything.

"my hand hurts," harry said truthfully, scared to move it in case it would start to hurt more.

louis stood up immediately, scurrying out of the room and returning with an orange prescription bottle that harry was so used to seeing.

"take this."

harry didn't look louis in the eye when he took it, he didn't even look at him at all. he kept his eyes on liam, who was staring sadly back at him.

then there was a glass right in front of his face. "here you go," louis said, his voice strangled with tears and lack of breath. harry took the glass of water with his left hand, which meant he had to put the pills on the bed. he couldn't hold two things at once. he stared helplessly at the bottle, before meeting eyes with liam.

"oh," liam exclaimed, grabbing the bottle and pouring two into his hand. he took the water from harry and let him put the pills in his mouth, before giving him the water back so he could drink it.

harry jumped when louis stood up again, kicking a nearby pillow on the floor. "i can't do anything freaking right!" he shouted, grabbing the hair on the back of his head, and harry could see how hard he was pulling by the straining of his muscles.

"louis, calm down mate," liam said softly, standing up and pulling his arms to his sides. "you forgot that he couldn't use one of his hands. it's okay."

louis glared at him. "it's not okay! he won't even *talk* to me, i swear, that just kills me," his voice was trailing off, and it was hoarse. it broke harry's heart.

"liam," harry called. louis looked over anyway, as if hopeful.

"make him leave."

it hurt him to say, crap, it hurt. and yeah, the look on louis' face as it dropped, it was shattering. his eyes literally lost what was left of their light, leaving a grey that used to be such a beautiful blue. his lips were trembling, his eyebrows furrowed in a broken, hurt puppy way. his shoulders sagged; his knees were shaking.

harry never knew that louis could look so absolutely crushed, so defeated.

and he never knew that it would be because of just three words that he said.

liam gave louis a hopeless look, and louis ran out of the room, not even slamming the door behind him. harry could hear him crying, but the sound was soon gone. it was replaced with a car engine running and harry burst into tears.

liam looked so conflicted. he shook his head. "i can't let him do something to hurt himself. harry, please don't do anything stupid. i need to go get him. niall and zayn are making popcorn in the kitchen if you need someone."

then he sprinted out of the room too, leaving harry alone in his room.

harry probably sat there alone, crying like the freaking baby he was, when niall and zayn came in hesitantly.

"we made you popcorn," niall said nervously, his step causing the floor to creak.

"okay," harry said.

"god, harry, we're so sorry," zayn rushed, plopping on the edge of harry's bed and wiping his tears away. "harry, we completely have been ditching you and that's *not okay,* it's not at all. "let's just talk, yeah?" niall added in, coming closer and putting the bowl of popcorn on harry's lap.

harry nodded. "yeah, that'd be wonderful," he whispered.

forty-two

niall and zayn sat down on the bed next to harry, careful not to move his hand. harry cradled his cast against his tummy, hoping that he wouldn't hurt it even more. he wanted to rip the bandages off of his wrist, to cut them again as he stared at his "best friends." niall's eyes were hopeful, zayn's were full of regret.

"harry, are you okay?" zayn asked quietly, reaching out and touching his elbow. "we have been such awful friends through all of this. crap, there are huge gashes in your wrists and we both know it's not because you fell."

harry stared straight back at him, knowing that if he spoke all that would come out was a whimper. he felt quite sick, but he ignored it.

"do you still love louis?" niall looked nervous when he said this, avoiding harry's eyes and instead playing with his fingers.

harry nodded. of course, he loved louis, so much. but he also hated him, he hated him with a burning passion. he hated what louis had said to him, he hated that louis was the reason he was going to have so many scars, emotionally and physically.

i hate him. i hate him i hate him i love him i love him.

harry repeated this mantra in his head while zayn and niall poured out their hearts, saying their multiple apologies and telling harry what they think he should do about louis. apparently louis had left, driving away and leaving liam standing there, about to talk him out of leaving. harry didn't want to think about where louis was going. he could go wherever he wanted.

and then he got caught on just *louis*. he had a million images going through his mind, and he couldn't hear zayn or niall anymore. his eyes locked onto the picture behind zayn's head, of him and louis. it was a picture jay had taken of them on christmas morning, of louis giving harry his promise ring.

his promise ring.

it was on the hand that punched the wall. when was the last time he wore it?

he let out a quiet sigh of relief when he saw it on his desk, on top of a few stacked books with the titles, "to kill a mockingbird," and "pride and prejudice."

"harry? are you listening?" niall cried, grabbing his shoulders and shaking him roughly and harry closed his eyes, the movement causing him to feel sick. it was probably the medicine.

"niall, stop!" zayn grabbed niall's wrists, and they made long eye contact for quite a while, a silent conversation, before niall removed his strong grip on harry's thin shoulders. harry felt his stomach churn, and he fluttered his eyelashes as the overwhelming feeling to throw up came over him.

"harry are you okay?" zayn said worriedly, and harry laid down on his bed, sliding his legs forward so they hung over the edge. his eyes were now closed, and he licked his lips quickly. he could feel his mind clouding, fading.

"check the symptoms on that medicine," zayn murmured to niall, and niall picked up the bottle.

"constipation, nausea, loss of appetite, drowsiness, fever, headaches, hallucinations."

their voices were so distant. harry was sweating badly now, he didn't like it, he hated it. he was cold and hot at the same time and his stomach felt so bad and he could feel the medicine kicking in because his hand didn't hurt anymore.

zayn sighed, leaving the room for a second before coming back with a wet rag. harry could feel a tear slipping down his cheek as the boy placed it on his forehead, a cold, moist feeling.

"let him sleep," niall said sadly, pushing a few curls out of his face. "we can talk to him later, when he doesn't look so miserable."

harry didn't have the energy to respond, he just sunk further into his mattress and tried to ignore the pounding of his head. the more unclear his mind got, the farther he slipped into sleep and the number he felt.

were those.. colors? he saw something, moving and fading in and out in his room. but weren't his eyes closed?

he was shaking, no he was still.

"louis!" i call. it smells like popcorn in here, i notice. my room is so small, and i wonder why. but all i can focus on is louis.

he's right in front of me, right next to my dresser. i like to watch the way he moves. his hands are fluttering around as he scurries around my room. why is he so nervous? "louis!" i say again, louder, and i cringe at the low tone of my voice that i despise. my curls keep falling in my face, and it's quite annoying. i want to focus, but i can't.

louis looks over at me, his lips in a deep frown. i want to see his sunshine smile. i love his sunshine smile, although i rarely see it anymore.

"louis why did you leave?" i ask loudly, but every time i step closer so i don't have to yell, he takes a step back. he's wearing his black vans and white tank top. i stare at his hands, and his nose. his nose is perfect, i think. he's really pretty, but i don't know if i can tell him that. he probably think's i'm annoying.

"don't you want me to leave?" louis says back to me, and i frown at him. do i want him to leave? i play with my fingers for a second. my fingers are so long, and my legs and i wish they weren't. my feet are hanging off my bed.

but i'm not laying down? i shake my head in confusion, my curls brushing against my eyes and cause me to blink. louis isn't looking at me anymore. why isn't he looking at me? i don't understand. i wish i could read his mind, it would be so much easier.

"louis i miss you," i say. wait. now he's in his football uniform. why? he's kicking a ball around, with a boy i recognize. i didn't know my room was big enough to play football in. louis passes it to mitchell. i stare at mitchell, and there's this really weird feeling in my heart and i think it's called jealousy. but louis doesn't like when i'm jealous, does he?

louis ignores my statement, and i feel my hands shaking. what's happening? is this is a dream?

"hi angel." i feel my heart flutter at the word. how come every time louis says that i feel like this? there's an aching feeling at the bottom of my ribs and my stomach feels like there's a lot of butterflies in it. he thinks i'm an angel.

"why do you think i'm an angel?" i ask, scrunching up my nose. he smiles, his sunshine smile, and shakes his head for a second before reaching out and touching my curls.

he doesn't respond though, and i make a mental note to ask louis later, when he's actually willing to have a conversation with me.

"louis what's happening?" i say. louis' eyes are sparkling, they're so blue. they're the color of a pool, or maybe the sky. either way, i want to paint my room the color of his eyes, as weird as that sounds. what if louis thinks i'm weird? i can feel panic growing in my chest at the question, and i try my best to push it out of my mind.

"nothing baby."

baby. *i love the way it sounds coming out of louis' mouth, especially after he shows me his sunshine smile. his sunshine smile is a present. it's like unwrapping a gift. it's unfair that he keeps giving me presents and i haven't given him anything good.*

well, what about.. what was that called? louis said it was making love. i called it a present, but i don't think he thought of it like that. i was acting absolutely ridiculous that night. i'm embarrassed. i feel a blush rise to my cheeks as i remember that night.

i feel sick, suddenly. louis just keeps looking at me, and now's he wearing the same thing he wears on my lock screen. my mind is spinning, and it still smells like popcorn. no, the cold sweat is back. no, i sweating, especially when whenever i touch my forehead it feels hot but i'm shivering so that must mean i'm cold, right?

"louis, i feel sick."

i wait for louis to say something, but he doesn't.

i notice the way he licks his lips. he always raises his eyebrows when he does it, and i love that. i love louis. louis looks at me, and i want to touch his eyelashes. is that weird? they remind me of a picture frame around beautiful art. because they encompass this really pretty blue that i'm going to paint my walls, and i swear sometimes they are actually sparkling. if i stare close enough, which i usually don't like to do because eye contact isn't fun and people are always judging me when they look into my eyes, but if i stare close enough i can see my reflection.

i wonder if some people smile at themselves when they see their reflections. i see them do that on movies, and it makes me think. what is a reflection? what does it really show? it's odd because we've never seen ourselves straight on; we've only seen a reflection of ourselves. i wonder if my reflection is what louis sees when he looks at me. it probably is, because that's what i see in his eyes when i look close enough.

i realise i'm rambling, in my own head, which i do a lot. it's awfully annoying, but it's better than talking. i hate my voice.

in fact, there are quite a few things i don't like about myself. like my hips. i lift up my shirt, which is white, but it keeps changing colors. i pinch the fat on my hips, on my tummy, and feel tears prickle my eyes.

i realise that louis is disappearing now, and i take a shaky breath before i speak. "louis, where are you going? i didn't tell you to leave!" i cry.

louis doesn't look at me. it's weird, because he's just fading away and i've never seen that happen before.

"harry!"

hey, he's finally talking. but wait, no, that's not louis' voice. louis' voice sounds like a soft blanket, like warm cookies and angels and soft things. i like his soft voice. it makes me feel warm inside. like drinking hot tea, because after it slides down your throat you just kind of feel warm all over. i wonder if louis feels like that when he drinks tea; he does drink it quite often. he loves yorkshire tea, i always catch him making it. he claims that sugar isn't good in tea, but he always puts a lot in mine anyway because he knows i like it.

i remember one time, after i told him to put a little more sugar in my tea, he didn't listen. i was really confused, because he usually always listens to me, i don't know why but he does. anyway, he just put my cup down. the mug was blue, a little bit darker than the color of louis' eyes. louis' eyes were only that color when he was about to kiss me, which confuses me but i kind of like it. in fact, speaking of that, his eyes are that color again, and i like that it matches the mug because i like when things match.

he had grabbed my hand, and his thumb was rubbing against my skin and it felt so soft, and i hope he knows how much i like soft things. i like how soft louis' skin is; it's softer than dove soap and blankets. i love how soft his skin is.

i also love how he smells like honey.. it wasn't as prominent then, though; the smell of tea on his breath was much more noticeable because of how close his mouth was to mine. he had cradled my jaw in his small hands, his eyes crinkling up a bit at the sides as he smiled. i love how small louis' hands are, and i love the crinkles by his eyes.

i took a deep breath when he had kissed me. i always am self-conscious of what i look like before i kiss louis. because he always looks so beautiful, so soft when he's about to kiss me. his eyes are closed, and like i said, i love his eyelashes. and his lips are always so moist, which i don't understand because mine are always dry and that's why mum told me when i was little to always keep a tube of chapstick with me because i always licked them. his nose was perfect like always, and sometimes i would be tempted to lean down and kiss it.

but. we were in his kitchen, his large kitchen that probably cost a million dollars to design and build. all of the appliances were stainless steel and the granite countertop was dark, and noticeably cold, especially when louis had lifted me up by waist and helped me sit on it. it was so cold because i was only in my boxers, and the cold granite against the back of my thighs caused goose bumps to rise on my arms. i was in my boxers because when we woke up, although the house was all sleeping, louis insisted that i put some form of clothing on. apparently it wouldn't be good if his mum saw me like that.

so there i was, shivering on the counter in my boxers with no shirt on. louis was shirtless too. i don't think i was shivering just because of the cold counter; every time louis rubbed his hands down my arms it caused me to get goose bumps.

"harry!" i hear a voice call, interrupting my recalling of louis that morning. but ignored it, instead trying to remember more. for some reason, remembering times i had with louis is bittersweet. of course, i know why it's happy, but i don't know why i'm so sad.

louis had kissed me softly. his lips tasted so good and they were warm and soft. of course they were soft; like i said louis is always so soft. the way he murmured angel into my mouth was so wonderful, i felt like i was breathing in everything he said and i hope he doesn't find the things i notice weird.

the counter was getting warm, probably because i was sitting on it. louis was standing between my legs; his sides were so warm as i squeezed my legs tightly around him. i moved my hands that were before supporting myself to his back. i dug my fingers into his skin, moving around his body and pushing my fingertips in between each bump of his ribs. i liked to feel his sides. he seemed to like it too, because he let out a quiet whimper in my mouth. i love the noises he makes.

"harry!"

i had kissed louis hard, and he was drumming his fingers against my lower back, against the dimples i had there but hated.

"harry styles, wake up! why are you crying?"

i could feel louis pulling away, he was crying now.

"harry!"

harry's eyes snapped opened.

his cheeks were moist, and his eyes were burning.

"niall," harry breathed out, reaching over and pulling him tightly to him.

niall hugged him back, and he seemed a bit confused. but harry didn't care, he just let out broken sobs into his shoulder. he could faintly feel zayn rubbing his back, but he couldn't see anything because his eyes were blurred, and his curls were sticking to his cheeks and he wanted to die.

his dream was so painful, so painful.

he ached to feel louis' touch again, but he also hoped louis would never come back. his contradicting thoughts were so annoying, and he wished they were never there. he wished louis hadn't left so long ago and made friends with mitchell. he wished louis hadn't cause him to wonder about whether or not he was cheated on.

just the smell of the popcorn sitting half empty in the bowl next to them made more tears come. his sobs were choking, he couldn't even breathe, and it wasn't long before he was screaming. niall held him tighter, rocking him slightly and zayn was telling harry comforting words helplessly.

he wanted to fall asleep again, because that always helped when he was this far gone, this numb, but at the same time he was scared if he fell asleep he would have that nightmare again.

so he battled with himself, he battled his thoughts and what to do and niall finally helped him make his decision when he carried him to the living room and laid him on the couch. zayn turned on the television, to a random cartoon, and niall came from the kitchen holding a gallon of ice cream.

"we figured you would break sometime," zayn whispered, cuddling next to him and kissing his hair. niall sat on harry's left, handing him a spoon.

harry was still crying, but he was starting to calm down. he was now hiccupping because of the uneven breaths he was taking earlier.

he stuck his spoon into the ice cream, which looked to be the flavor of peanut butter and chocolate. zayn and niall graced him with silence and instead turned their attention to the television. harry's hand was so shaky as he struggled to get some of the ice cream out of the carton. it looked quite good.

he finally got some on the very tip of the spoon, and he hesitantly put in his mouth, feeling the cold cream melt into liquid on his tongue. but he had trouble swallowing it because of the tears that had built up in the back of his throat.

he closed his eyes and tasted the peanut butter, feeling the coldness numb the ache in his chest.

don't dream.

forty-three

"you *have* to join a club. it's your senior year, it'll look good on your college applications," zayn nudged harry's shoulder, pointing at the wall of flyers and sign-up sheets in front of them. niall nodded in agreement, clapping harry on the back and laughing as others around him joked about joining glee or band.

harry personally thought the band members were cool, but he decided not to speak up.

"i don't think i would like any of these," harry said honestly, sticking one hand in the pocket of his skinnies and with the other hand he gripped onto his thermos of tea. "i'm not any good at sports; and i *can't* be in theatre."

harry wanted to cry at the thought. *he* was good at theatre; *he* rocked the stage and sang with all his heart. but no, *he* was never coming back.

"you can do water polo with me," zayn said hopefully. "'s not that hard, i swear it. it's bloody fun, is what it is!"

"have ye seen volleyball?" niall asked. harry nodded, looking down at the two of them with a nervous frown. "it's like that, except in the water. and you're tall, so it'll work out perfectly!"

zayn was practically hopping up and down. "yes, yes you have to come with me during eca. at least try it out, and if you don't like it you can quit. you can swim right?"

harry shook his head yes.

"well, i, personally, am joining the footie team."

zayn rolled his eyes. "i'm so surprised, niall."

niall punched him in the shoulder, laughing. "at least i don't swim like a loser." when harry gave a worried look, niall clarified, "no, i'm kidding. i think it's cool."

"okay," harry whispered, twirling the bracelet around his wrist. "okay, i'll think about it."

zayn smiled, a proud smile. "harry, 'm so glad you're feeling better. i thought you weren't ever going to come back," he whispered, tilting his head up so his lips were close to harry's ear. "i think you did the right thing, making him leave." he leaned back, bringing his voice back to normal. "i do miss li though."

"i do too, when's that bloke coming back? we need to play some fifa, he used to be the only one who i actually had to try against."

"hey!" zayn defended, making a pouty face, and harry tried his best to smile, to make them think that he was, in fact, okay.

when his attempt failed, and his lips were just shaky and he felt like crying, he put his thermos up to his lips, feeling the hot tea slide down his throat and he licked his lips. his throat was thick, and his chest ached. it was a normal feeling, the only thing he felt when he wasn't completely numb.

zayn and niall were in the middle of a conversation when the bell rang, signaling first period. harry checked his schedule really quick; he didn't have a chance to before because he was too busy getting himself prepared for the first day of school. his mum usually helped him and made him his favorite breakfast; today she slept in, which wasn't an unusual occurrence.

he had psychology, which he was actually quite interested in. he could relate, which was helpful.

so he said a half-hearted goodbye to the other two of his friends, who sent him off with a tight hug, and then he cowered into himself as students brushed past him with books in hand. harry had already put his books in his class so all he had was his tea.

once the hallway had cleared and he only had about a minute to get to class, he dragged his boots down the hallway until he saw the room number he was looking for. he rushed in with a deep breath and was in the middle of sitting down when the bell rang again.

he got a few odd glances, one from a girl with blue eyes and brown hair who looked quite.. interested. she gave a hesitant wave and harry just stared at his hands on his desk. whenever he tapped his fingers his rings would make a clanging noise, which he found himself enjoying the sound of.

every time he saw that hair color or blue eyes his heart would literally feel like it was tearing. he was trying so hard to stitch his heart together, but every little thing ripped those stitches out one by one. he missed him; he missed that smile that could outshine the sun.

he shook his head, causing his long curls to fall into his face. the teacher was saying his name -mr. thomas- and handing out the syllabus for the class. he avoided all eye contact when he took the stack of papers from the person in front of harry's hand so he could put one on his desk for himself. he gently took a paper off of the bottom of the pile, sliding it onto his desk before handing it to the boy across the aisle from him. then, he took a perfectly sharpened pencil from his binder, placing the tip slowly on the clean paper and scratching his name perfectly onto the top of the page. *harry styles.*

was it bad that he had sunken to hating his name now?

he ignored the tugging in his chest and tried to focus his attention on the teacher. he was explaining the rules of the classroom and what they were going to start on.

the steam coming from his yorkshire tea caused moist droplets to form on his face, as he was leaned over it, breathing in the smell and hoping it would mask the smell of that cologne.

it was louis' cologne, the cologne he used to wear every day when he was still a senior and going to high school. although harry loved the smell of that cologne, the thing he loved the most was those nights.

he could remember them clearly, and they seemed a million years ago.

louis would walk out of the bathroom and into harry's bedroom, pajama pants pulled a bit down, so his hips were showing, and the bottoms were pooling at his feet and dragging against the floor. his shirt wouldn't be on, showing his tan chest. his hair would still be wet, making it dark brown and it was messy. his eyelashes would also be wet, causing his eyes to shine more than ever.

and he would walk towards harry, a small tiny smile flitting across his lips for just a second, and harry would sit criss cross on the bed, hands shaking excitedly in his lap and his heart aching with so much love, he felt like he had to do something with how much he loved louis; he felt just saying it wouldn't do it justice. he wanted to announce it to the world, to kiss louis forever and let everyone know that louis was his. he loved that he had something -some- that was all his.

louis would say a few things like, "brush those messy curls, it makes you looks so beautiful and it's driving me crazy," or "i'm so freaking in love with you, you've no idea."

and harry would blush, sheepishly biting his lip and looking up at louis through a pair of thick lashes from where he would be sitting on the bed, his feet covered in a pair of plaid booties which louis had a matching pair of.

they got them at one of their many "girl's night outs," as louis called them.

and louis would sit down on the bed, draping his legs across harry's lap and his hands would cradle harry's jaw. and then he would just kiss him, gently and it was amazing. harry would never get tired of kissing louis, he just loved it so much.

harry shook the memory out of his head, listening to the teacher instead.

"you're seniors now. if you're in this class, it pretty much means that it's what you want to do when you graduate, am i correct?"

harry found himself nodding along with his classmates.

it wasn't long before the bell rang, and he carefully stacked all of his books before pulling them into his skinny arms.

his shirts and pants were slowly getting looser on him. harry was so glad he decided to go on a diet.

harry ran into niall right when he walked out the door. the blonde boy was beaming, his teeth that were now perfectly straight and white blinding harry.

"hi niall." harry felt his throat itch a bit, but he ignored it.

"did you like your first class?" niall put an arm around harry's shoulders and spun them around so they were walking down the hall, towards their lockers.

"yeah," harry said.

"i thought you would, it seemed to fit you, ya know?" niall smiled at harry, his bleached hair bouncing a bit as he practically skipped down the hall. "it's so cool being seniors."

harry nodded, biting his lip. being completely honest, he just wanted to go home.

***

"lunch is actually good today!" zayn cried.

they were in the cafeteria, surrounded by freshman that let everybody cut in front of them with nervous, scared eyes. harry felt bad for them; when he was freshman he was so freaking scared. he still was now.

"what is lunch?" niall asked curiously, cutting in line with the pair.

"cheeseburgers and fries," zayn responded, pulling out his phone and checking something before putting it back in his pocket. "and we get to go first, because," he paused motioning around the group with his hands, "seniors."

harry forced a smile, playing with his fingers down by his legs. his tummy churned at the thought of eating, especially something as greasy as they were having today.

his mind flashed back to the movie where a girl who was trying to lose weight kneeled in front of a toilet, throwing up everything so it wouldn't store the extra food as fat. harry knew it worked; by the end of the movie she was thin.

maybe he should try that. he wasn't losing that much from cutting down his eating. he would eat healthier, but healthy food is quite a bit more expensive.

they were in the front of the line now and harry snapped out of his trance when niall handed him a blue lunch tray. he took it and said a quiet thank you, before staring ahead of him and letting everything and nothing wander through his mind.

"do you want a cheeseburger, honey?" the lunch lady asked when he passed. harry looked around and was about to shake his head no when zayn answered for him, putting a hand on his arm.

"yes, he does. sorry, he's just quiet."

harry blushed, embarrassed and ashamed. he had the urge to throw up when she slapped a greasy bun with a burger and a handful of fries on his tray. she sent him off with a smile, clueless to harry was feeling.

he paid for his lunch quickly, sitting down next to his friends along with some of their friends as well. they all got quickly immersed in a conversation about clubs and how excited they were to be seniors but harry just picked up his hamburger bun and started picking it apart, with his long, delicate fingers. the smell was nauseating, he could practically see it just adding to the fat on his hips and tummy whenever he just looked at it.

"not hungry?" niall commented to harry, taking a large bite of his burger and harry's stomach turned.

"not really." his voice was almost a whisper.

"just eat something, you haven't had breakfast," zayn urged him. "you need energy."

"to sit in class all day?" one of their friends, ed, laughed, and harry was thankful that the attention wasn't all on him anymore. "we're not doing anything."

but when zayn and niall sent harry worried looks, he decided he needed to reassure them. so he spent his time picking apart his food, pretending to eat, and whenever they weren't looking he folded some of it into a napkin.

louis hates me, he thought. *he thinks i'm fat and ugly and i eat too much.*

he frowned, feeling his eyes blur with tears as he stared at his food. he didn't want to cry. not here, no. that wouldn't do.

so he took deep gulps and tried to clear the thickness in his throat, blinking the tears out of his eyes and letting his curls fall in his face to cover it.

his hands were in his lap, shaking as panic swept through his head. he needed to get out, to go somewhere other than this lunchroom where people were judging his every move. he hated that every pair of vans he saw walk by on their way to the bathroom made his heart drop to his stomach, heavier and weaker as every second passed.

zayn was in the middle of saying harry's name when the bell rang and harry picked up his tray and scurried to the trash can, careful to keep his head down so his hair was hiding his face, hiding his rimmed eyes.

he dumped the uneaten food into the trash can, putting his tray away before walking out of the cafeteria and back into the hallways of school. his heart was racing, and he felt so weak and tired and his stomach was rumbling. harry hoped nobody could hear it.

finally, it was his last class of the day: study hall. to say harry was relieved was an understatement.

he packed up his backpack, which only consisted of his binder and assignment book, before zipping it up. he ran a hand through his messy curls before lifting his backpack onto his shoulders. he pretended not to notice the way it made him stumble; although it was very light it caused his weak body to almost collapse, and he walked on shaky knees to study hall, the light headedness getting worse with every step he took.

when he walked in the door, it seemed as if everybody was staring at him, and his heart beat painfully hard in his chest as his cheeks heated up.

honestly, harry didn't know how he was going to get through this school year. not without his mum, not without his sunshine. no chance.

***

when he finally plopped his backpack onto the floor of his room, he was completely and utterly exhausted.

his shoulders ached, his stomach felt completely empty and hollow; he loved and loathed that feeling at the same time.

harry assumed his mum was at work, and if she wasn't she was locked up in her room, watching television or reading.

harry sat down gently on his bed, wrapping his arms around his stomach so each of his hands were on the opposite hip. there were sharp pains in his stomach; hunger pains. he ached to have his usual macaroni and cheese, but it was way too fatty with all of that cheese and the whole milk his mum always bought.

he had to close his eyes when he took off his tight jeans and his white shirt with the sleeves rolled up to reveal his shoulders. he threw them in the laundry, avoiding looking into any mirror, and he wanted to look at his body so bad, but he hated his body, he hated it, he hated it because he knew louis hated it.

and yeah, louis hadn't spoken to him in four months, but that's the thing; louis didn't love him anymore. louis thought he was ugly and harry knew that louis always thought that his curls were stupid and dumb and hideous.

he didn't have any homework, which he was grateful for. he laid down on the bed and closed his eyes, rising his right arm up so his forearm was covering his forehead. his ankles were crossed, his bare feet hanging off the edge and they were cold because the fan blowing directly on them. he was just in his boxers now, and the feeling of no clothes was comforting. at least, only when his eyes were closed.

and so he laid there, eyes closed so his eyelashes were brushing his cheekbones and his chest rising and falling as his breaths evened out. he felt calmer than he had in a while, except for the constant distraction of his hunger. he hadn't eaten a proper meal in a week now, he was getting by on a few bananas or granola bars, washed with water. he knew it was helping, but sometimes those hunger pains were so painful, and he would find himself rocking back and forth in the middle of the night, his stomach begging him for something *real* to eat.

but now, he was a bit okay, and he hoped that if he cried enough now then he wouldn't have to do it at school, where everybody could see him. they could see how pathetic he was, how weak and so freaking depressed he was since louis left, along with liam, never to be seen again.

and yeah, he was the one that told louis to leave, and he had such a good reason to.

he just didn't know it would hurt this much.

forty-four

"i can't do this," harry mumbled to himself, walking back and forth in the big stall of the swimming locker room restroom. "i can't do this i can't do this i can't do this."

he could hear the splashing outside, the laughter of some kids he didn't know, but he could make out zayn if he listened close enough.

he was wearing a pair of swim trunks, the swim trunks louis had given him so, so long ago. he never gave them back, he actually kind of liked them. but now it just caused his stomach to twist, especially since he wasn't wearing a shirt and he felt so fat, his tummy bulged out so much, it was awful.

he was sitting on the toilet, his arms crossed over his growling stomach, when he heard wet footsteps on the tile floor along with water dropping. "harry! harry why aren't you coming out here! come on, it's fun!"

"okay," harry responded, trying not to sound on the verge of tears.

he waited for zayn to leave, for his footsteps to disappear as he left the locker room. but zayn stood there, harry could see his bare feet under the stall.

"harry? come on."

harry was shaking now.

"okay," he repeated himself, struggling to even bite his trembling lip, when he tried a choked sob escaped his mouth, and he squeezed his eyes shut for a second. "okay, okay okay okay okay."

it wasn't long before zayn was at the stall door. "harry, open this door now or i swear i'll crawl under it and drag you out."

"okay okay okay," harry replied, and his head was spinning as he stumbled across the slightly wet floor towards the lock. he fumbled a bit before he managed to turn it open, and zayn burst through the stall before quickly pulling harry's frail body into his arms.

"c'mere," he whispered. "it's okay baby, it's okay, i know."

"okay," harry cried, he was crying and everything he said sounded like a distressed sob and he hated himself more every second he let zayn comfort him. zayn hushed him, rocking him slightly and telling him not think too much.

zayn didn't smell like honey and harry didn't like that. he always associated comfort and sleep with honey and laundry and *louis* and he didn't know if that would ever change. it was just the way things were, whether zayn was his best friend or not.

"i want louis," he sobbed, pushing his forehead further into zayn's shoulder. "i don't want louis but i want louis and i don't want him and i want him." zayn's bare shoulder was wet and cold against his forehead. he smelled like chlorine.

"harry, you don't want him. you think you do, when really you just miss your relationship, not louis."

no, harry wanted to scream. he did miss what they had, but he also missed the way louis smiled and the way his left eye twitched when he was talking and he missed louis as a person, not as a boyfriend.

but he also hated that louis had turned him into this.

he was trembling when zayn lifted his chin up.

"harry, you don't even look like you've been crying. maybe if you play some water polo, get your mind off of things, you'll feel better? is that alright?" zayn's voice was soft, it was compassionate and caring and it *wasn't louis'*.

it's been four months, harry thought. *get over him already.*

so he nodded weakly, and zayn gave him a really tight hug before releasing harry. they walked through the small locker room together, the whole time harry sucking his stomach in and it was really hard to breathe but it was better than being even fatter.

his stomach hurt so bad.

when they walked out, everyone turned to look at them. harry wished he could suck in his tummy even more but it didn't seem physically possible, so he just put his arms over it and hoped the rest of his body didn't look as ugly.

"finally! harry, you're going to be so good! you're really tall, it's perfect."

yeah, tall. like a freaking giraffe. harry scowled at himself, at his bare legs that he always shaved and his knobby knees. he was too long, he was too tall and big and he wished he was as beautiful and skinny and curvy and gorgeous as louis tomlinson, the person he *shouldn't be think about*.

"come on, jump in!" one of them, harry thought his name was duke or luke or something, he honestly didn't even care, called. but he stepped forward, careful to make sure zayn was always by his side, helping him. he stuck one foot in, flinching at the cold water. goose bumps ran up and down his body, and he hated the way it looked on his pale skin.

the large room they were in smelled of chlorine and it was humid. harry found himself breathing it in, closing his eyes and letting it take over his senses. once the water around his legs felt somewhat bearable, he lowered the rest of his body in the water.

the coldness engulfed him; he liked that numb feeling. he squeezed his eyes shut as he went underwater, feeling his curls float around his head like a halo.

angel.

he opened his eyes up under the water, and it burned and it was blurry but it was cool seeing his curls move around in the water and all the legs hopping up and down farther down in the shallow end; he was in the deep end.

so he dealt with the stinging, and he could hear his heartbeat in his ears as he held his breath. his lungs were aching, screaming at him to go back up for some more air. part of him wanted to ignore it, to just lose all of his breath and die now; peacefully and quietly, where all he could see was the light blue of the water.

but, he finally surfaced, taking a gasping breath. he shook the water out of his curls, blinking his burning eyes and licking his lips. harry could see zayn at the other end of the pool, throwing the ball to another player, laughing as someone tried to dunk his head underwater.

harry took a second to catch his breath, but even after that he couldn't breathe properly.

he decided to ignore it, and his heart was racing as he swam towards the boys playing water polo. some of them greeted him nicely, others looked at him as if he didn't belong there. he wanted to ignore them, he really did, but he was never good with judging looks.

"harry, you should be the goalkeeper!" zayn cried, his hands grasping the ball as he struggled to keep it away from the others. the current goalkeeper -was it duke or luke?- gave zayn a questioning look.

"zayn, i'm the goalkeeper." he had an australian accent, and harry watched as he chewed on his lip ring.

"just let harry try. i want him to experience all the positions."

harry blushed, the way zayn was talking making him feel like a shy child who was unable to speak.

but duke moved out of the way, and harry made his way into the goal, which resembled something similar to a hockey net.

"c'mon luke! you're on our team!" zayn smiled. oh. his name was luke.

"let's play," harry mumbled, putting on the helmet another boy handed him.

***

"you're so good!"

zayn tackled harry in a hug, despite luke's glare. "you should totally be the goalkeeper, you're so great at it! you don't let anything get past you!"

harry felt like he was going to die; he had used all of the energy left in his weak body on this game and it was taking a huge toll on him. suddenly food sounded a bit more bearable, but at the same time it didn't.

"yeah, go harry!"

harry whipped around in the pool, causing tiny waves to ripple the surface of the water. what he saw made his heart stop.

there, sitting on the bleachers looking down at the pool, was louis. he was on his feet, standing and clapping, at the same time cupping his hands around his mouth and yelling out encouraging words to harry. harry almost passed out there; he couldn't figure out if it was because of his lack of food or the fact that the one person he couldn't stop thinking about was standing there. his fringe looked the same as it did four months ago, swept across his forehead skillfully. his short legs looked so perfect in his black skinnies and white tank top.

harry burst into tears in the middle of the pool. "louis," he sobbed, ignoring the worried looks from the other boys on the team. "louis louis louis." his knees were shaky, and he knew that they would've given out by now if the water wasn't helping him stay up. his eyes were burning with tears, and he was crying so hard and his chest hurt, and he didn't know how louis was standing there, only about ten feet away. he waded his way towards the edge of the pool, hiccups and random words escaping his lips, as he was blubbering, his shoulders shaking.

harry didn't know what came over him, but really couldn't breathe this time, it felt like his throat was closing up. he squeezed his eyes shut, shuddering and he was gasping for air and *was he even breathing?*

"louis," he choked, and zayn was touching his arm, pulling him back, hushing him again just like he did in the locker room. "no!" harry yelled. "i wanna talk to him, i don't care if he hates me i just wanna touch him again!" harry's voice sounded so weak, so strained and harry knew that he was pathetic by the utterly sad look zayn gave him.

"harry, are you okay?" he whispered, reaching out and brushing a curl out of his face. "harry, louis isn't here."

"harry!"

the voice came from the same place, but it was different. more, girly. harry looked up again, his lips trembling, and no. no. eleanor was there, now racing as fast as her skinny legs could carry her down the bleachers. "harry are you okay?" she rushed, taking quick steps until she was kneeling, leaning down to meet eyes with him. "harry, i didn't mean to upset you, i was just trying to cheer you on. you were doing great!"

"go away," harry breathed, wiping his eyes furiously and trying to hold in the sobs that threatened to take over him, and he was shaking.

eleanor looked hurt. "harry, what happened? why are you crying?"

zayn finally stepped in, circling an arm around harry so harry could bury his face into his bare chest. he didn't smell like louis.

"eleanor, just go. he isn't mad at you, trust me. he just needs you to go."

"feel better harry," eleanor said helplessly, before taking a few hesitant steps backwards and then turning around and walking away. she gave him one more worried look though, right before she shut the door behind her.

"louis," was all harry could whimper in reply. it was eleanor, not louis. these freaking hallucinations, probably coming from his lack of food, they were so painful and that race that he felt in his heart was so awful. why was he so hopeful? even if louis was actually there, he wouldn't be cheering for harry. no, he would probably be visiting some of his other friends from the classes that were below him.

"i want to go home," harry begged, and zayn nodded.

"okay," he replied sadly, his voice unbearably soft.

***

zayn left harry alone at home, which the younger boy was extremely grateful for.

he wanted to cut so bad, but zayn and niall had hidden all of his razors, only allowing them when he promised that he only needed to shave, and then he had to give them right back.

so here he was, laying on his back in the middle of his bedroom, on the floor. the white color of his ceiling above him was fading in and out, turning black for a second before going back to white again. there were tears still coming from his eyes, sliding down his temple and onto the carpet.

his arms were crossed in front of him, his hands held together loosely and his rings rubbing together. he had changed into sweatpants and a sweatshirt, along with a green beanie. he had taken a shower to wash the chlorine off of his body; now he smelled like green apples and dove soap. it was odd, because every time he used soap it reminded him of louis. he didn't like soap anymore.

his mum was working, she actually had the decency to write a note this time. harry had crumpled it up and throw it away. the kitchen was spotless when he left it, shining and perfect the way he liked it. it seemed there were only a few things he could actually control these days; it bothered him immensely. he didn't like when things didn't go his away and it seemed that's all they were doing lately.

he jumped from his position on the floor when his phone rang. it was on his desk, plugged into a charger.

he let out a deep sigh, laying there for a few more seconds before getting up and walking towards his phone. he picked up his phone, not looking at the caller id when answering it.

"hullo?" he mumbled, and he was so sleepy. his eyes were drooping and he couldn't stop yawning.

"hi harreh."

their words were slurred, they were slurred but harry knew that voice anywhere. he knew by the way his heart stopped for a second and he kind of just woke up.

"louis."

louis was crying, harry could hear his sobs over the phone. he sounded a bit drunk.

"louis where are you?" harry breathed.

"i wanted to hear your voice."

he hung up.

forty-five

"you know i love phone calls with you, right?"

harry furrowed his eyebrows, snuggling closer to louis on his small bed. louis ran his fingers through the mess of curls on his head, humming little random songs as he let harry think of his response.

harry lifted his head so he was looking into louis' brilliant blue eyes. "why?"

louis sighed, a happy, sweet sigh where you could hear a hint of his voice, and his lips were turned up into a small smile. harry wanted to reach up and brush the back of his knuckles along louis' soft skin, against his perfect cheekbones and his stupid, adorable little nose. he watched the way louis looked into the sky, as if something on the ceiling interested him, but harry knew it was because louis had a habit of staring into the air when he was thinking. he was biting his lip and then licking it, an action that always made harry's heart speed up.

"angel, there's a lot of reasons why i love phone calls with you." louis circled his arm tighter around harry's waist, his fingertips brushing harry's bare hip. they were both shirtless, dark red sweatpants on louis' legs and grey ones on harry's.

"what's one?" harry liked to bury his face into louis' chest, because he radiated warmth. louis claimed that he was a heater, but that didn't make sense when he was so cold all the time.

louis let out a tiny, sweet chuckle. "well, one reason is that i can focus on just your voice, and i love your voice. it's low and slow and soothing and i could fall asleep to your voice, it's so beautiful, harry."

harry blushed, his cheeks heating up. he usually hated compliments, but this one made him melt.

"what's the other reason?" he breathed. louis fingers were drumming softly on his side, pushing in-between each of his ribs and it tickled a bit but it was bearable.

"you always talk to yourself, and i love listening to it. we'll be in the middle of a conversation, and then you'll say something, and then disagree with what you said, and then you pretty much argue with yourself. i love that about you."

harry frowned. "i didn't know i did that."

a little laugh escaped louis' lips. "you're adorable."

"will you always call me? to hear my voice i mean?" harry's voice was hopeful, nervous.

"always. your voice is a song to me. a song that i never get tired of."

"thank you," harry whispered. louis smiled, grabbing harry around the sides and pulling him so harry was pretty much laying on top of him. they were chest to chest, harry's curls falling in louis' face and causing louis laugh. harry found louis' laugh unbelievably attractive.

"that tickles." louis reached up, his eyes sparkling and shining, gently brushing harry's curls behind his ear. harry always was amazed with how beautiful and absolutely radiant louis looked, especially from this view. his rosy lips were in a tiny smile, as if he was holding in a laugh. there were crinkles by his blue eyes, and his eyelashes were dark coal black. his skin was tan and glowing, soft as always. harry could see every freckle that littered his nose, that weren't even noticeable from far away. he could see the blonde tips of his fringe, colored by the sun. he loved the faint specks of green in his smoldering eyes, and he loved the little curly pieces of hair that poked out *from underneath his ears and curled at the tips. he loved the vague tint of pink that was always on louis' cheeks, like a tiny blush.*

he was prepossessing, enchanting. captivating.

and he was harry's.

"louis!" harry yelled into the phone, even though the line was dead and there was a monotone beep coming from the speaker. "louis louis louis!"

there was no response. of course. why was he stupid enough to think there would be?

harry shook his curls out in frustration, feeling tears build up in his eyes. he couldn't decide whether to call louis or not.

he finally let out a groan and typed in louis' number, which he had memorized, by heart. then, he clicked call.

the answer was not immediate, no. he sat for minutes, when he didn't get an answer he called again. he knew louis has his phone; he knew louis was just ignoring him. who wouldn't ignore harry? he was irrelevant.

after a few minutes, louis finally picked up. "what do you *want* harry?!" he spit into the phone, and the drunkenness that was clear in his voice made harry's stomach twist. it was a painful feeling, as his tummy already was completely empty.

harry was dumbfounded as louis waited for harry's response. harry could hear his heavy breathing and whimpers, and it hurt him so much.

"i was wondering where you are? are you at home?" harry's voice was shaky.

"i'm in my flat, yes. curly, you're making me sad."

"you're making me sad," louis frowned playfully, nudging harry's knee under the table. "that bottom lip though. put it away. now."

harry wasn't meaning to pout, really he wasn't. but soy sauce wasn't really his thing, and they had drowned his rice in it.

"i don't like soy sauce," he murmured, sticking his fork in his rice and moving it around. "i can't help it my lip insists on sticking out." his voice was whiny.

"crap, harry."

harry lifted his head to look at the boy across from him. they were in a chinese restaurant, and chinese never was appealing to him, but they both wanted to try something different than their usual fast food restaurants they went to. they never liked fancy; cheeseburgers and chips were perfectly fine.

"what?" he asked, looking up at louis through his eyelashes. he left his fork, abandoned in his pile of drowned rice. his heart was in his throat as he stared at the boy across from him. his eyes were full of lust and want, and he whispered something inaudible as he twisted their feet together under the table.

"you're so," he paused, letting out a big breath and blinking rapidly. "you're so beautiful and i feel like i need to do something about it. like you're curls, their just. i just feel like i can't stop touching them and it makes me sad that you don't have somebody who is just as beautiful as you but then again, nobody can be anywhere near as perfect as you. but i freaking cherish you, okay?"

harry honestly didn't know what to say. he slowly fixed his lips so he wasn't pouting anymore, not breaking eye contact with louis. louis was breathing hard, as he had let out all that sentence in one breath.

they stared at each other for a few seconds, leaving their food untouched on the table.

"basically, you're making me sad, harry."

harry smiled.

"are you drunk?"

the question was rhetorical; both of them knew the answer.

"why are you calling me? i'm having so much fun here without you, you're ruining it."

"you called me first," harry frowned into the phone, picking at his nails and resisting the urge to bite them. when he was little, his nails were always bitten and short. it was quite a bad habit that he had picked up. "you said that you wanted to hear my voice."

harry wondered if louis knew that he was crying. harry could imagine the tears streaming down louis' face, staining his perfect, soft skin. he could imagine louis brushing his fringe out of his eyes, biting his lip to conceal more sobs that were threatening to escape. he had only witness louis like that a couple times; it was absolutely heart shattering.

"i don't want to hear your voice. it hurts harry. why did you make me leave anyway?"

the signal was a bit bad; every few words his voice would fade out. there was a loud noise in the background; harry couldn't make out what it was.

"where are you?" harry asked.

"why do you care?" louis snapped, his voice so harsh that it made harry physically flinch, and he placed a hand over his heart, because, crap. it just stopped for a few seconds.

"it's really loud and i want to know," harry said quietly. "where are you?"

louis faltered a bit, blubbering a few incoherent things that sounded like a few curse words, before speaking. "'m on the roof. outside. the flat's got a nice roof. can see the city and that. cool."

harry's breath caught. he was standing up, slipping on some socks before he put his boots on. he didn't care that sweatpants looked awful in boots; he just needed to drive to doncaster. now.

"tell me about it."

it was weird, trying to stay calm for louis. he was used to being the one out of control, having a panic attack, sobbing into the phone and waiting for someone to comfort him. but right now he felt eerily calm, although his heart was racing.

he listened to louis mumble and declare things that didn't make any sense as he ran outside and got in his mum's old car. she was going to sell it, but for now she was leaving it in the garage. the keys were sitting on her bedside table.

he turned the key, listening closer as the engine blocked out louis' voice for a second.

"...and i just walked outside, and there was this dog. it was purple, but it was also blue and i really liked its curls. they reminded me of you. not that you look like a dog, i mean, besides the curls. you know he had curly hair?"

he burst into giggles and harry held in a smile. louis was so, so cute.

"yes, i knew," harry chuckled.

he felt so light, like something big was happening. he knew that louis was on the edge of the roof; louis was describing how far away the street looked and how there were so many cars and it was weird because it was late at night.

but for some reason, he had this tugging feeling that louis wasn't going to try to jump off.

if only he knew.

***

"do you think i'm ugly, harry?"

he was so close, so close to doncaster. only ten minutes away. harry was growing restless, his hand tapping on the steering wheel, the other hand gripping his cell phone.

"i don't like my hair. do you think i'm ugly, harry?"

he was standing in his full length mirror, his hands running through his messy hair.

"no, i don't think you're ugly," harry said quietly, honestly. he really didn't know how to respond to that question, because it frustrated him so much that louis didn't see how beautiful he actually was. every single thing he did, even if it was lazily scratching his arm or letting out a big yawn, every single thing was extremely attractive and incredibly adorable. he could be covered in mud and dirt, but his blue eyes would just shine through and he would look perfect.

"really? because, you're all skinny and stuff-"

"no, i'm not."

"no, harry you are. you have this perfect body, i don't know how many times i have to tell you."

harry shrugged.

"i'll just keep saying it until you believe it, i guess."

there was a smirk on louis' face, but harry could see the honesty and truthfulness in louis' eyes.

"you don't have to worry about being ugly. you look like a freaking sun next to me, you literally radiate adorableness."

"is that a word?" harry's english accent was extremely noticeable on that sentence, he didn't know why.

the carpet of louis' room was soft beneath his bare feet.

"you're beautiful," is all harry said in response.

harry practically memorized the look of louis' flat building. he had stared at the picture for ages, trying to imagine everything that louis did in it.

he pulled into the parking lot, unable to tear his eyes away from the roof the minute he got out of the car.

he didn't see anybody, which he had mixed feelings about.

he didn't realise he was crying until he could taste salt in his mouth. he blinked rapidly, trying to get the tears out of his eyes.

harry honestly didn't know what he was expecting.

he just hoped louis was still up there on the roof, acting the drunken boy he was.

because that was better than killing himself.

forty-six

harry received many odd glances when he finally burst into the apartment building. it was set up similar to a hotel; there was a front desk and a few chairs. harry rushed past the couple making a deal with the person at the front desk. they were obviously excited, probably because it was their first "home" together.

'i'm coming, lou," harry murmured into the phone, but the boy was too drunk to understand anything. he just kept saying random things that didn't make sense half the time. "just stay there, stay right where you are." he stepped into the elevator, and the minute both his boots were in the clicked on the top floor.

the music, the peaceful, happy music was frustrating and he tried to block it out, because louis was on the *roof* and he was unable to do anything while he was stuck in this cramped place. he pushed his fingers through his curls, taking deep breaths and trying so hard not to cry.

"...do you think it would hurt if i jumped on top of that car parked down there. not as far as a distance, you know?" louis was saying, and harry shook his head, feeling his heart pound at the thought.

"louis, no, don't do that. no no no no louis no."

he could feel the panic filling his mind, although he tried so desperately to ignore it. no matter how hard he focused, his mind was still spinning and he hated that feeling. it was a faint, hollow feeling and he wanted it to go away so he could breathe properly.

but it didn't, it actually worsened with louis' eerily calm voice that was also shaky with tears.

harry knew his knees would give out, they almost did when he finally stopped on the top floor and saw the short set of stairs that led to the roof of the apartment building.

"louis!" he yelled into the phone, his voice echoing through the empty, slightly warm building. he stumbled up the stairs and held in his sobs as he looked around for louis. "louis louis louis no don't die, don't freaking die, i can't handle that," he choked, tripping over almost everything in his path as he struggled and failed to keep his mind focused, to not completely fade out like he always did when he got upset like this.

it was windy outside, so windy that harry pushed his sweatshirt hood over his head and he let out a little sneeze.

"your sneezes are so cute."

harry whipped around, lowering his phone from his ear and letting his tears fall as he saw louis.

it had been so long since he saw those glowing blue eyes, which were now shining as he was drunk. louis was smiling up at him, his head tilted really high and his eyes almost squinted shut. harry felt his heart flutter because *wow* he was adorable, but what wasn't adorable was the fact that his legs were dangling off the edge.

it wasn't an unusual thing to do; a lot of people liked to sit on the edge of buildings and let themselves enjoy the view. but louis was drunk, and that meant that one wrong move could kill him and harry would not let that happen.

"louis," he said shakily, trying to keep his calm. "louis, louis louis don't do that."

"are you not going to thank me for complimenting your sneeze or.." louis trailed off, before bursting into laughter.

"louis." harry held in a smile, feeling a calming warmth go through his chest. "louis, can you give me a hug?" he hoped louis would get away from the edge of the roof, but he also really freaking wanted a hug.

louis shook his head, and the lump in harry's throat came back.

"i wanna jump off, it'd be *so* fun, harry, so fun and you could maybe come with me." he furrowed his brows, before correcting himself. "no, i don't want you to jump, it's too cold, angel."

fondness and horror were an odd thing to be mixed together, and it caused harry to almost reel backwards. "louis, it's not fun to jump. it's scary." his voice cracked.

"i don't understand what you mean. it's a beautiful day out; the wind is giving me a rush." louis spread out his arms in the air, closing his eyes and letting a smile cross his rosy lips.

"no," harry pushed. "no, i don't want you to jump, louis. please, come here." harry's voice was getting louder, that awful panicky feeling was coming back and he hated it.

louis listened though, he grumbled a few odd things and stood up, walking towards harry. "what?"

he was only wearing socks, causing him to be a bit shorter than he usually seemed.

and he looked absolutely stunning.

he seemed a bit more sober than he was when he first called harry; he wasn't blurting out random things anymore, just holding his gaze with a goofy smile. his hair was blown back from the wind, causing little pieces to fall in his face. harry reached out and wrapped his long fingers around louis' short ones, holding their hands against his legs gently.

"thank you for listening to me," harry whispered. louis nodded, looking a bit dazed and confused, but harry could tell he was a happy kind of drunk, whether he really was depressed.

perhaps just as depressed as harry.

"you look so much like an angel right now, i swear," louis laughed, looking away as if somebody need to clarify. "am i right or am i right?" he squeezed his eyes shut and blew his lips out as he burst into giggles.

harry honestly had no idea what to do. because the love in his heart was so overwhelming and he felt like jumping up and down, like calling everybody and crying and screaming because louis was *so beautiful.*

"you're so cool, louis," harry smiled, and louis snapped out of his laughing fit. his stuck his bottom lip out, his eyebrows furrowed.

"now why did you say that?" he grinned and harry thought he was going to get whiplash from these mood swings. "that was unnecessary, young harold."

they were still holding hands, standing on the roof about ten feet away from the edge. the wind was picking up as night grew closer; harry could see the sun setting and sending a dim haze over the city of doncaster. the sky was purple and orange and yellow and it was amazing but harry couldn't stop looking at the even more breathtaking boy standing in front of him.

he was fascinating. harry just watched as he unhooked their hands and started to "shoot" harry in the chest. "pow pow!' he screeched, shooting, shooting, shooting. "poo, pow, bam, pam pow!"

his eyes were dazzling as he looked into harry's eyes. "it doesn't hurt does it?" he asked worriedly.

louis was twiddling and moving his hands, and harry held his gaze while he reached and gently stopped his hands, intertwining their fingers and bringing both of their hands into the air. he kept their hands there and smiled a bit before pushing his forehead into louis, their chests bumping, and then he captured louis' lips in an urgent kiss.

louis was taken aback, all of his breath that tasted a bit like alcohol being released into harry's mouth and harry just kissed him harder. louis' lips were warm compared to the chilly wind.

he pulled back for a second, and louis' eyes were wide, and he looked completely sober now. "louis, is this okay?" he untangled their hands and instead wrapped his arms tightly around louis' waist.

louis nodded, his breaths uneven and rushed. he gave a little smile. "i forgot how much i missed kissing you, harry angel styles."

harry's heart melted, it melted into a puddle of goo that he really didn't feel like cleaning up, so he just himself go, he pushed away all his doubting thoughts and protests and kissed louis again. they were still standing, except for the fact that harry was holding louis up, so that his sock-cover feet barely brushed the ground.

it felt like a movie star kiss, the one where the whole audience could feel it, where even the producers of the movie were caught off guard. their eyelashes tangled together and their lips moved together perfectly, in an uneven rhythm and harry honestly could feel his knees shaking as louis put his delicate hands in his hair. harry could hear his heartbeat in his ears, along with the rush of wind and whimpers escaping both of their mouths.

harry's heart ached, as it had been in pain for so long and it felt like it should still be but it wasn't, not as long as louis was here. he let out a sad sigh, though, when his stomach grumbled loudly.

louis pulled back, raising an eyebrow.

"hungry for my kisses, are you now?" he winked, but then, as he really looked into harry's eyes, a frown etched his face.

"harry, what's wrong?"

"nothing," harry began to say, but then he shook his head. lying wasn't going to do him any good.

"i haven't been eating," he whispered ashamedly. "because you left me because i was too fat. perhaps i still am."

louis looked taken aback; hurt, even.

"harry, i've told you a million times how much i love your body, have i not?"

harry didn't respond, just looked into the sky and let a breath shake his trembling lips, as tears threatened to escape. he wished he could go back to that happy state he was in just a few seconds ago.

"harry," louis pressed, reaching out and cradling his jaw. "harry, don't do this. please, don't starve yourself."

"okay," harry responded. was it bad that it felt like a lie?

"i'm keeping my eye on you, curly." harry was grateful for louis' attempt to keep the mood light, or at least not utterly sad.

"okay," harry said again.

***

"i have this tiny feeling that we need to talk, but i really don't feel up to it right now, to be honest." louis blew out air through his lips, handing harry a mug of tea as he sat down on the small couch next to him, so their knees were touching.

"i only have one question to ask, though."

louis rolled his eyes. "you never listen to me, styles. i said not to say cheese and you said cheese!"

harry looked at him confusedly, before he remembered, that day two years ago. he smiled.

"so what is your question?" louis' voice was quiet and soft now, almost as gentle as his hand was on harry's hipbone as he rubbed tiny circles on his skin with his thumb.

"why were you drinking?" harry whispered.

they were silent for a moment. the smell of louis' apartment was kinda wonderful and harry was surprised it didn't smell utterly awful. it was that honey, laundry, and boy smell that harry wanted to bottle up and turn into a fragrance that he could spray all of his crap with ever since he met louis.

"i think i could ask you something very similar to that, and you know what it is. i believe we'd have about the same answers."

harry nodded in agreement, taking a sip of his tea. the taste of it reminded him of so long ago. he could never quite make tea the way louis did, no matter how many teaspoons of sugar he put in or how many times he watched louis make it.

"has the perfect amount of sugar, doesn't it?" louis asked softly.

harry smiled. "yeah, it does."

"i missed you, harry." louis avoided harry's eyes. "but at the same time, i feel like this time away from you made me love you even more."

love.

whenever harry heard that word, he thought of louis, on instinct.

but he honestly didn't believe that louis still loved him.

"what about mitchell?" he murmured, almost inaudible.

"i love *you*." louis voice was firm and soft at the same time. "my angel. you are my angel. harry is my angel. angel."

harry blushed. "i-i uhm-"

"you uhm what?" louis asked when harry trailed off and sat in silence for a few seconds.

"i love you, uhm, too. yeah. i love you."

forty-seven

october 31, 2010

"i wasn't planning on dressing up, no," harry mumbled into the phone. "i'm a junior; isn't that too old?"

"harry styles, i am a senior and i'm dressing up, you twat."

harry perked up. "what are you dressing up as?"

"why, thank you for asking." his voice was quiet. "i am going to be a banana."

harry burst into laughter. "really?"

"yes, i am. and i knew that you weren't going to get a costume, so i took it upon myself to get one *for* you."

harry could feel excitement in his chest at the thought of louis picking out a costume for him. he wondered what it would be.

"i'm scared," he smiled, gripping the phone tighter.

"bye harry." harry could practically hear louis grinning, or maybe doing his sunshine smile.

harry hung up his phone, locking it and sticking it in his pocket. he was outside, sitting criss cross on his front porch.

it was an unusually warm day. the fall leaves were swirling around him in splotches of orange, red, and brown. there was a bowl of pumpkin seeds sitting next to him, and then another bowl of candy corn. harry was happy that halloween turned out to be such a beautiful day.

he reached over and turned the pumpkin he carved so it was facing him. he loved what he had done. it had two triangle eyes and a crooked smile, along with a triangle nose. there was a tiny candle burning inside it, causing it to glow in the darkening night. it wasn't quite dark yet; there was still a bit of light and he could see children running out of their houses, getting ready for an exciting night of trick or treating.

he had a large bowl of candy in his lap, filled with chocolate bars of many brands. he was tempted to eat them, but he decided that the kids were more important and he would be just fine eating his candy corn. he lifted one up, examining it's three different colors, before placing it on his tongue and savoring the taste.

it smelled of halloween and harry breathed it in. his grey sweatpants and white shirt provided just enough warmth for him to be comfortable, which he was thankful for. he had to admit that he was a bit anxious, waiting for louis to come over. louis claimed that trick-or-treating when it was still somewhat light out was childish and cowardly, so he said he would come a lot later. he told harry to save him a handful of candy.

harry hoped that the children would listen to his one-piece-a-person rule.

he smiled softly when he saw a little boy and girl, probably brother and sister, ran up. the girl was a princess, and the boy had a sheet over his head with two holes cut for the eyes. "trick-or-treat!" they yelled in unison, holding out their tiny pumpkin bags. harry said hello to both of them and put a candy bar in each of their open bags.

"have fun," he called after them, watching them run off and beg at the next house.

harry thought that halloween was an odd holiday; originally it was meant to worship devils and demons and scary stuff that he only saw in horror movies. now, it was just a chance for children to dress up like their favorite movie characters and get free candy.

he remembered when he was little, and he always insisted on being scooby doo. his mum would grumble about how he needed to try something new, something that didn't require him wearing the raggedy old costume that got bundled up in the attic every year. but he didn't listen, he just put on the worn out costume and messed with the scooby nose on top of his head that was about to fall off.

harry smiled to himself, eating another candy corn and closing his eyes as some of his hair was blown in his face gently. his lips were slightly chapped from the chilly weather that october presented; he just thankful it wasn't too cold today.

harry had handed out candy to a dozen more kids when louis' car finally pulled into his driveway. it was dark now. the moon was shining onto the ground, making it look scary, especially since it was halloween night.

louis came out of his car carrying two bags, one much larger than the other.

"look how cute you are, handing out candy and sitting like that!" louis called, grinning and running up the pathway that led to their front porch. "give me some of that candy."

harry held his breath when louis squat down and leaned forward, his hair brushing harry's lips as he dug through the variety of chocolate and tried to decide what kind he wanted.

"which one harry?" louis murmured and harry leaned back in surprise when louis' head shot up, revealing a goofy, crinkly eyed smile. "you can pick for me."

harry shrugged, pulling out a snickers bar shyly. "is this okay?"

"course it is!" louis said loudly, reaching over and ruffling his curls. "now let's go inside so we can put on our bad-arse costumes."

harry giggled. "okay." he moved the bowl off of his lap, before uncrossing his legs. he looked up and realised that louis was holding a hand out, to help him up. he smiled and grabbed it, letting louis pull him up.

"mum, we're going trick-or-treating!" harry called, leading louis into his bedroom and shutting the door quietly behind them.

"are you ready to see your costume?" louis grinned, wiggling the smaller bag in his hand along with his eyebrows.

"somewhat."

"it's perfect for you, i swear it."

"as if that helps," harry murmured.

"give me a second." louis bit his lip and sat down on harry's bed, unzipping the bag. "close your eyes, harold."

harry closed his eyes, feeling his eyelashes brush his cheekbone. the room was getting colder and colder as the night droned on, and he had goose bumps on his arms whenever he heard the yells of people outside. last time he checked, it was eight thirty, not that late but late enough for scary things to come out. he always got scared on halloween, ever since he started watching movies like the grudge or paranormal activity, he had been scared of supernatural things like that.

harry froze when he felt a slight breath on the back of his neck. it was warm and it smelled of chocolate and peppermint. "I-louis," he stuttered.

"shh, don't worry. louis is putting your costume on. it's only one thing, not that big of a deal. the rest of your costume is already on."

harry felt a shiver down his spine when louis brushed some curls off of the back of his neck, kissing the skin there gently. "so beautiful," louis whispered. the words caused a tugging feeling at the bottom of harry's ribs, and he tried to control his shaky breathing.

the sides of louis' arms brushed harry's faces as he reached over to move his fringe around a bit. harry flinched slightly when he felt louis slip something into his hair, behind his ears.

"what are you putting in my hair, lou?" harry asked curiously, very tempted to open his eyes and look in the mirror.

"just wait a second," louis murmured. "i'm fixing it so it's just right."

harry nodded, which made louis grasp his head. "stop moving, you fool," he giggled.

harry blushed, holding in a smile and trying not to jump up and down as he was growing impatient. the carpet was soft beneath his bare feet, and he focused on that feeling instead of the lingering of louis' hand on his face.

he could feel louis circling around him, so now he was in front of him. harry liked the way louis' socks touched his bare toes, the connection causing electricity to shoot up his whole body.

"i love when you close your eyes. i love your eyelids and your eyelashes and your lips and your eyebrows and wow, harry, you're pretty," louis murmured as he continued to move harry's curls every which way. harry felt his cheeks burn and his hands sweat.

louis leaned in and kissed him, which caught him off guard, but in a good way. "this halloween is going to be awesome, because your face is so perfect for your costume."

"it is?" harry responded.

louis led him towards what harry assumed was his mirror. "open your eyes." louis put his hands around harry's waist, resting his chin on harry's shoulder from behind. harry fluttered his eyes open, first seeing louis behind him in the mirror smiling fondly before he noticed the thing floating above his head. "you're an angel," louis whispered.

harry melted, he really did and he reached his hands up to touch the almost invisible wires that were holding the white sparkly halo above his head.

"thank you," was all harry could say, and louis pulled him in for a soft kiss before taking his costume and changing into it quickly. harry giggled at how small louis' face looked in the big banana costume.

"let's go, angel." louis held out his hand, the other hand clutching the two bags. "we're using these bags to put our candy in."

"okay," harry breathed.

***

"i can't believe this. it says take as much as i want but you still make me take one."

harry shrugged.

"harry, you're too sweet. 'let's save it for the other kids, they want candy too!'" louis mocked harry, but his eyes were teasing and there was a bright smile on his face. louis' hand that was sticking out of one of the banana arm holes was clutching harry's, and harry hoped his hand wasn't too sweaty.

"this is no time for child-play, angel, no, we are going on an adventure. a halloweenie adventure." this sentence caused harry to laugh, and louis smiled proudly.

"where are we going?" harry asked once he had recovered.

"we are going where the demons hide."

harry gasped, and louis burst into laughter. "you're so dramatic, baby. we're going into the woods. niall said that him and his friends were scaring the couples that always walk on that trail, with the mini jack-o-lanterns and romantic overhanging trees."

"the woods?!" harry spluttered. "but it's midnight, there could be a wild animal!"

louis kissed his nose softly. "the only animal there will be me."

harry found himself blushing and his body was hot, and just that sentence had so much meaning behind it and it bothered him very much, very much so.

"let's go, angel." louis reached out and swung a confused harry into his arms, so that he was carrying him bridal style. "louis will lead the way, no need to worry."

harry felt as if he should have been begging for louis to put him down, but honestly, he loved being in louis' arms. it made him feel small, but in a good way.

***

louis was right about the trail. it was quite romantic. the trees that were slowly being stripped of their leaves by the howling win hung over a newly raked trail, and there were tiny pumpkins that were glowing along the path. louis led them along, calling niall's name every now and then.

"he should be hiding here somewhere," louis said, confused. "these woods aren't that big."

harry pushed his forehead into louis' chest, feeling the butterflies in his stomach flutter as louis stepped, causing him to bounce slightly. he could hear the leaves crunching beneath louis' feet, and it was a soothing noise. for some reason, he didn't feel that scared, as long as there was a tiny bit of light and louis' strong, arms were around him.

"niall!" louis called, and harry lived for the way louis' wonderful voice echoed into the night sky of october,

louis almost dropped harry when someone jumped out of the brush, a scary mask with small black eyes covering the face of the person. "ahh!" they screamed, and harry's heart beat incredibly quick.

"get away!" louis screeched, turning them so his back was on the person and harry was facing away from them. "harry, run, that isn't niall. he was a clown."

harry never knew his heart could race so fast. he let louis gently lower him to the ground before he sprinted away, heavy breaths escaping his lips. he could hear louis arguing with the boy, saying something about how rude he was and how he smelled like a rotting pumpkin.

"reveal yourself!" louis cried into the sky, and was it bad that harry smiled?

"angel!" was what he heard next. "*angel get your scrawny adorable tiny little arse over here right now, he just ran away!*"

harry whipped around, and he couldn't see anything anymore. he didn't realise it, but he had wandered off the trail and he couldn't see anything anymore.

he also didn't know which way to go. it seemed as if the farther he walked the less he could hear louis, and every time he turned in a different direction louis' voice still faded.

"lou-" harry began to say, when he was bombarded by a huge force, causing him to be slammed onto the ground and he rolled a bit, leaves and sticks painfully poking into his back. "get off of me!" he screamed loudly, flailing his legs and kicking the mysterious person.

the person fought back and harry could barely make out that same white mask, with the black eyes and the boy had straight brown hair.

"louis!" harry was crying now, because the boy was on top of him, holding his wrists above his head. "louis help!"

he didn't know whether the crunching of somebody running towards them was good or not.

"who are you?" harry sobbed, because he was so scared and his halo had fallen off when he had been rolling on the ground and he wanted it back.

"don't cry!" the person behind the mask said worriedly and harry tried desperately to place that voice with a face, a name. "i was just kidding, don't cry."

"you-" harry began, when all of the pressure was lifted off of him and he squinted his eyes to see louis and the boy wrestling on the ground.

"get, off, of him," louis growled, pushing the boy away and running towards harry. harry felt his knees give out when louis finally wrapped his arms around harry, holding up all of his weight so harry didn't have to do it himself.

"angel, it's okay. i know who it is. they're not going to hurt you." louis squeezed him tighter. "although i want to hurt them." his voice sounded cruel, scary, foreign.

"liam, that isn't even freaking funny. don't even *touch* harry, and don't you dare tackle him to the ground. he isn't me; he can't just assume it's you and be okay with it."

liam turned on his flashlight, and he looked like he was about to cry. "it was a joke, harry, i'm sorry, i thought it would be funny."

harry looked at him through tear filled eyes. "it's okay," he whispered. "sorry, i was being overdramatic i was just scared, because, this happened to me, you know, before."

louis cradled harry in his arms. "I know, liam won't do it again, he didn't mean to hurt you. now how about us three go find niall and call it a night? i'm really in the mood for a good horror movie."

"okay," harry breathed.

"wait!" liam cried, reaching down and lifting a twisted object off the ground. "you're halo."

"you broke it," louis said sadly, reaching out and placing it in harry's head. "it's okay, he's still the most beautiful angel i've ever seen."

harry blushed, sniffling and blinking the last of his tears out of his eyes. liam reached in and hugged him.

"let's go find niall, and zayn."

***

"this isn't scary."

harry looked at niall, who was quivering next to him and louis. he had a bowl of popcorn in his lap, stuffing piece after piece into his mouth unless he was screeching.

"you're a terrible liar, niall," louis pointed out, lazily drawing nonsensical patterns on harry's hip.

zayn was cuddled up to niall, gripping the fabric of the polka dot long sleeve shirt niall was wearing. none of them felt like taking their costumes off except for louis, who was shirtless with pajama pants.

harry even had his crooked halo nestled in his messy curls. louis had spent the rest of the trip back picking out the leaves from his hair and placing tiny kisses to his cheek.

the movie was currently showing the boring parts that nobody cared about and harry was grateful for the break from all the suspense. the conjuring was a scary movie, whether any of the boys said it wasn't. louis had picked it out, claiming that him and niall watched it every halloween. he whispered to harry that niall always tried to make louis believe that he wasn't scared, but he usually ended up sleeping in his bed.

harry laughed at that, despite the fact that his heart was pounding as he anticipated what was going to happen next. there was a woman walking into the basement. harry never understood why people in horror movies, whenever they heard a noise, they were stupid enough to go investigate. personally, if he heard something growling in the basement or a scream in the closet, he would not slowly turn the door knob and look to see what it was. he would run, probably hide behind louis because louis always protected him from the bad guys.

harry smiled at the thought, balling up even closer to louis and laying his cheek on louis' chest. he could hear louis' steady, rhythmic heartbeat that always seemed to match his own. it was soothing, a gentle noise that did really good to distract him from all that was happening on the television. in fact, when the woman finally found who was causing the noise, harry was already asleep.

forty-eight

harry's favorite time was evening. he loved taking long hot showers and putting on pajama pants that he would end up taking off when he finally snuggled under his blankets. he loved looking out the window and seeing darkness except for the moon or a few scattered streetlamps. and here he was, sitting on a soft blue chair that louis had placed right next to the window overlooking the back of the flat. there was a parking lot and past that a few grocery stores and restaurants. they all had lights glowing from their signs, causing the sky to glow as well. harry watched as families and friends wandered in and out of swinging doors, sometimes holding hands or giving sideways hugs. he could see many clouds in the dark sky, signaling that it might rain later than night. harry was already growing use to the smell of louis' flat.

louis was in the shower. harry had already taken one, and now he was sitting criss cross on the blue chair and sending responses to zayn and niall. he was supposed to go to niall's house later that night. obviously, that wasn't an option now that he was in doncaster, drinking his third cup of tea and searching for some sign that he was sleepy. but with every sip he took, he just felt more awake. his lips were moist but a bit swollen, as him and louis had kissed on the couch for almost an hour.

he could still feel louis' burning skin on his, and the thought brought a blush to his cheeks. just as harry got up to get himself another cup of tea, louis claimed he needed a shower. harry had walked into the kitchen, trying not to think too hard about the beer bottles that littered the kitchen counter. instead, he refilled his cup with hot water and stuck another tea bag in the water. he watched it float, tinting the water a light brown color, and the steam rose and caused water droplets to form on his nose. the smell of yorkshire tea would never fail to remind him of louis.

and now, here he was, staring out the window and letting the quiet sound of the shower running soothe his senses. the blue chair was incredibly plush, of course it was. everything associated with louis was soft. even liam was soft. so was the blanket louis had wrapped gently around harry's shoulders before he disappeared into his bedroom. it was a bit chilly. harry didn't mind, though, because whenever louis touched him with his warm hands he felt it that much more.

honestly, harry was surprised he was being so calm. there was so much that he needed to think about, but like louis said, he didn't feel it at the moment. he didn't know what louis and he were anymore; were they friends, were they boyfriends again? he was trying to remember why he made louis leave in the first place. it was something louis had said to him that was mean, but was it really that important that he had to ignore him for four months?

harry frowned, heaving a deep sigh and wiping away a tear that was falling down his cheek. he didn't even know he was crying. he stared into his cup of tea, barely making out his reflection, and the surface rippled when a tear splashed onto it.

harry blinked rapidly, hoping this ache in his heart would go away with time. he placed his hand on his chest, feeling the faint beating rhythm against his fingertips. his thin white shirt wrinkled up when he touched it. he remembered putting it on this morning, and zayn had rolled up the sleeves for him. the bottom of the shirt reached his thighs; he didn't realise it was so long.

harry watched as another car pulled into the parking lot, shining it's headlights and causing shadows to run across the walls around harry. the only light on was a lamp next to the couch, causing the small room to feel cozy and warm. the carpet was white and surprisingly not stained. louis must've gotten better at picking up after himself. harry remembered when there was clothes all over his floor and his bed was always unmade. he wondered if louis' bed was made now.

louis' laptop was sitting on the coffee table, along with an open book and what looked to be a journal. harry had a tiny urge to open it, but he quickly shooed that thought away and took another slow sip of his tea. it wasn't as hot anymore, which he liked. there was a small television hanging on the wall, with a desk under it with stacked movies on top of it. an empty can of red bull also sat on that desk, accompanied by a half-empty bag of doritos.

basically, the messiest place in his flat was the kitchen, but that was only because of his drinking problem as there were bottles everywhere.

harry sighed again, drying his eyes once more with the hem of his shirt. he was checking the notifications on his phone when he heard the shower shut off. he quickly locked his phone, stuffing it in his back pocket and averting his eyes back to outside. he flinched when a tap hit against the window, and he squinted his eyes to see. it was raining, just as he had predicted.

"it's raining," he mumbled to louis, who walked out wearing just sweatpants and a towel hanging over his shoulders. his hair was all over the place; sticking up, partially wet, partially dry. it looked fluffy and sweet and it drove harry crazy. "i like your hair," he said shyly, unable to tear his eyes away from the boy.

there were still some water droplets on his tan face, and his eyelashes were dripping wet, causing his eyes to shine. his expression was soft and his lips were in a tiny smile. his torso was thin yet toned and harry knew it was because of football.

"thank you." louis paused, stepping closer, his bare feet sinking slightly into the white carpet. "i like you."

harry looked away, his cheeks warm. the rain was pounding harder now and harry gently placed his fingers on the cool glass. he could feel a bit of tapping because it was raining so hard.

"i see you like rain," louis commented, and his voice was incredibly close to harry's ear. it was also raspy, and soft and sweet and harry really loved louis' voice.

"i like rain, but not thunderstorms," harry replied. he watched as louis touched his forearm, running his fingertips across his pale skin, up his arm and down his side until his arm was wrapped across harry's belly. harry immediately sucked in his tummy, but louis shook his head, pressing a soft kiss behind his ear.

"you're beautiful, harry. i love your tummy, don't suck it in."

harry was embarrassed and ashamed, but he let out his breath and shakily traced louis' fingers with his own.

"'m sorry," he whispered. louis hushed him, nuzzling his nose against harry's shoulder. he was kneeling beside the blue chair, the towel abandoned on the floor beside him. there were still some droplets on his arms as he hadn't dried off all the way. he smelled like soap and shampoo, and harry couldn't help but lean his head back and breathe it in.

"you smell good," he commented.

"so do you. you smell like an angel." louis leaned in and blew a raspberry onto harry's neck, giggling and causing harry to squirm and laugh.

"cutie," louis laughed, tracing a finger along his jawline and pinching his cheeks. "my cute little angel."

harry smiled and hid his face in louis' bare chest. "'m not cute," he said weakly, his damp curls brushing against louis' collarbone.

"oh, harry styles. you don't even want to start with me."

harry lifted his head, hesitantly meeting eyes with a grinning louis. "what d'you mean?" he asked quietly, the end of the sentence ending in a whisper.

the darkness of the flat and the rain muffling their voices caused some kind of excitement in harry's rushing heart.

"i mean a lot of things. i'm just saying that i have this thing with a lot of things about you in it and if you really want to keep saying stuff like 'i'm not cute' then i can pull it out and slay you, but i don't want to slay you because you're too innocent and sweet.

"i'm not innocent or sweet," harry said, before he realised his mistake.

louis laughed a bit, his eyebrows raised in disbelief, but in a teasing way. "you did it again! i'm really tempted to show you. i think that your view on your nice little body will change when you read it, angel."

harry's eyes widened. "what does it say?" he asked in a hushed voice.

louis just smiled, the blue in his eyes looking so dark that harry's heart dropped to his stomach.

"i can see my reflection in your eyes," harry said.

louis leaned back a little, squinting his eyes at the boy. the smile on his face looked like it could cause his cheeks to break, and harry wanted to warn him, because he didn't want louis to break his face. no, that wouldn't do. but he didn't, instead he let louis stare at him, his eyes flickering over every feature of harry's face and harry was a bit uncomfortable because louis would start to notice things, that stupid arse pimple that he saw on his cheek this morning or the largeness of his nose or the size of his buck teeth. he would notice that harry hadn't gotten a haircut in a while so the tips of his curls were broken, and they reached past his jawline.

"harry." louis looked away, his jaw clenching along with his fist, that was still cradled against harry's tummy. "harry, i can't believe i ever hurt you."

"lou-" harry began, but louis kissed his words away, pressing another short kiss on his lips once harry was silent. his breath was minty, telling harry that he had brushed his teeth while he was in the bathroom.

"let me speak, baby," he whispered, nudging harry's forehead with his own and kissing him once more.

harry nodded, breathless and taken aback. louis whispered a quiet thank you, lightly running his fingertips along harry's cheek with a thoughtful expression on his face.

"i told you, way back when we went to blackpool with the other lads, i told you that when i saw you i promised myself to never come near you. to never hurt a soul.. what did i say?"

"as beautiful as harry styles." harry had memorized the words by heart, he had repeated what louis said in his mind over and over until it was burned into his *soul*. and for some reason, now, his voice was coming out as a whimper, and he remembered how brokenly happy he felt then.

"yes. and now i've left you more broken then you were when we started in the first place. and you have no idea how many things i've tried to hurt myself to make up for that. but no matter how much i drink, it doesn't help."

harry looked up at him through his eyelashes with wide eyes, his bottom lip quivering a bit, and he lightly brushed over louis' scars on his wrists with his thumb. there were cuts on his wrist too, not as old and still not healed all the way, but he hoped louis didn't notice that.

"but you keep making me think it's okay. every time you look at me i just forget that i should be letting you live a happy life, a life without you, and i just really want to hug you. i just love hugging you, because you feel so small in my arms even though i'm smaller and i love that, i love that your my little angel and nobody can touch you, and i just keep remembering when i put a halo in your little curls and you just looked at me and your lips were all dark red because you kept biting them, and your cheeks were flushed from the cold weather. your eyes looked so green; they still do. and when i think about you, i just want to hold you, you know?"

harry was crying, and he was shaking, and louis picked him up so he could let harry sit on his lap.

"i love you harry," louis said softly, pressing his lips against harry's temple softly.

forty-nine

"what is your definition of love?"

his voice was quiet, soft. not prying, just curious.

their empty cans of red bull were numerous, sitting side by side on the desk next to the blue chair harry had grown incredibly attached to.

the night was late, the rain still pounding hard against the window and hiding the night, hiding the closed shops and empty streets. louis' legs were tangled with harry's, his burning skin causing heat to flow throughout his body and send a fluttery feeling to his heart.

harry didn't know how to respond to louis' question; for some reason it made him feel warm inside, the way louis' whispery, sweet voice formed around the word love was enchanting, a lovely magical thing that harry could never in a million years explain.

"harry," louis nudged him, his voice growing impossibly softer, and harry watched as the hour hand on the small clock on the wall passed the one. he felt as if he should be tired, but he was more relaxed. he had only yawned once, and that's because louis yawned first.

"i don't know," harry whispered. the rain muffled his voice and for some reason harry found that exciting. "what's yours?"

"my definition of love?" louis drew back a little, his head titled and causing his hair to float in the air, dangling in little strands of what harry considered gold, and he reached his long fingers out to touch it. and it was soft, of course it was. louis smiled, the corners of his lips turning up just a little and the crinkles by his eyes peeking out, just a little. harry took a picture of it in his mind. he never wanted to forget it.

"yeah," harry nodded. "what's *your* definition of love, louis?"

louis paused, snuggling further into harry, his arms tightening around the boy. harry felt a bit better than he had in a while, since louis made him eat, just a bit, and now the hunger pains weren't as bad.

"my definition of love," louis hummed, "is short. but it can also be long. which one would you rather hear?"

"both." harry fisted his hand against louis' chest, trying to hide the smile on his face. louis smelled like soap, so much like a boy and harry hoped louis didn't mind the way he was messing with the thin grey shirt that the boy had put on when he grew a bit colder. the thin fabric wrinkled beneath his soft touch, and he rubbed it between his thumb and pointer finger.

"i'll say the long one first," louis decided. harry looked up at him, expectant and excited. he nodded when louis took a long breath, as if thinking deeply.

"love is a.. what's the word," louis looked into the sky, "love is breathtaking. it takes your breath away so much. when someone kisses you, it feels magical. you want to be with the person you love all day, and when they're gone it feels like there's something missing, like you're going to school without clothes on or just floating, not moving away or towards anything, just waiting for something, somebody, to come back. you obsess over every single one of their flaws because those flaws become your favorite part of that person. their sensitivity is something you cherish; you live for the way they come to you when they're sad. when they have tears, you want to be the one that kisses them away, the one that hugs them so tightly that neither of you can breathe. and it sucks sometimes, you both get jealous and want to break down sometimes but it's *okay* because you know that later you'll be okay, you'll be talking about your problems and your lives and unimportant things because your love is better than that, your love is better than jealousy and hate and ignorance. love is when you stare into somebody's eyes and you can hear every thought their thinking, and it hurts you physically when their hurting. when you can't fall asleep because you said one thing and the fact that you caused them any pain just kills you, it eats you away. love is when you watch the way that person blinks, when you stare at the curve of the bottom of their lip and the dimples on their cheeks and every curl of their hair. love is when you feel like you can't contain everything, when you feel like you're losing your mind when really you are numb to everything else around you but that person and you want to scream, you want to yell to the world that you love that person, that that person is yours and only yours and nobody can touch you because what you have it magical, it's unbreakable even by a million miles or a couple of guys that try to come between you. love is when you're willing to change, willing to do anything just to show that person that you care about them so freaking much it hurts, so much that you could burst. love is putting sugar in their tea even though it isn't needed and watching the way they make their bed and answer the door and stab each piece of macaroni on the tines of their fork, watching the way they mess up both sides of their hair and use two fingers to swipe it across their forehead. it's watching the way they watch you, and listen to you, when you're speaking. it's when you know that you would do anything, *anything*, to see them smile, to see that imaginary halo that's always floating above their curls that you've always wanted to touch but you know it's not really there. but it seems like it, it seems like you're standing next to an angel."

harry stared at louis, watching him lick his moist lips and catch his breath, the whole time maintaining eye contact with the boy curled up in his lap. he pushed his fingers harder against louis' shirt, feeling louis' heartbeat against his fingertips.

"and do you wanna know my short definition?"

harry just nodded, unable to say anything, as he was proper speechless.

"love is you."

harry's breath caught, but he finally could muster up some sensibility as he held louis' gaze.

"i love you," harry whispered.

***

"i burnt the popcorn a bit, but it's late, so."

harry leaned his head back, his curls falling over the back of the couch as he strained to see louis coming back into the main area of his flat. louis was walking towards him, but he was upside down, due to harry's view.

"that's okay," harry said softly. there was a movie, the boy in the striped pajamas, playing on the telly. harry had a glass of water in his hands, deciding that the taste of tea was getting old after drinking it so much. there were a few ice cubes floating in the water, clinking slightly when he moved at all.

louis sat down beside harry, immediately laying his legs across the younger boy's lap and leaning into his side.

he put the popcorn on his lap, close enough for harry to reach, and unpaused the movie. harry immediately knew it would be sad; he had heard about it before and the innocence in the little boy's eyes was so pure that he knew that something bad had to happen.

harry loved to listen to louis' little chuckles through the movie, or the little whimpers that escaped his lips whenever something sad happened. louis was holding his hand, bouncing both of their hands up and down on harry's lap, dangerously close to a certain area and harry tried not to make a big deal about it, but the tiny movements made him feel really hot.

at first, harry didn't think louis was doing it on purpose, but then he heard the mischievous chuckle.

"stop," harry whined, squeezing louis' warm hand extremely tight.

"angel, i'm not doing anything, i'm just watching the movie. look, you just missed it. bruno stole some of the bread and stuck it in his pants, stuck is right in there."

"that's disgusting," harry mumbled. "louis you're disgusting."

louis burst into laughter.

"i was just telling you what was happening, sweetie."

harry glared at him, untangling their hands. "'s not funny," he grumbled.

"oh, baby harold angel styles. i thought you loved me."

"not right now, i don't," harry was trying really hard to smile, but the way louis licked his face was kinda adorable.

"i'm a dog," louis yelled, and harry let out a low chuckle. "woof woof. bark." he licked harry's cheek again and harry pushed his face away.

"i told you that you were disgusting," he laughed. "what are you even doing? why are you acting like a dog?"

"because you're my kitten."

"i thought i was your angel."

"you are," louis said immediately. "you are my angel. you are. don't ever think you're not. did you think that you weren't?" he sounded worried.

"uhm," harry began.

"you are!"

harry giggled but was caught off guard when louis reached over and grabbed the sides of his face. "stop," he said pleadingly. "i'm trying to watch the movie and you've distracted me."

harry raised an eyebrow. "you distracted me first," he pointed out, trying to keep his breath even but it was kind of hard when louis mouth was so close to his, so close that he could smell the red bull on his breath.

louis pulled back. "let's go outside," he declared, grabbing the remote and turning off the television. "c'mon."

harry stumbled behind louis as he dragged him by his hand out the door of his flat. he felt as if he should be protesting, as it was cold and rainy, but he decided to keep his mouth shut. at least louis had gotten a coat. the hallway of the building was pitch black; everyone was asleep except for them. harry understood why; who would be awake at this time of night?

louis pulled the two into the elevator, waiting until the door was completely shut before he grabbed hair, lifting him by his waist and pushing him into the wall, kissing him hardly. harry took a moment to process before he was kissing the boy back, wrapping his legs around louis' waist and his arms around louis' neck. louis supported him by holding up his bum, whimpering incoherent things into harry's mouth.

then the door was opening, and louis didn't put harry down, no. he was still holding him, still touching his bum as he ran them through the entrance. harry tried not to think too much about the look from the tired person at the desk.

harry shivered when louis carried them into the coldness of outside. the rain was pouring down hard, sticking their hair to their heads and soaking their clothes in just a few seconds. it smelled of metal and fast food; the smell of cities never failed to make harry' heart beat excitedly.

"are you trying to act out a romantic movie scene?" harry laughed, having to put his lips very close to louis' ear for the older boy to hear him.

"no, angel. i'm trying to dance. get off of me, baby."

he gently lowered harry to his feet and harry had to hold onto louis a little before he caught his balance, although his knees were shaky and he was still disoriented from that kiss in the elevator. the wet ground soaked through his socks, causing his feet to squish whenever moved.

louis linked their hands, bending his elbows and holding their hands in the air. "stand on my feet," he whispered.

harry placed his wet socks on louis' bare feet, the squishing noise causing him to giggle a bit.

"let's dance now," he breathed.

"there's no song," harry argued.

"then sing. i'll sing with you."

harry shook his head immediately, blinking the wetness out of his eyes, although the rain continued to pour. louis hair was dripping wet, hanging in front of his eyes that were glowing and his cheeks were flushed pink.

he was captivating.

louis started to sing anyway, the same song that he sang to harry so long ago.

"you are my sunshine, my only sunshine," he paused for a second, swaying them back and forth.

"you make me happy, when skies are grey," harry whimpered, laying his head on louis' shoulder and letting louis lead their small dance.

"you'll never know dear," louis kissed harry's wet curls softly, "how much i love you."

their voices sounded beautiful together. "please don't take, my sunshine, away."

fifty

"where were you this weekend?"

harry gripped his lunch box tighter as him and niall walked slowly down the hallway. there were surrounded by the voices of their classmates and the slamming of lockers. "at home," harry lied, trying to keep his chill.

"you were supposed to go to my house," niall said sadly. "me and zayn were planning on having a movie night with you and everything. we even bought you gummy bears, because we know how much you love them. but you'd rather stay at home?" niall looked at his feet and harry felt guilt tug at his heart.

"i'm sorry," he whispered, following a frowning niall into the cafeteria. "i just didn't feel very well."

niall ignored him, sitting down at their usual table. zayn was already there, munching on a carrot and talking to luke. ever since water polo started, luke and zayn had become better friends. but harry could tell zayn liked niall better by the way his eyes lit up and he patted the empty seat on his other side.

harry remembered when perrie used to sit at their table. she was extremely loud; hard to miss. harry thought that she was really funny, but apparently zayn didn't like her very well as they had broken up a few weeks ago.

harry opened his lunch box, pulling out his mountain dew and peanut butter and jelly sandwich. he popped open the tab on his soda and took a long sip, feeling it bubble in his mouth and cause an odd feeling in his chest. zayn and niall had started their usual conversation about people that act like dolts in class. harry laughed along, but honestly, he couldn't keep his focus. his mind kept flashing back to that weekend, that unbelievably perfect weekend, and he ached to call louis, to hear his voice again.

he had drove back from doncaster on sunday, regretfully pulling out of the parking lot as louis walked slowly back inside. he was wearing grey sweatpants with no shirt and thick white socks.

harry didn't know he would cry so hard.

he frowned, picking at the crust of his sandwich and crossing his ankles beneath the table. he was wearing his boots, along with black skinnies and a flannel shirt. he had a beanie on his head; his curls were not being cooperative that morning.

harry could catch luke staring at him, and he stared harder at the table, hoping the boy would look away soon. the piercing made him much more intimidating than he already was. but then again, that's how zayn was in sixth grade. intimidating, scary, but then harry saw niall hanging out with him and figured he must not be that bad.

"harry."

harry lifted his head, taking a big gulp as he tried to clear the lump in his chest. the lights of the cafeteria were incredibly bright, as if shining on every single flaw he had. his hands were shaking as he struggled to hold onto his peanut butter and jelly. he didn't feel well, he felt dizzy and he wanted it to stop.

"yeah?" he asked shakily, putting his sandwich down. the churning of his stomach as he stared at it was familiar and he thought it would've gone away by now, but it hadn't. in fact, every second that passed he felt more and more sick.

"are you going to water polo practice after school? it's not mandatory yet, not until next month, but you should still come."

when harry just stared back at zayn, the older boy raised an eyebrow. "are you going?"

harry looked down for a second, taking a deep breath before shaking his head. "uhm, i don't really feel up to it to be honest," he mumbled, squeezing his eyes shut tightly so it could be dark for once. it was getting louder and louder, there were people from different tables laughing and talking so loudly it sounded as if they were screaming. harry wanted them all to stop talking for once, for there just to be silence.

"are you okay?" zayn asked and harry could tell niall was annoyed. why wouldn't he be? if niall was mad at harry, then zayn should be too. harry would feel better about that, because then zayn would leave him alone and he could have peace.

when harry didn't answer zayn's question, he thankfully didn't press any further. they ate their lunch in silence, except for a few comments from luke about random things. it was obvious he was trying to make the tense silence less awkward. harry just thought he was being absolutely annoying.

the bell finally rang and harry shot up to throw his leftover sandwich and soda away. it made a loud clang because of the angry way he threw it and harry ignored the odd glances that were sent his way. he turned on his heel and walked back into the hallway of his school, holding his breath until he reached his locker.

harry could faintly recall a time exactly like this. it seemed as if the pain of missing someone was worse than the pain of not having them at all. the fact that he could be with louis right then, that he could be cuddled up in his arms and singing stupid lullabies with him while watching cheesy movies, was awful. he was stuck at school, where he constantly got scolded for not finishing his homework, and half of his class thought that he was mentally ill and could not speak or interpret words.

harry sighed deeply, taking his books to math and struggling to keep his mind straight. everything inside of him was fuzzy, as if what happened only a day ago happened a few years ago. the world around him was hazy, and he felt as if his eyes were only half open. he hoped that this feeling would go away, or at least calm down. he decided that he needed to just stop thinking for a while.

the room was completely empty when he came in, as there were still three minutes left until the bell rang and most people liked to stay and talk to their friends until the last minute. harry slouched down into his seat, scooting forward until he was on the edge of his chair and his knees were touching the end of his desk. he dug the heels of his boots against the carpet to steady himself before laying his head in his arms, feeling his curls brush over his skin lightly and causing goose bumps to raise on his arms.

his desk was cold against his cheek, and he could feel the moistness on his face as he breathed into the closed space he had made with his arms. it smelled of air freshener and the spray they used to clean the white board. harry wished he could fall asleep, but even then he wouldn't want to dream. but maybe, he could take a little rest with these two minutes. harry fluttered his eyes shut, his mouth slightly open as he breathed, in and out, in and out. the steady feeling reminded him of when him and louis finally fell asleep, the next day in the middle of the afternoon. they were laying on the floor, side by side, playing would you rather and playfully nudging their shoulders together. after a while, when they the spaces between their words grew larger and larger, louis fell asleep, but not before threading their fingers together gently and placing their hands on his tummy. harry closed his eyes and fell asleep to the sound of louis small, even breaths.

it was how he felt now. tired, just so tired and it was as if the lack of sleep still hadn't caught up to him, either that or he had no energy because he hadn't eaten anything.

just a minute, harry thought, *just a minute of resting my eyes. then i'll be more awake.*

he slouched further in his seat, almost to the point that he would fall off of his chair.

one more minute.

***

"has he been sleeping this whole class?"

"i don't know. he sits in the back so i couldn't really tell."

"he doesn't even understand it and he still sleeps in class? what a joke."

"who even is that kid?"

harry's eyes snapped open, but all he saw was darkness, just a little lighter than what he saw before, the murmurs of his classmates were growing less and less distant as he came to his senses.

"harry styles. he doesn't talk. well, he does, but only when he's crazy."

harry now knew that they were talking about him, and his cheeks burned.

"mr. styles? are you awake?"

harry looked up, trying his best not to let his eyes droop, as that would give away that he was sleeping.

"have been this whole time, ma'am," he mumbled, the warmness on his cheeks spreading to his hands and causing them to sweat. he rubbed them on his jeans quickly, sitting up further in his chair and accidently banging his knee into the bar on his desk.

"ow," he said quietly, to himself, but everyone around him burst into laughter as if it was the funniest thing in the whole world.

harry felt like crying, he really did, and he was so embarrassed. why did he have to fall asleep during math?

the teacher was staring at him. "you have detention after school. i'll give you your slip after class."

harry was too exhausted, too ashamed and embarrassed to respond. he just bowed his head, hoping his curls would cover his flushed cheeks and watery eyes. he wished louis were there to wipe them away, to tell him that it was okay. that he wasn't a freak, that he wasn't crazy.

because it was extremely hard to believe.

***

"are you sure you don't want to go to water polo?"

harry looked at the shoes next to his. he was standing by his locker, just about to leave to go to the resource room for detention. they were black boots, completely unlaced.

zayn.

"i have to go to detention," harry replied. he bit his lip hardly, the taste of blood already there from when he was biting it earlier. the hallway was already clearing up; the buses had all left and everybody was going to their after-school practices. harry hoped that he wasn't running late for detention. the teacher never said a specific time that he had to be there.

"what?" zayn asked worriedly. "harry, how'd you get a detention?"

harry paused for a long while, turning around on his heel and resting his back gently against the lockers. he decided that he wasn't going to bring his backpack home as he had no homework and he had no plan on studying for his psychology test. he already understood it all, and he was too tired. "i fell asleep in class," harry said flatly.

harry was caught off guard when zayn pulled him into a gentle hug. just the kind way zayn kissed his hair caused harry to burst into tears.

"when you get home, i want you to eat some of your macaroni and cheese, then take a long hot shower and brush your teeth and then go to bed, and sleep and don't think about anything bad. don't stay up late, go to bed and get some rest. okay?"

"okay," harry whimpered. maybe he would sleep. but for now, he was going to detention. he gave zayn another hug and walked towards the room for detention.

***

the room was probably ten degrees colder than the hall, and goose bumps immediately rose on harry's arms. he shivered, walking to the seat in the very back of the class and plopping down in it. there were only two other kids there; one had light blonde hair and was wearing a much-too-big sweatshirt and jeans with big holes in them. harry knew that he had to avoid that boy by the devilish smirk on his face as he stared at harry. the other was a girl, with long black hair that hung in her face and a dark band shirt with black jeans and combat boots. she gave harry a smile, showing crooked teeth. her eyes were pale blue, and it reminded harry of louis.

the teacher walked in; a teacher harry had never seen before. he introduced himself as mr. yarrow, but harry decided to call him monkey because something about his nose and jawline reminded him of a monkey.

monkey said that they weren't allowed to speak, pass notes, or do anything but homework. he looked incredibly bored as he read off all the other rules, like no chewing gum or texting or getting on your phone. harry noticed the way he spoke with his hands. it reminded him of louis.

he finally stopped talking, sitting down in his large leather chair and propping his feet up on his desk, showing hairy ankles as his khakis slipped down his legs. he was wearing all black shoes. it reminded harry of louis.

harry tapped his foot to the steady ticking of the clock on the wall. he traced the word *kill me* that was engraved on the desk with his finger. the more time that passed, the more every single thing he saw reminded him of louis.

one of those things was the color of the chalk. it was yellow, a light pretty yellow. that color reminded him of sunshine. sunshine reminded harry of louis.

there was a halfway erased tic tac toe board on the white board. it reminded harry of louis.

harry knew that if he kept this up then the time in detention would go by unbearably slow, and that just wouldn't do. he decided that instead, he was going to draw. he took out a pencil from his pocket, pushing his thumb against the eraser so that a short piece of led stuck out. he first looked at monkey, at the way he rose his eyebrows when he read, before looking back at his desk. he gently placed his pencil on the desk.

it make a tiny noise, and he did it again and again, with a tiny smile. once it grew less and less entertaining he decided to start on his drawing. he only had to think for a moment before he knew what he was going to draw. first, he drew a perfect circle, making the line thicker and thicker and shading inward so that the darkest point was on the inside. the circle looked as if it was glowing.

harry added a few lines to the side of the circle, curving them to form wings and adding little feathers to the wings. the more he shaded against the rough desk, the better it looked. he drew on little beams coming from the circle, and then drew a halo.

there were only five minutes left when harry had finally become satisfied with his drawing. he hadn't added anything after he drew the beams, just shaded it better and fixed a few small mistakes. it was a sun, with angel wings and a halo. it was one of his favorite drawings, and he wished he could take the desk home with him and add it to the collection of drawings in his sketchbook. he couldn't take a picture of it because the teacher had already gone ape on the blonde boy for getting his phone out to check his hair with the reflective screen.

if only harry had his polaroid camera.

the teacher finally told them they could go, giving them a small speech about how they needed to quit acting up or they were never going to amount to anything in life. harry avoided his eyes when he left and set outside to walk home. zayn usually took him home, but his practice wasn't going to end for a half an hour or so.

the leaves around harry were red and orange and brown, and all the colors made him smile. there was a slight breeze, causing his curls to blow around him. harry liked the sounds of his boots crunching against the fallen leaves.

the air was a bit chilly and harry was thankful that he had brought an extra jumper. he tried not to burst into tears when he realised that it was louis' jumper, his footie jumper that he had got his senior year. it still smelled like him, and it said seniors with all of the boys names on it. harry ran his finger over louis' name on the back of the shirt and gave a watery smile, before pulling it over his head. the smell of honey was overwhelming and comforting at the same time.

the boy jumped when he felt his phone vibrate in his pocket. he took a deep breath before pulling it out of his pocket.

"hullo?" he mumbled, tripping a bit over a pebble. he blushed a bit, although nobody saw him.

"harry."

the skip of his heart was bloody huge and harry hoped that his knees wouldn't give out. he gulped thickly, squeezing his eyes shut and savoring the whispered tone at the end of louis' word.

"hi louis," harry breathed, wiping the tears off of his cheeks quickly and walking a bit faster. why did louis have this effect on him?

"i miss you, okay?"

harry nodded, biting his quivering lip. and he knew louis couldn't hear him, and he was just about to speak but louis beat him to it.

"i love the way you look when you nod. you always look flustered. you do right now. or maybe that's just because it's cold."

harry froze.

"isn't my footie sweatshirt warm enough? it always kept me warm enough. well, maybe it's because you're so tiny, so beautiful."

harry let out a surprised noise. "how do you know i'm wearing your sweatshirt?" he choked out.

"why are you crying, angel?"

"i'm not," harry lied, gulping and blinking his eyes rapidly.

"angels aren't supposed to cry."

the voice wasn't in his phone anymore, no; it was in his ear. and there were arms wrapping around his waist, warmly, gently, but firm at the same time. secure. he felt lips press against his jaw, softly.

harry about fell backwards, but then again he couldn't because louis was behind him, louis was letting out a little chuckle as he watched harry recover from the fact that *louis was right there.*

"it's okay, baby," louis smiled, twirling harry around a bit and squeezing his sides. "louis louis louis is here."

"louis louis louis," harry whispered.

and then louis leaned in and kissed harry, he kissed him until the world around harry was spinning, when the leaves were falling backwards and the sky was all around them and the trees blended in with each other. the air smelled of fall and honey and harry was glad louis caught him when his knees buckled.

fifty-one

"whoa baby, are you okay?" louis chuckled, holding harry's waist tighter and steadying him on the empty street. there were trees lining up and down, the wind pushing leaves to the ground with a whistling tune. this part of the neighborhood was always silent and peaceful; harry and his mum used to always take walk on these streets. there were only a couple of houses.

"i think so," harry breathed, his voice disappearing into the cool fall air. louis' fingers were gripping his hips, and he knew that if the older boy let go he would surely fall again. "how are you here?"

"i couldn't stand not being able to touch your curls," louis smiled, "they're so soft."

harry blushed and looked at the ground as louis brushed his fingers through his fringe, placing little kisses to his face the whole time. "cutie patootie. how was school today?"

harry shrugged. he didn't like to talk about school, no; that was something that stayed at school. he hated it, he hated the way people treated him and the ache in his chest whenever he thought about the fact that louis wasn't there. but now, louis was here, asking him how it was, and he had to answer louis because he was *louis* and louis was his best friend, his favorite person in the whole world.

"the kids at school think i'm a freak," harry whispered, hating the way his voice cracked. louis' eyes softened, even more than they were before, and he furrowed his brows as if he was hurt.

"you're not," he began, clutching harry's face in his hands, "you're not..."

harry jumped when louis backed away, grabbing his hair before kicking a stray pebble on the road. he looked... angry.

"why can't they see how freaking perfect you are?! you're so beautiful, how can they not see it? h-how?" the broken tone in his voice caused harry to feel some type of way, and he hugged himself, as he watched louis let out his anger, kicking every pebble there was and clenching his fists. he jumped when louis stormed towards him, holding his face again. his breathing was heavy, his cheeks flushed and his blue eyes wide open, watering, either from the breeze blowing or his tears. his hands were trembling on harry's face. "please, harry, please don't believe them when they say you're a freak. i can't describe how untrue that is."

harry stared at louis, his green eyes wide open and his hands still hanging at his sides. he didn't know whether louis was sad or mad.

"louis?" harry asked.

"harry," louis said.

they stared at each other for a while and harry didn't know why his heart felt like it was exploding, like it was about to burst. he liked to look at the pink tip of louis' nose, as it was getting chillier as night grew closer. he liked to watch the way louis licked his lips, the way he blinked his eyes slowly, hiding the color before revealing a glowing bright blue. he loved his cheekbones.

"i love you muches," louis smiled. he smiled so wide that there were crinkles by his eyes. harry loved that.

a thought crossed harry's mind for a second and he frowned, pushing his hands against louis' sides gently and digging his fingertips into his hipbones. "are you gonna leave again?" he asked quietly, nuzzling his nose into louis' thin white shirt, putting his ear on his chest to listen to the steady, strong beat of his heart. he fluttered his eyes shut for a while, and his mind was hazy and clear at the same time. the thought of louis walking away again caused a tear in his heart.

"i'm not going to leave," louis responded. "i'm just going away for a while. but i'm coming back."

"i don't like when you leave. school's scary," harry whispered, and he felt ashamed.

"scary? how?"

harry squeezed his eyes shut. "i can't breathe. it's scary."

louis cupped his small hand around harry's face, the side that was pushing into his chest. "why can't you breathe?"

harry stepped back, and louis looked at him for a while, before taking his hand and leading them to side down next to a tree. the leaves crunched beneath their feet; harry was wearing boots, louis black vans with black laces. louis laid his back against the trunk, before gesturing for harry to sit in between his legs. harry nestled himself so that his back was against louis' chest, and he grabbed louis' hands, holding them in front of his eyes and trying different ways to link their fingers.

the smell of crisp leaves was wonderful and mixed with the smell of louis was purely amazing.

"harry, why can't you breathe?" louis repeated gently.

harry paused for a moment, his breath caught as he struggled to think of a way to word his sentence right. whenever he tried to explain how he felt he always felt as if he was choked up, and he hoped that louis would understand why he took so long to respond.

"there's a lot of reasons," harry finally said.

"tell me one," louis nudged him, resting his chin on his shoulder. "just one."

"just one?"

"just one."

harry took a shaky breath, squeezing louis' hand a bit tighter. "one of the reasons, uhm, is, uhm." he gulped thickly. "one time a boy found me in the hallway on the way to class and told me i looked confused. then he offered to lead me to the special needs room, and he was being so nice about it, he even talked really slow because he didn't think that i understood him very well i guess."

it was silent for a moment, so silent that harry couldn't even hear louis breathing, not until he felt louis shake beneath him with a shuddered breath.

***

2 months later

flashing lights. strobe lights, sending a neon glow throughout the entire room.

could it possibly be that the smell of smoke became a godsend?

pounding music caused harry's head to throb, but he nodded along with it all the same.

the coldness of winter seemed as if it should be causing harry to feel cold, but he could see sweat on his arm that was laying across the top of the dirty, stained counter. perhaps it was the amount of bodies in this loud place, or maybe it was because he was sick. his nose was runny, but he was so tired, too tired to even blow his nose because it would cause him to go weak at the knees, so much physical exertion. and he knew that no matter how many times he went to these clubs, the dancing around him wouldn't make him any less exhausted.

harry let out a cough, closing his eyes because it was such a strain to keep them open. he could see a boy a bit older than him trying to catch his eyes with a soft but knowing smile. he even had an extra drink in his hand. did he buy that for harry?

harry avoided his glance, running a shaky hand through his sweaty, curls. he hadn't taken a shower in two days, which wouldn't be that bad except for the fact that all of this smoky, sweaty air was soaking into every inch of his body. but harry didn't want to take a shower, not after the last time where he collapsed when he spent too much of his energy trying to squeeze the last bit of shampoo out of the bottle.

he hoped that a swipe of deodorant and a spray of cologne would do the trick.

he cringed, tensing up for a second before he sneezed loudly. nobody looked at him though, because the noise just escaped into the air, as if it wasn't there at all.

for some reason, harry always had the urge to cry whenever anybody looked at him. he knew that he looked miserable; his eyes had bags under them and his curls were growing much too long for his liking. he wore black skinnies and a white shirt every day, but soon the white turned yellow because he had worn it so long without washing it. he was capable of it, but he tended to avoid and places his mum could be. she had started to leave the house for days at a time, not telling harry she was leaving, not even leaving a note.

harry was waiting for the day that she wouldn't come back at all, where she would turn visits to cross' house into a permanent living situation.

harry knew that a few months ago, the thought would make him sad, but ever since louis left back to college and he got so busy he couldn't visit, every feeling he had seemed a bit numb.

was harry being ridiculous? he thought he was, because he hadn't been this torn when he and louis weren't together, so long ago sophomore year. but it seems as if louis had buried himself somewhere deep inside harry, and whenever he left he took a part of harry with him, whether he wanted to or not.

harry missed louis. he missed him so freaking much it hurt. it seemed as if he was always in pain; emotional and physical. he hoped that he would grow use to the hunger pains, because his method really was working. he had already lost fifteen pounds. he hoped that louis would notice sometime soon, but he tended to lose weight in his legs instead of his face, and his face was all louis could see when they were skyping.

he knew louis missed him too. he knew by the ache in his voice whenever they both grew tired to even just stare at each other and he gave a tired goodbye. harry found himself having to turn off the camera early sometimes because he didn't like to cry in front of louis.

although, louis had cried in front of him plenty of times. he hoped louis didn't think he was a monster for not crying as well.

every time louis cried, he would grab a pillow nearby him and bury his face in it, mumbling incoherent things and harry would feel his heart tear just a little. sometimes louis cried because his practice was so hard, or others it was because they were talking about how they missed each other.

louis and harry had just skyped last night, actually. louis seemed concerned. his eyebrows were furrowed and his blue eyes were wide and curious as he struggled to get harry to explain what was wrong. harry couldn't exactly say it was because he wanted louis to quit everything, to quit his dream and come live with harry and protect him from all these bad guys. there was at least one mean comment every day, and it hurt worse every time. so no, he didn't want to say that, because that would be selfish and harry hated being selfish.

so he said that he had stayed up the last few nights studying, which was completely untrue. it seemed as if his studying consisted of sleeping and resisting the urge to cut because his tummy hurt so bad and he needed something to distract him.

he soon found himself here, at this club that was about twenty minutes away from his house. he hated the way the bartender always offered him drinks. he didn't want to drink anything, no; he wanted to sit here and drown his sorrows by watching other people have the time of their lives.

but after coming here for a while, he realised there were a lot of people that thought like him. he could see a girl from over here, smudged black eyeliner circling her eyes thickly, bringing out the purple circles under her eyes. harry could tell by the drips of mascara on her flushed cheeks that she was crying, or at least had been crying. her eyes were watery, and he had a slight notion that she was doing drugs of some kind. the thought of drugs made harry cringe; he couldn't imagine doing something like that.

but then again, every single time that smell of smoke came near him, he found himself breathing it in, despite the slight sting in his throat and the watering of his eyes.

he pulled out his phone. *louis i miss you,* he typed.

it was only a minute when louis responded.

harry i love you.

there was a little sad face next to it, with furrowed brows. harry felt his lip tremble just a bit and he let out a choked noise, struggling not to cry.

there's a boy staring at me.

this time the response was immediate.

i am suddenly wondering where you are, harold angel styles.

harry smiled a little, feeling a tear drop down his cheeks and land on the dirty countertop. he was sweating even more now that the group of dancing people were gravitating towards him, bringing all their drunken laughs and body heat with them.

i'm at a club. i'm actually a good dancer.

what kind of dancing?!

just kidding.

harry knew that he wasn't funny, but he also knew that louis laughed at almost every attempt of a joke he made. that was one of the reasons he loved louis so much.

tell that boy that your beautiful wings are off limits, angel.

for some reason, harry found himself holding his phone against his chest, closing his eyes and biting his quivering lip, smiling but also crying and *wow* he loved louis.

he screenshotted the text, adding it to his small camera roll of four pictures. it was annoying that tears were so hard to wipe away from his screen.

fifty-two

"i don't know what i'm supposed to get him," harry said sadly into the phone, running his fingers across the fabric of all the different color shirts. "whenever i ask him he tells me not to get him anything."

"what'd you get him last year?" zayn asked, and harry must've looked like a fool, the way he was blushing in the middle of american eagle.

"i don't remember," he lied, his voice quiet and nervous.

the other end was silent for a moment, before zayn let out a quiet, "oh.

"anyway," harry said, embarrassed, "if it was your birthday, what would you want? i mean, i guess i have time, his birthday's in three weeks, but i'm not going to have much time away from him starting tonight."

zayn started listing off suggestions that harry knew were all too expensive, and he walked out of american eagle and started to stroll through the mall, holding his phone against his ear and avoiding brushing anybody's arms. he didn't know his way around this mall, as it was about two hours away from where he lived, and he usually shopped at the local mall.

"..maybe cologne or something. i don't know. do you want it to be, like, personalized or something? i don't know like, something that reminds him of you, like since you're always away, you know?"

harry sighed deeply and sat down at an empty chair in the food court, crossing his ankles and playing with some of the rings on his fingers. he actually kind of missed the way his hair tickled the back of his neck, but niall had insisted it looked ridiculous and dragged him to the hairdresser. it was now in a curly fringe across his forehead, the ends at his ears.

"hey, i gotta go, but i'll keep thinking, yeah? i'll call you if i think of anything good."

"okay," harry said quietly.

zayn murmured something else that harry couldn't understand before he hung up. now, he was alone, alone with his thoughts and himself and *wow* this mall really smelled too much like pizza.

he drummed his fingers on the small table he was sitting next to before shaking out his curls and standing up. his boots squeaked whenever he moved them against the shiny tile floor. a few girls were at a table a couple feet away and harry could feel them staring at him. he avoided eye contact with any of them, scurrying away, flustered.

"what would louis want, what would louis want," he repeated to himself, glancing into every store and hoping something would stick out to him. he was tempted to text the boy and ask him, but he knew louis would never respond, or at least he wouldn't tell him.

he didn't want to rush, no; whenever he rushed he did stupid things. but louis was meeting him here in less than an hour and he hadn't a clue what he was going to get him.

he decided he would sit here and wait, hoping something would come to mind, anything.

and that's when he remembered that he had left his polaroid camera in the car.

and he also remembered that day, about two years ago, when louis found it under his bed, and his face just lit up and he told harry that he loved polaroid cameras. and harry could remember making a mental note in his mind to give it to louis one day. it was a present from his aunt, who had died when he was about twelve.

he smiled to himself, glad he finally had a path in mind. now all he needed was a box and some wrapping paper. he could wrap it at louis' flat when he was showering or something.

now all he needed was to wait.

***

harry thought that waiting for louis was a good plan, but soon he grew restless and he really needed to go the restroom.

so he gathered himself off the ground, where he was sitting, laying against a wall. he gave one more glance around for louis, who hadn't answered any of his calls, and quickly walked towards the entrance of the mall, where the restrooms were, he assumed.

he could say that he was annoyed with all the looks he got from passing teenage girls, but he was more just uncomfortable. he hoped that they weren't staring at him because he was ugly, or because he always looked like he was going to burst into his tears. that wasn't his fault.

maybe they were staring at the haircut. he knew it was a bad idea. he liked his long curls.

he blew air out of his lips and adjusted the rings on his fingers as he walked into the restroom. it smelled of lavender air freshener and soap. there were only a couple other people in there, one was a middle-aged man and another was a little boy who looked to be his son. harry smiled at the boy, who looked away shyly and continued drying his hands with the brown paper towel.

harry walked into a stall and quickly relieved himself. he could hear the people he saw leave, their voices fading as the door shut behind them.

but when he walked out, his heart dropped to the bottom of his stomach.

louis was there, and he wanted him not to be there because he wasn't *prepared,* he wasn't ready for this kind of meeting because he hadn't been able to bring down his blushing and not look like a complete fool in front of the boy who he was foolishly in love with.

so he just stood there, trying to keep the stupid smile off his face because *wow* that was his boyfriend, his stupidly adorable cheesy sunshine boyfriend standing there in a pair of black jeans and a big baggy sweatshirt, his hair messed up in the back, and harry could see in the mirror how concentrated the boy was on washing his hands. harry loved how louis' head looked from behind.

it probably took louis two minutes before he saw harry, he washed his hands, scrubbing every finger gently, then he dried his hands and fixed his hair in the mirror, a nervous breath escaping his lips. only then did he finally decided to turn around.

he jumped so high he was harry's height, and he let out a little squeak mixed with a gasp. "harry!" he exclaimed, not moving at all.

harry didn't think he could move either, what with the way his heart was racing and his hands were sweating. all he could do was stare, stare at this boy who he had missed so much, who he had cried over for days and days even though crying wouldn't have brought him any closer.

it seemed as if louis was the same way. harry could feel himself shaking under louis' intense, non-wavering gaze.

and when they met eyes, when harry could finally see the wonderful blue of louis' eyes that a laptop camera could never reveal, louis walked towards the younger boy, his pace growing with every step. soon, harry found himself being pressed gently through an open stall.

louis shut the door behind them gently, carefully locking it while still keeping one hand on harry's waist softly. "louis missed you," he whispered, an ache in his voice that harry had heard before, but never this prominent, never this heart breaking. harry smiled up at him, trying to steady his quivering lip as he looked at louis.

louis was still shorter than him, but only a little. harry liked being taller so he could see the curve of his eyelashes, and the mussed up top of his head.

"i missed you too," harry finally replied, grabbing louis around the sides and lifting him so his black vans were on top of his boots. he was light as a feather, so light and that made harry's stomach flutter with millions of butterflies.

and then louis was kissing him, pressing their lips together in an urgent kiss that really was absolutely wonderful, because harry loved kissing louis, and he was just so happy that louis was here with him, after three months.

three months. it didn't seem that long, but to harry it seemed like a lifetime. the only things that kept him grounded were the nightly skype calls and zayn and niall.

but nothing like that could even compare to what harry was feeling right now, the emotions that were rushing through him like a dam bursting through. crap, he had almost forgotten the taste of louis and that scared him. he let his fingers dig into louis' hip bones and squeezed his sides, because that part of louis was one of his favorites.

louis let out a whimper into harry's mouth, pressing his forehead hardly against the younger boys and holding both sides of his face, so gently yet so securely. harry hoped nobody would walk in the bathroom, that nobody would hear how freaking loud they were being, they were being ridiculously loud and louis kept whispering cheesy things like, "i love you more than the moon loves the sun," in between kisses.

after a while, the small stall became cramped and harry pulled back slightly, watching the way louis' eyes sparkled and shined. "let's go to your flat," he suggested, reaching out and touching louis' hair, because now he just couldn't keep his hands off the boy, it was too impossible with the way louis was smiling up at him.

***

"i don't even want to drive in different cars," louis whined, tightening his hold on harry's hand as they walked through the parking lot to get in their cars. it was very, very cold outside, especially since the wind was blowing so hard. "i can't stand being away from you for another minute." his voice was quieter now, more shy and sad. "it was awful not being able to kiss you or hold you or watch the way your hands shake when i call you angel."

harry blushed. "is that why you call me that?"

"one of the reasons. another is because you are one, silly." louis smiled at him, swinging their hands high in the air. "don't you know that by now?"

harry shrugged shyly, biting his lip to conceal the smile that threatened to break out on his lips.

"love, we have to separate now. you need to follow my car, okay?"

harry nodded. "i'll drive behind you."

louis sent him away with a kiss and a hug and harry stumbled to his car like the clumsy person he was. it wasn't much warmer when he finally shut himself in his car, and he hastily turned the key and turned the heat all the way up. after a while, the vents were blowing warm air and causing his curls to fly around a bit.

he knew he wouldn't get by with wearing a white t-shirt for much longer, as the temperature lowered by a few degrees every day. he didn't fail to see louis' worried glance at the goose bumps on his arms. he knew that if louis had been wearing a jacket he would've given it to harry.

harry waited for louis' car to pull out of the parking lot before he pushed his foot onto the break, starting out slow and moving forward to follow the boy. he turned some music on, bobbing his head to it and trying not to miss any of the turns louis made.

***

"please don't comment on the cleanliness. i hate it. i'm tempted to trash up the whole apartment again."

harry smiled and raised an eyebrow. "then why'd you clean it in the first place?"

"because," louis groaned, "mum visited a couple days ago to bring me my birthday present which i'm supposed to open on my actual birthday, and she insisted that the way i was living was inhumane and she never thought i would sink that low. honestly, i kind of gave up on the whole clean thing after my friend spilled a glass of coke on the carpet and i didn't clean it up. it's like a chain reaction, you know?"

harry nodded. the smell of louis' flat reminded him of that time long ago when they stayed up all night, watching movies, talking, and of course, kissing in the rain. it was still one of harry's fondest memories, but it was also was a memory that, if he thought of it at the right time, made him cry.

"so, basically, harold angel styles, welcome to your new home for the rest of christmas holiday." louis smiled widely before throwing a pillow at the boy.

fifty-three

"is it bad that i'm nervous?" louis chuckled quietly, standing by the door and shuffling from foot to foot. his arms were crossed over his chest and his shoulders hunched, and he was biting his lip. harry could easily tell that he was, in fact, nervous.

"why would that be bad?" harry asked, tilting his head. he wished that the way louis looked right now didn't affect him so much. harry couldn't decide whether he liked the tightening of his chest when he looked at the older boy. he reached out and brushed his fingers across the white, thin material of louis' football jersey. it was white, a few faded grass stains on it, and the number seventeen written where it belonged. the sleeves hung loosely around his skinny, tan arms. his skin looked so soft.

"because i'm usually quite confident," louis paused, brushing his fringe out of his eyes and pushing his water bottle against his hip, "but for some reason i'm getting all shaky and i don't like it. it's your fault, harold."

harry scoffed. "i did nothing."

louis smiled, his eyes crinkling for a moment, before leaning in and kissing harry softly. "you'll be my good luck charm, angel." he whispered, and the way his breath fanned over harry's lips caused his cheeks to burn. harry had to step back, just a little, an overwhelming feeling washing over him as louis reached out and ran his thumb over his bottom lip. harry shut his eyes slightly, tilting his head towards the boy at his light touch.

"you'll do great," harry whispered. "you didn't practice all this time for nothing. it's your first game, and it's inside so you don't have to worry about the cold. i'm sure you'll do perfect."

louis sighed. "i hope your right, babe. i couldn't sleep last night, too nervous," he admitted.

"why didn't you tell me?" harry asked quietly. "i could've sang to you."

louis' eyes widened, and he took a deep breath. "that'd would've been so wonderful." he laughed lightly, caressing harry's curls with a bit of wonder in his eyes. harry still wondered why louis was so intrigued and fascinated with his curls.

harry blushed again, every second louis was staring at him unnerving him even more. he adjusted the watch on his wrist before meeting eyes with the boy again.

"let's go to the game."

"'course. i got you front row seats."

***

"are one of the players your brothers?"

"no," harry said.

"family?"

"no."

"boyfriend?"

harry didn't respond, but he had to turn his head when he heard the long sigh escaping the lips of the person sitting next to him. they were both in the front row, so close to the field that if he reached his hand over the fence far enough he could touch it. harry missed when louis had games in high school and the seating was random, depending on who got there first. now, though, it was college footie, and it was serious. harry smiled at that, before he remembered the boy sitting next to him.

"what's wrong with that?" harry said defensively, finally meeting eyes with the boy. his were ocean blue, a little bit less blue than louis'. he had full lips and pale, porcelain skin. but harry couldn't examine him for long before the boy was jumping back, eyes wide and regret clear on his face.

"there's nothing wrong with that!" he said quickly. "no, no my boyfriend's out there. see? number five. dark brown curly hair? his name's darren."

harry wasn't one for stereotypes, but he wasn't surprised that the boy was gay by his high, feminine voice. the reason he liked louis' because it had a deep, raspy tone to it, a soft, wonderful whispery tone that he could never get enough of.

stop thinking about louis for once.

when harry didn't respond, the boy laughed and looked around before speaking again. "what's your boyfriend's name?"

harry stared at him for a while. he didn't look him in the eye; no, he was still uncomfortable with that. but instead, he looked at his forehead and blond highlights, his heart beating rapidly in his chest as he pondered whether or not he should share his louis with anyone. although he was playing on the field, and he *was* the captain, harry still felt as if louis was his little secret, somebody he loved and kept with him in their little corner of the universe.

but, he decided that the smiling boy would find out sooner or later, so he said proudly yet nervously, "louis. louis tomlinson. number seventeen." he beamed, pointing to his boyfriend, standing on the field with his hands on his hips, his head held high and a determined look on his face. he was telling the players something, but he was all the way across the field so he couldn't hear him. but he could see him, and that was enough. he loved the way louis stood, the way he crossed his tiny little ankles and swayed from hip to hip.

harry didn't realise the boy was staring at him with a wide smile until he turned his attention back off the field to him.

"what?" harry asked, insecure.

"never seen anything like that," the boy said. "i don't even think i look at darren like that. that was some deep stuff right there."

harry raised an eyebrow.

"you care about him," was all the boy finished off, about to look at the field again, when harry stopped him.

"what's your name?"

the boy smiled, showing short teeth and letting out a small chuckle. "chris colfer."

he nodded. "harry. harry styles."

chris laughed a bit and tilted his head. "sounds like the name of a movie star."

"does it?" harry blushed, feeling like a fool as images of stardom flashed through his mind. he saw himself on stage, singing and acting, or maybe starring in a movie. he would never admit it to anyone except lou, but that had been his dream since he was a little boy with blonde hair and chubby cheeks. louis insisted that his cheeks were still chubby and adorable, and he never failed to poke his dimple every time he smiled wide enough.

"it does," chris nodded, giggling, and opened his mouth to speak again when harry pointed to the field. the game had started.

***

"go, go, go," harry mumbled under his breath, watching louis skillfully dribble the ball down the field towards the opposing team's net. every second on the clock that passed, the more anxious the boy got. the two teams were tied and harry could tell louis was extremely frustrated because of it. he was fanning his hands in the air and letting out puffs of air constantly, and his nervousness made harry nervous as well. at least it was inside, or it would've been freezing. harry could see his breath walking into the building.

harry observed closely, ignoring the little chants chris was making beside him, as louis shouldered anyone near him out of the way, biting his lip and occasionally fluttering his eyes closed. harry always had wondered why louis played with his eyes closed, but the other boy always said it was because it helped him focus and "become one with the ball." harry didn't understand it that well, but he decided that if louis could always play that well, then it didn't matter how he did it. especially since he always looked hot doing it.

harry smiled as louis took a large kick, rearing his foot back and nailing the ball, but then his heart stopped. because crap, louis was falling, he was slipping on the soft, green grass, his eyes wide with fear, but harry knew he was still watching to see if the ball went in. he was that passionate about football, that he ignored the way his ankle was twisting underneath him, making everyone in the crowd cringe as he crumpled to the ground. harry was about to jump over the fence when chris grabbed him. "hold on. don't go out there. wait until someone brings him to the bench."

harry felt his heart clench when louis finished his fall by banging his head on the ground and rolling over in pain. and harry teared up when louis puked in the grass, before grabbing his ankle, and he was close enough that harry could hear the loud whimpers of pain that escaped his mouth.

at least the ball had gone in, and the scoreboard changed to 3-2, but it seemed as if none of his teammates cared about that. they all huddled around their captain, asking him worried questions and offering to help him up. harry's breaths quickened, and he bit his lip as tears leaked out of his eyes. "lou," he breathed out, leaning into chris' comforting hand on his shoulder. he jumped when the boy chris was talking about, darren, rushed over to them.

"what happened?" chris asked. "is he okay?"

darren licked his lips, looking away before meeting eyes with harry. "do you know him? louis? he told me to come get you."

harry immediately gripped the sides of the fence and hopped over, stumbling through the grass to louis. he didn't wait for darren to follow after him.

"louis!" he yelled, staggering his steps and falling in the grass next to the boy who they had managed to carry to the sidelines. they decided to carry on the game now that the initial worry was over. but he was still hurt, harry knew he was in severe pain by the way he was closing his eyes and his cheeks were sweaty and flushed, more than they had been on the field.

harry grabbed the ice pack the coach had been making, zipping it faster than he had been, before gently placing it on louis' ankle.

"are you okay?" harry whispered, leaning in and placing his head against louis' chest. he could hear his heartbeat, his rapid, uneven heartbeat. "i'm right here, sunshine," he breathed.

"'m fine," louis managed to get out a smile, and harry reached out and wiped his tears away.

"you made a goal, lou," harry grinned at him sadly, and he just absolutely loved the way louis' eyes lit up for a moment, as if he wasn't in pain at all.

"i did? we're winning?"

harry nodded eagerly. "and only two minutes left for them to get you guys back. i bet you're going to win."

louis lowered his eyes to the ground, his face sad again. "what if i can't play for the rest of the season?" he whispered, struggling to get the words out. "i hope it's just a sprain. a very, very bad sprain."

harry pursed his lips, biting his tongue to prevent himself from saying any negative words. the injury seemed pretty bad, and they were going to the hospital as soon as the coach let them.

he just hoped it would be okay.

***

"go to sleep. the more you sleep, the faster you heal."

"it's just a sprain, angel. it'll heal by tomorrow."

harry rolled his eyes, wiggling his toes underneath the thick layer of blankets on louis' bed. "i guarantee you it won't," he said, partly sympathetic.

"i don't know. c'mere. my feet are cold."

harry scooted towards lou, who was being extremely goofy ever since they got home from the hospital. he had a black boot on his foot, meaning he couldn't drive. harry had to ask chris to take his car, which he was very reluctant to do since he had just met the guy, but louis assured him that his boyfriend, darren, was an honest guy.

and now here they were.

"your feet are sweating, you dolt," harry mumbled quietly. louis' boot was lying beside their bed, and now all louis had on was a thick black sock. harry couldn't fathom how the boy could be cold.

"why can't you let me find a less embarrassing way to say, 'i love you and i want to cuddle you and listen to your breaths and sing a song in my mind to the beat of your heart'?"

for some reason, this sentence made harry melt into a pile of goo in louis' arms, and he snuggled so close that their chests were touching and their legs were tangled together.

"because i want to hear you say it," harry whispered.

fifty-four

"that jacket isn't warm enough."

harry jumped as he was pulled back into the flat by an arm wrapped around his waist, gently.

"i'm fine," harry smiled sheepishly, lowering his head and staring at the floor. he was wearing a pair of fuzzy black boots.

"your cheeks are flushed," louis murmured, kissing each side of his face before placing one more kiss on his nose. "kitten's too cold to go outside."

"i was only outside for a second," harry laughed, a blush rising to his cheeks by the way louis was holding him. he was caught off guard when louis pulled his coat off his own shoulders and wrapped it around harry's, sending warmth throughout his whole body. he shivered at the temperature change, smiling foolishly as louis hugged the coat around him.

"too cold outside," louis whispered.

harry nodded.

"now let's go get our christmas tree, shall we? i'm hosting a christmas party."

harry pulled back in surprise. "really? but your flat's so.. small, lou."

"so is my group of friends," louis chuckled, and harry laughed along with him, giggling and stumbling as louis pulled them both down the stairs and out the door of the building. snow covered the ground, the trees, and the cars in the parking lot. harry could tell just by the weather that christmas was coming in less than a week.

"harry, do you think it's a good idea to host my own birthday party?" louis asked, genuinely curious. louis was holding both of their hands over the vents, letting the air warm their skin. his car smelled of leather and honey, just that musky scent that was *louis*. harry could even smell part of the football field, grass and that, a part that louis had brought with him into his car. the floors were spotless except for an occasional penny or gum wrapper. harry had to drive since louis still had on his boot.

"i think it's a good idea," harry said quietly, turning the key in the ignition. the car roared to life, and he turned on the windshield wipers to get rid of the pieces of snow blocking his view. "are you dressing up for it?"

louis turned his head to look at harry as they pulled out of the parking lot. "what do you mean, am i dressing up? do you want me to be santa claus?" he scrunched up his nose, in this adorable way.

"i'm dressing up," harry whispered, staring ahead with wide eyes at the wonderland in front of them. it wasn't snowing so hard that they couldn't see, but it was pretty... white. it wasn't dark enough to see any christmas lights and harry couldn't wait until it was night and the city and houses would be lit up with rainbow and yellow lights. he loved the way they reflected off the sparkling snow.

"what are you dressing up as, an angel?"

harry turned the wheel, listening to the turn signal clicking, a sound he absolutely loved for no reason whatsoever.

"no. i'm not telling you," harry huffed. "i want you to see on your birthday."

louis just smiled, leaning over a little and kissing harry's cheek softly. "as you wish," he whispered.

harry smiled to himself, looking at his lap with his eyes closed for just a second before looking back at the road. he liked that he didn't have to be on guard with louis anymore. louis used to yell at him every other sentence, but once he started taking his medicine regularly, it just, stopped. the odd thing was, harry kind of missed that sassy, mean side of louis. he had no idea why. maybe it was because that part of louis, that part he saw when he was just a sophomore; he fell in love with that just as much as the other parts of him. and he hoped louis would never lose that spunk, that sass that was still there, just not as harsh.

"do you know how to get to the place where you get the, ehm, trees?" harry asked, stumbling over his words as he tried to think while focusing on driving at the same time.

"turn left," was all louis said.

"turn left where?" harry blurted, blinking rapidly as suddenly a billion left turns passed by.

"on the turn," louis chuckled.

harry took his left hand and pawed at louis' shoulder. "stop," he whined. "just tell me."

"calm down, kitten."

harry rolled his eyes, deciding on driving straight forward until lou would cooperate with him.

"okay, turn left right here," louis mumbled in defeat, but harry ignored him, just to make him mad.

"harold!" the boy screeched.

"hmm?" harry hummed.

"we're gonna get lost now. all i can see is trees. look what you did, you dumb bum!" louis shrieked.

harry couldn't help but laugh as louis started to pretend to cry and little whimpers escaped his lips. he just drove, on the road that was conveniently straight forward. louis was right, there were trees surrounding them now, an overhang that caused everything around them to be darker.

"we're supposed to be getting the tree," louis grumbled into his hands. "you've no idea how bad i wish i could drive right now."

harry blushed. why was he blushing? why was it that louis always made him blush? he decided to blame it on the heat of the car.

they drove in silence for about twenty minutes, just listening to some christmas radio station and humming along with it. at least louis was. harry was listening to him. he could listen to louis' humming with his high little voice all day long.

finally, harry stopped the car. they were in the middle of nowhere, the place between the city and the country. the farther they got, the denser the layer of trees and snow got.

"harry," louis paused, taking a deep breath before reaching out and moving some of harry's curls out of his face, "what are you doing babe? i'm trying to let you do your thing but it's killing me."

harry looked over at him, his green eyes burning into louis' blue ones. louis looked so beautiful it hurt, it actually caused a pain in harry's chest. harry didn't think he could ever describe how louis looked without it being an understatement. the best writer or storyteller in the world could attempt but could never match the feeling harry had in his heart as he looked at louis.

basically, his eyes were shining so bright, a light pale blue. his lips were dark red and slightly chapped from the cold weather, his skin was flushed from the warm air of the car, tan compared to harry's pale skin. his hair was in a messy fringe across his forehead, part of it sticking up and part of it flat. and wow, why were his eyelashes so long?

it seemed as if louis was doing the same thing to harry, running his eyes over every single feature. he even went so far as to reach his hand out and run it over the place harry's dimple was when he smiled.

"we're so lost," louis said lightly.

"we'll find our way back," harry said in response.

***

after about thirty minutes, harry managed to drive them back into civilization, and louis told him the directions to the tree farm. they pulled into a gravel driveway, the wheels crunching against the snow and rocks. nobody else was there except for a few men dressed in big coats with fuzzy beards.

"let's go pick out a tree," louis smiled, reaching out and squeezing harry's arm.

they walked out of the car, louis immediately skipping to a small green tree and calling harry's name.

"angel, angel baby harold this is the one! this is our tree!" he screeched sliding on the rocks and turning around, hopping up and down. it reminded harry of a kangaroo.

harry flinched when he heard laughter from a nearby tree.

"stop laughing at me tree," he whispered, wide eyed. he watched as his breath dissolved into the air. he could hear louis squealing in the background and it made his heart stutter.

"louis, stop acting like a fool!" the tree called. harry almost fell backwards, tripping over his own feet.

louis was by his side in a second.

"don't fall," he said softly, wrapping his arms securely around his waist. "come with me. ignore darren. we need to buy our tree."

"oh," was all harry said. it was darren.

louis led harry towards the small tree. it was about louis' height, dark green and fluffy. harry immediately fell in love with it when someone he already was in love with started hugging it.

"how's this?" louis smiled, not even flinching when darren started walking towards them and saying they looked like they were in a commercial.

"louis, smile for the camera!"

harry turned his head to see chris right next to darren, leaning into his side with a camera in his right hand. louis squealed, hiding behind the tree. "no, don't take a picture of me!" he called, despite the looks he got from the men that supposedly would be cutting their tree for them.

harry was caught off guard when louis reached out his hand, pulling him by his sleeve to hide with him.

"let's take a selfie," louis said in a girlie voice.

***

"there's something missing."

harry was sitting on the couch, sipping from his steaming cup of coffee and scrutinizing the tree, his eyes squinted and his neck craned forward to see even closer. he had been sitting there for a few minutes, trying to find what louis meant when he said, "there's something missing" for the fifteenth time.

there were only a few ornaments they had bought at the dollar store. louis claimed that you had to build your ornament collection over many years, instead of buying them all at once. they had wrapped rainbow lights around the bottom of the tree, but then they ran out and had to use yellow ones for the top instead. in result, they had a multicolored tree with dark spots because louis really didn't know how to wrap lights around a tree.

his flat smelled overwhelmingly like coffee and the sugar cookie scented candle harry had bought louis for an early birthday present.

"i don't see anything missing," harry said after they sat in silence, watching louis as he stared at the tree with judging eyes. "stop judging, lou. the tree didn't do anything. i think it looks beautiful."

louis' eyes suddenly lit up as if a lightbulb had gone off in his head and harry cowered as louis charged towards him. "what are you doing?!?" harry screamed when louis grabbed him around the waist and threw him over his shoulder.

"there needs to be an angel on the top of the tree."

harry couldn't decide whether he should laugh or cry because louis was struggling to put harry's legs around his shoulders.

"help me out here, babe," louis laughed, breathless.

"how do you expect me to *be* on the top of the tree?" harry asked, incredulous, but he positioned himself so he was sitting on louis' shoulders anyway. he had to duck his head a bit because he was a little too tall.

"let's go," louis said in a low voice, bringing them towards the tree, ignoring harry's protests.

"louis put me down now," harry begged, trying not to laugh as louis continuously walked in and out of the tree, making some ornaments fall to the ground. luckily, they didn't break.

louis finally listened to him, but he didn't let him go. he just pulled harry so he fell backwards on the couch and harry fell right on top of him, and then harry fell in love all over again when louis hugged him until he couldn't breathe and then started kissing him senseless, and the coffee mixed with the peppermint was a wonderful, christmasy combination.

harry couldn't wait for the party.

fifty-five

"help me decide!" louis exclaimed, running his hands through his hair roughly as he stared ahead at his computer screen. there was a recipe for red velvet cake and for another for chocolate. "i can't pick one, harry! stop pressuring me!"

harry raised his eyebrows, a bit taken aback. he had just been standing there, looking over louis' shoulder as he tried to plan for the party tomorrow. louis had been stressing all night. it was now one in the morning.

"let's just hang the lights," harry suggested. "so we can get one thing done with." he hugged his arms around himself and stumbled a bit over his own feet as he began to walk towards the box of lights. they were all rainbow, as louis had a slight obsession with all things rainbow. even his sheets had little rainbows on them.

"okay," louis sighed. harry could tell louis was trying so hard to not be mean, but he also knew that louis got quite sassy when he was mad, and especially if he was tired. in this case, he was both. so harry decided not to take anything the shorter boy said *too* personally. instead, he took a deep breath and placed both of his hands on louis' waist.

"get on my shoulders," he said gently. "i'm not tall enough on my own."

louis gave him a questioning look. the lilac color beneath his lids and the disheveled state of his honey brown hair made it clear that he was not in the mood for anything fun. what he needed was to get under his rainbow sheets and cuddle up to his pillow while harry did all the work. but, harry wasn't tall enough. he gave louis an empathetic smile before sitting down in front of the boy. harry was surprised when he heard a little chuckle behind him.

"you have no idea what is going through my head right now," louis said, his voice tired but it had a hint of something exciting. harry couldn't help but smile. rolling his eyes and grabbing the back of louis' legs to move him over his shoulders. he smiled when louis' legs pressed against his cheek, and then he smiled even wider when he realised that louis' legs were so short and his bare feet barely went down his torso.

"grab the lights before i stand up," harry said fondly, watching as louis struggled to reach over and pick up a string of lights. harry clutched the clips that the lights would hang on in his right hand and he held onto louis' knee with his left.

"should i even have this party?" louis asked, letting out a loud yawn as harry stumbled over to the wall. he handed louis a clip to put on the wall, and then louis clipped a part of the lights on. they continued this method as they circled around the room. it was cool to look outside and see all the city lights and occasional cars that caused shadows to reflect all throughout the dim lit apartment. harry couldn't wait to plug the lights in and see what they looked like.

"am i too heavy?" louis asked worriedly, after a few minutes of silence. "i feel like i'm weighing you down. you're breathing all heavy and that."

harry stopped. "i'm not breathing heavy at all, lou."

the boys sat there for a few seconds, harry giving louis a break for his arms as he repeated the words he had always said himself when he stopped eating for a few months. he hated hearing something like that escape louis' lips, especially since louis' body was one of his favorite things in the world. he loved the curve of his waist, and he loved the way he could always grip onto louis' hips. he was soft, so soft and he didn't want louis to dislike that about himself.

"let's just get this done with it. i feel like i'm gonna fall asleep on your shoulders and that wouldn't be good."

harry nodded, spinning them in circles a bit as he examined the room. he couldn't tell what it looked like because they weren't plugged in, but he couldn't plug them in until they were done. they probably would need another few minutes.

soon, harry found himself tiredly rambling to louis, who, being completely exhausted, was a wonderful listener. harry told louis about all of his past times of christmas, when him and his mum still celebrated holidays together. he told him about how he used to hang lights in his own room and just lay in there for hours, and how cool it looked whenever the lights reflected his tears and everything blurred together. harry recalled when he was little and everybody hated him, and his room would be the only place where he felt completely safe, completely alone. christmas time, though, was the time he was in his room the most.

louis let out little noises of anger or sadness whenever harry mentioned the people the bullied him, and he even dropped all the lights whenever harry brought up the time in primary school where a kid drew a very mean picture of harry and showed it to all of his friends. it didn't seem like a big deal now but harry had been so embarrassed by it back then. he honestly didn't know why he was telling louis all of it right now, he was blushing at just the thought of it, and not in a good way.

"louis?" harry asked, when the boy had strung the last of the lights and leaned over and laid his forehead on the top of harry's curls. he let out a heaving sigh.

"harry, can you keep talking to me? please? just keep talking."

harry shut his mouth, suddenly realizing how much he had been talking. never in his life had he talked that much, that long. did he like it?

he decided that was too deep of question to think about at two in the morning, and he quickly tried to push it out of his mind.

"harry?" louis asked again, gently touching his curls as harry lowered him to the ground. there was no light, now that the computer just shut off.

"yeah?" harry whispered, the dark room giving him the feeling that he needed to be quiet.

"can you always tell me stuff like that? i like hearing you talk about yourself. i never do.." he trailed off, sliding onto the floor next to harry.

harry didn't respond, just crawled to the outlet and plugged the lights in. the room immediately lit up, sending a rainbow glow throughout the small area. harry smiled widely, meeting louis' eyes with his own wide ones.

louis' face was practically glowing, his eyes shining as he stared back at harry. he suddenly didn't look so tired, more just.. happy. harry liked to see louis like that. harry liked louis.

harry scooted towards louis again, which was a bit of a struggled because his socks slipped on the carpet.

"let's go to bed, but keep the lights on," he suggested when he finally got a spot next to the boy. he jumped a bit when louis reached over and intertwined their fingers, holding their hands between both of their chests before leaning in and kissing him gently, his lips were soft, so soft, and he tasted like peppermint. harry took the hand that wasn't holding louis' and placed it on the small of his back, pulling louis closer to him.

"let's not," louis whispered against his lips, before kissing him harder, grabbing the back of harry's neck and wrapping his legs around the younger boy's waist.

harry pulled back, furrowing his brows. "i thought you were tired."

"i never said that," louis said, but betrayed himself when he yawned, right in harry's face, actually.

harry burst into laughter, watching as louis' cheeks flushed a deep shade of red. "i'm sorry," he said shyly. "i didn't mean it."

"it's okay," harry laughed.

"not s'not!" louis pushed harry's shoulder playfully. "i'm embarrassed and you're laughing! meanie."

"let's just go to bed. we're already staying up late tomorrow," harry reminded him.

"fine. if you carry me."

***

"no! i'm not greeting people!" harry lowered his voice. "i'm not social," he whispered. he flinched when he heard a knock on the door, cowering into louis, who was in a much better mood after getting a bit of sleep.

"harry, you look so cute. i want everyone to see you."

harry blushed, placing his hands in his hair. after much searching, he had found christmas lights that did not need to be plugged in, and he threaded them gently through his curls and around the little halo louis had bought him a couple years ago.

basically, whenever he looked in the mirror, it hurt his eyes because of all the lights. harry loved to think back to when louis first saw him in it.

louis had just kinda smiled, and he was blushing and harry was wondering why *he* was blushing when harry had to be the one who put on this costume, and *wow* he felt like a fool. but louis just walked towards him and wrapped his arms softly around the younger boy, kissing him and softly pushing his fingers into harry's hair, pressing gentle kisses along his jawline and whisper sweet nothings, that really did mean *something* to harry. harry asked him if he liked it and louis nodded eagerly into his shoulder, although he had to stand on his tiptoes a bit, but harry helped him by holding him by his waist and leaning back slightly.

basically, harry was kinda hoping the party wouldn't start, because that would mean louis would start *not* paying attention to him, and he wanted louis to pay attention to him. louis was his. his louis.

"i don't wanna! i'll go get the cake out of the oven," he volunteered urgently, touching louis' elbows and desperately trying to avoid the door. he was not going to be social. only with louis, niall, and zayn.

one person at a time, harry. one person at a time.

before harry knew it, louis was lifting him up bridal style and bringing him towards the door, where there was urgent knocking, probably because the cold weather outside.

"put me down, lou," harry whined, not moving at all.

louis sighed and placed him in front of the door, putting his hands around his waist so he wouldn't move.

"greet. the. people," he whispered, his lips brushing harry's ear slightly. harry shivered at the contact, unable to disobey the boy by the way he was holding him. he reached his hand out and turned the knob, feeling louis slowly release his tight hold the whole time. he finally managed to open the door while trying not to let his knees buckle because of the way louis was touching him.

he couldn't help but break into a huge smile when niall came in and tackled harry into a hug, so much that they fell on the ground, zayn following right behind.

"harry!" niall groaned. "we missed you so much!"

"oh my god, h, don't ever leave us again. you smell too good." to prove his point, zayn sniffed harry's shirt. "never mind. you stink of louis now."

"hey!" louis exclaimed, just as a few more people walked through the door, people harry recognized as louis' team mates. "get off him, you twats. you're ruining his beautiful curls. those are mine to touch, not yours."

zayn rolled his eyes, before sticking his tongue out at louis and ruffling harry's curls. harry blushed, closing his eyes as niall kissed his cheek multiple times. wow, he really loved his friends.

louis reached over and grabbed harry's hands, pulling him up before lifting him up so his feet were brushing the floor. "go socialize, louis' going to get the food."

harry smiled to himself. "okay," he whispered, following louis with his eyes as the shorter boy practically waltzed into the kitchen.

if only he knew what was going to happen.

fifty-six

"liam texted me, he's going to be here in a few minutes," louis said excitedly, tugging on harry's shirtsleeve and putting his phone back in his pocket. harry could smell the peppermint schnapps on his breath, although it was only an hour into the night. still, he leaned into the older boy's touch, smiling when louis kissed his cheek.

"angel, don't you wanna talk to zayn and niall? you haven't seen them in forever."

harry stared straight ahead, nodding. something didn't feel right, he just didn't know what it was. it was a tugging sensation at the bottom of his stomach and he definitely did not like it. he didn't tell louis this, just nodded once more and met his blue eyes for a few seconds, before louis was walking away and leaving him alone. he felt empty, right away. his left arm was cold, his heart aching for louis' presence, as if it would rid the awful feeling in his gut. louis was his protector, the only person he felt completely safe around. and now he was leaving to go talk to his new donny friends.

he frowned sadly, reaching over the bar in the kitchen to grab a mini candy cane. he unwrapped it slightly, sticking the end in his mouth and letting the taste of peppermint overcome his senses. he could see niall and zayn having an intense conversation with a few other lads in the corner, and they were obviously on the same side. harry could recall them gaining up on him like that whenever they were trying to decide what restaurant they were going to go to. harry recognized one of the boys, but he didn't want to think too much about it. he was already exhausted from staying up last night.

"hi harry."

harry looked up through his lashes, pulling his candy cane out of his mouth slowly and licking his lips. a little light slipped out of his curls and hit him in the forehead. he didn't try to fix it.

"hi," he said quietly, clearing his throat when his voice cracked. the room was becoming suffocating, and he tried not to look to frantic as he searched for louis. he finally saw the boy standing in a corner of the flat, his arms hugged around himself, and he was laughing really loudly at something.

harry recognized the person standing in front of him as the same one he saw that was talking to niall and zayn. just the way he smiled made harry's hands shake. harry couldn't even look him in the eye, that's how freaking lame he was. he felt like he was at school again, where everybody around him judged him for his lack of social skills. it wasn't a good feeling, no; he looked at his hands and played with his fingers as he waited for the boy to say something.

the worst thing was, he didn't expect to see the boy again. he thought that after the boy graduated everything would be okay. why did louis even invite him here? he wanted to tell louis that it wasn't okay, but that wasn't his right. was it? did boyfriend's tell each other who they were allowed to invite to a party? he didn't want to be clingy or over-protective or bossy.

but he also was really upset that louis invited *him*.

harry scowled at him, cowering in on himself as signals to run away overcame him. he felt cornered, and he desperately wanted to run into louis' room and hide. he couldn't read the look on the taller, bigger boy's face, and that scared him even more. he hated trying to read people. he hated it.

"are you normal yet?" was what harry heard after a few moments of silence, and he stepped back as if he had been slapped. he didn't say anything though, just continued to stare at the ground.

"oh, so you didn't grow out of it? did it get worse? i see you can't talk. so sad, autism sucks, doesn't it?"

harry took another step backwards, each blow hitting him worse than the first.

"do you hear what i'm saying? i hear your brain doesn't work right. freak."

harry flickered his eyes back and forth and blinked them rapidly, because *wow* he forgot how much this *hurt*.

"can't tell if i'm kidding or not? i'm not." the boy smiled, and harry looked up just a second, to see his doncaster college sweatshirt that looked very similar to the one louis had.

speaking of louis.

harry took a few more steps back, desperately trying to catch louis' eye.

louis finally looked over, and when he saw harry was looking at him he gave him a wide smile, but then he frowned quickly when he saw the troubled frown on harry's face.

"harry?" he mouthed, and his eyes widened when harry was shoved into the doorway of the kitchen. harry's breath caught in his throat, and he stumbled over his feet until he was sitting down, his back against the wall of the kitchen.

"we should drive to get louis a present. i forgot to get him one. we'll be back before he notices."

harry stuttered a bit before any actual words came out of his mouth.

"louis already noticed," he whispered.

"oh, so you can talk? not that loud, i see." stan grinned, and harry winced when he stepped between his legs, kicking his feet apart with his black dress shoes. he shut the door with his left hand, locking it before turning back to the younger boy, who was trying to back up into a wall that wasn't going to move.

"I-leave me alone," harry begged, shivering when stan brushed his shoe against the inside of his thigh. "i didn't, i-i d-didn't do anything to, to you, stan."

"i thought you said you were done being friends with louis."

"i-i never s-said that." harry had goosebumps on his arms. no. why was his head spinning? he hadn't experienced this in so long.

"harry? are you okay?" louis yelled through the door, knocking on it loudly. "who locked this door? who's in there with you?"

harry opened his mouth to respond, but then stan was kneeling on the ground, putting his hand over harry's mouth. harry's eyes widened, and he shook his head, squeezing his eyes shut. stan chuckled to himself.

"you're really beautiful," stan smiled, and harry saw warmness in his eyes. wait. wasn't stan mean?

"no i'm not," harry said as stan took his hand off of his mouth. same thing he said to lou.

"no, you really are. your eyes are so freaking pretty, did you know that?"

harry's heart stuttered at the compliment, and he didn't know how to react.

"harry! answer me, babe," louis begged, his knocking becoming less frequent. harry jumped. he had forgotten about louis. stan made him forget, for just a second. how the heck did he do that? he felt troubled, but then smiled and pulled in his attention again.

"you should kiss me. you have pretty lips."

harry shook his head frantically. "no, i love lou-"

"lucas. you love stan lucas."

harry flinched, taken aback at his words. he was so confused. "no, stan. i don't. i love louis. i love louis. did i say i loved you?" he said worriedly, afraid that he might have said it on accident. that would be betraying his louis! no, no that wouldn't do. why was stan saying these things? he didn't love stan, not at all. why did stan think that?

"harry! what's wrong, angel?"

harry watched as stan physically flinched at louis' words, a look that harry couldn't read burning in his eyes and it scared him. and one minute stan was standing between harry's legs and then he was grabbing harry around the waist roughly, kissing his lips so hard that it hurt and he bit harry's lip and harry could tell it was bleeding by the copper taste that soon greeted his mouth.

"stan, what are you doing?" harry breathed, rubbing his lip and at the same time trying to free himself from stan's strong grip. he wasn't very strong; never had been. he was suddenly regretting his disinterest in sports.

"we're going to get louis' present."

"why'd you kiss me?" harry cried, pushing him away and hiccupping a bit when tears came to his eyes and clogged his throat. his vision was blurred. there were now a lot of the people at the kitchen door.

"is there another way in there?" he heard niall say, and it was silent for a moment while stan dragged harry out the door that led to the staircase. stan pulled them down the stairs and through the lobby, until they were going through the exit doors. they were greeted with cold weather, snow cascading onto the ground at an unbelievable speed. the lights in harry's hair reflected rainbow colors off the snow. he got distracted by it for a moment, and for some odd reason his compliance made stan stop for a second.

"what is it?" stan asked, breathless.

"look at the lights," harry said, his green eyes wide as he watched the rainbow colors sparkle and glitter against the dark night. the wind was causing harry's curls to blow into his eyes, and he blinked them rapidly.

stan was snapped out of his trance with harry when the door of the building opened once more, little bells signaling it's jostling. harry whipped around, shivering and trying to rub away the goose bumps littering his skin. it was definitely below freezing, but he was too upset and confused to care.

"harry!" he could see louis under the light of the entrance, looking around until his eyes landed on the taller boy, whose presence was clear since he lit up the small area around him. harry thought that louis looked absolutely breathtaking at the moment, standing under the porch light, his eyes shining and a red santa hat upon his head. harry didn't know what was going to happen tonight, especially since stan was dragging him towards his car, but he did know he loved louis.

"happy birthday louis!" harry called into the air, just as louis started to walk towards them.

but then stan was shoving harry into his car and running to his seat and louis was now running towards them. "stan, i didn't freaking invite you! what are you doing! let go of harry!"

"happy birthday, lou," harry whispered, prepared for stan to drive away and get whatever louis' 'present' was. but then louis was opening harry's door, before stan could drive away. and he pulled the taller boy out, and harry could feel him shivering because of the cold weather. louis kissed him hardly, before pulling him into another hug and asking him if he was okay.

"you do know he kissed me," stan said from where he was sitting.

louis froze, pulling back and meeting eyes with harry for just a second before he opened his mouth and whispered, "harry?"

harry didn't lie to his louis.

fifty-seven

"harry?" louis asked shakily, taking a step back from the taller boy, his eyes flickering between stan and harry. harry whipped around to look at stan, and he was smirking, his dark eyes calm as he stared back at louis.

"that's why he locked the door."

harry felt his heart pounding. "i didn't lock the door, louis. stan did." he was saying the truth. as long as he was honest, it would be okay. he just wished that all this bad stuff wouldn't be happening on louis' birthday.

louis stepped back once more, his lips quivering as he struggled to maintain eye contact with harry, who was looking at the ground and the sky and everything but the beautiful boy standing in front of him. the wind was blowing his curls into his face, and he cringed whenever he felt the wet snow stick to his cheeks and hair. the only light was from stan's car and the rainbow colors in harry's hair.

"did you kiss stan, harry?"

harry, honestly, did not know the answer the question. was louis asking him if he initiated it? because the answer to that question would be no. but if he was asking if their lips touched, if they actually did kiss, then that answer was yes, sadly.

he decided it was the latter, as he knew louis didn't like to get into specifics and he didn't want louis to misunderstand.

"yeah, we kissed," harry whispered, flinching when louis grabbed the back of his neck, turning around and kicking his foot into the tire of a nearby car. "louis," harry said quietly.

louis ignored him, yelling a string of curse words into the air before turning back to stan. "why did you kiss him, stan?" he asked, his voice eerily calm and his blue eyes darkened to a deep, cold color. "do you honestly think he knows what he's doing? do you know how freaking fragile this boy is?" his anger and volume grew with every word, with every step closer he came to stan.

stan maintained his composure, although harry could see him shivering because of the cold wind blowing into his car. harry didn't know what was going on, but he did know that he did not like the tone that louis was using, and he didn't like the way that louis was talking about him.

"louis, i'm not fragile," harry furrowed his brows, hugging his arms around himself and biting his lip. "how could you say that?"

stan interjected. "you know, lou, i can punch him to see how fragile he really is. then you guys don't have to argue about it."

louis looked like he was trying so, so hard to keep his calm, but harry knew just as well as the boy himself that after a while, some medicine wasn't enough to do that job. harry hoped that stan liked seeing them both in the worst state of their mental issues.

louis had anger problems and harry didn't even have the brain to interpret what the heck was going on. oh, what a wonderful match that was.

"stan, why are you here?" louis placed his hands on his hips. "nobody freaking wants you here, nobody, not harry, not me." he looked at harry, his glance a bit troubled and nervous. "right, harry?" his voice cracked at the end, and something about the heavy way he was breathing and the obvious anger in his eyes made harry falter in his words.

"uhm, erm, i guess, so," he whispered.

"harry, just be sure of yourself, for once!" louis yelled, hitting the side of stan's car loudly and causing harry to flinch. "you don't even know how to form a sentence, or stand up for yourself! and you can't even look guilty for freaking cheating on me! how do you think that makes me feel!? how could you do that, on my birthday, on christmas, on the day i was gonna, i was gonna…" louis trailed off. his eyes were shining with tears, his hands shaking and the next thing harry knew stan was laughing.

louis looked absolutely furious as he turned to look at stan. "i can't believe i was ever your friend," he spit.

stan continued to chuckle like a fool and harry didn't know why but that made him quite annoyed, quite irritated that he was laughing at louis, who was obviously having a breakdown.

and it was quiet for just a moment, before stan whispered quietly, "faggot."

harry felt his heart drop to his stomach at that word, and he felt numb for just a tiny second, and he was so unbelievably cold. just that one word made him want to burst into tears, to bring back the memories of hiding under his bed and screaming out all the things that he was to freaking nervous to say. he wanted to run into louis' arms and hide in his sweatshirt and say how hard it was, how hard it was to hold in tears when there was an ache in the back of his throat and a burning in his eyes. he wanted to tell louis how much he wanted him to be there when he was crying so hard he couldn't breathe, when he was gasping for air and trying to calm the pain in his tummy whenever he went without food for too long.

he wanted louis to know how hard it was to go to school without him. because he heard just that one word one too many times a day, and each time hurt worse than the first. he heard somewhere that the more you hear something, the more numb you become, the less meaningful it becomes to you. harry didn't agree with that all. especially with this word.

especially since he could see the hurt, stung look in louis' eyes as he stared back at stan.

"you know how much i hate that word," he whispered. "you know how much i hate that word, you piece of crap, i hate you so much, i hate you so much and harry hates you too-"

"please stop speaking for me," harry said, and everybody was silent, even stan, who was beginning to yell things back at louis.

"angel," louis began, reaching his hand out to harry, but harry just started to cry, not a loud cry, just quiet and he wiped the tears out from under his eyes and tried to steady his breathing. he knew this feeling all too well, and louis could tell that all of this fighting was getting to him.

"please just go, stan. please go. i can't watch harry do this to himself. please, if you care about either of us at all, just drive away and we can settle this tomorrow without harry, but just leave."

harry's head was spinning, and all of the lights blurred for a few moments before becoming clear, but then they would blur again. he could taste the salt of his tears on his tongue, and he hoped it would rid the taste of stan. he hated that he had ruined louis' birthday, he hated it and he hoped louis would forgive him. but why should louis forgive him? harry kissed stan, and harry yelled at louis.

"do you think i care at all about either of you? louis, you're a jerk, you ditch everyone and you can't be trusted to not leave after things start to get hard, even though you're the reason they do. and that piece of sensitive crap sitting over there doesn't get anything, he probably doesn't understand anything that's going on, he's just a little kid. his brain can't put things together right."

harry's breathing was getting heavier with every word, his vision was getting more blurred. he could feel this awful panic in his heart, and he wished he was normal so he wouldn't have to worry about breaking down.

way louis was screaming at stan was perhaps the reason harry lost control of himself, the reason he passed out in the snow for the second time in his life, and he felt pain shoot up his legs when his knees hit the pavement. his feet were cold, his body was cold and louis' touch was feather light when he finally felt it. he felt like a ghost.

he didn't know if stan ever drove away.

***

when harry woke up, he didn't open his eyes, he just pushed his head into louis' chest. they were sitting somewhere, and the room was dark and quiet, the only noise was the sound of their breaths. louis, though, for some reason knew that harry had woken, for the second harry began to play with the hem of louis' shirt, he whispered, "go to sleep, angel."

louis' arms were wrapped securely around harry, and harry wanted so badly to know what happened but he knew that he was safe, so that was enough.

well, it was enough until harry woke up a few hours later and his stomach was hurting because of this awful thing called guilt. he didn't realise the harshness of what he had done until he put himself in louis' shoes. when he thought louis had kissed mitchell, he knew how painful that was, he knew how betrayed he felt. yet here louis was, holding him so tightly and warmly although harry had kissed stan and harry had yelled at him. louis was here after having his own breakdown and having no one to hold him, instead having to hold harry to keep himself together.

harry wondered where stan was, where stan could be on this cold morning of christmas. the clock read one, and for some reason that made harry feel depressed. louis' birthday had been a mess, and it was all his fault.

"louis?" he whispered, and his lips were so incredibly dry. he needed a drink. when louis didn't move, he maneuvered his way out of the older boy's arms and stood up. when he looked around, he realised he was in the living room of louis' apartment. he wondered why they weren't sleeping in louis' bed. maybe louis was too tired to take them in there.

harry frowned, but when he looked at louis, sleeping so peacefully and innocently, he felt some type of fondness, some type of comfort. louis could be the sweetest person in the universe, and even when he was yelling and he couldn't control his own emotions he was still a beautiful, strong person. he got mad when he was hurt, not for no reason at all.

"louis," harry whispered again, hoping he would wake up. he didn't, he just snuggled further into the couch and wrapped his arms around himself. harry sighed and walked into the kitchen, grabbing a glass out of the cupboard and gulping away the knot in his throat as he filled it up with water. the flat was way too quiet for his liking, it reminded him of his room when his mum was away and he was completely alone. he had grown very used to louis' loudness, to his tendency to blurt out whatever was on his mind and laugh at his own stupid jokes. he even talked to objects, like he sassed the television when it didn't work and he apologised to the remote whenever he dropped. those were the moments when harry was so in love with him it hurt.

harry took a sip of his water, and he flinched when he felt a warm tear slide down his cheek. maybe it was because he hated to remember what happened last night. maybe it was because the silence was getting to him, or maybe it was because of the way stan's words kind of pushed their way into harry's brain and he couldn't shove them out. all he knew was, he was crying, and a minute later louis was walking towards him, his hair frazzled and a tired look in his eyes. harry could only see him because the moon shining through the window of his kitchen.

soon louis was hugging him, hugging him so tight he couldn't breathe and he was sobbing into louis' chest and yet he felt so happy to be there, to feel louis' skin against his because neither of them were wearing shirts and all of his guilt faded away for a moment and all he cared about was that he was in love with louis.

he was so in love with him.

fifty-eight

"don't cry angel."

was it possible that louis was real? he was tragically beautiful, breathtaking and alluring and so soft as he stood in front of harry, his eyes flickering over every inch of the younger boy's face. it was a painful thing to witness, to watch louis' lip quiver ever so slightly, a tiny giveaway that this ordeal was perhaps just as hard for him as it was for harry. harry knew he was trying not to cry because someone had to stay strong between the two of them, and it was achingly obvious that the shy harry styles was not that someone. especially since if he ever encountered anything close to fighting, he would be crying. he didn't like that about himself; perhaps that could be his new year's resolution. to stop being so darn sensitive.

he wasn't to focus on that proposition, no. he was to watch the way louis' eyes practically glowed, the pale blue contrasting so very well with his skin that looked quite pale because of the moon shining through the window. his lips were a dark, pretty rose color and his messy hair tangled and swooped in just the right places, brushing against his eyelashes and over his curved eyebrows. he looked way too agonizingly stunning, exquisitely beautiful; a kind of divinity that was enough to stop harry in his tracks, enough to make his knees buckle and his heart stutter for a few seconds.

but louis was always there, he was *always there* and perhaps that was one of the main reasons harry fell so hard for him, one of the main reasons harry found himself wanting to touch louis every second of the day, to kiss him every second of the night. when harry fell, louis was there to catch him, to help him on his feet. he knew he shouldn't take advantage of it; he should be learning to stand on his own and to speak for himself, but he wasn't quite sure if he was ready for that. louis, although his tendency to yell and scream and break down, was so strong, a strong harry strove to be.

"wait," harry whispered, his whisper disappearing into the silent air, a quiet plea for louis to come back. but the thing was, louis was right there, his arms wrapped tightly around the taller boy and the soft material of his pajama pants brushing against harry's legs and sending goose bumps throughout his whole body. harry felt as if he needed to correct his wording, because he had something to say, he just didn't know how to say it.

"wait for what?" louis breathed against harry's curls, his fingers tangling in the hairs on the back of his neck gently. his breath was warm, his lips were moist. harry leaned further into his touch.

"don't leave," harry whimpered, and there was still this ache in his chest, an ache that spread to his throat as he held his breath, trying not to let the tears slip past his eyelids. there was a pushing feeling in his stomach, a pang at the bottom of his ribs that was so painfully familiar, reminding him of the dull burn that he had endured for so many years. "please don't leave me louis, please please please."

louis shook his head quickly, his forehead pressed up against harry's chest. he was on his tiptoes; harry could tell by the way louis was leaning into him. "i'm not gonna. why would you think that?"

"stan said you would leave." harry laid his forehead on the top of louis' head, breathing in his unique smell. harry knew he was taller, but at the moment he felt so small, as he was asking so much of louis and all of his happiness lied in the fate of another boy's heart.

"stan doesn't know what he's talking about, angel. please don't take what he says to heart. i'm going to stay as long as you'll allow me, promise," louis murmured into harry's chest, his arms tightening around harry's waist in a long, comforting hug.

"i'm tired," was what harry ended up saying, and louis shook a bit as he laughed.

"then let's go to bed. it's only one in the morning; we still have seven hours of sleep." louis pulled back but kept his hands on harry's hips. "and then it's christmas morning."

"do you feel twenty yet?" harry asked quietly, and for some reason his own question caused a tightening in his chest. louis was twenty years old. his louis that he was in love with since he was seventeen was twenty.

louis sighed deeply. "no. i want to be eighteen again. those were the days, man."

harry stopped in his tracks, turning his head down to look at louis with his brows furrowed. "these aren't the days?" all he could remember when louis was that young was louis snapping at him every second, and being insulted by anyone near him if he slipped up.

louis shook his head quickly, grabbing harry by the arm and pulling him into his bedroom, shutting the door behind them. the room was lit up with christmas lights, sending a yellow glow across louis' face.

"no, this is better. this isn't something i'm going to look back on, because it's never gonna stop. you're forever, harry. you're in my plan of forever."

harry stumbled a bit as louis pressed him harder against the door, as if urgent.

"trust me, louis isn't going anywhere," the shorter boy whispered, cupping harry's jaw in his hands. "now catch me." his tone trailed off, and harry was a bit confused for a second before louis was jumping into his arms, wrapping his legs around harry's waist tightly. harry whimpered and pushed his forehead against louis', then he pressed his lips into the other boy's.

"'m so lucky to love you," louis breathed, before kissing him harder and wrapping his arms around harry's neck. all harry could think was *wow,* he really liked kissing louis, and he felt dizzy and faint and all he could do was accept this beautiful gift of affection while trying not to smile.

but, he failed miserably at his attempt and soon he was grinning widely as louis kissed him, and he led them to fall onto louis' bed. "i love you," harry said against louis' lips, and louis let out a deep breath and nodded quickly before leaning in and kissing him again. his lips were warm, feather light then assertive and rough. and harry just wanted to kiss him, all day. louis' nose brushed his cheek when he turned to catch his breath, and since harry really loved his nose it just made him want to dance, and he leaned in to capture louis' lips again.

since louis was on top of harry, harry rolled them over and placed one hand on louis' cheek and the other on the bed to support himself. louis, on the other hand, tangled his fingers into harry's curls and held the back of his neck gently, and harry really tried to ignore the ache throughout his whole body whenever louis pushed his hips into his.

they kissed lazily until they were tired, until harry yawned in his face and caused louis to laugh.

"happy birthday," was what harry said when louis tangled their legs together and he was staring wide eyed at the ceiling. there was a click when louis reached over and turned off the lights, covering them in darkness.

"it's not my birthday." louis paused. "but thank you."

"g'night," harry mumbled, smiling when louis brushed some of his curls out of his face, and leaned over and kissed his lips softly.

"good night, angel."

***

"we have so much to do, harry. we're going home tomorrow and mum is expecting me to bring the red velvet cake. i'm not going to make you make it... but can you make it?"

"you might as well make me," harry murmured, smiling at his hands while he pushed a few rings on his fingers. he liked to have them on at all times, even when he wasn't dressed. currently, louis was throwing a pair of pajama pants and a soft white shirt at him so he wouldn't be opening presents completely naked.

"thanks sugar plum," louis smiled at him, and harry turned around slightly to look at him. he looked beautiful in daylight as well, but in a different way. harry liked the way sun shined through the window and caused a shadow to cast across only part of his body. he was wearing harry's sweatshirt, and harry just kind of loved that.

"i can't wait for you to open your present," harry said quietly, slipping on his pants.

"oh really? i thought it was you?" harry cringed when he winked.

"that isn't funny." harry blushed. "i was so stupid. i'm so embarrassed."

harry was caught off guard when louis started shaking his head, sighing deeply before running towards harry. "what are you-" harry began, his words caught in his throat when louis lifted him up around the waist and twirled him around, and he put his hands in louis' hair as a laugh escaped his lips.

"you are not stupid. that was the best day of my life, don't ever say that."

harry furrowed his brows as louis put him down. "the best day of your life?"

louis laughed. "either that or the day i first saw you."

harry tried to control the racing of his heart when he replied. "you're so cheesy," he said quietly.

"let's go," louis smiled at him, his eyes crinkling up and his eyebrows raised in expectation, his arm held out. harry smirked before walking next to him, his arm wrapped around louis' shoulders while louis' arm snaked around his waist. "i'm expecting you to make me breakfast, you know that right?"

harry scoffed. "i'm not even that good a cook. you overestimate me."

"i'm proud of you. you have the best cooking in the world."

harry raised his voice excitedly. "have you had my mum's..." he trailed off, before there was a deep frown on his face, and his heart clenched. "never mind."

they were both quiet for a moment, standing in the middle of the hallway. louis turned and put his other arm around harry's waist as well, laying his head on harry's shoulder. harry really loved when louis hugged him.

"it's okay, harry."

"she hasn't spoken to me in two months," harry whispered, staring straight ahead at the tree in the living room. "two months, lou."

"have you tried calling her?" louis suggested. "whenever i hung out with both of you, it seemed like she loved you so much."

louis' words caused a tightening in harry's chest. "that's what i thought," he whimpered. "i don't know what happened to her. she was so accepting.... and then she wasn't. i think it's ross' fault."

louis stiffened at the name. "i can believe he thought he had the right to tell you what to do, and to turn your mum against you. he's just her boyfriend, not her husband. even then, he still doesn't have the right to do that."

"let's just not talk about it right now, yeah?" harry said in a lighter voice, letting go of louis and walking towards the kitchen. he reached up and pulled some pancake mix off the shelf, placing it on the counter before opening up a cabinet and grabbing a bowl. "can you get the eggs?'

louis frowned, a worried look in his eyes, but he got the eggs out of the fridge and placed them gently on the counter in front of harry.

"harry, are you okay? can you smile for me?" louis titled his head and leaned in front of harry, giving him a closed mouth smile and reaching out to run his thumb under harry's bottom lip.

harry gave him a halfhearted smile, but lou wouldn't accept it.

"you know how much i love your smile, harold angel baby styles. do it for lou."

harry closed his eyes for a second and then smiled, blushing when louis' eyes flashed with some type of emotion and then he was beaming.

"you're so beautiful." he shook his head, reaching his hands out and running them across harry's chest and down his sides, then over his cheekbones. "too beautiful for anyone."

"anyone but you," harry whispered.

fifty-nine

christmas went quite perfectly, not a surprise to either of the boys.

was it possible that it was *too* perfect? harry had read many romance books where the people in the couple got suffocated from being together so much, and they needed some alone time after a while. back then, he thought the idea of being away from louis for just a second was unbearable, that he would miss him too much. but now, after spending all christmas with him and almost crying with fondness at louis' reaction to his polaroid camera, he actually did crave some time alone.

was that wrong?

he honestly didn't know how relationships worked; he had only been in one relationship his whole life. he figured maybe louis would agree that he needed a tiny break, though, because louis was understanding. sometimes.

so, on the day after christmas he dressed up in his black jeans, brown boots, and black calvin klein sweatshirt. he ran a hand through his curls, softly, and looked at himself in the mirror for a good while. he was incredibly pale, especially since it was wintertime. he licked his chapped lips, running a hand across his face for a second before exiting the bathroom of louis' flat and crossing through the living room.

he saw louis, standing in the kitchen and talking on the phone with somebody. harry assumed it was his mum by the way he was speaking so softly and kindly like he always did with jay. harry admired his patience whenever jay was upset, he just shushed her and said quiet, soothing words. it seemed he only had that type of patience with two people. everybody else could get him mad pretty easily, and harry thought it was very mean when people tried to do that. he could control it, but only to a certain point.

louis looked up when harry picked up his keys off the counter, and they met eyes for a second before louis blinked and looked away.

"okay, okay mum, i know. bobby gets like that sometimes. just calm down, have some wine-"

it was obvious he was interrupted, and he flinched a bit at what jay was saying. harry stood there, frozen, watching louis, as louis' eyes flickered back and forth between the ceiling, in thought, to harry, who was standing there with his hands on his keys.

"where are you going?" louis mouthed, his eyebrows furrowed and his finger pointing to the keys. harry shrugged, because honestly, he didn't know where he was going. he just needed to get away for a few hours.

and louis walked towards him, and harry was caught off guard when louis kissed him, hardly, putting one hand on his cheek and the other covering the mouthpiece of the phone.

"just come back," was what louis whispered, and harry nodded and kissed him shortly again, before turning around on his heel and stumbling a bit, flustered. he was always, *always* dazed after that boy kissed him, no matter how many times he caught him off guard or touched him.

"okay," harry breathed, before practically falling out the door. he felt this attraction, this need to go back in there and kiss louis again, it was like a gravitational pull and *wow* he really needed to pull himself together.

he sighed deeply, fumbling his keys into the pocket of his sweatshirt and walking down the stairs of the building, his boots echoing into the empty hallways and bouncing off the walls. the minute he was in the lobby he felt excited, like he had done something wrong, when all he really did was just leave by himself for the day. he felt some type of guilt in his chest, and he willed it away with furrowed brows and shaky hands, running his car and ducking his head to avoid the falling snow, tumbling to the ground like rain.

his car was cold when he got in it, and he turned the key in the ignition, rubbing his hands together and hoping the heat would kick in soon. this was a cold winter, a snowy one at that. there was mud and slush on the road, and on road signs as well from wheels pulling it from the ground and spraying it everywhere. there was a large wind blowing in the air, and the minute harry shut the door all of the whooshing sounds disappeared.

he gave one last glance at louis' flat building before taking a deep breath, pushing his foot on the pedal and carefully pulling out of the parking lot. the farther away he got, the closer he got to his undecided destination, the guiltier he got. it weighed on him heavily, and he found himself struggling to drive away. he would call the older boy but that would defeat the whole purpose of what he was doing. he needed alone time, so why was he so scared?

perhaps it was because louis was the only person he felt safe around. even though it was nice that he could finally think to himself, think *for* himself, the passenger seat next to him felt empty, like it needed louis' big perfect bum sitting there to accompany him on this drive to nowhere.

enjoy this. he said to himself. *lighten up. go somewhere.*

harry had never been one to listen to his thoughts, because he never trusted himself enough. he liked to rely on other decisions to move him along. was that a bad thing?

well, he never knew the answer to that question.

harry squinted his eyes and squeezed his hands on the steering wheel as he drove on, the sounds of the city surrounding him like a blanket. he could hear cars honking, probably driving to the mall to do some returns as it was the day after christmas. the parking lot of every store was packed with cars, and harry watched as all the colors of each car zoomed by him, bringing their own sound with them, bringing their own people and their own lives with them. he turned his windshield wiper on, trying to clear his windshield so he could see better, but it was foggy and *why* were people driving in this weather?

harry knew he was being a bit hypocritical, as he was driving and he had no purpose, except to be alone. maybe this would be good for the both of them.

he was over thinking this, way too much.

he sighed loudly, reaching his left hand over to turn on the radio. it was stuck on a christmas station, although christmas was over. maybe people considered new year's part of the christmas season.

and maybe, just maybe, the snow falling roughly against harry's windshield and the music playing softly through the speakers of his car, made so many memories, of louis and his parents, to come to his mind, to make all the sounds of honking and braking and loud music fade away.

"that's beautiful, harry," anne smiled, taking the white ornament with little stick people drawn on it out of harry's tiny hands. harry smiled up at her, putting both hands on the opposite hip and tilting his head to watch his mum hook the ornament he made on the tree. his teacher had told him that he had made the best one out of the whole second grade class, even ellie, who was known as the best artist. harry was quite sad about that, as he loved to draw and especially paint.

he had wanted to be an artist ever since.

anne leaned down, grabbed both sides of harry's face, and kissed his forehead. "i love you, sweetie. so much. okay?"

harry blushed, shying away and goose bumps rose on his arms because although the house was warm anne's fingers were freezing.

"i love you too mummy," he whispered, and he just felt so happy, because his dad was there, watching them from the couch with a smile on his face and a cookie in one hand and a coffee in the other, and it was snowing outside. harry had played in the snow earlier, and he hoped the storm wouldn't knock over the snowman he and his dad had made.

"des, come here. you have to put an ornament on the tree or else it'll only be harry and i's," anne smiled at harry's father, and des got up from his chair, putting his cup and cookie on the table. harry watched curiously as des kissed anne lightly, and the happiness on her face when he pulled back was so pretty to watch, harry didn't know what it meant but she was so pretty, harry thought his mum was the most beautiful mum there ever was.

his father reached over and picked up the last ornament, a purple one with lace linings, and he chuckled slightly and smiled at harry before putting it on the tree.

"you put it in the wrong place!" harry exclaimed, pointing to where it should've gone, a blank space where no ornaments were.

des laughed loudly, as if harry was the funniest boy in the world, and he leaned over and picked up harry and twirled him around before propping him on his waist. "that's not the wrong place, buddy. that's where daddy puts it, that's where it stays."

and harry loved his dad, he really did.

but then des told anne that they were going to go check on the batch of cookies in the oven, and when the door shut behind them in the kitchen he put harry on the counter, standing between his legs. "you're going to love daddy tonight, i'll sleep in your bed and keep you warm, okay?" he whispered, and harry looked at him, confused.

before harry could say anything des left the kitchen and harry was alone, alone with his seven year old mind.

harry could feel tears rolling down his cheeks at the memory, at the memory of his father who he used to admire so much but now he hated with a passion.

and he cried even harder when he thought of how well louis treated him. louis treated him like a prince.

"babe, that's not gonna work. but keep trying, you're cute when you're concentrated."

harry looked up from where he was trying to unwrap the present without ripping any of the paper. he was peeling the tape off, well, attempting to, and this paper was so thin and he didn't like how hard this was.

and louis was smiling at harry, with his eyes all crinkled up and his lips pressed together and he really actually looked like sunshine, and wow he was so fond.

"i love you, so much, harry." he shook his head, looking away and picking at his nails. "and i'm not going to let anything touch you, or anything hurt you? okay?"

harry blushed, looking at his unopened present and trying so hard not to cry because he just loved louis, so so much and there was finally someone, finally, who loved him, and cared about him, but actually stayed with him, protected him.

harry honestly didn't know why he was crying so hard.

he pulled in front of a bar that louis and he had went to a few weeks ago. it wasn't that crowded, probably because of the bad weather.

harry shut his car off, taking a deep breath and bracing himself before opening his door. he was greeted with a cold, icy breeze blowing his curls back and snow blocking his view.

"'s cold," he mumbled to himself, hugging his arms around himself and running inside. he didn't like that he was getting his boots wet, but that wasn't not the point. the door had a bell over it that jingled when he opened it, and the sound made him smile, as silly as that sounded.

only a few heads turned when he walked in, and the others were laughing at something another man had just said. it had something to do with sex.

of course.

harry walked up to a random table, pulling the hood down from over his head and shaking the snow out of his hair. he sat down quietly, letting a yawn escape his lips and he hoped that it wasn't noticeable that he had been crying.

he sat in that bar for a couple of hours, drinking a glass of water and munching on some cheese fries. and he had a good time, he did, but he also felt alone.

the storm was worse when he finally got back in his car to drive home. it was ten at night, and the streets were very dark, almost impossible to see in. the snow was falling faster, the wind was blowing harder. harry sat in his car for a while just to watch the trees sway back and forth and the snow build up around him. he could hear snow plows going around, as well.

he needed to get home, he decided.

harry pulled out of the parking lot, leaving the bar behind and trying to decide whether this night out had a point or not. louis was probably worrying about him, and he didn't want that at all. although, he wouldn't be surprised if the boy was, as it was practically a blizzard out here, a terribly beautiful blizzard.

harry really liked snow.

and perhaps, that was why he was staring out the window when he was driving down the highway and he missed the black ice, and why his car off the road.

maybe he loved snow too much.

sixty

so many moments can take your breath away, so many things can change your life in the blink of an eye and it moves too fast for you to change anything. but the earth keeps spinning, other people's lives keep continuing on while yours is crashing down, while your cutting yourself trying to pick up broken pieces too small to see. perhaps that is a good thing, that one person's problem doesn't affect the whole world, yet just their small corner of the universe, but then again, it's not. harry knew, right when his shaky hands slipped a bit as he struggled to stay on the road, he knew that this bit of his world wouldn't just affect him, it would affect louis. it would affect louis and his friends and maybe even his mother, and that was one of the scariest things harry could've imagined in the two seconds of silence he had before his tire screeched against the icy road and his car began to turn over. he was holding his breath, his heartbeat in his ears as he curled in on himself, his only restraint his seat belt.

he squeezed his eyes shut, just like he always did when he was scared, and he was *so freaking scared*, and his head hit hardly against the back of his seat as the car crashed into the snow, off the road and under some nearby trees, but he was still breathing. he was breathing and holding in a scream as he was thrashed around and hit into the side door and the steering wheel slammed into his chin and glass came flying towards him, and he felt a cut, a stinging cut on his cheek. it was perhaps the most painful and peaceful thing in the world, his arms wrapped around himself and his eyes closed but all these crazy things going on around him, just like he was all his life. the silent one, the scared one in so much pain while everyone else went on through their chaotic lives without him. he was quiet, he was alone right now, and all he wanted was his car to stop *moving*. for the objects getting hurled against his chest like knives to stop moving. for everything to quit hurting him.

and it did, after his hands were bleeding and he passed out, still strapped in his seat belt.

and it seemed just seconds later he opened his eyes, his phone ringing loudly from his back pocket, and he was so cold because his car had crashed and the heat shut off, and now he was in his car laying sideways in the snow. there were tears running down his cheeks, and his head was pounding. harry was sure he had gotten some type of injury, just because when he touched his forehead he felt something warm and sticky and it was red.

harry put the phone to his ear, unable to speak because he was in so much pain and he was so cold, the snow soaking through the broken window and causing his coat to turn damp.

"harry? i made dinner, why aren't you home yet baby?"

harry sobbed into the phone, but it hurt because every breath he took caused a sharp pain through his ribs and lungs, and he was almost sure he had never been in this much excruciating pain before, at least not physically.

"l-l-lou, lou-is," he choked out, before he was coughing and he couldn't stop. he coughed so hard and it hurt his lung, there was an agonizing pain all throughout his chest and he could barely hear louis' worried voice over the phone.

"harry, harry where are you? oh my god are you okay? where are you please tell me i'm going to come get you harry, harry please just breathe for me," louis rushed.

harry squeezed his eyes shut when a pair of headlights shone on him, a stray car stopping next to him. he could see a woman rushing out, her coat wrapped tightly around her shoulders and a horrified look on her face. "are you okay?" she yelled over the loud wind, her red hair blowing everywhere. she held her phone in a shaky hand. when harry didn't answer, she came closer and knelt down. "i'm calling 911," she said softly into his ear, and harry was shivering too hard now to respond. he just stared, wide eyed into the sky, his vision blurred by the falling white snow, spiraling to the ground in uneven motions and jumping with the wind.

quiet, it was, except for the woman's breathing, her worried, heavy breathing that turned into a gasp when her eyes flickered up to harry's head. "you're going to be okay, i promise," she said. harry didn't quite believe her when he started coughing and he could taste blood, metallic and sharp in his mouth, and it started dribbling down his chin. he could hear louis over the phone, he was crying.

the woman picked up the phone. "hello?" she said, her head whipping back and forth as if searching for the ambulance would make it come faster. her voice, frantic as she gave directions to louis, faded out as harry blinked his eyes slowly, trying to see or feel something. he wasn't in pain anymore; he was just numb, clutching the woman who said her name was lindsey's arm and struggling to keep his breathing straight, but his lungs.. they weren't working. there was a deep weight on his chest, pushing hardly and causing him to choke every few seconds, and he couldn't lift his head up because the whipping of the car had hurt his neck. lindsey finally realised what harry was trying to do, and lifted his head up on her leg. she must have been cold to, sitting in the snow, and harry would tell her to go back to her car if he could talk.

soon there were sirens, illuminating the empty highway around them with red and blue, and lindsey was being taken away. harry didn't know her, but he wanted to thank her.

but he couldn't.

he only saw a glimpse of louis' face, streaked with tears and full of worry, before he was throwing up blood and an oxygen mask was place over his lips. it hurt too much to take a breath, though.

he fluttered his eyes closed, feeling a warm hand slip into his and squeeze tightly for just a second before he was loaded onto the ambulance.

then there was a needle pressing into his arm for just a second before everything went black.

***

maybe it was because i trusted him too much. or perhaps it was the wide-eyed look he gave me after i kissed him, or the second glance i failed to give whenever he left.

whatever it was was the reason for my guilt. for the burning guilt in my chest and stomach, for the physical ache in my heart. it was perhaps worse than someone coming in and tearing every part of me in half, seeing harry getting picked up out of the snow with a dazed look in his watery, half-open green eyes. there was blood on his face, but not just there, it was on his arm and his shirt and i wanted to wash it all away, to make him clean and okay again. i wanted him to be *okay*, to come home from wherever he drove off to and stumble into my arms like the clumsy little angel he was, and i could kiss his forehead and stand on his feet so i was taller than him and admire the curls on his head and the curve of his eyelashes. i could push my fingers in between his shoulder blades, my secret favorite place on him, because that's where his wings were, his invisible wings.

he was an angel, and although that thought caused a churning in my stomach now, he was. he was selfless, so caring and so unknowing of the terrible world he lived in. he just let it happen to him, thinking he deserved it but *crap*, he didn't, he didn't deserve any of the insulting comments he let just push him down until he was too weak to get up on his own. he deserved the world, more than i or even the kindest of the kind could give to him.

and i couldn't even see him. the nurse told me he had a collapsed lung, and a cut that needed staples on his head. he had a concussion, and he broke a lot of bones in his body.

basically, he was freaking wreck and it was all my fault.

i never knew i could cry so hard from someone else hurting. i used to be so selfish, only caring about my mum getting hurt and everybody else could get punched in the face and i wouldn't bat an eye. but harry, just the thought of him cringing in pain, of the fear in his chest and the knot in his throat when he was crashing; it was too much for me to bear. i would take his place in less than a heartbeat. i think what killed me the most was his face when he looked at me.

"is he going to be okay?" was what i heard behind me, and i saw niall, his blue eyes wide and his lip quivering. his blonde hair was a frazzled mess, as if he had just gotten back from a party. i didn't know what to say; i had heard that collapsed lungs could be fatal, because it cuts off air. it depends on how quickly you treat it. so i just shook my head, shrugging my shoulders, only able to look at the ground. if i moved my eyes it would let tears escape, and my eyes were stinging too much for that to happen.

soon, the blonde boy's arms were around me, squeezing tightly. hugs were the one things that made me break, that pushed down the dam of my emotions. i let out a choked sob and buried my head in his shoulder. he smelled like the cold air of outside, if only i could describe it. the tightening in my chest was utterly awful. "liam's coming, you know. he wants to know if you're okay."

i pushed back, furrowing my brows. "if *i'm* okay? what about harry? how does liam think *he* feels? he has a collapsed lung, niall! he couldn't even breathe out there-" i began, and smashed my lips together and squeezed my eyes shut as a shaky, overwhelming feeling of needing to cry came over me. i squeezed my fists together, sitting down on a nearby chair and ignoring the worried glance of the receptionist.

"louis," niall said softly, and i lifted my head as i saw zayn walk in slowly, his boots barely lifting off the floor and his shoulders hunched.

"how's harry?" zayn asked quietly, biting his lip, and his accent was so thick i could almost not hear what he said.

"i don't know," i whispered. "i don't know, okay? if i knew i wouldn't be in here! you guys are such idiots, stop asking me! i'm not a freaking nurse, i'm just louis. i'm just plain, boring, useless louis. get used to it."

never had i felt so pathetic, so empty because i couldn't do anything to help him, i couldn't even run my fingers through his soft curls and kiss his pale skin and tell him how much i cared about him, how much i loved him.

and when liam came in with anne, when i saw the tears of guilt in anne's eyes, that was where i couldn't handle it anymore. i pulled my knees up to my chest and sat in a chair, burying my face in my knees and letting the numbness take over my body, letting the unknown wash over me until i could know.

i just wanted to know.

sixty-one

i loved the way he breathed.

it was perhaps my favorite song, if i may say, to listen to. to place my hand on his chest and feel it rise and fall beneath my fingertips as he slept, his heartbeat strong and pure. i could hear the small breaths escape his lips and disappear into the air, into my ears where i would remember the sound forever. his breathing made part of me feel alive, as if whenever he let out a little whimper in his sleep or held his breath as he turned on his side i would feel it too. i loved to watch the way his mouth opened and closed, as if he was murmuring to himself in his sleep. i liked to grab his long fingers and find all the ways i could intertwine them with mine. i loved his fingers, they were the same ones that brushed across my cheek and jaw before we kissed and the ones that always managed to squeeze my hipbone before they cupped the small of my back gently.

his skin was softer than mine, although he always told me that i reminded him of dove soap. it was one of those things that he had in his mind, those final things that he always repeated. that was part of harry, repeating things and wanting them to remain the same. he told me that he never wanted me to change the way i make tea, and always to put my laundry into different piles. i liked to kiss him when he was saying those things.

and his chocolate curls. they were always so soft beneath my touch, slipping from my fingers every time i ran my hands through his hair. i loved the way the back of his head looked, when all of his curls were pushed forward and they poked out from behind his ears.

but i couldn't see the back of his head right now, because he was laying down, he was still sleeping, his lilac lids closed to reveal a curtain of dark coal lashes. there was an oxygen mask placed over his lips, fogging up every time he breathed. i hoped to god that he would be able to breathe on his own soon.

the doctor said only one person could visit at a time, and of course that meant anne got to go first. i hope she could feel my stare of pure resentment as my eyes followed her until she disappeared into the hallway. i was tempted to ask her where ross had went, if he had decided to become less of a coward and finally face the fact that the boy who he tore down, the boy he separated from his mother, was hurt. i hope he was guilty, that all the words he said left a burning feeling in his mouth, a churning feeling in his stomach like yesterday left mine.

the doctor said that his collapsed lung wasn't too late to be treated, and if he stayed on a ventilator long enough it would heal on its own. i bet niall was secretly laughing at me because of how hard i cried, how freaking wide i smiled when i knew. i knew he was going to be okay.

but then again, what is the definition of "okay?" i took it upon myself while anne was busy begging a sleeping angel for forgiveness to look it up on my phone. it said, "satisfactory but not exceptionally or especially good." and i wondered. would harry be okay with having broken ribs, a fractured wrist, and staples in his forehead? would he be okay with his mum finally visiting and realizing that there had to be a car accident for her to finally be there for him?

was he okay before the accident? i wouldn't know, i was too busy talking to mum on the phone to grab him by his arm and ask him. i wish i had, because maybe that would save him a lot of pain.

but now, here i was, trying to ignore the obvious presence of anne in the waiting room outside, and admiring the curve of harry's jaw and cheekbones. how could one be so beautiful, so breathtaking? yeah, anne was pretty and i had never met his dad, des, but i had never seen someone as perfect, prepossessing, as this boy laying down right here. there was a bandage covering the cut just below his hairline, and a blue cast on his wrist. and i knew that when he woke up it would be hard for him to breathe because his ribs were fractured.

i held his hand tightly in mine, jumping a bit when i heard footsteps behind me. i whipped my head around, surprised to see a doctor. it wasn't the doctor who had spent all night repairing harry, but a different one.

"where's the other doctor?" i asked. i looked at his name tag. dr. lucas.

he chuckled, running a hand down one of his forearms before stepping closer to me, pathetic little me who was kneeling beside harry's small bed. i held in a frown when anne came in, but felt a bit better when niall, liam, and zayn followed behind her.

"he took the night shift, i have the day shift," he explained, and i squeezed harry's limp hand tighter when anne walked closer. she looked tired, her hair frazzled and dark circles beneath her green eyes that looked so much like harry's. the little bit of pity in my stomach faded away as quickly as it came.

"so what are we going to do when he wakes up?" liam asked, his eyebrows furrowed. he looked at me worriedly, as if asking if i was okay. i nodded slightly, and he gave me a small smile.

"well, when he starts showing signs he is going to, i'm immediately going to inject some paracetamol into his iv along with some ibuprofen to bring down the inflammation of his ribs and wrist and also to bring down the pain he's going to be feeling. broken ribs take about four weeks to heal themselves, maybe longer for harry because he fractured his pretty bad. he's going to have a hard time breathing for a while, it's a bit like sharp pains, both in his ribs and his chest. but before i give him any anti-inflammatory pills i have a few questions i feel anne might have the answer to." i watched as niall gestured for him, liam, and zayn to leave.

i was going to protest, but i knew that anne probably knew more about his medical history than i.

"does harry have a history of stomach bleeding or ulcers, heart disease, high blood pressure, or kidney disease?"

i raised my eyebrows. whoa.

anne shook her head, looking at harry and her eyes were shining with tears.

"does he have asthma?"

this time i shook my head.

"okay, then i think he'll be fine when it comes to some ibuprofen. "

i nodded, not exactly sure what all of this meant but he was a doctor so he must be right.

"he needs to take it easy for a while, no activities that cause heavy breathing. his wrist, i've heard, has been broken before. but, i will still give you each a paper about how to treat it when he gets home from the hospital. we need to keep him here to ensure that his fractured ribs don't cause any damage to his internal organs, and also we need to make sure to avoid him getting pneumothorax, hemothorax, or a chest infection. louis, what is your relation to mr. styles?"

"boyfriend," i said, just as anne said, "friend."

dr. lucas blinked, sensing the awkwardness between the two of us. "okay. is he living with you?"

"yes, he is staying with me right now." i pointedly glared at anne. what made me really mad was how well she treated harry and i before ross came along. it was as if she completely changed. i began to wonder if that was her fault, ross', or both of theirs.

"i think it would be a good idea to bring some of his things over here so he isn't completely bored. he's going to be here for a week or so."

i sighed in relief. this whole time, i was thinking he was going to die, but he was going to be fine. a little beaten up, but alive. his heart was still beating, his lungs, although damaged, were still working. now all i needed was to see him open eyes, to watch the nervous way they always flickered around, filled with wonder and ambiguity.

it seemed as if dr. lucas read my mind, and he smiled. "don't worry, harry will be waking up in a few hours at the least. that gives you some time to go home, shower, eat, and take a bit of rest. i'm sure staying up all night wasn't pleasant."

i shrugged. "more pleasant than what harry went through."

anne stood up, brushing off her jeans as if there was something on them in the first place. she brushed her dark hair out of her face, meeting eyes with me for half a second before looking at dr. lucas. "thank you for this, for everything. i would thank the other doctor as well, but he's not here. you have no idea how much this means to me."

i narrowed my eyes at her. "stop lying," i murmured, but i secretly hoped that she heard me.

apparently she didn't; either that or she didn't want me to know that she did. dr. lucas followed her out the door, after shaking my hand and telling me he hoped harry would have a speedy recovery.

i hoped so too.

***

the smell of chicken noodle soup was quite overwhelming, especially since it was the first thing harry smelled when he woke up. he felt numb all over; he couldn't decide if that was a good thing or a bad thing.

"where am i?" he murmured to himself, knowing he wouldn't get a response. all he saw was white walls, a television, and a chair. oh, and the bowl of soup sitting on the table next to him.

then he made the mistake to take a deep breath, as he always did when he had just woken up. he felt a sharp pain in his lungs and ribs for a second before he was coughing, coughing so hard he couldn't breathe. he couldn't even do anything but widen his eyes when louis came rushing in, the louis he completely left behind.

"lou," he coughed, his eyes watering. "lou what's," he coughed loudly, "what's wro- ong, with me-"

"shh, shh baby stop talking. it'll make your chest hurt worse." harry continued to cough as louis put the little red button labeled nurse on the remote by his bed. soon, there was a nurse with her blonde hair pulled into a messy bun running in, her eyes filled with concern.

"is everything okay?" she asked, before she saw harry, who was bent over the bed, yet to get any relief from the constant coughing and his eyes were watering, partly from tears of pain.

she calmly came over, grabbing harry's arm gently and propping him up on the bed again. he was crying, struggling and wincing every time he coughed. "you need more pain medicine, baby," she said softly, kindly. louis immediately liked her. he watched as at first she put the oxygen mask over his lips, and a pillow behind his back, then injected some more pain medicine into his iv. "you're going to be coughing a bit, but it won't hurt as bad if you have some more paracetamol. i'm going to bring you an ice pack to help with the pain honey. just try to take deep breaths, you're coughing because your lungs are trying to clear the fluid." harry watched her with wide eyes, and louis reached his thumb over to brush a tear out from under his eye.

louis leaned in. "you're okay, angel," he whispered, before kissing his cheek. "you're okay."

the nurse, who's name tag read, "hannah, registered nurse," smiled. "yes he is. tell me if he starts coughing up blood."

she laughed as louis gasped.

"it's not a big deal, it happens all the time with patients with fractured ribs. it probably won't happen, as long as he keeps taking these pain killers and he doesn't move around too much. his right lung still is very weak, so if he's every having trouble breathing just hand him this oxygen mask. okay?"

louis forced a smile. "of course."

hannah leaned in, her lips touching louis' ear. "you better not kiss him too long; it can make him breathless."

louis blushed, watching hannah's playful smile as she winked at harry, patting his shoulder. "i'll go get you that ice pack. by the way, i'm going to be your nurse until you are released. harry, do you need some water?"

harry nodded quickly, and louis frowned. "i'll get it for him. i don't want him to wait."

"there's a water bottle in the small refrigerator. pour it in a cup and get a straw from the drawer over there. i'll go get you guys a menu so you have something to eat for dinner."

harry watched louis get the water for him, his hands moving delicately and gentle like always. the pain medicine was starting to kick in again, and he hesitantly took off his mask. he took a few doubtful, careful breaths and luckily didn't break into a hacking cough.

louis came over to him, handing him the water.

"harry, you have no idea how much i've missed you," he breathed, leaning in and kissing his temple.

harry smiled.

sixty-two

harry never knew how painful broken ribs were until he had them. it was like a knife pushing in between your sides and twisting every time you took a breath. luckily, whenever the pain got too severe, hannah would come in and inject some more pain killers into his iv. it was nice to have her there, even though he had just met her. she was one of those people that talked a lot, and harry was thankful for that, because he didn't talk much.

louis stayed at the hospital for the whole day, watching television with harry, telling him tons of childhood stories that were quite pointless, but harry loved to hear louis tell them, nonetheless. he loved the way louis told stories. he would always put a dramatic tone in his voice on the sad or scary parts, and whenever he got excited he would put wrap his fingers around harry's arm and squeeze tightly, unable to stop moving in his seat. he would run out of breath and laugh through a large smile and harry would just watch him, wide eyed, not smiling but not frowning, just watching. he would nod his head along with what louis was saying, his gaze steady on his face.

you would think that being in a hospital wouldn't be fun, but it was perhaps one of harry's favorite things in the world, being able to lay in bed and listen to louis talk without any distractions beside a slight ache in his sides and a few coughing fits. his collapsed lung was already healing, as he didn't need the oxygen mask anymore and he could breathe on his own without coughing for a long time.

but of course, louis had to leave sometime. he needed to shower, to sleep somewhere other than an arm chair. harry would have loved for him to sleep in his little twin sized bed, but there were too many things hooked up to him for that to be comfortable. so at about six thirty, hannah came in to give harry his nightly meds. she suggested that louis go home and get some rest, maybe take a break from the hospital. louis looked quite reluctant to leave, but harry nodded at him and let out a small cough before giving him a smile.

"yeah, lou," he murmured, clearing his throat and blinking quickly. hannah reached over and touched harry's shoulder.

"i've got this. he's an easy patient, if anything happens i promise i'll call you, okay?"

louis furrowed brows. "if anything happens? is something going to happen?" he stepped back, meeting eyes with harry before looking back at hannah.

harry went into another coughing fit just as hannah shook her head. hannah gently helped him put his oxygen mask on his face before looking back at lou. "no, louis. go home. i'm not trying to be mean but you're going to get sick of this hospital if you stay here all day."

harry glanced at him, slowly taking the mask off of his face as he felt his throat clear up, and then he looked outside. it was snowing, not so much that he couldn't see but it was. seeing the white snow caused his chest to tighten. the thought of louis driving in a car made him feel nervous, although louis had never gotten in an accident before. "be careful," he said softly, blinking over and over as if it would make the snow go away. his lips parted as he got distracted, distracted by the way the setting sun shone on the ground and pushed through the trees, causing a sparkle to reflect off the window. he loved the orange, pink glow to the sky, shining bright and pure through the falling white snowflakes. perhaps snow was one those things that could cause harry to feel a flutter in his heart, a beauty he could never quite understand, something that always made him stare in wonder.

he felt louis bury his nose in his neck, breathing deeply and whispering, "beautiful, isn't it?"

harry nodded, wide eyed.

"reminds me of you. i love you." louis kissed his jaw softly, hugging him around the waist while being careful not to tangle himself with his iv drip.

"i love you too," harry murmured gently, unable to tear his eyes out the window.

"bye, angel. just keep watching."

harry felt louis' fingers ghost across his cheekbone and nuzzle his hair before they were gone, disappearing along with his favorite person in the world.

***

"you have a visitor," hannah smiled the next day, carrying in a tray with some water, macaroni and cheese (at harry's request), and a spoon.

"louis?" harry perked up.

hannah shook her head with a sad smile. "but i think you'll be equally happy that it's your mum!"

she looked confused when harry frowned deeply, looking out the window. "why is *she* here?" he huffed. he flinched when hannah put the tray on the small table that she hooked over his bed, before placing her hand on his arm.

"what's wrong, harry?" she asked, concerned. he shrugged her hand off. just the thought of his mum made him want to cry. did she come visit him when he crashed? or did she just find out about him now? she probably didn't care, just wanted to say "i told you so," or something like that.

"is she allowed to come in here?" hannah asked quietly, respecting harry's space and stepping back. "you have the right to decline her. you're eighteen."

harry didn't move, just gulped thickly and tried to calm his racing heart. it just made it harder for him to breathe, and he didn't want to have another coughing fit. there were blisters on his throat. his head hurt quite a bit, stinging whenever hannah touched it with the ointment he had to put on it twice a day. he just couldn't wait until he got out of this hospital. yeah, he got more time with louis, but he literally sat in bed all day, he was going to until he didn't have the iv attached to him.

"harry. is your mum allowed in here?"

harry nodded, ever so slightly. "whatever," he muttered, reaching his hand up and running a hand through his curls.

"are you sure?" hannah asked.

"yes." harry clenched his teeth, and it hurt his jaw and his head but he was so angry, he was so angry with anne.

louis still wasn't ready to talk about the accident, the only thing he could really say was, "i thought i lost you." and when harry asked him more he said he wasn't ready, that it was too early to talk about it. harry thought it would be more of a traumatic experience for him, but he guessed not. he couldn't remember much, except for that red haired woman that helped him. louis claimed that he hadn't seen her, and that made harry so sad. he was disappointed; he wanted to talk to her, to thank her for everything she did. if it weren't for her he probably wouldn't be sitting in the hospital room.

anyway, louis hadn't said anything, and so harry knew nothing of his mum. he didn't know if she came right away or if this was her first time visiting. doncaster, being a couple of hours away, wasn't that hard to get to.

hannah had just left the room with his tray when anne came in. harry felt his heart skip for a moment. she looked different. her dark hair was longer, and she wasn't wearing makeup. harry hadn't seen her for a couple months, but it felt like a lifetime ago when they had sat down together and had an actual, kind conversation. he honestly didn't know what to say to her. he was never very good at sticking up for himself, and the longer he looked at her tired eyes the more his anger dissolved and sadness replaced it.

"harry," she breathed, walking towards him hesitantly. harry could see her struggling to keep her arms at her sides. why would she want to hug him? why would she want anything to do with him? he turned away from her, facing to the right where the window was. he had grown to really like the window, because if he stared at it long enough, the sky would shift colors as the day went on. cars would pull in and out of the parking lot, leaving muddy snow behind them that was soon going to be plowed up.

anne came a bit closer, and harry froze when she touched his shoulder, his shoulder that was covered by the horrific hospital gown he was handed after he changed out of his old clothes. what he wanted to do was take a shower, but he had too many stitches and again, he was hooked up to too many things. he still hadn't stood on his own. every time he moved too much it was hard to breathe.

"harry, i'm sorry."

i'm sorry. never had the words seem so hollow, so meaningless, but at the same time they caused an ache in harry's heart. they brought back memories, memories that he had in the car and memories that he had pushed out of his mind. but his mum was there, she was there and conscious and not leaving all the time to go off on some date. her attention was on him, and for the first time he wished it wasn't. he wanted her to go away, to take all of her problems with her and say her apologies to someone else, although this whole holiday harry had been thinking about her, she was always in the back of his mind. he loved anne, he loved his mum, and he couldn't see how someone that was so kind to him before could turn on him so suddenly.

"why are you here?" harry asked quietly, turning to look at anne. she was standing by his bed, her green eyes that looked so much like his were wide.

"i don't deserve to be here," she shook her head. "but i miss you harry. i miss you. and i can't believe it took a car accident to make me realise that but i love you so much. i know you hate ross but i love ross. but that doesn't mean i'll let him tear me away from you ever again. i don't care who you are, who you love. because you're my harry."

harry had mixed feelings about her small declaration. she loved him, but she loved ross. he was her harry, but that was incorrect. he was *louis'* harry. he was louis'. louis was his. anne was just his mother.

"how can you love ross?" harry asked, confused. "he's so mean to me, and i assume that means he is mean to you as well."

anne's eyes flickered to the ground, and she probably stared at harry's bowl of cheerios for a full minute before meeting eyes with harry again. he looked away awkwardly, the feeling of someone's eyes looking into his always hard for him. it used to not be with anne, but sadly, now it was.

"harry, how is your head feeling?" she asked warily, reaching her pale hand out to touch his forehead. harry was even paler than her. louis claimed that it was one of his favorite things about the younger boy, but harry disliked it. louis had this tan, warm, soft skin and he really just loved louis' skin.

"fine."

"how did you crash? did somebody run into you from behind?"

"i slipped. on the ice."

anne had opened her mouth to speak, when hannah came in. "mrs. styles?"

anne shook her head. "it's mrs. twist," she said politely.

"well, you came in quite late in the day and i'm afraid visiting hours are over."

anne nodded, leaning in to squeeze harry's arm, but he leaned away from her. "bye," she whispered, hurt flashing in her eyes.

harry didn't respond, but he raised his eyebrows at hannah when she closed the door. "since when were there visiting hours? louis sleeps in here all the time."

"there's not." hannah paused. "i just think you could use some sleep and i could tell you needed a break. i came in here to check your fluids, that's why i'm in here."

"i think i need to sleep," harry said, staring straight ahead. "tell louis i said i love him."

hannah smiled. "he's not here."

"tell him i love him," harry repeated, insistent.

"okay."

sixty-three

"why are you in here?"

harry eyes fluttered open at the hushed voice that came from behind him. he was wrapped in blankets, facing the window with an oxygen mask placed over his lips. he didn't like to sleep without it on because he would be constantly waking up when he needed to cough, to clear the fluid out of his healing collapsed lung.

he didn't move when he heard his mum's voice respond back to louis'.

"because harry is my son, and he's hurt." anne said, obviously offended. "i have more of a right to be here than you."

harry bit his lip to keep from speaking. anne was wrong, so wrong, and he wanted to defend louis and telling him that yes, he had the most right to be here out of anyone.

"i may not deserve harry, but i sure deserve him more than you. and keep your voice down, i don't want harry to wake up and miss some of the rest he needs, unlike you," louis huffed. harry could practically see him crossing his arms, giving his signature glare. harry moved his head a little on his pillow, and louis immediately came over to sit down next to him.

"really, why are you here?" louis asked, sitting on the bed and gently running his hand up harry's back before caressing his curls softly. "anne, honestly. do you know how much you hurt him? and me? i trusted you, i always thought you were so cool and accepting, when really, you leave when things get hard." his voice was low and angry, but his fingers were lightly squeezing harry's shoulder before he rested his hand in harry's curls. harry hoped louis wouldn't notice the goosebumps that went up and down his arms and the shiver that lightly shook his body. no, he wanted to hear what his mother really had to say.

"i care about harry, so much it hurts and i feel so bad-"

"anne, i don't want to yell, because i don't want to wake up harry, but you can't just freaking come back here like saying sorry is going to fix everything. guess what? it's not. it took me so long to get harry to trust me again, and even then i still don't deserve him. but at least i didn't sit around while he was getting abused."

it was quiet for a moment, the only noise the three people's breathing and the whir of the heater. hannah had come in and turned off the television, harry assumed. he had his eyes closed, and he wanted so badly to open them but decided that he could wait.

"you sat around." anne said. "you sat around while he was getting abused."

the bed lifted as louis stood up. harry knew he was mad; he recognized his heavy breathing. "don't say that. i didn't sit around, anne."

"you left harry when he was abusing himself, louis. do you think i didn't see his wrists, or the razors he left on the sink because he's too oblivious and never knows how to keep things secret? he can't hide things from me, he's an open book that can't read, louis. i could see how torn apart he was when you left him, i can read him clearly. but he takes everything literally and can't read people for the life of him! so i know, i know that what you did was just as bad as what i did, because i can tell. you ruined him. you ruined my son."

harry was already shaking with every word that escaped him mother's mouths, and he flinched when he heard a crash.

"don't you dare say that again," louis snapped, the anger in his voice growing with every second.

"he doesn't interact with anybody anymore. he just stares at things stupidly because he doesn't know how to be in love without being absolutely ridiculous. and i know he wasn't good at that before but now you've completely ruined him."

harry let out a choked sob, curling in on himself and biting on his knuckles to stay quiet. he pulled his knees up to his chest, shaking more and more with the blows his mum was giving him. yeah, it freaking hurt when his friends said that. but for his mum to call him stupid, ridiculous, ruined?

it stung, it burned.

"get out of here, anne! just get out, you freaking heartless-" louis began, when the door opened.

"what's going on in here?" it was hannah.

"get out!" louis screamed. he had lost his temper. harry broke into a coughing fit when all of the rushed breathing became too much for him.

"i'm going to have to ask both of you to leave. i'm sorry louis," hannah said quietly.

"hannah, no! i have to see harry! harry, angel, baby are you okay?" louis rushed over to harry, and harry whimpered when louis touched his arm.

"stop being mean to my mum," harry breathed out, flinching away from him.

"louis," hannah said, more firmly. "you need to go to the waiting room. *now.*" harry turned around and watched as louis kicked a chair into the wall as hard as he could, and he could see the pain flashing in his eyes and he wanted so badly to hug him, to comfort him.

it was weird how quickly the room could transition from loud and intense to calm and quiet. hannah was standing there, her hand on the doorknob as she watched louis disappear down the hallway while yelling things all the way.

"i brought you breakfast. i have good news. you're getting discharged in a few days, harry."

"i want louis."

"harry, you just told him to go away. i think it would be best if you calmed down and ate some of your cheerios."

harry wiped the tears off of his cheeks, and he felt like a child as he looked up at hannah with his green eyes wide. "i want louis," he repeated.

"please, eat your breakfast first." hannah put the tray on his lap, and harry glared at her before pouting and looking at his bowl of cheerios. it had too much milk, and he couldn't eat it.

"i can't eat this," harry murmured. "too much milk."

"harry, it's fine. it's not going to hurt you."

"there's too much milk!" he said louder, pushing the tray off of his lap. "and my socks aren't white and i'm not brushing my teeth with crest toothpaste and i'm not wearing my boots and louis isn't happy and i'm not wearing my black jeans and i'm not waking up at six o'clock and *i want to go home!*" he screamed, throwing the blankets off of his legs. "louis!" he yelled.

"harry, calm down," hannah said hurriedly, holding his arms and harry started crying when she pushed a button on her waistband. "please, take some deep breaths for me. we'll get you a new bowl of cheerios and it'll be okay."

"i just want louis," harry begged. "i want to sleep, please."

"harry, louis isn't here. okay?"

"no! it's not okay!" harry cried, struggling in hannah's grasp. "this room isn't clean!"

and then he started rambling, naming off all the things that weren't the way they were supposed to and how much it freaking bothered him and it seemed as if he had finally broken, because everyone breaks sometime, right? but hannah was asking for help and harry was screaming.

and he couldn't remember much after that, but louis was holding him and he could finally, finally calm down.

because everything didn't need to be perfect when louis was there.

***

"my head hurts," harry mumbled.

he still had a few weeks until he was getting his staples out, and also the stitches from a couple of the cuts throughout his whole body. basically, everything hurt and he couldn't do much about it but take some pain medicine and pray for it to be *stop hurting.*

"do you want to take a shower? i can put some waterproof bandages over your stitches and there's a bar in there and a shower seat so you can sit down," hannah said gently, changing her gloves before getting out a bottle of peroxide. "but first, we need to clean those cuts of yours."

"yeah, i want to take a shower," harry said shyly.

"okay, i'll get you some shampoo and soap." hannah put some cotton balls on the table next to her, unscrewing the lid of the peroxide and placing it right next to it. "what first?"

harry shrugged, before reaching his hand out. he had stitches going down his palm, and another set on his wrist. it was a cut that had already been there before, except this time it cut deeper.

she was putting the medicine on the cotton ball when louis walked in. "hi," louis said quietly. he met eyes with harry. "angel."

harry stared at him, the nerves in his stomach because of his soon encounter with the burning medicine suddenly washing away, melting away with the softness in louis' blue eyes. "hi louis," he whispered. he could see hannah smiling and looking between them but he honestly couldn't care, because louis' stare just pulled him away.

yeah, he was still mad at louis for talking about anne that way. he was also mad at anne, but she had done so much for him when he was little and he wouldn't let louis speak to her like that. then again, he wouldn't let anne speak to his favorite person in the world like that either. he was in a pickle.

"harry, prepare for some stinging. but it's going to hurt if it's going to heal. it needs to stay clean. okay?"

harry took a shaky breath and nodded. "okay."

"wait!" louis said just as she began lowering her soaked cotton ball to his hand. he knelt down on the floor and reached for harry's other hand. "squeeze my hand to distract you from the pain." he gave harry a soft kiss on his temple.

harry braced himself, and right when she put the cold liquid on his cut it burned, it burned so bad that he was afraid he would squeeze louis' hand off. louis looked upset.

"it's okay, just look at me," he whispered, his eyebrows furrowed. "this is killing me," he groaned when harry let out a little whimper.

"louis, it's okay. he's fine. right harry?"

harry gave a tiny, shaky smile. "yeah," he began, but immediately stopped talking when she put a new cotton ball on his head, the worst injury of them all.

hannah continuously apologised, and afterwards she dabbed each cut with gauze. "it's so important that you keep these dry. moisture softens the skin around the cut and increases the chance of a suture coming out, and that wouldn't be good. so if you happen to notice them getting wet, dab them with a clean towel." harry nodded.

"also, you need to clean these with soap and water every day," she paused, chuckling, "and i know that's ironic because i told you not to get them wet, but when you're cleaning them you do, although you have to dry them right afterwards. use warm water and regular soap, not the scented kind. change the bandage at least every five hours, and if you start to feel numbness, or tingling, you need to tell the doctor, or if it's while you're still here, you can just tell me."

she stood up for a second, getting a box out off the little cart she wheeled around. "i want you to watch me put these bandages on your hand, they look the same as the ones we're giving you, except these are waterproof. we're giving you both waterproof and regular."

as she was dressing each of his cuts, louis began speaking. "hannah, i'm sorry about how i acted yesterday. i get that way sometimes, and i'm sorry."

hannah shook her head, giving him a smile. "i don't hold grudges, louis. it's okay. i know what your intentions were." she looked at harry and poked his nose with her temporarily free left hand. "i just wanted to get this mister over here upset," she teased, her earrings jingling as she giggled.

"i'm sorry too," harry whispered.

hannah taped over the bandage on his hand and motioned for him to lean his head forward. "you," she said softly, "have nothing to be sorry for."

for some reason, this made harry blush, and his cheeks burned even more when louis squeezed his hand.

"okay, you can go in that bathroom." hannah motioned to the restroom a few steps away from them. "if you need help just put the red button on the wall."

"you're prepared," louis chuckled, but stopped laughing when he saw harry's cheeks flush light pink.

"louis, can you help me stand this tall twig up?" hannah smiled, and louis got up, nodding. first, they helped him pull his sheets to the foot of his bed, and then they both picked him up under his arms.

"i can walk," harry began to protest, but hannah and louis quickly shushed him.

"you can't be breathing heavy for a while," louis said, and hannah nodded.

and so they led him into the restroom, and louis and harry stared at each for a few seconds before harry shyly asked him, "can you help me?"

louis nodded, avoiding hannah's eyes and thanking her. "we've got it from here," he murmured.

hannah nodded. "remember. red button."

she shut the door to the room behind her, and louis also shut the door to the restroom. it was a small room, with white tiles on the floor and a set of towels. hannah had called for another nurse to bring him his things. there was a mini bottle of shampoo, green apple at harry's request. harry wondered if they had every single scent there was.

louis caressed harry's jaw lightly before unbuttoning his hospital gown, running his fingers between his shoulder blades, like always. his skin was soft and warm, burning beneath his fingers.

louis' touch was like a feather, and harry shivered, closing his eyes and biting his lip. louis leaned down and kissed his hair once more and then released his gown so it fell to the ground, pooling around his feet. when harry opened his eyes, he saw them both in the mirror, and he smiled softly, the sight making him weak at knees.

louis was hugging him around the waist, forehead rested on harry's shoulder. and harry just loved the way his messy bangs hung there, the honey color contrasting perfectly with harry's pale skin.

"hi," harry whispered, and louis shivered before responding.

"hello, angel."

and harry watched as louis first started the shower and checked the temperature before taking off his own clothes, then he pulled them both under the gentle stream of warm water.

louis kissed him softly before squeezing some shampoo on his hands. he rubbed it together and, being careful to avoid his forehead, massaged the bubbly shampoo into his curls, his fingers firm and gentle at the same time. harry went pliant against him, having to sit down when breathing began to hurt a bit. they were silent, quiet as louis washed his hair for him and helped him wash his body.

harry pretended not to shiver at times, but whenever it became a bit much louis would kiss it away and he could breathe again.

"are you still mad at me?" louis asked once he had towel dried harry's hair while avoiding his cuts.

and harry nodded, before leaning in and kissing him as light as a feather. "and i love you."

"i love you too."

harry didn't even pretend not to see the unbelievably happy smile on louis' face, his eyes lit up and he just looked like sunshine.

sixty-four

"we need to check on you before we release you, love," hannah smiled, before motioning for harry to sit up. "i'm going to listen to your lungs, and i know it's odd, but i need to see if you're breathing clearly." she pressed the cold stethoscope up to his chest, causing him to shiver a bit.

"take a deep breath for me," she said softly, and harry took a quick glance at the door, his eyebrows furrowed, before he breathed deeply. ever since louis left he had been on edge, and on the verge of tears for no apparent reason. after they had gotten out of the shower, louis had kissed him deeply and hugged him to his chest, and then he started crying. harry didn't know what to do when he ran out.

"hannah?" harry asked, brushing his curls out of his face and letting her gently fold the covers off of his hospital bed, before placing them on the little cart she wheeled around with her. the room was incredibly warm, but harry shivered a bit when his legs came into contact with air for the second time that day. he was still in a hospital gown, despite his protests. hannah claimed it was easier to check up on him when he didn't have to take off his clothes or anything. he blushed when she said that.

"yes?" hannah questioned, gently taking harry's wrist in her small hands.

"why did louis leave me?"

she furrowed her brows, and harry bit his shaky lip as he tried to recall anything mean he could've done to the older boy. "what do you mean, why did he leave you? didn't he just, you know, take a shower with you a few hours ago?"

harry nodded. he let hannah work on unwrapping his bandage while he stared at the door, stared at the ground where louis had been walking earlier. why had he been crying? was it because he remembered something? harry was dying to know, but he was stuck in this hospital until hannah had finished his check up and the doctor gave him a release.

hannah sighed when she realised harry wasn't going to answer her question, and instead said, "your cuts are healing up nicely. the stitches should be ready to come out in a week or two. see this?" she held up a tube of what looked like polysporin. "put this on those cuts every time you change the bandage, and if there's any puss or yellowing or anything gross like that, call the doctor and we'll have you come in." they both turned when they heard the door creak.

it was the doctor. "hi harry," he said politely, taking his hand out of the pocket of his scrubs and revealing a shiny watch before shaking harry's hand. "how are you feeling?"

"okay," harry said quietly, staring at the little striped pattern on his hospital gown. hannah continued to gently dress his cuts, rubbing some ointment on them and then placing a bandage on it carefully, rubbing all the sticky ends to make sure it wouldn't fall off.

"how are you breathing?"

"okay," harry said again. "i can't take too deep of breaths, though, because it makes me cough," he said honestly.

"that'll be gone in a couple of days. i don't want you doing any exercise or physically exhausting activities for probably two, maybe three weeks, just to be safe. make sure you drink a lot of water, okay?"

harry nodded.

"well, it's been nice to meet you, harry. i want to see you next week, so we can get those stitches out and make sure your ribs and lungs are doing okay. don't wear tight clothes or wrap something around your waist, it's not good for it. they're still healing, so i don't want you to be walking much, and definitely not be bending over. do you have a job?"

harry frowned. he didn't have one. why did he not have a job? "no," he said, biting his lip.

"well, don't get one." dr. lucas laughed, signing his name on the paper he had been filling out and handing it to harry. "see you next week, mr. styles. hannah, can you help him carry his things out? hopefully, you have someone to drive you?"

harry looked worriedly at hannah, before nervously looking at dr. lucas. he was just about to say no when zayn came running in, breathing heavily. "i'm taking him home," zayn smiled, before waving at harry. harry smiled at the older boy, his presence making him feel a bit better.

"hi zayn," harry whispered quietly.

zayn nodded at him, looking hesitant for a second before pulling harry into a hug. "hi, harry," he said softly, placing one of his hands in his hair and the other gently around his waist. "are you okay?"

harry could feel himself crumbling beneath the boy, hugs always being his breaking point. so instead of speaking because he didn't know if he could due the knot in his throat and the weight in his chest, he just shook his head. zayn let out a sigh and hugged him tighter.

"i'm going to take you home. any special instructions?" zayn asked, not pulling back from the hug, and harry was grateful that he could hide his face in zayn's leather jacket. he smelled like cologne and cigarette smoke.

"we told him all. we'll give you a paper with extra things we might have missed and hannah will escort you to the receptionist so you can check out and get your next appointment time scheduled. nice to meet you zayn."

they left, zayn releasing harry as they followed hannah back to the front of the hospital. they got their next appointment time and a print out of the doctor's note, along with special directions about how harry can't work or drive for about three days. just as they were about to leave, harry stopped and turned around.

"hannah?" he asked shyly, and she looked back. harry held his arms out, and hannah smiled sheepishly, before accepting harry's hug. harry breathed in her smell, hand sanitizer and a bit of perfume, but then he was being released and back to his friend.

"let's go," zayn said gently, squeezing his shoulder quickly before they walked out of the hospital.

***

"anywhere you need to be?" zayn asked about ten minutes into their drive. he had just finished talking all about his christmas break, which he spent with his family. apparently niall had gone off to see his relatives in ireland, like his cousins, aunts, and uncles.

"not exactly," harry said warily. "i honestly don't know where i'm supposed to be."

"well, there's a week left of christmas break. do you want to stay at mine for a few days? niall's coming down to visit, he says he missed me too much." zayn let out a chuckle, letting the steering wheel rotate beneath his fingers as he finished a turn. "mum made like a billion sugar cookies, i swear there is no room to do anything in our kitchen, and it smells horribly like chocolate and sweets."

harry smiled slightly. "can i bring louis?" he asked warily.

zayn immediately nodded. "of course. i've missed him. i didn't get to talk to him much at the hospital." he paused. "do you want me to go pick him up at his flat or are you just going to call him?"

"can you call him?" harry suggested nervously, picking at his fingernails and staring at his lap.

zayn gave him a quick, questioning look, biting his lip, before looking back at the road. "sure," he said lightly, but harry could hear the confusion in his voice. of course he would be confused. louis and harry had been inseparable for harry's whole hospital stay, actually his whole christmas holiday. they were dating. yet harry was a bit scared to call the boy.

harry sat quietly in his seat, doing and undoing the buttons on his black coat. his hair had grown quite long, down to his shoulders again. louis had never told him what he preferred on the younger boy. his arms and legs were unbelievably pale, and so was his face, making his green eyes more vibrant than ever. he was wearing his light brown boots with his black jeans, along with a big baggy grey sweatshirt. he didn't want to wear tight long sleeves shirts one, because he didn't like them, and two, it would hurt to roll up his sleeves with all the cuts on his arms and hands.

harry looked at zayn. he couldn't help but notice, just like everyone that took the time to admire zayn, his unbelievably long eyelashes and pretty hazel eyes. harry was very jealous of zayn's godlike looks. he always managed to fix his hair into a perfect quiff, although now he had shaved the sides of his head and put the top part into a man bun. harry laughed quietly. man bun.

zayn was telling louis the same thing about coming down to visit him and niall at his mum's house. "yes, harry will be there." he rolled his eyes, but then he was furrowing his eyebrows, staring ahead at the road as he listened to louis speak.

"why are you crying?" he asked, and harry practically dived to the other side of the car when he heard those words when they escaped zayn's mouth.

"give me the phone," he begged, his eyebrows knitted together and his bottom lip trembling. he supposed that he looked like a child, staring at the phone with a worried look on his face, leaned over the center console. louis was crying. no, louis couldn't be crying. harry didn't like when louis cried.

zayn handed him the phone, giving him a warning look.

harry grabbed it, putting it up to his ear as quick as possible. "louis?"

the end was silent for a moment, before louis said, "harry."

"are you coming to zayn's?"

"yeah." louis cleared his throat. "yeah, i am."

"why," harry lowered his voice, "why are you crying?"

louis let out a watery laugh. "i tell you at zayn's." then he hung up.

harry looked at the phone, confused, before giving it back to zayn. "he's coming," harry said softly. he looked out the window. it wasn't snowing, but there was snow covering the ground thickly. there were bare trees scattered everywhere, but some of them were fallen to the ground, probably from the heavy winds they were having earlier. harry still loved thunderstorms as much as he did when he was little.

the two boys stayed silent for about the next half hour of the drive, both lost in their own thoughts. harry himself was tired, tired of laying down for so long, tired of doing nothing. he laid his head on the window, which was wet and a bit cold. it made him shiver.

"what do you want to be when you go to college?" zayn asked, breaking the silence.

"a psychologist," harry immediately responded after a long pause. "what about you?"

"i'm thinking of becoming an english teacher. maybe i can play water polo in college, too."

harry looked at him. "water polo? you're really good at that."

zayn laughed, shaking his head and blushing. "thanks, harry." he reached over and ruffled his hair. "so are you. you are a heck of a goalie."

"thanks," harry whispered.

***

"niall!"

harry walked through the front door to zayn's house, watching as his two best friends tackled each other in a sloppy embrace.

"zayn," niall breathed, twirling him around and burying his head in zayn's neck. harry stood in the doorway, smiling at the two fondly, when niall finally made contact with him. he smiled, he smiled really wide before walking towards harry. harry practically fell into niall's arms, letting the blonde boy hold him up and pushing his head against his chest.

"hi, h," niall whispered.

"hi niall," harry responded.

niall let out a yell when something shoved into harry from behind. "liam!" zayn screeched, in his odd accent that he used sometimes. niall released a dazed harry, who stumbled into a nearby wall before shaking his head. dizzy, he was.

"i brought cake!" liam shouted, so loud, and harry didn't mind but he also wondered why the three felt the need to yell everything. he laid his head against the wall, trying to steady his breathing when he felt a bit of pain in his chest. *no heavy breathing for the next few weeks.*

"harry, get your flat little arse over here," liam began, and was coming toward harry when the most beautiful boy harry had ever seen jumped onto liam's back, one hand fisted in the air and the other holding liam in a chokehold.

"who is this twat on my back?" liam exclaimed, smiling.

"louis," harry whispered. hugging his arms around himself as he watched louis greet his old best friend. liam leaned his head up and kissed louis on the cheek, which caused louis to burst into laughter. harry loved to watch him laugh. his eyes would crinkle up, his head thrown back. he loved how his fringe fell into his eyes and there was a rosy tint to his cheeks when he ran out of breath. and yeah, harry was tired, he was so tired, but he could just stand there and watch louis be happy forever. he was absolute sunshine, and harry had yet to figure out how he deserved someone as wonderful as louis william tomlinson.

and everything was silent, everything blurred around him and his friends laughs echoed into the background when louis finally met eyes with him. he smiled, before mouthing, "i love you." and harry felt weak at the knees as he watched louis turn back to liam and whisper something absolutely inappropriate about the way they were holding each other, and perhaps just knowing that they were all together and the fact that he had louis was enough for him.

sixty-five

"what are we celebrating?" louis finally asked when he jumped off liam's back, careful to avoid knocking over the cake in liam's hands. harry watched as he flicked his fluffy fringe out of his eyes, a move he had memorized by heart and sometimes did it himself because he was around louis so much.

"the fact that our own harry styles is okay. you are okay, right?" liam teased, running and tackling harry in a hug, burying his face in harry's neck and letting out a laugh. harry smiled and pushed his forehead into liam's shoulder.

"yeah, i'm okay," harry grinned.

he hugged liam for a few more seconds, before liam was getting pushed out of the way and louis replaced him, except this time harry was lifted up in the air and twirled around. he could tell louis was avoiding his ribs, instead holding him by his hips. harry let his head hang forward, resting his forehead on the top of louis' head so his curls hung in louis' face.

"angel angel angel," louis sung, putting him down and kissing his nose then his lips. "how is my harry on this windy day?"

harry furrowed his eyebrows and cleared his throat before asking quietly, "why were you crying on the phone?"

louis immediately stopped smiling, holding harry's worried stare for a second. "i'll tell you later." his voice was hoarse, and he let out a cough. this reminded harry of when louis told him about how his dad had lung cancer, and that scared him to death. *stop overthinking things, harry. he's probably still upset over the accident.*

"niall!" harry whipped around when he heard a female voice with an accent very similar to zayn's. he watched as niall was yanked into a hug.

"hi tricia," niall murmured. "nice to see you." he was smiling widely, hugging tricia tightly.

zayn watched them both fondly, and harry couldn't help but join in on the hug. he loved tricia, she was the one person that could make him feel better with good food and warm comforting hugs.

"hi, sunshine," tricia smiled, reaching over and kissing harry's cheek. "how are you, sweetie?"

"okay," harry responded, and then they were all going to the kitchen. tricia claimed that she had spent all day making the perfect dinner for all of the boys. harry believed her, it seemed like something she would do. the kitchen smelled amazing, and harry could see what zayn was saying when he saw all the homemade baked treats sitting on all the granite counters. all three of zayn's sisters were already sitting down. harry always had adored waliyha, she was fourteen years old, and the second youngest of zayn's sisters. doniya was the oldest, only a year older than zayn, and harry didn't like her very much because she always bossed harry around and she tried to teach him how to get a girl. the worst part was, she knew he was gay.

harry chuckled, although what he was thinking wasn't that funny. he watched waliyha blush when he waved at her. niall ran over and kissed each of their cheeks, and harry smiled as he looked at his second family. he actually had three families. well, if he counted his mum anymore. the other two were niall and louis' family, and zayn's family.

the dinner looked absolutely amazing. harry always thought himself a good cook until he saw what tricia could make. he sat down next to his boyfriend and niall as tricia served everyone's plates. she had made fried chicken with mashed potatoes and green beans. "thank you," harry murmured, when she gently put a plate in front of him.

"you're welcome, honey," zayn's mum said in her thick accent, and harry blushed.

"harry harry, always so polite." niall laughed and shook his head, and harry's cheeks flushed even redder than before.

"awe, look at him, he's blushing," doniya said, smiling, and louis reached over and grabbed his hand, gently intertwining their fingers, and it gave harry some kind of comfort.

except for the fact that louis' hand was shaking and sweaty. harry turned his head to look at him, his eyes wide and his eyebrows furrowed. louis didn't look back at him, just bit his lip and let out a small cough. harry continued to watch him as he ate, taking small louis-like bites and avoiding harry's intense stare.

niall was talking, telling everyone about his trip to ireland, and how nice it was to see his little cousins. he said that his nephew, theo, was his favorite little thing in the world. harry finally stopped staring at louis when tricia asked him a question.

"are you healing okay, sweetheart?" she looked absolutely worried as her eyes flickered over the bandage on harry's forehead and the other ones on his right wrist, which he was using to hold his fork. she couldn't see that he was having trouble breathing, but every time he took a breath he felt a bit of pain in his ribs. he hoped the constant ache would go away soon. whenever louis let out a cough, though, it made his chest hurt worse because *what was wrong with his sunshine?*

harry nodded. "yeah, just hurts a bit, is all."

"how long until you can drive and exercise again?"

"a few weeks," harry replied, clearing his throat before taking a bite of his chicken.

"well, i hope you feel better."

"thanks," harry gave her a warm smile, although he still found it hard to make eye contact with her. well, anyone besides his best friends and of course his louis.

he thought he was done being in the center of attention when waliyha spoke up. "harry, do you have a girlfriend?"

harry's heart sunk. he thought doniya was the only one that was going to do this to him. now waliyha, the girl who he taught how to ride a bike because her dad was gone and zayn still didn't know how? harry, niall, zayn, and waliyha used to go camping in zayn's backyard, and harry remembered that safaa was upset because she never got to go because she was too young and tricia wouldn't let her. growing up with zayn's sisters surely affected who harry was, because now he knew how to treat children and how to put on eyeliner and how to make a girl stop crying.

he also remembered that he used to have a lot more panic attacks when he was younger, and anne had to come over and take him home so he could calm down, and harry started to scream and cry when he realised that safaa was scared of him. doniya, being the bossy and mean older sister she was, used to tell always tell her friends about her annoying little brother and his friends.

basically, zayn's family was like harry's own, and when waliyha asked him that when she knew that he in fact liked boys, was a bit upsetting. either she forgot or she didn't *want* harry to be okay. she was only an eighth grader.

"no," harry said quietly, and he felt louis squeeze his hand. should he tell them? he didn't have much time to ponder the question when louis spoke up in his hoarse voice.

"he has a me." louis smiled.

the surprised looks on all of their faces scared harry, but when tricia smiled and let out a laugh, he knew it was going to be okay. "harry! why didn't you tell me?" she cried, brushing some hair out of her ear. she turned to zayn pinching his cheek. "or you, mister?"

"guess i just forgot," zayn chuckled, gently holding his mum's hand for a second before picking his fork up again. "but yeah, louis and harry are together."

harry avoided waliyha and doniya's eyes, and instead looked at safaa, who was grinning.

harry watched as louis winked at the little girl, who was only in sixth grade, and he didn't know his heart could go from so low to so high. he was so proud to be louis', and for louis to be his.

***

"niall, you're sleeping in zayn's bed like you used to." tricia paused. "i feel like you all are little boys again, having your little sleepovers. you used to keep me up all night, pretending to be robbers and tiptoeing louder than elephants." niall, zayn, and harry all looked at each other, grinning knowingly as they remembered.

"me and harry could sleep in the guest bedroom," louis suggested, meeting eyes with harry as if asking if it was okay.

"that's fine. liam, you sleep wherever you want, honey. i just want to let you know that zayn is like a wild animal in his sleep." niall nodded feverishly. "so you can sleep wherever. but please don't keep me up. i'm old now, boys. i need my beauty sleep."

they all laughed. "you are beautiful, mrs. malik." niall said, and tricia laughed and waved him off.

"good night." she hugged them all, before disappearing down the hall and leaving the five boys standing in zayn's room. it was quite warm, and harry was reminded just how much he loved zayn's room. it didn't have christmas lights like harry adored, but he had posters of some pretty cool bands and tons of soft bean bags and a queen sized bed, making his room feel extra cozy. there was a picture of zayn and niall on his nightstand, and then a picture of zayn and harry right next to it. they looked sixteen, and harry was surprised with how much older the other two looked. he thought that he looked about the same.

"so, do you guys want to do something?" liam asked, breaking the silence. harry looked at him, nodding slightly.

"let's play truth or dare!" niall screeched.

zayn groaned. "do you think we're in middle school?"

niall lightly punched zayn in the shoulder. "you're never too old to play truth or dare. me and dad played it by ourselves when we were camping once. it's not a child's game, trust me." he looked completely serious, and zayn and niall had a silent conversation that harry had grown used to seeing before zayn nodded and met eyes with harry. "okay?"

harry nodded, and louis did too. liam laughed loudly when niall made them all sit criss cross in the surface as he played some arctic monkeys on his phone.

"youngest first!" liam called, and harry frowned.

"hey, that's not fair," louis protested. harry blushed when louis gathered him into his arms, as if he was a doll, and he hugged him gently and pressed a tiny kiss to his temple. "i got your back, angel," he whispered.

"fine," niall stated, "oldest first."

louis sighed, causing the tips of harry's bangs to fly up a bit. "fine." he cleared his throat, coughing a bit, and harry frowned.

"truth or dare, tomlinson?" niall grinned.

"dare," louis said immediately. harry smiled at his louis. he was always so sassy, he even shook his hips a little, harry could tell because his head was on louis' lap.

niall let liam whisper something in his ear, and then zayn also told him what he thought niall should ask louis. they all looked at each for a second before niall smiled widely at louis. "i dare you to sing a song while dancing with a broom for two minutes."

louis let out a laugh, causing harry's head to lift up a bit off of his lap. "you guys have the worse dares," he chuckled.

he gave harry a quick kiss before gently lifting his curly head off of his lap, and zayn went to get louis a broom while louis tried to think of a song. he snapped his fingers and nodded when he thought of the song, and when zayn gave him the broom he immediately started dancing.

harry didn't think anyone understood how much he loved watching louis dance. louis dancing was perhaps the most beautiful thing in the world. for one thing, it was a package deal. he got to see his sunshine smile, he got to see his eyes crinkle up as he entertained himself, bouncing on his tiny little feet and sliding on his socks. harry loved the way the yellow light in zayn's room reflected off of his blue eyes as he dipped the broom, singing *hello, goodbye* by the beatles. harry was surprised at how raspy louis' voice was, but that made sense because of how hoarse he was all night long. and while niall, zayn, and liam were laughing their butts off at louis, harry just gazed at him through hooded lashes, feeling his chest tighten with this overwhelming feeling of love for this wonderful boy. and then he was jealous, because why couldn't he be the one being twirled around and held instead of that stupid broom?

zayn, being his best friend, could practically read his mind, and soon, he was being pushed to his feet and he stumbled towards his favorite person in the world, admiring him for a few seconds and listening to his beautiful singing voice.

louis eyes were closed, and he was really getting into the routine. but when harry stepped about a yard away from him he reached his arms out, dropping the broom and pulling harry to him. "angel," he said.

and they danced together, just like they were in their own little world, until louis broke into a coughing fit.

sixty-six

"are you okay?" harry rushed, unwrapping his arms from around louis' waist and gently placing his large hand on the boy's back.

"yeah," louis choked out, eyes watering. "yeah, harry, i'm fine." louis reached his hand behind and gently grabbed harry's, digging his small fingers into harry's palm. he looked so small, harry thought. it was odd, for louis to look so tiny, so vulnerable when harry himself was the smallest of them all. still, harry looked down into his blue eyes and brushed his fringe out of his face, running his finger along louis' cheekbones and caressing his jaw.

"do you want to keep playing?" harry whispered softly, leaning down and resting his forehead on louis' shoulder. louis was on his tiptoes now, his arms wrapped around harry so he could comfort harry too. harry let his fringe fall over his shoulder for just a second and he let his eyes flutter shut for a moment. "louis."

louis took a deep breath, and nodded. "yeah, yeah, i do. i'm okay." they both turned back to their friends. liam looked worried, staring at louis, but niall and zayn were making weird noises and pretending to kiss each other, mocking harry. harry rolled his eyes at them.

"let's continue then," louis said, grabbing harry's hand and pulling them both so they were sitting on the ground. he squinted his eyes, looking around the circle. niall was hiding behind zayn, as if his brother couldn't see him. it made harry smile.

"liam," louis finally decided, and liam pretended to cry.

"you have the worst dares," liam groaned, falling back and flailing his legs in the air like a child. louis laughed loudly.

"you know, you can choose truth, liam," zayn pointed out, before stuffing taking a sip of his glass of water. "i guarantee you louis isn't as good at those."

liam furrowed his eyebrows in thought, and harry looked at him wide eyed with excitement.

"truth," he finally sighed.

louis laughed, rubbing his hands together. harry raised his eyebrows, before reaching over and taking one of his hands silently. he quite loved louis' hands. he tried to ignore the knowing look zayn gave him. dumb zayn, and his dumb antics. always making fun of harry. harry chuckled to himself.

louis, who was about to say something, heard harry and smiled to himself and glanced at harry, meeting eyes with him and winking before turning back to liam, who was rolling on the floor for some unknown reason.

"have you ever fantasized about anyone in this specific bedroom?" louis asked, leaning back and crossing his arms. harry blushed at the question, even if it wasn't directed towards him. liam looked in thought. harry knew it was a sensible question. liam had been friends with zayn for two years, meaning he could've been in his room quite a bit. especially since tricia was always bugging zayn to have his friends over. harry sometimes thought she liked him just as much as zayn did.

harry knew liam had remembered something when he cringed in on himself, before shamefully looking at the floor. "yes," he said quietly, almost inaudible.

"what was that, liam?" zayn put a hand up to his ear, signaling him to speak louder.

"yes, okay? yes." liam's cheek flushed red, and niall seemed very interested in this answer, as he begged liam to tell him who it was about.

"that's two questions," liam shrugged. "anyway. zayn, truth or dare?"

zayn puffed out his chest, before pounding it like a gorilla. harry burst into laughter, and *wow* he really missed his best friends. "dare," zayn stuck out his bottom lip.

liam thought for a moment, but harry had a feeling he had already come up with the dare. "switch underwear with the person sitting next to you without leaving the room and without taking your pants off."

harry looked at him, biting his lip. what kind of dares did these people come up with?

zayn looked at harry, then at niall. "niall," he said.

then they both took about three minutes to wiggle their underwear through the leg holes of their pants and louis was dying of laughter as niall accidentally gave himself a wedgie. it was a long, awkward process and harry was cringing when they finally had switched underwear.

"that was great," liam leaned back and pretended to wipe sweat off his forehead. "wonderful." he clapped a few times.

"next question, little mate," louis smiled widely, pinching harry's cheek and using his sweetest voice. harry melted, blushing and trying not to be fond as he asked niall truth or dare.

"truth," niall said easily.

"what quality about the person sitting next to you do you dislike the most?" harry asked. was that lame? he hoped not.

niall looked at zayn, biting his lip and wincing. "i don't know, h. i don't want to hurt the poor boy's feelings."

harry shrugged.

"you can't chicken out, ni," louis protested. niall looked conflicted as he looked back and forth between his two friends, before he grabbed zayn's face.

"please don't get mad at me z," niall begged, and zayn waved him off.

"i guess... that he always sings naughty boy whenever we drive anywhere." niall groaned. "so good to finally get that off my chest." he flinched away when zayn punched his arm, and liam burst into laughter.

"i do not!" zayn cried, before looking at harry. "i don't sing naughty boy, right harry?"

harry shook his head, but quickly buried his face in his knees.

and harry felt happy for a while. because liam payne was laughing like a hyena and louis was holding him around the waist, giggling into his shoulder in between little kisses, and zayn and niall were bantering like idiots. the room was getting quite warm because of all the body heat, and harry hoped his next dare has something to do with taking his clothes off. it was louis asking him, after all.

"angel, truth or dare?" louis leaned back and looked at harry with a challenging look. harry pretended not to notice the subtle way he would cough and clear his throat but afterwards acted like it never even happened.

"dare," harry smiled.

"i dare you to use your best flirty voice and describe in detail sexual intercourse, and it's benefits." louis leaned forward. "and at the same time, give a striptease."

harry had never blushed so much it in his life. well, he probably had, but this was pretty bad. niall was cackling like the jerk he was, and harry glared at him menacingly. the blonde just laughed harder, clapping his hands and there were even little squeaky noises escaping in between laughs. was it that funny?

harry, being the awkward boy he was, fidgeted quite a bit and started out being very quiet before he got into this dare.

louis nodded at him encouragingly when he stood up, a bit shaky in his boots. *look at louis.* he told himself. *that's all you need to do, and you'll be fine.*

"sex," harry began, wiggling his eyebrows, and *wow* he was an idiot, "is very important. it is the process where a man pushes into another man, or into a woman. preferably a man though." he shook his head, squinting his eyes shut. he didn't sound flirty at all. he took his shirt off, and niall let out cat calls while louis just stared at him. and no, harry didn't fail to notice the way he bit his lip and his eyes got a bit glossier.

"it starts out when they're, you know, kissing." harry coughed. this would be so much easier if he could just make up something about his favorite bands. but no, he had to describe sex. he smiled cockily, before taking his belt off and snapping it with his hands, twirling it around his head and hitting his leg lightly with it and flinging it at louis. "and louis slowly takes off-" he paused. crap. he just said louis, instead of the boy. zayn was on the floor, snickering like a middle school boy in sex ed.

"takes off his shirt, and you run your hand over his beautiful curvy waist, feeling the warm skin beneath your fingertips." harry put his hands in his hair to slowly untie his headband, which was just a green bandana. "and then you, uh, you cup their cheek and tell them how much you love them."

"lame," liam coughed out, and louis reached over and slapped his cheek.

"and then they make love to you, and you kiss them the whole time because you love them." harry took the bandana in his hands and walked over to louis, wrapping it around his neck and gesturing for him to stand up. louis lightly patted his bum, and kissed him quickly.

"you're perfect," he murmured.

"how was it?"

"sexy, was what it was." louis leaned in. "you didn't take your pants off though."

harry's cheeks flushed, and he just pulled louis next to him.

"that was great," niall chuckled. "now stop acting like lovebirds, you're wasting time."

"niall," harry glared, "truth or dare?"

"dare," niall said, holding his hands up as harry smirked.

"kiss zayn."

the room was silent. the boys reactions were all different. harry was looking around worriedly, wondering if he went too far. louis and niall were having a quiet conversation with their eyes, and liam was staring at zayn, gauging *his* reaction. zayn, himself, was staring at the ground.

but then the blonde boy reached over and grabbed zayn's face, kissing him quickly but deeply. and harry felt his heart beat fast as he watched his lifelong friends kiss, it was quite a weird experience. he had no idea how he even came up with the dare, but he knew he didn't need to regret it when both of them laughed and pulled back, relieving the tension.

but liam, liam. harry had no idea what to say of his face. it made no sense, and he sucked at reading people.

"do you wanna play this tomorrow?" louis yawned, which then resulted in a horrible cough. "we're tired, and we still have quite a bit of time until your christmas holiday is over."

harry nodded, grabbing his shirt off the floor before grabbing his louis off the floor.

"let's go," harry said.

he was leaving when he got tackled in a hug. it was niall and zayn, both of his best friends.

"are you going to be okay?" zayn asked, ruffling his curls, but being careful to avoid the cuts on his wrists.

"yeah," harry said quietly.

"i love you," niall kissed harry's cheek, a sloppy wet kiss that zayn immediately wiped off with his sleeve.

"i love him more," zayn argued.

"oh." niall stepped back, before pulling zayn in a headlock. "no you don't."

zayn laughed, and wrestled him to the ground. then they were both wrestling and harry was caught up in watching them when louis grabbed him by the hand and dragged him to the guest bedroom. he shut the door behind them both, turning the light off and gently pushing harry onto the bed. the room smelled like clean sheets. harry could recall sleeping in here whenever zayn didn't want anybody to sleep in his room. a lot of the time he liked to be alone, and harry respected that. niall, on the other hand always tiptoed back into his room and harry would wake up and hear them snickering through the wall, most of the time watching youtube videos or telling pointless stories. harry would walk over and just listen. harry was snapped out of his memory when he heard louis sniffle.

"louis," harry said weakly as he struggled to see louis in the dark. for some reason, louis wouldn't let him turn the lights on.

he was crying.

"louis, are you okay?" harry asked again. his hands were shaky and sweaty as he stared at louis' silhouette pacing the floor. "louis, louis louis why are you crying?"

"harry," louis cried, hiccupping on his tears, and that was perhaps one of the most heartbreaking sounds harry had ever heard. louis walked over to him and pushed his face into harry's chest. harry furrowed his brows and kissed louis' fluffy head, and *gosh* he hoped his louis was okay.

"h-h-harry," louis choked out, "i have lung cancer."

sixty-seven

tears had never been one of harry's favorite things, especially when they were sad tears. they made his eyes sting and there was always a knot in his throat. perhaps they were necessary though, because he always felt a bit better after he cried a bit.

but this time, the weight on his chest wasn't going away, no matter how much he cried and hugged himself. louis had excused himself to go the restroom, unable to look harry in the eyes for more than a few seconds before he was locking himself in the room across the hall.

so, here harry was. laying on the guest bed, too weak to even lift the covers and crawl under them. alone, choking on his own sobs and letting out small whimpers and screams into his pillow, as if it would give him some kind of substance. but no, all it did was further the aching in his heart, intensify the chills that racked through his body. and harry was praying, pleading that louis would come in and comfort him, hold him even though the boy was broken too.

he cringed into himself when he heard the door open, and he started to thrash when he felt arms wrap around him tightly, holding him.

"get away! get off of me!" he screamed, choking as he struggled to breathe through his tears. the person kept their hold on harry though, and harry decided that he had never felt so miserable before, never felt so small than he did in that moment. zayn wiped his tears off his cheeks, although new ones formed a few seconds later. and niall followed in behind, wrapping his arms around harry, but not squeezing too tightly due to his healing ribs. harry began to sob harder when zayn kissed his cheek softly, whispering comforting words, although he had no idea what harry was so torn up about.

a few minutes later, after niall had calmed him by gently pushing his fingers through harry's curls and zayn had talked himself into silence, the door opened. harry didn't flinch, no; he pushed his head further into his pillow and squeezed his eyes shut as another stinging tear threatened to slip past.

zayn got up when louis whispered, "is he asleep?"

niall followed right behind him. "i think so. he's so upset. what happened?" he lowered his voice. "did you do something to him?" niall had always been so protective over harry.

"i guess you could say i did." the bed collapsed as louis sat down, and harry bit his lip as louis gently reached his hand up and put it under his shirt, tracing nonsensical patters on his hip bone with his warm fingers. that was perhaps one of harry's favorite things about louis; his soft, gentle touches that could calm harry down in just a few seconds. harry whimpered slightly into his pillow, but, luckily, the boys didn't hear him.

"what do you mean, you guess?" zayn asked quietly.

"i'm the reason he's like this." louis paused. "even if it's not my fault."

"what's going on?" niall asked.

"i'll tell you in the morning. right now i just need to go to bed, mates."

zayn let out a sigh. "do you honestly think niall and i can sleep after seeing our best friend like that, louis? you do realise we love him too, although in a different way? i care about him so much it hurts." as if to prove his point, zayn walked over and placed a hand on harry's cheek, and his hand was a lot more rough and cold than louis'. harry felt his broken heart melt a bit when he heard those words come from zayn's mouth.

louis moved a little on the bed when niall sat down as well. "lads." he paused, taking a shuddered breath, and harry knew just by the shakiness of his voice that he was trying so hard not to cry. and harry just wanted to tell him that it was okay to cry, it was okay to show emotion and be sad because this topic *deserved* tears.

harry almost let out a scream of surprise when louis gathered him into his arms by pulling him around the waist and into his chest. harry buried his face in louis' chest, biting his lip hardly as he struggled to hold in his sobs. he couldn't though, and he coughed a few times and his shoulders shook as he fell apart in his louis' arms.

louis kissed his temple softly before whispering in his ear. "i knew you were awake this whole time, angel."

harry blushed a bit, and it made his cheeks sting even more. and soon, louis was cuddling him and telling the other boys what happened. liam came in when he heard niall bang his fist on the wall. apparently liam was the kind of person that went to bed first, so he hadn't heard harry earlier.

"what happened?" liam rushed, running into the room. the only light was the lamp zayn had turned on, cascading a yellow glow throughout the whole room. all harry could see was black though, because he refused to move his face from louis' tummy. louis didn't mind though, just gently played with harry's hair and scratched his back underneath his shirt as he talked calmly. he wasn't calm the first time he said it, and harry liked it better that way. he didn't want them to be calm about it. he wanted to scream even louder, to cry even harder, if that was possible, or made any sense.

harry wished there was a way to block out noise without using your hands. he wished that he could just wish to not hear, and then he just.. *wouldn't*. but no, he had to hear for the third time his least favorite thing in the world. that louis had lung cancer. it hurt worse every time he said it, because it made it more real. and harry sure didn't want it to be real.

all of the other boy's reactions were different. zayn was silent. harry had never heard him so quiet, he was even quieter than harry himself. niall was mad, and liam was just absolutely heartbroken, and immediately started asking louis about what they were going to do about it.

"can we talk about it in the morning?" louis finally sighed, after he explained why the doctor had even had him tested for lung cancer. apparently he had noticed that louis was coughing and had a hoarse voice, and he was complaining about chest pains. why had harry not noticed that? why was he such a sucky boyfriend?

"yeah, yeah," liam said, and harry didn't fail to notice the crack in his voice.

and they slept. well, louis did. harry just cried.

***

"good morning!" tricia called the minute harry took a few tired stumbles into the kitchen, wrapped in a blanket, eyes drowsy and dark circles underneath them. the minute harry looked in the mirror he noticed the lilac color of his lids and his flushed cheeks, still tear stained from last night. never had he felt so miserable.

"good morning," he heard someone mumble behind him, before there were a pair of short arms snaking around his waist, picking him up off the ground and swinging him around for a few seconds.

"hi louis," harry whispered, not even pretending to smile when tricia let out a little squeal.

"i wish i could get a picture of this," she sighed happily, before turning back to the stove. "i'm making pancakes and bacon and some strawberries."

harry knew that before last night he would absolutely jump at the chance of eating anything that was made by zayn's mum, but now his stomach churned at the thought of eating anything. he tensed up a bit when she put a plate on the counter and gestured for him to sit down. "you look tired harry. did you not sleep well last night?"

he shook his head. "not really."

louis knew he didn't want to eat just by the way he played with his bacon, tearing off little pieces and spreading them around his plate. the older boy sat down next to him, graciously thanking zayn's mum when she gave him a plate as well, before looking back at harry. "angel, please eat," he said quietly, and *god* why was his voice so hoarse all of a sudden?

harry was distracted when zayn and liam walked in the kitchen as well. liam had a major case of bedhead and his eyes were half open. "morning, mrs. malik," he murmured, and zayn reached up and kissed her cheek.

"good morning, mum."

tricia looked around. "did i miss something? why are all of you so tired?" she narrowed her eyes. "did you stay up last night even though i told you not to?"

"you could say that," zayn said sadly, sitting down next to liam and resting his head on the other boy's shoulder. "yeah, you could say that," he repeated.

"well, you're lucky you didn't keep me awake, or i wouldn't be making you this delicious breakfast. do you like it harry?"

harry forced himself to take a bite of his bacon, and he wished it didn't taste so good. "yeah," he lied.

she smiled at him, and harry absolutely adored zayn's mum, he really did, but he just wanted her to go away. he actually wanted everyone to go away, even louis. he wanted to be alone, in his bedroom, preferably under his bed listening to ed sheeran or my chemical romance extremely loud. he wanted his mum to hug him and tell him that everything was going to be okay.

but here he was, sitting in zayn's kitchen as he watched liam and zayn talk quietly to each other and avoided looking at his boyfriend. louis and he hadn't properly talked since he found out, and he couldn't say that he wanted to talk to louis. he was afraid he would say something that hurt the older boy's feelings.

niall was still asleep. harry remembered when they were little and zayn and him would always walk around together outside or in the house and play games while they waited for the blonde boy to wake up. that's probably why harry was always closer to zayn, he just knew him more emotionally. harry loved niall to pieces though, and he knew that if he wanted somebody to protect him it would be niall.

there would be an awkward silence except for the fact that the girls came into the kitchen, one at a time, and tricia went on asking them how they slept. just that question could set two girls off for hours, they were always ones for conversation. harry did catch waliyha staring at liam a few times, though.

liam didn't look much different than a couple years ago. he still had a curly (not as curly as harry's hair though), honey fringe across his forehead and a bright smile. well, he wasn't smiling right now, but.

harry looked up with wide eyes when louis got up from the table, thanking zayn's mum once more for the breakfast before he was walking down the hallway and into the guest bedroom. harry looked around, nodding at the other boys and also thanking tricia before he followed behind the boy. he didn't have to walk faster, just took longer strides until he caught up with the shorter boy.

"louis," harry said softly. "louis."

louis turned around. "angel, c'mere," he sighed, putting his head down and letting his hair hang in his face. he held his hands out, and harry practically fell into them, breathing in the smell of louis for the millionth time. *wow* louis smelled amazing, and he would never get over it. he was so soft, so warm, and he just loved louis so much and he really didn't want to *lose* louis and louis was the reason he didn't act like a socially awkward idiot every second of the day and he couldn't live without louis, louis louis louis.

that seemed to be the only word that went through his head nowadays.

louis and harry sat in the bedroom for about ten minutes before all three of the other boys came in. niall didn't look at harry, just immediately walked up to his step brother and hugged him, hugged him so tight and the sight almost made harry cry, but he didn't cry because crying would just make everything worse.

and they were silent, quiet for a few minutes until louis finally spoke.

"i have one request."

harry looked at him.

"don't treat me any different. please, lads. that's all i ask."

and they nodded, but harry just stared at him.

sixty-eight

the next few days were... hard. louis apparently had a doctor's appointment on monday, which was in a couple of days. harry really wanted to come with him, but he had school that day. it was quite a disappointment.

but, today was friday. after two nights of truth or dare, the boys were growing tired of the game and decided to take a break. harry, actually, loved it, especially when the dares included him and louis. harry let out a chuckle.

he was standing in the guest bedroom, in front of the full length mirror. it was the afternoon and he was just now getting dressed. he had on a pair of black jeans with his black boots, and a long sleeve white button down, which he rolled up to his elbows, and a checkered blue and white bowtie. it was one of his favorite outfits, especially because of the memories that went along with it. he remembered shopping for it with louis, and wearing it on one of their many dates over christmas break. on his wrist was a silver watch that louis had bought him, and *why was everything incorporated with louis?*

harry frowned at himself, hugging his arms around his body and swaying back and forth, realizing how convincing his pouting face could be when he saw it in this mirror. his hair was swept forward, framing his pale face and curling below his ears and just above his eyebrow.

"harry."

harry smiled to himself and looked at the ground when he heard his voice. it had turned from wanting to fall on the ground sobbing to just smiling, because now he just wanted to appreciate him, he wanted to breathe every inch of him in without a care in the world.

"hi louis," he said quietly, adjusting his watch on his wrist.

the first thing he saw was louis hair, peeking over his own head as he stood on his tiptoes, placing a kiss to the back of harry's head. his small fingers brushed across the small of harry's back before sliding forward to hug around his tummy. harry leaned back into him, tilting his head back so it was laying on louis' shoulder. louis stepped forward so feet were on the outside of harry's, causing harry's bum to press against the front of louis.

"liam wants to go out to dinner with me tonight. says he misses talking to me. 's your fault, angel. you're hogging all my attention, and all you have to do is just stand there and look beautiful."

harry blushed deeply, turning around in louis' arms and letting louis rest his chin on the younger boy's shoulder. "i love you," he whispered, and just those words caused a dull ache in his chest.

instead of answering, louis leaned back and gently took harry's chin in his left hand, and cupped his jaw in the other. his pale blue eyes were still sparkling, his lips still moist and soft, his cheekbones still sharp and prominent. harry thought he was captivating, alluring, dazzling. when louis closed his eyes, the way he always did before he kissed harry, harry loved to watch how his eyelashes delicately brushed his cheekbones, because they were so, so long. harry lifted louis up on top of his boots and tangled his fingers in louis' honey fringe that he knew would be gone soon, and with his other hand he steadied louis by his waist.

and then louis was kissing him, tenderly, and every breath he took just pulled harry in more, entranced the younger boy more with his intriguing magic. he tasted like sugar cookies, and harry couldn't get enough of it. he pulled louis closer to him, wrapping both arms around his waist and holding their hips together. louis' black vans felt like feathers on top of harry's boots, and he was the perfect height. harry loved the way their foreheads touched and they now knew which way to tilt their heads and when, and they both kissed perfectly to match the other.

when harry finally pulled back, louis didn't jump up off his feet, just leaned back a little and looked at harry with heavy eyelids, biting his lip before releasing it.

"i have to go, li's waiting. don't have too much fun without me."

harry was prepared for louis to jump off and walk away, but he was caught off guard when he was tugged into a rushed hug, in which louis buried his face in harry's chest and squeezed him tightly. although it hurt his ribs a bit, it was worth it.

harry watched louis with wide eyes as he walked out of the room, dressed in his black jeans and harry's blue sweater.

and he was still staring at that same spot, lightly running his fingertips over his tingling lips, when niall and zayn came bursting through the door.

"harry!" zayn yelled, while niall just ran up and hugged him.

"hi guys," harry said. "what's up?"

"well, since liam is taking louis tonight, we're taking you. it's about time you guys separate for a while." niall frowned. "and it's been a wee bit, well, a lot bit, depressing seeing you stare at him all the time. we're all upset, but harry, you look as if he's died."

zayn cut in. "babes, he is in the first stages. it's not serious yet."

harry furrowed his eyebrows at them. "why are we talking about this?" he asked quietly.

niall and zayn met eyes, and it reminded harry of what his parents did when he was little. he sat down on the bed, putting his head down and laying his hands in his lap. he had on his rings, and the let out a little *clink* noise when he crossed his fingers. the room was quiet for a while, and harry didn't mind that his friends were having a silent conversation like they always did, ever since they were little, he just hoped that he could get a little more silence. it was unusual, because he hated the sound of himself thinking, but thinking about louis was better than talking about louis. and he also liked that instead of putting a lot of pressure on him by telling him everything, they slowly laid things on him so he could handle it better. he didn't want to be treated like a baby, but he really just didn't know how to handle things when they were all coming at him at once.

but apparently this wasn't them trying to decide to tell him something, just an agreement. harry knew by the way they nodded and smiled.

"we're taking you to dinner and then somewhere else that is a surprise."

harry narrowed his eyes. "where's that?" he asked.

"he said surprise, h," niall smiled, reaching over and ruffling harry's curls. "let's go. you're ready. so are we."

"has louis already left?" harry asked.

zayn rolled his eyes. "yes. him and liam are going to dinner. not where we're going to dinner."

harry just nodded, bouncing a bit on the bed before standing up. "let's go then."

***

"you guys know," zayn paused, looking around the table for emphasis, "mum got really offended when she found out we were all going out tonight. she asked me if you all were lying when you said you enjoyed her meals."

niall burst into laughter, and harry just smiled and shook his head.

"your mum is so funny," niall commented, before taking a bite of his fried chicken. harry wasn't very hungry, so he just occasionally stabbed his salad and ate it before putting his fork down. he'd rather listen to his friends talk.

he forgot how much he loved it. he loved to watch the way niall's eyebrows went crazy as he told them about his favorite movies, and he adored when zayn blushed because he said the word "like" too many times. he never could get enough of their stories, enough of their ridiculous moments where they acted like bigger dorks than even harry.

but, there came a time where they wanted that from him. and yeah, he lived just as much as them, but he didn't have as much to say. he felt like he was a boring person, even though his life was the opposite of boring.

"harry, what's your favorite movie?" zayn asked out of nowhere.

"the notebook." harry said.

niall looked like he wanted to laugh, but when he realised zayn was being serious he bit his lip and met eyes with harry.

zayn didn't say anything, just stared at him, and harry raised his eyebrows. "what? you already knew that, zayn."

"why?" zayn leaned in further, causing harry to laugh.

"because it's sad and ally and noah are cute together."

"have you watched it with louis?" niall questioned, putting his arm around zayn and leaning in so him and zayn's heads were touching.

"yes, why?" harry asked, exasperated.

"tell us the story behind it." zayn smiled at him, nodding in encouragement. harry shook his head when he realised what they were doing. they always did it when they were little. they asked him small questions with short answers until it led to a story, and they always made harry tell it.

harry *hated* telling stories. he hated being in the center of attention, and he always felt like whatever he said was lame and cheesy and unoriginal. of course, zayn and niall never said that, but why would they? they were his best friends.

"please," niall begged, holding his hands together in front of the younger boy's face. "for niall."

harry sighed, which resulted in both of the other two letting out whoops and clanking their forks on their plates.

"okay. fine. ehm, we were on the couch, eating, ehm, those curly things, yeah, uhm, noodles. macaroni and cheese. yeah, okay. so, i told louis to put the notebook in, because i had brought it with me when i came down to visit for fall break. louis let out a little scream, because, ehm, he apparently loves that movie. yeah. so, we watched it and we ended up, ehm, snogging on the couch. end of story."

zayn nodded approvingly while niall burst into hysterics, just like he always did when harry told stories. the curly headed boy had grown use to it, actually he grew quite fond of the way niall always spilled things on himself when he laughed. he tended to flail his arms and bury his head in his hands.

and then, the rest of the dinner they spent taking turns talking, while harry listened and sometimes commented his thoughts. zayn claimed that he loved harry's advice, that he listened to it more than he listened to niall's. harry was flattered when he found out.

***

"time to go to your surprise!" zayn called into the night air as they walked outside. they were greeted with sparkling darkness, with the whooshing of cars passing by and the voices of people on the sidewalk. it smelled of coffee and fast food. "niall, blind fold him."

"no!" harry protested.

niall didn't listen, though, and neither did zayn. he took the bandana that harry always carried in his back pocket or in his hair and whipped it around his head once, whooping like a cowboy and causing zayn to snort. then, he wrapped it around harry's head, covering his eyes. he could still hear clearly.

harry told them about his sister doing this game with him when he was little the whole time they were leading him to "his surprise." when they got there, niall ripped the bandana off of his head and zayn said a loud, "ta da!"

it wasn't what harry expected. it was a crafts shop, simple and sweet. on the counter was a black pack of pencils with a bow, and a tag with harry's name on it. harry walked towards it, looking around and making sure zayn and niall were with him.

"what is this?" harry smiled.

"new, pretty, perfect pencils. the ones you wanted when you were younger. when you *still drew*." zayn put emphasis on those two words, before scooting the box towards him. "you need to draw again."

"what should i draw?" harry asked.

"whatever you want."

sixty-nine

"thank you so much," harry murmured, looking at both of his friends and giving them a smile. "i can't wait to use them when i get home." and he wasn't lying. he didn't realise how much he missed drawing until zayn said that. he still had a sketchbook under his bed, half full of sketches. a lot of them weren't finished.

"speaking of home, we need to go before traffic gets bad." harry frowned, and looked at zayn questioningly when the dark haired boy shot niall an evil glare.

"no, niall," he said through his teeth, shaking his head slowly, and the blonde slapped his forehead.

"oh yeah," he chuckled, "i forgot. h, your surprise isn't over mate."

harry's eyes widened, and he held the pencils to his chest tightly, looking back and forth between zayn and niall. they were both smiling at him, like the cheesy friends they were. zayn reached out and took his pencils, slipping them into his bag, before meeting eyes with harry again. "let's go babes," he said.

"where are we going?" harry asked incredulously. "you just bought me these pencils, and they're the really expensive kind. it's okay, guys, we can go home."

niall shook his head, causing his blonde bangs to fall into his face. "nope, we've already planned it out. we have a few more surprises. c'mon, h, let's go to the car." niall grabbed his left arm, while a smiling zayn grabbed his left, and then they started skipping which meant harry had to skip also, but halfway to the car his ribs started hurting from the heavy breathing.

"okay," harry huffed, "let's stop."

niall didn't stop, just unlocked their arms and ran the rest of the way, the keys in his hand jingling loudly.

"i don't know when he decided that he could drive my car," zayn chuckled, walking besides harry and wrapping an arm around his waist. "but it's okay. he looks hot doing it."

harry stopped in his tracks, before tilting his down a bit to stare at zayn. "zayn," he said.

zayn looked at him, and if it wasn't so dark harry would really be able to tell if he was blushing. but he did know that he was smiling, by the way his crazy perfect teeth shone and his eyes crinkled up at the sides. harry leaned in to give him a hug right then, because he loved zayn.

they were on the sidewalk, a few more strides from the car, when niall yelled into the air, "let's go boys!" in his "female" voice, that he used quite a bit. he sounded a bit like his mum, maura.

"we're coming, grumpy pants," zayn yelled back, pulling harry harder down the sidewalk until they arrived at his car. niall scoffed.

"i'm not grumpy. we just have a time to meet."

again, zayn glared at niall, shaking his head.

"what are you guys talking about?" harry whined, stomping his foot on the pavement, but he stumbled a bit when the heel of his boot caught on the curb. this caused niall to laugh loudly, and zayn picked him up to put him in the backseat of the car, like a child.

"you can't handle walking, h," zayn chuckled, shaking his head, before climbing into the backseat of the car. niall went around into the driver's seat, pushing the key in the ignition, and the car shook a bit as it roared to life. harry frowned when he realised that they had completely ignored his question. oh well, he would find out later. maybe.

so he leaned back in zayn's leather seats, breathing deeply and letting the warm air in the vents relax his aching muscles. he had been up all day, because tricia made them do chores because they stayed there. she used to have niall and harry's names on the fridge with daily chores, because they were over there so much. harry liked it. it was routine, and he loved routine.

harry listened to niall and zayn's conversation in the front seat as they drove to the unknown destination, and an occasionally he would comment or tell them to turn up the music. zayn, of course, was listening to naughty boy, the thing niall said annoyed him. but niall was bobbing his head along with the song as he drove, laughing loudly whenever zayn said something funny.

"harry, what are you planning on doing for your birthday?" zayn called to the backseat, turning the volume of the music down a bit so he could hear the boy.

harry shrugged, before saying, "i don't know. i haven't really thought about it. i'll probably just eat cake and watch disney movies," he said honestly, twisting his ring around his finger over and over. he liked listening to the *whoosh* noises as they passed a car on the highway. it didn't scare him, although the doctor predicted it would. he wasn't afraid of cars. and he was so thankful that he wasn't. louis was, though.

"psht. boring," zayn deadpanned, and harry glared at him in the rear view mirror. "you need to do something fun, babes. your turning nineteen. it'll be the last of your teen years. it's bigger than turning twenty."

harry squinted his eyes. "i think twenty is a bigger deal," he said.

niall immediately shook his head. "no. it's not. you can ask louis. it's like asking the difference between a book and a movie."

harry furrowed his eyebrows. "a book," he said, just as zayn said a movie.

"duh, h, a movie. now, if you aren't going to plan something for yourself then me and zayn will." niall looked at zayn for a moment, wiggling his eyebrows before turning back to the road. "and you know how me and zayn's parties are."

harry shook his head. "i actually don't. when did you guys throw parties?"

"every friday, silly!" zayn laughed, and harry just stared at him in confusion.

"since when were our sleepovers parties?"

zayn just reached back and pat his cheek.

"we have arrived!" niall cried, pulling into a small parking lot. there were the christmas lights, and it was the coffee shop that harry used to visit all the time.. with louis.

harry looked at the building with wide eyes, and he couldn't stop smiling like a fool as zayn guided him out of the car and into niall's. why was niall's car here? he closed his eyes and sighed happily when he was finally sat down in the seat, though, because yes. this was where him and louis had spent the night a couple of days before christmas, and when harry first told louis that he loved him. he felt his lip start to shake as he thought about the moment, because they were so young.

"why did you take me here?" harry asked, trying to hide the fact that he was crying.

zayn laughed, pulling something from his back pocket. it was a folded piece of paper, with something written on it in sharpie. zayn handed it to him. "here babes," he said.

harry took it reluctantly, unfolding it to reveal louis' chicken scratch handwriting.

Harry Harry Harry, it read.

"louis louis louis," harry whispered, squeezing his eyes shut and holding the paper to his chest, squeezing it between his papers as he bit his lip tightly. he would always hold that fond memory in his heart. it was still in his sketchbook. wow, he just absolutely loved louis. he looked through the passenger window, and he watched the way the light twinkled, the same way they did more than a year ago. but the thing was, they weren't near as pretty when he couldn't see the way they reflected off of louis' pale blue eyes. niall and zayn laughing and teasing him as they tackled each other in the backseat was muffled in his ears as he looked wide eyed around the small area and just let his heart remember everything, remember the way he felt when that same night louis asked him to be his boyfriend.

but then he thought of louis now, and he almost began to sob, sitting there in niall's cold car, staring at the lights as they blurred due to his tears. he shivered a bit, licking the tears from his lips and tasting salt.

"c'mon, h, we're not done adventuring."

"yeah," harry choked out, "yeah okay. let's go."

and they walked back to the car. harry took small steps behind his two best friends as they continued to knock each other over the heads, before wrapping each other's arms around their waists. harry smiled when he saw it, sniffing a bit and blinking the last of his tears out of his eyes.

when they got in their heated car, zayn decided to drive this time, and niall complained about three minutes of their short drive.

"where are we going now?" harry asked. he wasn't sure why they were taking him to these places, but it was starting to tear his heart.

and tearing his heart was an understatement when they pulled in front of his house.

"why are we here?" harry asked, whipping his head back and forth in search of his mum's car. it wasn't there.

"no, harry, your mum isn't here. louis talked to her-"

"louis talked to her?!" harry asked incredulously. louis and anne hadn't been getting along well lately. well, neither had harry and anne.

"yeah," niall waved his hand, turning back to look at harry. "it's okay, mate. just trust us, yeah?"

harry nodded reluctantly, following them into his house. the minute he stepped in, he breathed in the smell that *god,* he had to admit, he missed so much. it brought new tears to his eyes, and he wanted to throw himself in a corner, roll into a ball, and cry. because this was home. this was his hiding place from the rest of the world when nobody was there. he only had to take a few long strides and he was in his bedroom, with his made bed and pictures of his friends and gemma and his mum, and his sketchbook and his extra clothes that weren't in his toothpaste. there was still a stain under his bed on the carpet from when he spilled his drink there, and the ring gemma gave him that he used to carry everywhere, except in his pocket. he was about to go in there, but zayn told him, "later. come here."

he pulled harry into his kitchen, right in front of the fridge. then, niall handed him another folded up note. harry raised an eyebrow in question, leaning against the fridge and crossing his ankles before taking the note from niall. he unwrapped it carefully, holding his breath as he awaited what it was going to say.

I want you.

and harry had to search all the way to the deep dark corners of his uncluttered mind for this memory, because it obviously meant something important to his louis. and then zayn cleared his throat and asked niall, "what would you like to drink niall?"

"a mountain dew," niall said loudly. zayn reached around harry and opened the fridge, before reaching in the fridge and tossing niall a mountain dew. he laughed when niall dropped it on the ground right after.

"what do you want louis?" zayn asked to the air, and harry froze, gripping the paper tighter in his hand, so tight that his fingernails dug into his palm.

"you," harry whispered, and he laid his head against the fridge roughly, closing his eyes. and then he smiled, letting a little laugh escape his lips as the feeling he had when louis first said that came over him. he was nervous, shocked, and so darn excited.

"get your sketchbook and let's get out of here. the darkness of this house is scaring me," zayn shuddered, and niall burst into laughter.

harry ran into his bedroom after tucking the note safely in his pocket. he fell down onto his bed, breathing in the smell of his blankets and himself and he never realised how much he missed home until now. he reached under his bed and grabbed his sketchbook, before getting his promise ring and exiting his room.

and then he left his mum a note saying he loved her.

"c'mon, let's go harry! we're not done here!" niall shouted from the car, starting the engine and bouncing in his seat. he had the music blaring, and harry was surprised zayn wasn't telling him to turn it down. he was the sensible one, and he knew that it could hurt his friend's speakers. but he didn't say anything.

they spent the whole car ride singing *thinking out loud* by ed sheeran at the top of their lungs, and harry found his voice cracked a bit because he was crying. but having all these memories was making him so emotional. he blushed when zayn complimented his voice for the millionth time.

"we're here!" niall screeched, taking a left turn before turning into the parking lot. harry looked up and saw the local mall. it closed quite late on fridays, so it was still open.

"let's go," zayn smiled.

harry looked at them in confusion, letting the two boys drag him out and across the parking lot as he let out little noises in protest. "zayn, niall. why are we here?" they didn't respond, just opened the doors for him and they walked inside. the minute the door shut, niall was running to the food court, zayn following not close behind.

harry fast-walked behind them, tripping a bit over every single thing he could trip over because he was just clumsy like that. people were looking at niall and zayn odd, who were arguing.

"this is the right one!" zayn said, sitting criss cross on top of a small square table and narrowing his eyes at niall.

"no, this one is. i'm positive. it has the green gum on the bottom like he showed us yesterday!"

"oh," zayn said, jumping off the table, and blushing. "yeah, you're right." he walked over to harry, who was standing there in his boots, lost. the mall was quite empty, due to it being about eight thirty, but people were watching them, nonetheless. harry shook his head, his mind in a jumble as he tried to decipher what the heck was going on.

zayn sat him down at the table niall was standing by, in a blue chair. and as harry looked around him, asking his best friends why they were torturing him like this, a wave washed over him. he recognized the trash cans a few feet away, and the auntie anne's that was visible. he recognized the tile pattern of the table and the bathrooms that he could go to if he walked straight long enough.

it was his and louis' first kiss.

and this time, he didn't burst into sobs. he just buried his head in his arms, his face burning with a blush although he wasn't embarrassed, and he was smiling so wide he thought his face would break. the memory made his heart beat faster, made his hands sweat with excitement and he felt like he was at the mall two years ago, a flustered mess. he heard niall talking quietly to zayn, and he seemed a bit more far away than before. harry jumped when the table moved, and the screeching of a chair moving hurt his ears a bit.

he lifted his head, and he almost turned into a pile of goo in his chair because louis was sitting there, sitting on top of his hands and giving him a huge closed mouth smile, causing his eyes to crinkle up, almost like they were closed. "hi angel," he said, before his face softened and his blue eyes were wide, and harry felt a pang in his heart as that beautiful blue color hit him, as if it was something physical.

"louis," harry smiled. "where's liam?"

louis jerked his head to the left as a gesture, and harry could see liam standing next to zayn and niall, showing them something on his phone.

"hi liam," harry waved, and liam waved back, but he was still looking at his phone.

"harry?" louis met eyes with the younger boy, leaning forward over the table. "do you know how much i love you?"

"i think so," harry said.

"i don't think you do."

"oh," harry laughed. "how much do you love me?"

"I was hoping you would ask that," louis grinned, and leaned in to kiss harry before beginning his speech. "i love you, harold angel baby styles. you are the reason i smile, you are the reason for my deepest happiness that i never thought i could find. i love watching the way you blush whenever i say anything, like you are now, and i love the way you push your fringe out of your face with two fingers. i love your nose, and your green eyes, and i love how shy you are. i love when you tell me stories, because you are the best story teller i have ever met." niall snorted, but it didn't snap harry out of his trance, not one bit. "you are the most beautiful person i have had the fortune of laying my eyes on. you manage to entrance every single person that sees you. niall and zayn treat you like a princess, because you are one, yet you don't demand anything, everybody just does stuff for you because you deserve it and you are so wonderful and humble and kind and unknowing of the power you have over people. more the power you have over me." louis paused, leaning in and brushing some curls out of harry's face.

"i love how you always bite your lip and you always forget what you are going to say, and i love that you laugh at everything i say even though it isn't funny, and i love the little stupid jokes you make under your breath that you don't think anyone can hear. i love your little boots and i especially loved how you used to always wear black high tops. i love your curls, and i love the way you smell. i love that you're my harry, and your flaws are perfect to me. i love you more than allie loves noah, and more than jack loves rose." louis lightly touched harry's nose, and his eyes closed for a moment and harry just took the time to first catch his breath he had been holding, and two to watch the way his eyelashes draped across his cheekbones.

"you're my angel." harry watched as louis took something out of his pocket, unwrapping it and holding it in front of harry's face. the first thing harry noticed was the drawing of an angel, with jagged lines and a stick figure body with a simple circle halo around its head.

Will you marry me?

and when harry read that, he about passed out. his knees were weak, and he was thankful he was sitting down. he could hear his heartbeat in his ears, and he could taste the tears before he knew he was crying.

"yes," he choked out, "yes yes yes."

there were many people surrounding the two now, about half of the people that were in the food court and of course niall, liam, and zayn. they cheered loudly, and louis got up out of his chair, coming around the small table to go to harry, who was still frozen in his chair, bawling his eyes out like a baby.

louis grabbed him kitten-style and lifted him up, twirling him around, and harry kissed him, saying "i love you" between kisses and laughing the whole time. everyone around him cheered and whistled as harry lifted louis up on top of his shoes just like they had that morning, and he kissed him harder and more passionately than he ever had before.

"i love you so much, harry," louis said against his lips, and then he hugged harry so tight that harry started to cry all over again.

seventy

"give him the ring! give him the ring!"

the chanting of everyone got louder and louder as other people in the mall joined in. harry usually would be embarrassed by his tear stained cheeks as he let out little happy whimpers into louis' shoulder, but at the moment he didn't care about anything else in the world except for the fact that louis and him were getting married. they were getting married and something happy was happening other than what they found out a few days ago.

he didn't let that sad thought cross his mind for more than a second, just kissed louis again and practically fell into his arms when his knees went weak. the words i love you were said so many times that the word echoed in his mind, and he just wanted louis to know how much cared for him.

louis wrapped an arm around his waist to hold him up and kissed his temple once more before taking his left hand and reaching into his jacket pocket. he came up with a small blue box, the perfect size box for a ring. harry was shaking as louis opened up the lid with his thumb, and it flipped up to reveal a beautiful silver ring, with small little diamonds embedded along it.

"put it on," harry whispered, biting his lip. louis unwrapped his arm around his lower back to take the ring out.

"look on the inside," louis said into his ear, handing the ring to harry. harry gently took it from him, squeezing it so tightly he thought he might drop it. his hands were shaking as he struggled to read the inside. and when he did read it, he started crying all over again.

a halo for my angel.

it was simple, but it was something louis would say to him, and it was the best thing that could've been engraved on the inside. louis took it from him gently, taking his left hand. harry watched with wide eyes as louis pushed the ring on his finger, and it slid on perfectly.

"i love it so much," harry breathed, holding his hand out before putting in on his cheek. he stared at louis in adoration and louis stared back just the same. zayn and niall were now beside him, shaking his shoulders and hugging him but everything was slow motion and silent as he looked into louis' eyes. they took him some place that he could never describe, a beautiful quiet place deep within his soul that absolutely pained him to be, it caused an ache in his chest and a knot in his throat and he would never want to be anywhere else in the world.

but soon louis was hugging liam, and liam was giving harry thumbs up over his back. people went back to their seats after saying their congratulations and life moved on, people moved on while harry was still stuck in the moment, still stuck in slow motion.

and there was no place he would rather be.

***

christmas holiday was finally over, which meant harry had to go back home and face the problem that was his mum. louis had to go back to uni and his football practices, which meant they wouldn't be seeing each other much anymore. but, harry promised to always drive down whenever he had an appointment with the doctor, which was tomorrow.

the house was dark and quiet when he arrived, walking through the entryway and into his room. he dropped his suitcase on the bed, unzipping it and beginning to unpack it. he folded every clean thing carefully (him and louis had did laundry before he left) and put it in its correct place. he made sure to make his bed back to perfection once he took his bag off the bed and put it in the top of his closet. after that, he changed into his pajamas and brushed his teeth.

it was six at night, which harry assumed meant his mum was working. he vaguely remembered anne telling him at the hospital that she had gotten a job as a waitress at the restaurant ross owned, and she said that she got tipped more than she ever could have imagined. for some reason, harry understood that. his mum was very beautiful, although she was slowly getting older and older, just like everyone around him.

harry was dreading the time where ross would come through the front door. harry thought his mum could do so much better. he had a very prominent jawline and a short forehead, with black hair that was way too long. he needed a haircut. the ocd part of harry wanted to take a pair of scissors and cut it himself. he had blue eyes and small lips, along with a very small nose. he was always dressed in his stupid leather jacket and a dark pair of jeans. nothing about him was attractive, nothing at all. well, maybe that was just because of his personality.

harry sighed and walked into his living room, plopping down on the couch and slipping on the pair of socks that he brought with him. he turned on the telly and changed the channel to say yes to the dress, a show that him and louis had grown quite obsessed with for some odd reason. over the holiday they had spent many snow days lazing on the couch, kissing occasionally while watching crappy tv shows. it was one of his favorite things in the world.

harry felt a tug in his heart as he thought about his boyfrien- wait, fiancée. louis was so far away. it had only been a few hours and he was already missing his company, already missing his small arms wrapped around his waist and his fluffy head on his chest. harry bit his lip and twisted the ring around his finger, and it took all of his self-control to not go back in his car and drive to doncaster.

he jumped when he heard a car door slam, reaching for the remote and turning off the television. he felt as if he needed to hide, although it was just his mum, but he didn't know where to go. so he decided to sit on the couch, putting his ring into the front pocket of his sweatshirt and crossing his legs. he played with the soft strings of his pajama pants and swallowed thickly, flinching every time he heard a footstep on the driveway. when the front door opened, his heart sped up.

"...and i almost slipped, ross. i really need you to shovel the driveway because i'm quite sick and i'll probably get worse if i'm out in the cold for a long time." anne's voice was tired, and she sounded congested. whenever harry heard ross' name he cringed in on himself.

"anne, i just picked you up at work and took you out to lunch. why are you always asking things of me?"

when they walked into the living room, their faces were different. harry avoided both of their eyes, squeezing a fist with his hand so tightly that his fingernails were digging into his palms. he bit his lip hardly, so hard that he could taste blood.

"harry," anne said, her eyes wide as she stood there in her big fluffy white coat, snow still in her hair. harry never had felt so vulnerable, with ross' hard stare on his face while he sat there in his pajama pants with his hair now very curly because of his recent haircut.

"hi mum," harry said quietly, his voice thick with some type of emotion. "christmas holiday is over, so i decided to come home. i need to go to school." he cleared his throat awkwardly as his mum, instead of responding, shook her head and stalked into the kitchen, leaving harry and ross alone.

harry honestly wanted nothing to do with the man, so he turned the television back on and turned the volume really high. he had just gotten into a show of spongebob while nervously glancing between the television and ross, who was standing there like a stone, when ross quickly came over and grabbed his hair.

"ow!" harry cried out, reaching his hand up to grab ross' and slap it away. he let go easily, letting out a little chuckle.

"you're such a complainer. your whining is worse than your mothers," he snapped, grabbing harry's head once more and slamming it against the back of the couch. harry felt tears come to his eyes and his heart started to hammer in his chest. was it bad that ross scared him?

"you don't know anything about my mother. she never complains," harry murmured to him, flinching away and standing up off the couch so he was far away from the taller man. "and neither do i."

his voice was shaky and he was sure that he sounded like an absolute coward, but he didn't care about that now. he just wanted ross to get out of his house.

ross had just started to walk towards him when anne came into the room. her eyes were partly closed and she looked absolutely miserable. harry just wanted to hug her and take all of her exhaustion away, to take away the bags under her eyes, and to fill her with happiness she had so many years ago, when harry was a little boy.

harry didn't have a good relationship with his dad, but anne always did. harry loved watching the way her eyes lit up whenever he got home, and she would fix her hair and put a huge smile on her face when she greeted him at the door. sometimes she was tired though because when he was little his panic attacks were a lot worse.

"sweetie, what do you want for breakfast tomorrow? i'll make you whatever you want."

harry tried to hide the surprise on his face but it was impossible. hearing her call him sweetie was a rarity in itself, and the way she forced a smile on her face caught him extremely off guard.

"i'm just eating cheerios. you know that," harry replied, taking every chance ross was looking at anne to step away.

"aren't you tired of those?" anne sighed. "it's all you eat."

"i know. that's all i want to eat," harry said.

"just try breaking your habits, harry. it's annoying."

harry glared at her. "no. i'm not 'breaking my habits', mum. do you not know me at all?"

this is when ross stepped in, and harry wanted to break down and yell at him because *wow*, he hated ross.

"you're a baby, harry. the whole world doesn't revolve around. you eat what we give you and do what we tell you and you like it," he growled, his voice gruff and stern.

"you're not my dad," harry said under his breath, and when ross put his hand up to his ear in a condescending way, asking for him to be louder, he almost lost it.

"you're not my dad, ross. you never will be my dad, i don't want you to be my dad!" his back hit the wall from stepping back as ross came closer to him. his eyes were full of anger, a sight harry hadn't seen in a long time. he was used to being around louis, who was so kind and gentle, and he just wanted to be back in his apartment, dancing to old music and drinking tea.

something that made harry even more upset was the fact that his mum was just standing there. she didn't look helpless, just as if she didn't care, as if she had given up on trying a very long time ago. harry looked at her with wide eyes, begging her to do something about the fact that ross was coming towards him.

ross was much taller than him and stronger. harry's arms weren't very muscular at all and even if he was strong he didn't have the emotional strength to hit anyone. so when ross grabbed his wrists and held his arms above his head against the wall, harry didn't flinch, just stared at his chest because he was too scared to look him in the eye.

"what did you say, faggot?" ross' breath was hot and smelled of coffee, and harry held his breath and closed his eyes. he wanted ross to go away, to leave him alone in his own house.

"you're. not. my. dad," harry whispered, keeping his eyes closed, and his breath caught when he felt a sharp, burning pain on his cheek, as ross used on hand to keep his wrists above his head and the other to hit him across the face. harry let out a gasp, and he was surprised when he heard his mother's voice over ross calling him awful names.

"ross! stop! stop hitting him!"

this only made ross hit him harder, punching both sides of his face back and forth, getting harder and harder. his knuckles made his cheek bruise and throb, and harry couldn't help but cry, but he kept silent. his vision blurred and went black for a second, though, when he was kneed between the legs.

he could barely bend over because his arms were above his head, so he just in the urge to throw up and groaned loudly.

he was kicked there again but then his mum was coming in, pulling ross away as she started to cry, begging for him to stop. harry was blinded by pain but the minute he saw ross slap his mum, he couldn't control himself. he grabbed ross around the waist and threw him against the wall, screaming the whole time and choking on his sobs.

"stop! stop stop stop stop stop!" he shouted, reaching to punch him in the stomach, but ross caught his hand and with his left he hit him once more in the face. harry could feel blood trickling from his nose and his face hurt so bad, but he couldn't stop.

everyone froze when harry's phone rang, and ross stared at him, as if daring him to get it. harry was breathing heavily, and they sat there for a few seconds before harry made a dash for his phone. ross chased after him but he got it before he could be stopped.

"hey angel, i miss you alre-"

"louis!" harry sobbed. "louis, please come to my house, ross is-"

he was cut off when ross grabbed the phone from his hand, throwing it on the couch and pushing harry into the armchair.

"go away," harry begged, cringing in on himself. he could hear louis yelling through the phone, and ross just ignored it.

"why are you here?" ross snapped. harry watched as anne walked out of the room, tears streaming down her face.

"because it's my house," harry retorted, sticking his hand in his pocket and twisting the ring in his hand. for some reason, when he felt the engraved words beneath his fingertips, it gave him courage, and that made his heart swell as he stared at ross.

but that courage could get him nowhere, nowhere but a peaceful place somewhere deep in his heart. he needed to leave, to put this behind him. so he turned around and stalked out, going to his room, slamming the door, and locking it. then, he called 999.

"hello?" the operator asked. harry could hear ross banging on his door, before going to anne's. he hoped to god anne was hiding somewhere.

"hi, there is someone at my house right now that is abusing me, and he's trespassing." harry recited his address to her, and she promised they would be sending police over as soon as possible.

and with that, harry tuned out the screams of ross and laid on his bed, closing his eyes and falling asleep. because for once, he honestly *didn't care.*

seventy-one

family.

that word would always mean the world to harry. no matter how bad things got, his family would always be first on his list, alongside louis. and they would be the people that he would protect over himself, even if they had done so much wrong to him. because that wasn't right, to not protect the people that knew you better than you knew yourself. that wasn't routine, to ignore it when your family was hurting.

harry remembered when he was about fourteen, gemma was walking to the bus stop with him. she hadn't learned how to drive yet, so they still rode the bus. she was in the phase where she completely ignored her younger brother, and she thought that her problems were too mature for him to understand. she was probably right. but harry still loved her, still loved to watch her straighten her hair in the bathroom in the morning like she always did. he loved that no matter how much they fought; he would still come down to an empty bowl with the box of cheerios sitting next to it. she knew not to pour it for him because there would sometimes be too much milk or not enough, and then it would result in a panic attack, which gemma did not know how to handle correctly.

and so, as they were crossing the street, a car was driving towards them, and gemma didn't see. so, she kept walking. harry automatically pushed her out of the way, and it resulted in him almost getting hit by the car. and while gemma was laughing and hugging him and thanking him, he was crying, sitting on the sidewalk and sobbing. it was the kind of person he was. because in that moment, he thought that his sister, his family, was going to be in pain, and that absolutely killed him.

gemma told him she loved him before he fell asleep, kissing his forehead after he had set his alarm to the perfect time. and he just smiled, hoping she could see it.

and now, he still would risk his life to protect his family. so when he was laying on his bed, his curls flattened out like a halo around his head and his ankles crossed, and he heard his mother scream, he didn't hesitate for a second when he jumped out of his bed.

"ross! please stop! you always do this!" she was yelling, and harry burst through his door, out into the hallway. he could see his mum, cowering against her closed bedroom door, as ross held her elbow tightly in one arm and hit her across the face with the other. she was crying, cringing away from him at every chance she got. harry let out yell and ran towards them, standing between the two and punching ross right in the jaw. he could feel his knuckles throbbing, the skin burning.

and when ross took his head and slammed it against the wall, he saw stars for a second and there was blood running down his face. ross had opened his stitches up again. he pushed out a few more punches, making sure to stay standing in front of his mother, before his head was pounding too much and his vision went blurry then black. he fell to the ground, hoping the sound of sirens would fill his ears soon.

and ross was continuing to kick him, saying the most disgusting words and calling him gay, and harry didn't know if he could last much longer before he passed out. but soon, the constant kicks against his stomach and back were gone, and ross was being pulled away.

harry could taste blood on his tongue, and the cut in his head was burning more than it was when he first got it. he let out a choked sob, curling in on himself. he could feel anne kneeling besides him, crying and apologising and telling him that everything was going to be okay.

but when harry finally had enough strength to lift his head and open his eyes, the sight was heartbreaking. louis was there. his louis. and he was screaming out a million curse words while slamming ross into the wall, punching him over and over. his blue eyes were wide, and harry could see from his position on the floor that he was shaking, shaking with anger, and this was louis. this was the louis that he had first met, the one that got angry very fast. but this was a reason, a legitimate reason, and harry couldn't find any reason to be mad at him as louis started crying, hitting ross continuously and losing energy and strength as he went on. ross had given up. he may have been stronger than harry, but not louis. it was probably because he lifted weights for football.

louis was leaning his head on the wall, biting his lip, his shoulders shaking as caught his breath. he was breathing incredibly hard, tears dripping off of his face. harry could see from here his red, bruised hand, and when he started to cough, harry knew things weren't good.

he was thankful when there were sirens, and anne was crying, and harry never knew that he would be in a situation like this one. he felt as if he were in a movie, and louis was his knight in shining armor. except for the fact that louis wasn't heroic, and he wasn't okay, he was coughing so hard he couldn't breathe. and harry wanted to do something, to tell him that it was okay, but he couldn't. and that absolutely killed him.

"he's never been this bad before," anne was saying, still hunched over his shoulder, running her fingers through his hair. "just wait a second honey, the police are coming, and we're going to take you to a hospital."

whenever she spoke, it caused a hammering in harry's head, and he cringed away from her soft but firm voice.

"i'm so sick of the bloody hospital," he said weakly, and anne let out a sad chuckle, before reaching down and kissing his cheek. the gesture was sweet, and it caught harry off guard, but he was too tired to do anything about it.

"are you ready to stand up?" anne looked at louis, who was currently groaning in pain, keeping his hand on his chest and wincing. his knees were shaking as he struggled to stay up while coughing at the same time. "louis, sweetheart, are you okay?"

sweetheart?

"he has lung cancer," harry said quietly, blinking the black dots that appeared in his vision away. he stumbled and bent over as anne helped him stand up, guiding him towards the entrance of their house. louis followed behind them, not leaning on anne, just taking heavy breaths and grimacing every few seconds.

anne let out a shocked gasp, looking at louis, who didn't say anything. well, even if he wanted to, harry didn't think he could. he met louis' gaze, staring into his watery blue eyes. louis looked very mad when he saw the cut on harry's forehead, but again, he didn't say anything.

ross was laying on the ground, groaning in pain, but harry couldn't find the strength to care.

about anything, actually.

***

"i think this is a bad sign," louis stated.

harry lifted his head to look at him. they were sitting on his couch, staring at each other and television, although the volume was turned off. harry had ice on his ribs, because they had just gotten worse due to ross' kicking. he still felt a sharp pain every time he breathed, but there was nothing the hospital could do for him other than tell him to take it easy and follow the same instructions he had before.

"what's a bad sign?" harry asked, twisting his shiny ring around his fingers. he and louis both had bandages on their knuckles, due to punching ross' *rock-hard* jaw. the police had taken him in, due to abuse, but they had not arrested him. he just had to stay there until they could make a decision. harry looked at the clock. it was twelve thirty at night.

"it's only been a few days of us being engaged and we're already having problems."

harry furrowed his brows, although it caused his head to hurt a bit. he had a mild concussion, and again, he had even more limitations on what he could do. basically, he was going to be a couch potato for a month and a half. "louis, *we're* not having problems. like, i love you."

"i love you," louis immediately replied.

"but this isn't a problem between us."

"i'm sorry i went all crazy earlier. but i saw ross hitting you and i completely lost it."

harry didn't respond, just looked at him and stared into his eyes, giving him a smile as if to say it was okay.

"speaking of that," louis said sadly, and harry could hear the disappointment in his voice. it worried him.

"what?" harry asked.

"i have to, ehm, i have to stop taking my medicine. my, ehm prozac."

harry's eyes widened. "are you serious?" he squeezed his ring tighter in his grip, the texture of the engraved words actually keeping him calm. "isn't that what keeps you from.. you know.. ehm.."

"from yelling at you every few seconds? yeah." louis scooted towards harry, before leaning in and touching their foreheads together. "harry, i need you to promise me something, okay love?"

harry cleared his throat. "y-yeah, any-anything," he stuttered.

"if i ever say something mean to you, especially if i say i don't love you or that something you do annoys me, please don't take it personally, or seriously. because i'm telling you now that i don't mean it. you mean the world to me harry, everything about you is perfect. so don't believe my insults. i don't mean them, angel."

"i'm scared," harry said honestly.

"of me?" louis asked incredulously.

"of everything," harry admitted. "i'm scared for you, i'm scared to go to school, i'm scared of what is going to happen with ross, i'm scared for mum, i'm scared for niall and zayn-'"

"niall and zayn?" louis asked curiously. "why are you scared for them, honey bun?"

"i think there's something going on between them that could ruin their friendship." harry frowned, staring at his phone, which was locked.

louis raised an eyebrow. "i saw that too. i don't think it'll ruin their friendship." he smiled. "my selfless little harry."

harry blushed, avoiding louis' intense gaze because it would only make his cheeks flush more. the room was dark and quiet, completely different than it was a few hours ago. anne was asleep in her bedroom. she was so exhausted she could barely even say good night before she was walking into her bedroom. harry understood. now that he was what ross could do, he realised that he must've been doing it this whole time. and that pained him to know, because that means he wasn't protecting his mother, who protected him his whole life. now he had louis, and she had no one.

"stop thinking so hard, harry," louis sighed, leaning back against the couch and gently taking harry's wrist. "stop thinking."

harry looked at him, biting his lip. "why should i?" he asked.

louis pressed a gentle kiss to his lips. "because you're sad. and i hate when you're sad. it makes me sad."

"what is there to be happy about?" harry asked weakly, his voice cracking as he lifted his hands into the air. "my mum has been getting abused. you have *lung cancer."*

"we're getting married, angel," louis said softly. "we're getting married and i'm going to be fine, we're going to be married and live our happily ever after, okay? you're going to be accepted into your dream college and become a psychologist like you've always wanted to be, and i'll play football and dedicate every goal to you, my fiancé."

and harry hoped to god that someday, that would come true.

seventy-two

"you all are off to a bad start. have you forgotten the classroom rules? because some of you need those to be refreshed in your brains. do you need that?"

harry kept his eyes on his paper, gently tapping his pencil on the edge of his desk. his curls weren't long enough to fall in his face anymore, so he could see the teacher staring at him with an odd expression. *don't look up,* he thought. *he'll look away after a while.*

and to be honest, harry had no idea why he was looking at him when he was the only one in there following the rules. everyone around him was talking about their christmas break. for one, he didn't want to talk about his. and two, he had no one to talk about it with rather than zayn and niall, and they weren't in his math class, because they were both a level up.

his technique of avoiding mr. thomas' gaze did not work one bit, because now he was walking towards harry, his eyebrows furrowed. harry wished he could read people, but he was completely blanking on what interest mr. thomas had in him.

"mr. styles." his voice was low. harry's face burned when he realised all of his classmates' eyes were on him. he didn't respond though, just stared at the carpet and tried to keep his breathing even. all of this attention on him was causing his heart to race and his hands to shake.

"harry. answer me." this caused everyone in the room to laugh, some nervous, some amused. harry gripped his desk, before biting his lip and looking at mr. thomas, as if saying *what?*

"let me see your left hand."

harry immediately yanked his hand off the desk as if it burned him, and stuck it in the pocket of the sweatshirt he was wearing. "why?" he asked defensively. he didn't know why he didn't want to show off his ring to everyone. maybe it was because they would all start talking about him, and the one thing he hated the most was being in the center of attention.

"okay, if you're going to talk to me that way, i'm going to make you do more than show me your hand. stand up." he gestured with his hand for harry to get up, and harry knew that he was on the verge of tears, he could feel the lump in the back of his throat and the burning behind his eyes.

"now go to the front of the classroom." harry's cheeks flushed an even deeper shade of red, and he took small steps with his boots towards the front. the carpet was stained with highlighters and pens. the room around him got hotter and hotter as he walked up to the board, and he felt himself start to sweat nervously. *louis, come here.*

"now i want you to tell the class the story of how you got that ring. i wasn't going to make you do that, i just wanted to see your ring, but now that you're being disrespectful that isn't an option anymore."

harry was shaking with anger and embarrassment. he was being asked to do the hardest task he could do.

"go on," mr. thomas nodded, which resulted in the snickers of his classmates. harry looked at the wall, unable to make eye contact with any of them.

"they proposed to me," he whispered, and mr. thomas cleared his throat before putting a hand behind his ear.

"*they proposed to me!*" harry yelled.

instead of getting mad, mr. thomas just nodded and encouraged him to go on.

"and they kissed me. and now we're getting married."

"do we know your fiancé?"

"no." harry shook his head back and forth as fast as he could.

"isn't it louis tomlinson?" somebody from the back of class, and harry stepped back, stung with betrayal, when he realised it was eleanor. she didn't seem to notice that he was upset with her, just smiled and waved at him. "i'm so happy for you two," she smiled.

he didn't even look at the faces of his classmates. "*leave me alone!*" he screamed, bursting into tears and running out of the room.

***

"why is everyone staring at us?" zayn asked, taking a bite of his chicken sandwich. niall, like always, wasn't in their lunch. zayn had sat them down at a table full of kids that harry knew were popular, but hadn't interacted with, not even once.

harry shrugged. it had already gotten around that harry stormed out of class. people treated him like a child and he was growing quite tired of it, especially when they asked him every question gently and flinched when he spoke up a little bit. beyond frustrating.

"hey, h, i was thinking about you, me, and- wait. what happened to your face?"

harry reached up and lightly ran his fingers over the bruise on his cheek. it wasn't that bad, most of his injuries were covered by his clothes and the stitches on his head were hidden by his hair. and of course, he had bracelets over the bandages on his wrists.

"nothing, why?" harry asked, trying to keep his voice steady.

zayn reached his hand out and ran a finger along his jawline, squinting his eyes in concentration. when he pulled back, his jaw was set and his arms crossed, and harry knew he had no way of getting out of this one.

"what. happened." zayn raised his eyebrows in expectation, and harry sighed deeply, taking a bite of his peanut butter and jelly and taking a sip of his mountain dew before he finally decided that he was going to try and muster up the courage to tell zayn what ross had did to him, did to louis.

"it happened when i came home," was all he ended up saying.

"harry, i don't think anne can-"

"it wasn't mum," harry interrupted, biting his lip. his lunch looked less appetizing every time an image of ross flashed across his mind, like a movie. he clenched his fists, the thought of louis getting hurt and breathing heavily angering him once more. he couldn't stand the thought of louis in pain. it physically hurt him, and he didn't care if that wasn't normal.

"then who was it?" zayn asked, incredulous.

"ross," harry whispered, staring at the table and crossing his hands in his lap. he was tired of talking about himself, he was tired of talking about ross, and *wow* he hated school. he hated everything about it. he had water polo afterwards, which meant that he didn't get to go straight home and take a much needed nap. louis had already gone back home, but of course not after giving harry a long goodbye kiss and a promise to visit as much as possible. his doctor's appointment was tomorrow, and harry didn't care that he was skipping school to go to it.

"where's he at now?" zayn asked, wrapping an arm around harry's shoulders comfortingly as the overwhelming feeling of being about to cry washed over harry.

"he's at the police station. we're not sure what's going to happen to him," harry said, and zayn opened his mouth to say something when harry felt someone's presence next to him as they sat down. he tensed up. taking a deep breath before looking to see who it was.

"oh. hi eleanor," harry said quietly. "what do you want?"

she looked taken aback. "i'm here to apologise," she said, looking away. "but if you want me to leave i-"

"no. it's fine."

zayn nodded in agreement. "why are you apologising?" he asked.

eleanor frowned. "because i said something in class that he didn't want anyone to know. i told everyone that him and louis were engaged.:"

zayn sat there for a moment, as if deep in thought. "harry, why don't you want people to know that you are engaged to louis? he's one of the best looking people ever, even i can say that."

"yeah he is," eleanor smiled, and harry glared at both of them.

"mine," he whispered, and eleanor smiled at him fondly while zayn burst into laughter.

"we know, harry. no need to bite."

harry blushed, smiling sheepishly. but he wasn't going to take it back. he would be lying if he said his heart didn't automatically clench when he heard anyone talk about his louis. louis was his, no matter what. and he had a ring on his finger to prove that. he looked at it and ran his finger over the diamonds, pressing his thumb hardly into the engraving as if it would give him some kind of substance.

"so then what happened, after you said that?" zayn asked, wrapping an arm around harry and squeezing his shoulder.

 eleanor met eyes with harry, frowning and looking confused as to whether she should say or not. but when she opened her mouth to talk, harry interrupted her.

"i told them to leave me alone and ran out," harry said quietly, tracing the letters on his can of mountain dew. it was cold against his finger, and the water got onto his finger. he watched it intently as it dripped down the side of his hand and onto his wrist. he titled his head as he watched it circle around his arm until it slowly disappeared and the water began to dry on his skin. he could vaguely hear zayn talking, but he was too distracted at the moment. the water brought memories.

it reminded him of the time him and louis and niall went swimming. niall spent the whole time going on the straight down water slide, although it made his back red and he had a headache from going into the water so fast. harry couldn't stop laughing when he couldn't see for a moment due to the fast motion.

louis and harry spent the whole time attempting to make up a dance in the water. louis would twirl him around, causing little waves to form around them. despite the fact that he was underwater, when they kissed, their hair floating around them as they held their breath, he felt utterly weightless.

he smiled at the thought, but was quickly snapped out of it when zayn started lightly hitting his cheek.

"what?" he asked, holding a hand over his cheek and frowning. zayn rolled his eyes.

"why aren't you listening to me? i was trying to give you a pep talk, babes."

eleanor leaned forward. "he was telling you all about how not to listen to the haters. it was a good pep talk harry."

harry shrugged. "school's almost over anyway," he said.

zayn put a hand over his mouth, gasping. "oh my god, harry, that's right. harry, eleanor, this is one of the last times we're going to eat in this cafeteria." at the sound of his surprise, a couple of the people at the table looked at them.

"and the last time i'm going to have to protect harry from the bad guys!" zayn complained.

eleanor laughed. "awe, you guys are you cute!"

"well, really, that used to be me and niall's job. and then louis turned from a bad guy to completely fawning over him and now he doesn't need us anymore," zayn frowned.

harry buried his face in zayn's shoulder, ignoring the snorts from the people beside them. "i need you a lot," he said truthfully, breathing in the wonderful smell that was zayn. whenever he felt zayn's warm hand on his waist he was immediately comforted.

"he seems a bit mental," someone commented, and for once, harry just ignored it.

and by ignoring it, he motioned for zayn to follow him and he got up and walked away.

there was only so much he could take.

***

"how was your first day back at school?" louis' face was blurry as he moved back and forth on the screen, adjusting his position on his bed so that his elbow was holding him up.

"it was okay," harry said, and he felt his heart ache as he stared at the gritty image of louis, as he watched how louis' blue eyes never managed to be hidden, even by a bad quality camera. the minute harry appeared on the screen he was smiling, his sunshine smile. "better now," he said honestly.

"what happened?" louis furrowed his eyebrows. "what did they say?"

and harry almost burst into tears right there, because louis could read him even over the crappy signal of their laptops.

"the same things," harry murmured, a knot in his throat. "about me being mental and that."

louis sighed deeply. "you know what, i guess we are mental. both of us."

harry's eyes widened. "what do you mean?"

"it seems the normal is being complete dickheads. and you're the kindest angel i've ever seen in my entire life. so yeah, you're mental in that way, because your different, even though it's in the best kind of way. and i'm mental because i have to take tons of pills every day and i used to snap at you all the time."

"not anymore," harry smiled.

"but soon," louis said sadly.

"how was football practice?" harry asked, changing the subject because he was growing sadder and sadder as the conversation went on.

but it was not the right kind of question. because that's when louis squeezed his eyes shut, biting his lip, and harry knew that something he said had made the boy cry. he let out shuddered breath as he struggled to compose himself, and it broke harry's heart.

"harry, i can't play football anymore. i have lung cancer, remember?"

harry fell back on his pillow, sighing deeply as regret washed over him. "i'm so sorry," he whispered. "i'm so so sorry."

louis looked at him. "i'm not perfect, but i have you."

seventy-three

harry awoke the next morning with his laptop under his pillow, his blankets tangled by his ankles. he took in a deep breath through his nose, squeezing his eyes shut for a moment as he yawned quietly. it wasn't that cold, which was surprising for january.

it was six, of course, and he had school one more day until the weekend. he could get through it.

the first thing he did was put on a pair of sweatpants, a sweatshirt, and his running tennis shoes. he hadn't gotten around to running, but it was a hobby he was going to pick up if he wanted to stay in shape. he ran his fingers through his curls and brushed his teeth before walking into the kitchen.

his mum was there, sitting at the table, alone. her dark brown hair pulled into a ponytail with her bangs hanging in her face. harry could see the visible bruise on her left cheek, and it hurt his heart.

harry hesitantly walked towards her, taking a deep breath and sitting down across from her. "good morning," he said quietly.

she lifted her head, before smiling softly and pushing a bowl full of cheerios towards him. "i poured you some cheerios." she then motioned her head to the gallon of milk on the table. "there's some milk, sweets."

"like gemma," harry whispered, before smiling at his mum. she had no idea how much he appreciated her doing that, since a few days before she was saying that his habits were annoying. "thank you mum."

"of course, harry." she blew her bangs out of her face, leaning back in her chair. "i usually don't get up this early. i don't see how you do it every morning. i could use a few more hours."

"then why'd you get up?" harry asked curiously. "not that it's bad, i'm just wondering." he poured some milk into his cheerios, careful to get it to the perfect amount. then he took the spoon sitting next to his bowl and pushed the cheerios so they were all covered in milk.

"i wanted to talk to my little boy."

harry blushed. "i'm not little, mum. i'm turning nineteen in a month."

anne looked like she was about to cry. and it turned out she was. her lip quivered for a bit before she buried her face in her arms, her shoulders shaking as a small sob escaped her lips. it took all of harry not to cry with her, because seeing others upset was his weak spot, especially if it was his mother.

"mum, mum what's wrong?" harry asked worriedly, getting up in his seat and going behind her, laying his body across her back and wrapping his arms around her waist in an awkward but comforting hug. "did i say something?"

she took a deep breath and lifted her head, harry went back to where he was sitting. her eyes were watering, and she pushed her bangs out of her face as she tried to compose herself so she didn't look so sad.

"you're almost nineteen and i feel like i've missed it all. i've missed all those years." she looked away. "i didn't even celebrate your eighteenth birthday. how awful of a mother am i? i just miss when you were my little baby boy, when i could just hold you in my arms and rock you back and forth when you were crying."

harry felt a wave of sadness and emptiness wash over him at that sentence. was it bad that he missed it too? he missed having to go to his mum for all of his problems, he missed coming home from school every day with his problems and letting her rock him back and forth in her arms. he missed baking cookies with her and his dad when he was little and eating half of the cookie dough. he missed being that little blonde boy who wore cargo shorts, power ranger shirts, and a stupid newsboy cap.

anne bit her lip. "is it bad that i miss your father?"

harry shook his head before pausing, and nodding. "a little." he took a bite of his cheerios and shrugged his shoulders.

anne rested her cheek in her hand. "i guess i just miss when we were a happy family, harry."

and all harry could do was sigh, because yeah, he did too.

***

"guess what babe? it's friday. which means-"

"no school tomorrow!" niall, liam, zayn, and harry all yelled in unison. harry smiled to himself, looking at the boys that were all lounging around niall's room, snacking on whatever they could find in the kitchen. liam had a bag of chips, zayn some leftover cake, and niall a king size bag of sour patch kids.

all harry had was his laptop, gazing at louis' face and trying not to look too fond.

"and guess what else it means?"

"what?" harry asked, furrowing his eyebrows.

"you're coming to my doctor's appointment tomorrow."

"wasn't that supposed to be today?"

louis frowned. "yeah, i had to cancel because i got snowed in."

"what do you mean?" harry asked, quickly looking out the window. "it's beautiful outside."

niall snorted. "right. *beautiful.*"

harry turned to glare at him. "it is."

louis cleared his throat. "either way, you're coming to the doctor's with me tomorrow morning, i don't care if niall was planning on taking you guys to a movie. because nobody goes out without me."

"oh you watch us lou!" liam yelled, laughing loudly and stuffing some more chips in his mouth. harry wasn't sure what he was doing. it was something on his phone that made him scream in rage all the time. harry didn't understand why people liked to play games that angered them. i mean, why waste your time doing that when you could be face timing a beautiful blue eyed boy with hair like feathers and a smile like the sun?

"i talked to my mum today. like i really talked to her," harry said nervously. niall and zayn looked up, probably confused with him offering to talk about something about *him.* either that or they wanted to know what happened. harry didn't care. they shouldn't be surprised. it was louis.

"i'm so proud of you," louis said gently, smiling at him and looking to the side before meeting harry's eyes. "so freaking proud of you."

harry blushed, but he didn't tear his gaze away from louis'. the only thing that broke it was liam making gagging noises. "you two are disgusting. stop it." it resulted in niall throwing a little sour patch kid at his nose, which then caused liam to sneeze. harry had to admit liam sneezing was quite adorable. but louis was cuter.

"so what did she say, angel?" louis asked curiously. he was laying on his bed, his head leaned against the backboard. harry loved the way his small body looked in his oversized doncaster college sweatshirt harry had given him as a gift of congratulations. it was so big that it slid a bit down his arms, and it revealed his perfect collarbones. he couldn't stop staring at louis' fluffy hair and his stupid adorable little nose and pale blue eyes framed by a pair of dark, coal lashes. breathtaking, louis was.

"she told me that she missed me. being little, i mean," harry explained. "and she wishes things were the way they used to be."

"what's that supposed to mean?" zayn asked, scooting over to sit next to harry. "harry, life goes on. you can't just be waiting for the past to come back, because it's not going to be."

"i know," harry sighed. "and i don't know what she expects me to say that. i'm sorry i turned out like crap, apparently? i don't know." he lowered his voice. "and she said she missed my dad."

louis' eyes immediately darkened and he frowned deeply, while zayn just leaned over and gave him a hug. "i think she just misses your family, babes."

louis groaned, looking at the ceiling. "i wish i could hug you like that." he pointedly looked at zayn. "because he's mine." then he turned his attention back to harry. "and i think he's right. she misses him, not what he did. you know what i mean?"

harry nodded reluctantly. "i think so. but i mean," his cheeks flushed red, "i kind of do too."

louis narrowed his eyes. "harry."

zayn grabbed his arms. "really harry. elaborate."

harry furrowed his brows. "i don't miss, ehm, *that.*" he could feel his cheeks burning, and it was worse that liam and niall were now listening as well, coming to sit next to him as well. "i just miss, when, he like, he used to like, he used to lift me up in the air and twirl me around and tell me he was, ehm, proud of me, i guess. yeah. and he would like, say he was the luckiest dad in the world. that's what i, ehm, miss."

louis looked like he was about to cry, the other three just looked as if they didn't know what to say.

"i'm sorry," was what liam finally blurted out. "you don't deserve any of this, harry. at all."

harry just looked at his keyboard, gently running his fingertips over the raised keys. he loved that feeling. it kind of tickled, though. he chuckled to himself. it was nice, distracting himself from what was going on around him. that technique also helped when his head was hurting. every time he got in the shower the hot water burned all of his cuts from the crash that ross had reopened.

zayn leaned over and hugged harry again, except tighter and more meaningful. niall joined in, and then liam. harry could feel tears prickling his eyes, and he met louis' eyes in the camera over niall's shoulder. louis just nodded at him, and harry felt a dull ache at the bottom of his ribs when louis mouthed *i love you*, before saying out loud, "you can handle this. you're strong. you're a champion."

niall laughed loudly, while zayn commented, "well, he is a great goalie. for water polo."

louis' eyes widened. "really? harold, why haven't you told me this babe?"

harry shrugged. personally, he didn't think he was that good, but zayn acted like he was some professional. it was amusing, really, but flattering at the same time.

"well, i'm going to come and watch your games." louis looked at zayn, who had pulled out of the hug and was sprawled out on the floor, one of niall's sour patch kids between his teeth, as if he was just holding it there. "zayn, when is your guys' next game?"

"saturday!" zayn shouted after he had swallowed the candy. "not this one, the next one."

harry felt a pressure on his chest. why did he not know this?

"zayn, i'm not ready," he said weakly, leaning back onto the foot of niall's bed, adjusting the laptop of his thighs. "i haven't been in the water for a while and i'm only getting my stitches out in a few days. four days isn't enough day to practice."

zayn glared at him, turning on his stomach. harry thought it must be uncomfortable, the way he was resting his elbows on the carpet.

"harry, you haven't practiced as near as long as luke and you're better. you don't need practice, my friend. you are a harry prodigy."

harry laughed, putting his head down. "okay," he murmured.

when he looked up he realised that louis was just watching him this whole time, and that frightened and intrigued him at the same time. what could there possibly be to look at? he was normal. but louis apparently didn't think so, because when he saw that harry found out what he was doing. he just smiled wider and whispered, "what an angel you are, styles."

harry would be lying if he said that didn't cause a jump in his heart, a moment where he could barely breathe at all.

"i can't breathe," he said quietly, and he widened his eyes. why did he say that?

but when he looked around, niall and liam were busy setting up the play station so they could play fifa. he sighed in relief. but louis heard him, because then louis responded.

"it's okay, baby harold angel styles. i'm used to being breathless."

seventy-four

"i'm so nervous," harry breathed, tapping his foot on the floor. louis put his hand on harry's knee to make it stop bouncing but it wouldn't work.

"me too." louis glanced at the boy. "they just got my results in so they don't know what stage i'm in. i'm gonna find out today."

there was silence between them, a comfortable but nerve-racking silence, and harry could practically hear his breath and his heartbeat in his ears. harry was dreading but longed for the nurse to come out and call louis' name. he wanted to know, but at the same time, he didn't want to, and he was so utterly torn.

louis seemed just as nervous, humming along to every song even if he didn't know it and biting his nails. it was a habit he had always had and told harry that he wanted to break. so harry reached up and gently grabbed his hand and pulled it away from his mouth, placing it instead in his lap.

"do you think that's gonna help me?" louis whispered breathlessly. "move my hand a little farther up."

harry blushed deeply, pulling louis' hand up to his chest and resting his cheek on it.

louis reached over and kissed his head gently and for a long time, before he whispered in the boy's ear, "i can hear your heartbeat, angel."

and harry almost broke down there, he almost fell apart right there in the waiting room. because *wow,* he loved louis so much, more than a million words could express, more than anything in the world. and the fact that his love was in the fate of another boy's heart was one of the scariest things he could ever imagined. louis could just leave, the lung cancer could be too much and *poof,* he's gone. and then harry would never be able to get over it, he would never be able to live with himself, never be able to *live* again, to *feel* again.

"what are you thinking about harry? are you okay?" louis asked quietly, extending his arm to brush a few stray curls out of harry's eyes. the younger boy nodded automatically, but then he started shaking his head, biting his lip and struggling to hold in a breath he was needing to release. he was afraid if he did that he would start crying, and he didn't want that to happen.

"babe, it could be a lot better than you're thinking. see? louis is fine." louis leaned in and kissed harry. "i can kiss you still. okay? i-i'm not dying." he lowered his voice. "i'm not dying."

"louis tomlinson?" there was a nurse standing in the waiting room, a clipboard in her hand. she looked middle-aged, about thirty to forty years old. louis stood up immediately, taking a deep breath even though he had to let out a few coughs a couple of seconds later. harry smiled at him sadly and let louis lead them hand in hand to follow the nurse.

"come with me, love," the nurse said to louis. "my name is drew, i'm going to be your nurse for today." she led them towards a room down the hall, and had louis sit down on the table with crinkly paper. harry sat in a nearby chair, watching as drew sat down at the computer and typed a few things in.

"okay louis. so your tests have come in, babe. the doctor will be in after i fill out all these necessary questions. any shortness of breath?"

"yeah," louis said quietly.

"discolored urine?"

louis squinted his eyes, before shaking his head. "uhm, no."

"have you stopped taking prozac yet?" drew looked at him sadly whenever louis looked at harry before shaking his head.

"louis, you need to stop taking it as soon as possible. if we put you on treatment, the prozac could interfere with it."

"but i looked it up and it said that it could help cancer!" louis argued, frowning.

"they're still testing that," drew said. "all we know is that it does affect treatment, and we can't try anything unknown on you unless absolutely necessary. okay?"

louis grumbled. "yeah. my harry is going to hate me."

"is this your harry?" drew smiled, finally looking at harry for the first time since she called louis out. harry blushed immediately when her eyes landed on him, and his heart sped up.

"yeah, i'm harry."

"nice to meet you harry. i'm aware your louis' boyfriend?"

louis snorted. "no. he's my harry."

harry didn't know whether to smile or frown at that, so he just looked at drew and shrugged. drew laughed loudly.

"you two are adorable!" she grinned. "let me just get a few more things from you and then you'll be consulting with the doctor."

louis and harry shared a nervous glance, before nodding.

***

"nice to meet you both! i'm dr. williams." louis immediately stood up to shake his hand, and harry did as well. his hand was big and warm, completely surrounding harry's. harry knew immediately by dr. williams soft smile and light pale blue eyes that he liked him. he had soft skin, the color of dark chocolate, and a low smooth voice. harry could tell louis liked him too, by the way his eyes lit up.

"louis, you know that dr. lucas? that told you that you have lung cancer based on your x-rays?" he shook his head, as if disappointed. the next time he spoke, it was more a mumble to himself. "idiot. half the doctors here don't even do half their research before they give a diagnosis. who just tells someone they have lung cancer and sends them on their way to do tests?" he looked at louis. "dr. lucas, the twat, didn't even know for sure."

harry looked at louis with wide eyes, who was breathing heavily and staring at dr. williams. he was sweating, probably from nerves.

"what do you mean?"

"your chest ray showed a very obvious clogging of your lungs, a very dark white spot." dr. williams reached over and grabbed a folder, before pulling a picture. "this is your chest," he said. harry scoot his chair closer so he could see it. there was a big mass of white on one side of his lung.

"that looks like cancer to me," louis began, "but then again, how would i know?"

"this could mean a lot of things, not just lung cancer, and i think it's absolutely ridiculous, unprofessional, and a horrible thing to do to a patient and tell them that they have lung cancer."

harry wanted to say, *hey, i like dr. lucas, he saved my life,* but then he realised that dr. lucas wasn't the night shift doctor that did all the saving. so he just nodded along in agreement.

"so what you're saying is," louis breathed, grabbing harry's arm as if it was an instinct.

"... your mri shows that you have tuberculosis, not lung cancer."

louis sighed in relief, and harry almost burst into happy tears, but then they both realised: what was tuberculosis?

as if reading their minds, dr. williams continued. "tuberculosis is a bacterial infection that spreads through your bloodstream to any organ in your body. in louis' case, it was his lungs." dr. williams gave them both a grim look. "it is highly contagious."

louis furrowed his brows. "how?"

"airborne. we're going to need to test anybody you've been close to in the past month."

louis let out a flat chuckle. "that's not that many people." he met eyes with harry. "there's angel, niall, zayn, liam, stan, ehm, mitchell, and then my team."

"well, if you can send them all a message to get an appointment to get tested here as soon as possible, that would be good. how about i get done getting all of your antibiotics we're starting you on subscribed, and then we're going to take some blood and skin tests from harry."

harry didn't know what to feel. first, he found out that his louis didn't have lung cancer. he most likely wasn't going to die. louis wasn't going to die; he wasn't going to have to go through those awful treatments. they would be okay.

but then he was also reeling over the fact that louis was in contact with stan and mitchell in the last month. he didn't bring it up in the doctor's office, but he made a mental note to ask later.

***

"why do you have a fever!? i thought you were on antibiotics!" harry asked worriedly. he started to step into louis' bedroom when he was lightly pushed back by jay.

"baby, don't go in there. we don't want you getting sick with what he has." harry couldn't help but burst into laughter when he realised that jay had a mask covering her mouth and nose, as the disease was spread through the air.

"jay, if anybody was going to get infected, it would be me." harry pointed out, before meeting eyes with louis. his light mood immediately dropped when he saw the sweat on his forehead and the dullness of his eyes. "louis," he whispered, before making his voice a little louder. "louis, are you okay?"

louis shook his head, before letting out a cough. "this is the second fever i've had in the last month."

harry rushed in. "why didn't you tell me the first time?"

"it was before they said i had lung cancer, and i didn't want to tell you so you wouldn't tell me i shouldn't be playing football." louis shook his head. "there's no point in playing the game if you have a fever, i can tell you that." he gave a gentle smile and laughed softly.

"you're so stupid!" jay cried, before sticking out her bottom lip and putting a cold rag across louis' forehead. "my poor baby." louis closed his eyes and let out a tired breath, as if he had just been running. it broke harry's heart.

"i'm so tired," he coughed out, and he shook his head profusely when jay offered him a bowl of soup that was sitting on the bedside table. "no. i'm not hungry."

"lou, you haven't eaten anything for about two days. are you sure you can't eat anything?"

"i'm not hungry," louis repeated.

"you haven't been taking your medicine either," she sighed, turning around and picking up an empty cup.

"i have to been taking my antibiotics!" louis yelled weakly, before breaking into lots of coughs.

"not your prozac," jay frowned, and before louis could respond, she left the room. harry took the opportunity to walk all the way in, sitting in the chair he had set up by louis' bed. louis was allowed to stay at home from college while he was sick, especially since he was contagious. harry could tell jay liked having louis there, even if he was as sick as a dog. harry just wished that louis wasn't so miserable. whenever he held his hand, it was shaky and cold, but his tummy and forehead were burning hot. despite that, louis was cuddled up under a million blankets and shivering like crazy.

"hi angel," louis did his best to smile, and harry almost started to cry.

"hi louis," harry whispered lightly. he missed the sunshine, and when the sun wasn't shining, he wasn't happy. it was as simple as that. "i think you look so beautiful," he said honestly, reaching out and wiping louis' sweaty fringe out of his face. "even when you're sick you're my favorite person in the world."

louis gave a weak chuckle. "i feel crap, and i'm sure i look it, no matter what you say, harold. having tuberculosis sucks, but the fevers are the worst. i feel like someone took my energy in a bottle and ran away with it, giggling and laughing at me as i sit in this stupid bed for the two billionth day."

harry shook his head. "no, you don't look crap. you just don't look happy, and you look tired. but your eyes are still really light blue, you know?"

"i know, angel."

seventy-five

"harry. harry you look so handsome."

harry stared at himself in the mirror, and he felt tears welling up in his eyes. the suit fit him perfectly, complimenting his broad shoulders and fitting comfortably around his waist. he stood there and let his mum adjust his collar and fix every button. he could feel his shaky legs beneath him as images of louis flashed through his mind.

"thank you," he whispered, slowing turning the ring on his left finger and smiling at the way it sparkled. he could practically see the engraving beneath it, and that made him smile wider. he could hear his mum and jay gushing about how beautiful he looked, but he honestly couldn't take the time to think about it.

it didn't matter what suit he was in. it didn't matter if it was in the church jay wanted or the chapel his mum wanted. he just wanted to marry louis tomlinson.

louis tomlinson wasn't here with him right now, and that upset him. louis claimed that he didn't want to be around when the younger boy picked out his suit and that. harry, on the other hand, hated not being around him, ever since he got so sick that he couldn't even speak. harry didn't think that louis realised how much that scared him.

it turned out that nobody got it except for harry, and harry was so thankful for that. it took him a while to get through it, and he had to miss a lot of school, but now that he was graduated and planning on going to college that didn't matter. he had a high gpa, the only grade that wasn't an a was math, but at least it was a high b.

harry remembered the day of his graduation clearly. he remembered anne sobbing and hugging him, saying that harry wasn't her little boy anymore, and harry cried too, he really did, *of course* he did, but he was happy. he was happy that he was finally out of that school, that school that brought so many bad memories. he could practically see louis a couple of years ago, yelling at liam about ruining a copy of the book he was writing, and then when he cried louis hugged him in the middle of the hallway. it seemed so long ago, a lifetime ago, when louis and harry barely knew each other and louis was always yelling at him.

he kind of missed it.

"harry, harry i am so proud of you." harry smiled at his mum in the mirror. jay was crying already, just like she always did when anything big happened. niall claimed that she sobbed on both of their birthdays whenever the party ended.

"i seriously can't believe my son is getting married," she said quietly, burying her face in her hands. "i don't know how i'm supposed to process this. louis is getting married. and to one of my favorite boys in the whole world. harry, you're already a son to me.'

harry looked at her, feeling an ache in his chest. when he saw he smile, and her eyes, there was so much of louis there. the bit of attitude she had was so much like louis, and they had similar smiles. it was heartwarming to see her.

"you're like a mum to me," harry said honestly, quietly. there weren't that many people in the store they were at, so it gave off a very quiet vibe. he liked it, though.

jay smiled at him fondly, her bottom lip wobbling a bit. harry knew that crying would be a huge problem for him. he knew that on the day of the wedding, the minute he laid eyes on louis, he would break down. that's the way he loved louis. the kind where he went insane when he didn't see him for a few moments, the kind where he would do anything to keep him.

"i'm scared," harry whispered to himself, and that's when his best friends came in. that's the kind of stuff they knew how to cope with. they just didn't know what suits looked good, and that was okay.

"harry styles, why are you scared?" niall said from where he was sitting next to jay, sipping from a straw and nodding his head to the beat of the music in the store.

"am i ready?" he asked, staring at his own eyes in the mirror, watching the way they widened with every word he said. these were the eyes that louis was constantly staring into, although he didn't think that they were that special.

"are you?" zayn asked, coming up behind him and touching his waist softly. harry shuddered a bit, closing his eyes. it seemed that almost every time he closed his eyes, he saw his fiancé's face. and it always brought a smile to his face.

"what are you thinking about, h?"

"your hands are soft."

i smile at louis, squeezing his hand softly and he squeezes back. his hand fits perfectly in mine, and i love the way his fingers gently rest against the back of my hand, sometimes drumming lightly and sometimes squeezing.

it's warm outside, just like it always is in the middle of summer. summer evenings are my favorite. i love to sit by the tree in my backyard and feel the breeze blow through my hair, picking it up and releasing it. today, i can smell freshly cut grass, a sweet tang that mixes perfectly with louis' natural smell, his cologne, and just fresh air.

i take a deep breath and fall in step beside louis as we walk down his driveway. the sun is shining, but not as bright as him. he gives me his sunshine smile when i clumsily trip over the curb, laughing and wrapping his arms around my waist firmly to help me balance. i love when does that. sometimes i fake a trip just so he will do that. the way his fingers feel brushing my hipbone is a feeling i will never get tired of.

louis looks beautiful today. his hair is fuzzy and soft, as he hasn't cut his hair in a while, but it just curls out a bit from underneath his ears. it's swept across his forehead and it takes all of my self-control not to brush it out of his pale blue eyes. i love to watch the way his eyelashes drape a shadow over his cheekbones, especially when he's looking down at his feet. speaking of his feet, they're small next to mine, covered in his sneakers. i sometimes wonder why he always has me tie his shoelace for him. he likes to put his foot on my thigh and then give me his puppy dog eyes, which i couldn't resist if i tried.

i like to listen to the pitter patter of our feet against the sidewalk as we walk. i smile and listen to it, chuckling a bit to myself. louis looks at me, stopping in his tracks and meeting my eyes. his cheeks are flushed red from the warm summer air, his eyes shining. i'd like to think that there is no one in this whole entire world that is as beautiful as louis tomlinson. i think i'm right.

"what are you laughing at, angel?" as he says this, he lifts my chin with his right hand and cradles my cheek in his left. my right hand feels empty without his in it though, so i decide to just rest it on his waist and i can't help but give it a little squeeze.

"nothing," i say.

louis leans in to me, so close that are hips are pressed together. "harold."

i find it hard to maintain my composure, and i struggle to keep my breathing even as he blinks slowly, hiding the beautiful blue of his eyes for just a second and i miss it, but then he opens his eyes again and i go weak at the knees. "what?" i say, my voice shaky and a thickness in my throat.

"smile again, please," he whispers, before gently pressing his lips to mine for a few seconds. his lips are so unbelievably soft, and he tastes like the red soda we were drinking earlier. i find myself reaching out for more, my eyes still closed and my breath still held as he pulls back from me, immediately opening his eyes again and giving me a tiny smile. the way his eyes crinkle up from just that small motion will always be one of my favorite things, along with the way he licks his lips and how his hair never fails to fall into those breathtaking eyes of his.

"i have so many butterflies in my stomach that i think i'll fly away," louis breathes, and i let out a long sigh, resting my head on louis' shoulder and letting him hold me in his arms for a few seconds.

"i'm in love with you," i whisper. the word love causes my heart to race, my hands to go limp against his waist. "so freaking in love with you."

"and i'm more in love with you," louis smiles. "now smile at me, angel."

angel. angel angel angel angel. i've always thought that louis was the real angel, but he insisted that i was.

i gave him a big smile, and just the action of him staring at me fondly made me laugh.

"i like the sound of the pitter patter of our feet," i state. the way he looks to the side and then looks back at me, biting his lip to contain his smile, it reminds me of zayn. zayn had always told me that i was funny, though i didn't agree with him. he said that i always said things that were completely random but adorable at the same time. niall said that he thought my mind was a deep hole full of randomness that nobody could understand.

"i like your feet." louis scrunches up his nose. "and i usually don't like feet, so that's a compliment honey bun."

"thank you," i blush. whenever i blush, i feel like it's worse than it actually is. because my cheeks burn up, just like they did when i walked into class the first day of second grade and i had my shirt on backwards. that was absolutely horrific.

louis pokes my cheek. i can feel the toe of his shoe pressing against the toe of mine, and i gently kick his to motion for him to stand on top of mine. he giggles a bit and steps on top of my converse, as light as a feather. i steady him by his hips. i cannot stress to anyone how much i love the curve of louis' waist and the softness of his body and skin. sometimes, when he's asleep next to me, i like to run my fingers along his collarbones and hipbones, his burning skin against my hand causing my heart to stutter in its steady beating.

and when louis smiles again, i have to speak.

"the sun is shining bright today," i say, not looking anywhere but into his eyes.

and he laughs, his head tilting back to look at the sky. i can't help but stare at his jawline, and the way the sun shines so brightly on his face.

"it is, isn't it harry? what a wonderful day to be alive!" he spreads his arms out and twirls in circle, right there in the middle of the street. i watch him, fascinated, before he is skipping towards me and taking both of my hands in his. he pulls me out gently, spinning us in circles, and i can't help but laugh loudly, and he does too, and our laughter echoes into the summer sky.

soon he is dragging me into my front yard, laying down in the grass and pulling me down with him. his breathing is heavy, and i find myself liking the sound of his breaths, because even they have part of his voice in it.

"harry, look," louis says into my ear. his hand slips into mine gently, and we intertwine our fingers easily. with his right hand, louis points to the sky. it has gotten significantly darker since we walked out here, but it's not that cold. there are stars in the sky, but i can still see a hint of the sun. it sends a pinkish orange tint throughout the whole sky, and i can't help but stare at it in awe, my lips opening a tiny bit. louis leans over and kisses my cheek, and i close my eyes for a few moments.

"it's so beautiful," i say quietly, blinking and making sure it doesn't go away.

when i look at louis, he is turned on his side, playing with my fingers, staring at me. "i know," he smiles.

louis has always been the kind of boy that drives me crazy. he is always jumping from subject to subject, unable to keep one thing on his mind for more than a few minutes. i fell in love with his spunky, sassy attitude, and his motivation to always do something, to be something special. i used to find it hard to follow his train of thought, as it always switched, but now, as i look at the way his face lights up, i know that he wants to go somewhere. with me. and the fact that louis tomlinson wants to go somewhere with me makes me feel like the luckiest boy in the entire world.

he gets up off the ground, hopping to his feet in one swift motion. i find myself on my side, facing his ankles. beautiful ankles, he has.

louis leans down and grabs me under my arms, pulling me up before i can do it myself. and i can't help but smile at the gesture.

"let's go, sweets." and louis is taking my hand in his once more. it never fails to sends shivers through my body, tingles up my arm. louis takes big strides with his short little legs and i follow behind him easily as he drags me down the street.

i end up running next to him instead of behind him and he leads me to the playground that we have in our neighborhood. there are a few people there, sitting on the benches and soaking up what is left of the beautiful summer night. louis waves at them, and they wave back.

i find myself sitting on a swing, my converse touching the dirt beneath me. in front of me is a louis tomlinson, smiling widely. beautiful view, i think.

he kisses me for a few seconds before going behind me. now i see a play set. there's a slide, a set of monkey bars, a merry go round, and and some teeter totters.

before i know it the wind is blowing gently against my face as louis pushes me, his small hands pressing up between my shoulder blades. i feel empty whenever i go forward, the feeling of his hand on my back wonderful. he doesn't make me go very high, and i like it that way. it feels good for the wind to be against my hot face. once i get a hang of the swinging, louis walks around to sit on the swing behind me. he is careful to stay at the same pace as me, so we are swinging in unison. and we swing in silence for a few minutes, listening to the birds and the crickets. i feel happy.

and just when i think that nothing could get more perfect, louis starts singing softly. his voice is sweet like the flowers growing on the ground beside us, with a hint of a rough tone that adds an edge to his voice. he actually sounds like an angel, due to the falsetto he sings in. he is singing "you are so beautiful," by joe cocker. i jump in and harmonize once he gets to the chorus, and he meets my eyes with a small grin, continuing to sing.

i have to admit, i love the sound of our voices together. i love the way my low voice contrasts with his high one, and his is clearer than mine. he begins to harmonize me as i sing the melody, and i feel my heart begin to ache with something, something like joy.

once we finish the song, louis drags his feet against the ground to stop himself, and i follow suit. he runs behind the slide. i trail behind him.

my breath catches when he wraps his arms around my neck, looking up at me through his lashes. i automatically slide my arms around his waist, pulling him so that his front was pressed up against me. we dance slowly, back and forth, and i kiss louis' hair when he rests his head against my chest.

the crickets get louder as the sky gets darker, and my eyes are closed as we dance. louis is still humming the same song we were singing earlier, quietly, and my heart swells. when he looks up at me, his light blue eyes are practically glowing in the dark night, and i almost groan at the sight of him. because wow, he is beautiful.

the moon shining on his face accentuates his sharp cheekbones and flawless jawline. and i can't help but lean in and capture his lips with mine, letting out a sigh into his mouth. he kisses me back just as urgently, murmuring my name and tangling his fingers in the hair on the back of my neck. when i take a breath through my nose i smell honey and grass, and it sends a buzz through my head.

"you really are so beautiful, angel," louis pulls back and stares into my eyes for a few seconds, and i feel my cheeks burn. but then he is kissing me again, his lips warm and soft. i move my hands up his waist and to each side of his face.

"you're more," i whisper back.

"are you ready?" zayn asked again.

"yes," harry whispered.

seventy-six

Louis

"I can barely breathe," I say, squeezing my eyes shut. I can still taste Harry on my lips from last night. I can feel his hands cupping my cheek and quivering as he struggled to keep his composure. And I just want to see his face again, when he fell as a heap into my arms with a heavy breath, his curls falling into his face and his eyes fluttering shut.

"Louis. It'll be okay, mate. I wish you could realise how much Harry loves you." Liam lets out a huff. "It's a lot. And he's not afraid to show it."

"With our luck, some guy is going to come in with a gun and crash the wedding." I close my eyes. "Or Harry is going to realise he belongs with the angels, and he's too good for anybody." It's true. Harry is the most amazing boy I've ever met.

I take a deep breath and look in the mirror. The first thing I notice is my pale blue eyes that Harry seems to love. I don't see anything special about them. I step closer, and Liam sits down on a chair in the corner of the small room we're in. The pants of my suit bag up a little once they reach my feet, which are sporting a nice pair of black dress shoes. I smile at myself, cringing at the crinkles by my eyes. I wish I was looking at Harry. Who wouldn't want to look at him?

Who wouldn't love him?

"My baby!" Jay cooed, and I jumped a bit as mum burst through the door, glowing in her beautiful light blue dress. It matches out colors, blue, light purple, and white. I give her a shaky smile, reluctantly walking out of the mirror's view. Liam stands up next to me, dressed in his waistcoat. For some reason, when mum took my arm gently, her lilac painted fingers gently brushing against the material of my suit, I felt butterflies in my stomach. I gulped quickly.

I, Louis Tomlinson, am marrying Harry Styles.

I let out a mix of a laugh and a sob, and I get weird looks from two of my favorite people.

Mum looks at me. "Louis, honey, Niall and Zayn say that they made Harry look beautiful. Aren't you excited to see him?"

I scoff. "He always looks beautiful, mum," I say, and she squeezes my arm with a laugh. The whole walk Liam talks to me about the steps I have to take and the words I have to say. I act annoyed, but secretly, I am grateful that he goes over it with me. I give him a hug when we get to the doors leading into the chapel.

Mum suddenly gasps and grips my arm. "Louis!" she screeches.

"What?" I say, whipping my head around and searching for what could possibly be wrong. No. I knew it. No matter how much planning Harry, our mum's, and I did, there would always be a problem,

At least that's what I think until I hear my mum speak.

"You saw him the night before the wedding!" She slapped her hand on her forehead, blowing her bangs out of her face.

"Had sex with him too," Liam said under his breath.

I burst into laughter.

harry

"stop crying. your eyes will be all red and it starts in an hour."

zayn snorts, and i give him a look. i am sitting on a bench in the chapel. my hands are sweating, and i wipe them excessively on my pants. i want to see Louis. i want to see his Sunshine Smile. i miss him.

zayn asks me if i'm scared. i shake my head, then nod, and he takes me hand. every time i think of Louis i get a million butterflies in my stomach. is that normal? i don't know. i look around the chapel as niall adjusts my bow tie for the hundredth time. it is decorated with pretty lilacs and white roses. i can smell the burning candles on the altar. my heart skips a beat, and i twist my engagement. i decide to keep it on my right finger and until Louis puts the wedding band on my left.

what if he doesn't want to marry me? what if he leaves? i bite my lip and struggle not to let out a little whimper as i think about it, and niall and zayn give me concerned look.

"you okay h? you'll do fine babes. you are the hottest guy in here, trust me."

niall scoffs at zayn, slapping him on the shoulder, but zayn just continues. "and to think. in third grade we said that niall was going to be the first one out of us to get married. now look at you styles. you're getting married."

"yes he is," i hear behind me. i jump a bit as the front doors of the chapel close behind mum. she comes up behind me and places both hands on my shoulders. i shiver as she places a kiss on the top of my head and ruffles my hair, which results in a glare from niall.

"we just fixed that hair," he says flatly, and mum pulls back, laughing nervously.

zayn and niall were planning on fixing my hair into a quiff, but i wanted my hair to be the same as i always had it. swept across my forehead, curling underneath my ears. i hope louis likes that i kept it the same. just like my boots. they are still the original brown ones i've had since sophomore year.

i smile nervously as mum stands in front of me. she looks beautiful in her dress, and i tell her. then i see tears in her eyes. why is she crying? i don't understand.

"why are you crying?" i ask. "did something happen to Louis?" i shoot up off the bench. i can feel my heart pounding way too fast in my chest. "is he okay? what happened?" i bite my lip and my eyes widen as mum looks away. what is she looking at? i grip her arm. "where is he? did he leave?"

i hear zayn and niall laughing like the hyenas they are, and i glare at them. mum leans in and kisses my cheek.

"you are so cute." she says softly. "no, Louis is fine. i'm just.... you're not my baby anymore," she frowns. i don't understand why she is upset. i furrow my brows.

"i haven't been a baby for like nineteen years. i don't know what you are talking about," i reply. i watch the way her eyes flicker to the ground for a bit before looking back at me. her smile somewhat reminds me of Louis' Sunshine Smile, although not as bright.

she doesn't say anything. she leans in and pulls me into a soft hug. i smell her strawberry shampoo mixed with hairspray. it makes me sad, for some odd reason. i bite my lip as she pulls back, and her eyes are still shining with tears. i brush it away as one slips past.

"don't cry," i whisper, my lip wobbling. "it'll make me cry again."

niall pulls me away. "anne, you are going to have to stop. harry is at a breaking point. we cannot afford any more tears before Louis sees him." i laugh flatly, wiping under my own eyes. the tears are warm on my skin, and i am tempted to wipe them on my suit but i don't. i look down. i can see my lilac bow tie.

the purple color reminds me of grapes. i used to love grapes when i was younger. when i got home from school, mum would have some grapes and a peanut butter and jelly sandwich waiting for me. i was usually sad because of the mean kids at school, and she would just run her hands through my hair and let me cry. dad was there too, giving me pep talks on how to be a "big boy". he said that mummy can't always fix my problems. and i asked him, what about daddy? he told me that daddy couldn't either.

so i just ate my grapes in silence, keeping my eyes trained on the table as dad started to kiss mum. it was always awkward for me, seeing dad do to mum what he did to me. i never understood what it meant.

now i do.

i squeeze my hands in to fist and close my eyes, trying to make the memory fade from my mind.

"where are you going for your honeymoon?" zayn asks, and i snap out of my daze, meeting zayn's brown eyes.

"paris," i whisper, staring at the flame from a nearby candle as hundreds of scenarios flick through my mind, like a movie. i can't wait to go to paris with Louis. Louis says it's his favorite place in the world.

"that sounds so romantic," mum coos, and i ignore her, raising my brows in confusion when niall and zayn do another eye conversation thing and begin to walk towards the altar. there is a door on the left near it, so i don't have to go through the front to exit.

"people should be coming soon. they're supposed to be here in twenty. so we need you to wait here and calm down for a second so then you can walk down the aisle," niall says to me as i follow them down the aisle i will be walking later.

"just remember h," zayn says in front of me, turning to look back at me for a few seconds. "you're sexy."

Louis

"Remember. Stand here, and then, just wait for Harry to walk towards you," Liam says. The place is filled with people, mostly my friends and family and some Harry's. I see Eleanor on his side and I smile at her, waving softly. She waves back. She looks beautiful in her simple blue dress with white polka dots.

The buzz around me seems kind of silent as all of Harry and I's best men line up around us. Harry chose Bobby to walk him down the aisle, claiming that Bobby was his second dad because he was over there all the time.

"Harry must be so nervous," I say, shakily taking a step onto the altar and nervously putting my hands in my pocket and taking them out. Just the thought of him walking down the aisle towards me, probably blushing like the cute thing he is, makes me smile at the ground, and Niall meets my eyes.

"Good luck," he says softly, reaching out and touching my hand for a second. The minute he touches me a wave of comfort washes over me. I bite my lip and nod at him. Zayn gives me a similar look.

I used to hate Zayn, back in high school. I used to think Niall and his friends were annoying. Especially Harry. I chuckle. Now that I see them now, I realise I am ridiculous. Niall is the best stepbrother I could ask for, and Zayn is actually a pretty cool guy. Harry, well, that's a different story.

He's just somebody I like quite a lot. He stood out to me.

And now I'm marrying him.

seventy-seven

harry

"go," she whispers in my ear.

i feel a million butterflies flying clumsily around in my stomach, causing my head to feel dizzy and my knees to shake. i want them to go away, but no matter how many times i gulp and blink, it stays. i feel as if the wind blowing against my back as i stare at the closed doors of the chapel will blow me over, as if i'm so weightless i can fly. i take a huge breath, the way Louis always makes me when i'm upset or scared.

right now i'm just so excited.

mum steps in front of me and opens the door, and i can hear soft, beautiful piano music playing and echoing through the small room. i close my eyes for a moment, breathing in the smell of burning candles and a mix of tons of different perfumes and colognes. i can feel the anticipation, the expectancy of everyone surrounding me in the benches decorated with pretty flowers.

and then i make the decision to stop looking at my feet, as i sway slightly to the flow of the music. mum is pulling my arm, desperately trying to tug me forward, but i stay planted.

and when i lift my head, causing one of my curls to fall into my eyes, i see Louis.

no words, *none,* can describe how beautiful Louis Tomlinson is. there are a million ways to put a sentence together, to make it have more feeling, but not even the best sentence can begin to tell you how absolutely prepossessing, alluring, and incredibly handsome he is. i can feel my hands shaking as he meets my gaze. he has on a light blue tie, and even a few meters away i can see that they match his vibrant, pale blue eyes.

and when i trip a little bit over my own feet, that's when the Sunshine Smile comes. it starts out slow, before it blows into a huge grin, so that his eyes crinkle at the sides. i hold in a little whimper, because, wow, he is so beautiful. mum can feel me shaking, so much that i think my legs might collapse beneath me, and she lets out a small chuckle before wrapping her arm around my waist, a small motion of encouragement. i walk forward, and suddenly the piano music is gone, there is no sound. mum's hand disappears, and i'm practically flying as i stand on the altar. because Louis is in front of me. and when Louis is here, the rest of the world doesn't matter.

i have to look down a bit, and when i do, his eyes are locked on mine, shaded by a curtain of thick lashes. his pants are baggy at his ankles, and i can see his hips and curvy waist that i absolutely adore.

"lou," i say quietly. i can feel a slight blush on my cheeks from all the people looking at me, but it fades away as Louis gives me a wobbly smile, touching my waist softly.

"harry," he responds. he licks his lips and my heart skips a beat. i wonder what is going through his mind right now. i've never been good at reading people. i chuckle to myself, receiving a cheeky wink from Louis.

and then the minister speaks.

Louis

I wish I could say everything that the minister said when we got down there. I just remember exchanging nervous glances with mum and then looking back at Harry, who's gaze pulls me in like a rope. But then what the minister says catches my attention, and I keep my eyes locked on Harry's as he continues.

"-marriage is an act of faith and a personal commitment as well as a moral and physical union between two people. Marriage has been described as the best and most important relationship that can exist between them. It is the construction of their love and trust into a single growing energy of spiritual life. It is amoral commitment that requires and deserves daily attention. Marriage should be a lifelong consecration of the ideal of loving kindness – backed with the will to make it last. " The minister ends his long list of what he has to say, before meeting my eyes.

"The two grooms have decided to make up their own vows." He lowers his voice. "Go ahead." I watch as he takes a step back and then I have the floor.

And then it's just me and Harry.

I gently touch his waist, knowing that he needs comfort because he's probably very nervous in front of all these people. I can see it. I can see every nervous habit he has. Rubbing his sweaty hands on his pants, biting his lips, the way he squeezes his eyes shut and gulps multiple times. It takes everything in me not to pull him in and kiss him right there, to draw out whatever embarrassment or panic he is feeling.

But I don't. Instead I squeeze his hip, wishing I could feel his soft, warm skin instead of the rough material of his suit. And he gives me a shaky smile, his breathtaking green eyes glowing with anticipation and excitement. I practically fall apart at the sight of him.

"Harry." I look down and smile a little before lifting my head. "Angel, I mean." A warm blush beautifully spreads out over his pale cheeks, and I see a bit of his dimple peeking out.

"Yeah?" He whispers quietly, asking me out of habit. I recall in the middle of night, when I wake up due to a scary dream. I watch Harry sleep for a while, the sound of his even breaths comforting. And then I wake him up, and there are still scary images in my mind, and he asks me in his groggy voice, "Yeah?" And I kiss him deeply, loving the way he arches his back underneath my hand.

"You are the most beautiful person I have ever had the fortune to lay my eyes on." I begin. And the way he bites his lip to conceal his smile makes my heart stutter in its beating. "And when we met, you were just a sophomore at our school that hung out with my little brother. And the first time I saw you, I reckoned that you were too innocent and pure for someone like me. And sometimes I think I'm right, but I'm too selfish to do anything about it." I pause, taking a deep breath and glancing at our families and friends, before grabbing Harry's hands. "I fell in love with you. Every single time I spoke to you, every time I held you while you cried over something *i* did, I felt like I was free falling, without any control, and I was falling right into your heart."

Harry's hands are shaky in mine, and I squeeze them. "And I was afraid you would fly away, what with those angel wings you have," I reach around his back and find my favorite spot between his shoulder blades, and Harry melts beneath my touch. I can feel him shudder, and I have to close my eyes for a second. "Right here."

"You're sensitive. You're shy. You turn the worst situations into a cheesy joke that only you understand. And I love that about you. I love how smart you are, no matter what teachers argues differently. I love that just seeing a bit of your smile can make my whole day a lot less awful." I can feel my bottom lip wobbling, bubbling hot tears threatening to slip past my eyes. But I don't let them. I have to finish.

"Angel, you're my favorite person in this whole entire world. You belong in the most pure, amazing place on Earth, and god, I will never let anybody hurt you, or harm you again. I'm gonna protect you and take all of your pain away in a heartbeat, because I care about you so much, so so much." I feel a tear slide down my cheek, and I let out a wet laugh. "And no one, *no one*, will ever love you as much as I do." I cup his face in my hands, admiring the slope of his nose, the curve of his bottom lip, the drape of his lashes and his dark eyebrows.

He's crying too, but of course he is. He's my angel. The way he puts his heart into everything is so amazing. "I love you," I breathe, "And I can't wait until I have the privilege of calling you my husband."

Harry pushes his cheek against my hand, like a small kitten, and I struggle not to tell him how utterly adorable he really is.

"Louis." Harry looks at me for a second, giving me his cheeky little smile. "Louis Louis Louis." I hear a chuckle from the congregation, and my heart swells with pride. He's mine.

"I uhm... Oh god this is hard," He runs a hand over his face, laughing. He has no idea how funny he is. To prove my point, everyone else laughs as well, and Zayn reaches forward and pats him on the back in encouragement.

"I love you too, I love you so so much. So so much. A lot."

The way he speaks never fails to make me smile.

"And, ehm, you're so beautiful. More beautiful than me, actually," he laughs to himself, looking down at his shoes. His hands are shaking so hard that I have to hold them against my stomach. "And..."

He looks like he's going through a mental checklist. "Sunshine Smile," he states. "Yeah, that. I love your Sunshine Smile. It makes me smile too, really really wide. And I love that you like to follow my silly routines, but to me they're not silly, but you call them silly so I guess they are."

"I love that about you," I whisper, and he shushes me playfully, and when he leans forward a little bit his forehead bumps against mine, resulting in us both giggling.

"I love that you make my tea the same, always. And I love that you make me feel safe, always. And you always give me your jacket when I'm cold and I love when you ramble to yourself, and you talk, because I really really love listening to you, always."

I smile at the amount of times he says always.

"You always..." he trails off, looking lost for a moment, and I swear watching him get distracted by the flicker of the candle on the altar is the most beautiful thing in the world. He looks back at me though, and smiles sheepishly.

"Louis, uhm, I love your style, and I love that you can always make me feel better even when I go numb and my head spins like that sometimes, and you make me feel beautiful for just a second, and you make me forget about the bad things, and I always laugh a lot when I'm with you because you are so funny, so so so funny. Your passion about football turns me on."

When he realise what he said is a bit inappropriate, and the congregation doesn't fail to remind him, the redness of his cheeks seems almost impossible. I am laughing so hard that I'm sure I might fall over, but Harry, like always, is there to steady me, even when he's embarrassed.

"You're so adorable," I say through rushed breaths, and he blushes even deeper.

"I want to marry you. So, so so so so much. So much."

And then we go through the short general vows, but I feel like I'm underwater, with Harry, like we were when we went swimming, and I kissed him but we were floating.

All I can seem to hear is, *you may kiss the groom.*

And before I can even move, Harry is grabbing me tightly around the waist, his fingers pushing gently against my hips underneath my jacket and he puts me on his feet. And then he kisses me so hard that I'm breathless and I don't need air, I just need him, and I breathe in all of his emotions and his thoughts and *him* and it is the most amazing kiss I have ever experienced. The clapping is muted in my ears and all I can hear is Harry, the little whimper he lets out when I pull back, the way he catches his breath and smiles, and the gentle way he always whispers *i love you.*

seventy-eight

louis' hair smells like green apples, harry thinks. green apples like the ones he used to eat when he was little and wasn't allowed to have junk food for a snack, so mum gave him apples. he wonders if louis still uses his green apple scented shampoo or if that scent is embedded in his soft, fluffy hair. he likes the way it slips through his fingers, like silk, and flops back onto louis' head.

"sleepy, sleepy, sleepy," harry murmurs, the hum of the airplane soothing him. "sleepy husband."

louis shifts in his seat and harry lets out a noise of disapproval when it involves his hair being pressed up against the window. "lou," he whimpers, and he wants so badly to wake the boy up, but he doesn't. instead, he rests his head in his lap, wishing louis was awake to play with his hair and use his soft soothing voice to talk him to sleep.

as he rests, feeling louis' tummy rise and fall beneath his cheek, he thinks back to the reception. he smiles at the thought of niall dancing like an idiot which zayn stood behind him, holding his beer in the air and laughing.

they were only twenty, but they were wild. senior year brought out the worst in them, and the fact that graduation was less than a month away made it even more exciting. they made sure to schedule the wedding on spring break so that they could have a long honeymoon.

harry feels himself smile in trepidation at the thought. he gently slips his hand underneath louis' shirt, so that his fingertips are brushing the warm skin of his hip bone. "i love you, lou," he whispers.

louis made a wonderful toast at the wedding, never failing to meet harry's gaze every few seconds. zayn and niall both acted like idiots at first but got serious halfway through. harry's mum started crying right when she started, so jay just took over. it was one of the most amazing things harry had experienced, listening to his favorite people in the world talk and say their congratulations. there weren't many of harry's friends at the wedding, well, because, he didn't *have* any. but eleanor surely filled the shoes of about ten people. she practically died at the sight of his ring.

"harry?"

harry tilts his head up, meeting louis' gentle, sleepy eyes. the sky is dark, and the lights from the city below them send a glow into the sky.

"yeah?" he asks quietly, closing his eyes as louis brushes a few stray curls out of his face.

"have you been awake this whole time?" he is grinning. "i like the way you sleep."

harry blushes when he realizes his head is right.. there. but when he moves to adjust, louis grabs his hand and leans down to kiss his forehead. "don't move, angel."

"okay," he says lowly. the heavy breaths of people sleeping on the plane around him make him want to speak quietly, and louis follows suit.

"i'm excited," harry whispers.

louis eyes are smoldering as he responds. "believe me, i am too."

***

'Wise men say, only fools rush in.'

I take his hand, the rush of people forming a circle around us causing a jump in my heart.

'But I, can't help, falling in love with you.'

I melt into his embrace, the touch of his hand on my waist causing me to shiver, goosebumps running down my arms. His jacket is rough beneath my hand as I move to slide my arms around his neck, brushing my fingertips across the warm skin of his neck, tangling my hands in the curls that tickle my skin.

'Shall I stay, would it be a sin, if I can't help falling in love with you.'

Harry rests his forehead on my shoulder, and I smile as I hear the rushed breaths he always takes. I can feel mum taking pictures of us, but all I can focus on is him as we dance, back and forth, and our heartbeats match, and when he moves to the left, I do too. I pull him as close as possible, so that our chests are touching.

And we dance. Although our families are watching, it's just us. and it's absolutely amazing. "Husband," I whisper lightly.

***

"le meurice."

harry has never been here. he's actually never been to paris. but when he sees the sparkling hotel, it sparks familiarity, and he doesn't understand why.

louis grabs his hand, thanking the taxi driver one last time before falling into step beside harry. harry felt small beside the huge building, but once he is beside his boyfriend- wait, husband- he feels larger than life.

when they arrive at the hotel, harry is enamored of the elegance, faltering a bit in his step as someone immediately comes up to greet them. for some reason, the man knows that harry and louis can't speak french, and he greets them with a simple, "hello," and gentle smile. his accent his prominent, sounding beautiful in a weird way.

they are led up to their room, and harry doesn't even have to take his bags. he can't seem to make his eyes any less wide as he looks around, but he begins to smile like a fool when louis dances with him in the elevator to an upbeat song.

louis twirls harry around before pinning him against the wall, so their noses are touching. "you look breathtaking," he murmurs softly, capturing harry's eyes with his in an unbreakable gaze. and harry almost falls forward to kiss him, when the elevator dings and the doors open. and one minute harry is against the wall and the next louis is grabbing him around the waist, dragging him towards their room.

their luggage is already waiting inside when he opens the door. harry reaches to turn the lights on, to look around, but louis gently cups his cheek and pulls his hand away, locking the door behind both of them.

"keep it dark, yeah?" he says softly. the roughness in the back of his throat causes a twist of pleasure in harry's stomach.

"okay," harry whispers, and is about to say more when louis kisses his words away, pushing his lips into harry's. harry feels a flutter in his heart, an ache at the bottom of his ribs as louis draws out all of his emotions at once, every soft touch taking his breath away.

"angel," louis hums, squeezing harry's waist and pulling him gently towards the large bed in the middle of the room. harry's breath releases when he falls onto the bed, and he arches his back as louis kisses him deeply, placing his hand underneath the sweatshirt he had worn on the plane.

"love you so much," harry says, hugging louis to him for a moment and breathing in his wonderful smell.

louis mumbles an incoherent reply, his breathing rushed as he practically falls on top of harry, his hands placed next to harry's head to hold himself up.

louis' hands leave a burning trail as he gently runs his fingertips over harry's cheek, then down his waist. harry lifts his arm as louis pulls his sweatshirt off, and he shivers in the cool air of the hotel room.

harry whimpers as louis kisses him fervently, touching every part of him. louis' soft shirt brushes against him. this, harry decides, needs to come off. he pulls it off by holding onto the hem, and then he takes a moment to just... watch.

louis has harry's favorite type of body. he is curvy in the waist, and he's skinny but he has a bit of a tummy that harry loves the feel of against his own. he is tan and warm and beautiful anyway. his lips are swollen and kissed, his eyes glowing blue in the dark. harry reaches up to brush his thumb under his eye, over his cheekbone. "beautiful," he says, but it comes out more as a moan when louis decides at that time to touch him through his sweats.

"lou, lou oh my god," harry cries out, biting his lip hardly as louis palms him, with skill, because he knows exactly what makes harry squirm the most.

"love you so much," louis says breathlessly, occasionally kissing harry but mostly just burying his face in harry's shoulder so that his hair falls limply against harry's soft skin.

"s-stop, that feels so good," is all harry can say, and he bucks his hips when louis puts his hand under the waistband of his sweatpants and lightly runs his fingers over his thighs before taking harry in his hand. "l-louis," he says weakly.

louis doesn't respond, just strokes him gently as if harry isn't falling apart beneath his fingers. the burning desire in the pit of his stomach grows as he kisses louis' shoulder, the soft skin beneath his lips making him even more of a wreck.

"pants off, angel," louis finally says, and his voice is shaking, raspy. "c'mon." he pulls them off, throwing them on the floor, before taking off his own. harry barely has time to look before louis is distracting him, holding him around the waist tightly and kissing him, a passionate kiss that was perhaps so slow and so careful that harry didn't know if he could contain the amount of love he felt in his heart. the words *i love you* remained lodged in his throat as louis quickly pulled lube out of the front pocket of his suitcase and clicked the cap open.

"y-you ready, harry?" louis asks, his voice small and warm with love and care.

harry just nods, not caring how eager he looks. louis hastily spreads the gel over his fingers, his hands shaky.

"c'mon," harry whines, desperately clinging to louis' arm, loving the way it flexes beneath his grasp.

it isn't long before louis is pushing two fingers inside him, and although it hurts it feels *so good*, and harry shudders, a low moan rising from deep within his throat.

"lou," he squeaks out, and louis kisses over every inch of his face, focusing on his lips, as harry adjusts to the size.

"beautiful, beautiful, so so so beautiful," louis murmurs, his hot breath fanning over harry's lips, and goosebumps rise on harry's arms and legs. when louis pulls his fingers out, he feels empty.

"are you ready, angel?" he asks, and harry feels a jump in his heart, a desire from deep within him, and he desperately clings to louis as his husband pushes into him.

"married, husband, yours," harry starts to murmur, but he ends up yelling it when it all becomes a bit much.

"you're all mine," louis growls, but his voice is still gentle, as it always is when he talks to harry. harry cries out in a mix of pain and pleasure when louis goes in farther, and he collapses on the mattress with a whimper when he finally pushes all the way in.

"louis, louis louis louis," he chokes out, each movement louis makes sending a sensitive pulse through his whole body. and when he moves to grab himself, to relieve some of the throbbing tension, louis pushes his hand away.

"let me," he whispers delicately, softly touching harry's skin, gripping his hips and thrusting every few moments to emit a loud groan from the younger boy.

it doesn't take long before louis says harry's name and harry releases all over both of their stomachs with a low moan, and he collapses on top of louis, his breaths rushed and his world spinning. louis closes his eyes, hugging harry tightly and tensing up before riding out his high as well.

"i-i-i," harry begins, but he is unable to finish his sentence, and he tiredly lays his forehead on louis' chest, now loose around louis.

"you love me?" louis is still breathing heavily, and he rests his hands on the small of harry's back.

harry nods quickly, kissing louis' neck softly.

"well, i love you, angel."

"husband," harry says.

"husband," louis replies.

epilogue

i can see him from here.

he's smiling.

i can see his Sunshine Smile.

the sun is shining on his face.

i run a hand over my skin. it feels like it's burning.

he's mouthing something. i squint my eyes and yell at him to ask louder.

he runs towards me, and is very hesitant when he stops.

"did you get it?" he asks breathlessly. his eyes are glowing pale blue, like always. my heart flutters, like always.

i nod at him. "yeah."

then suddenly i am being lifted on the ground, twirled in circles. we fall into a heap on the grass, and i put my face in his chest as i laugh.

"i'm so happy for you, angel. i knew you would get it."

i did get it. i got a job. a school psychologist.

mum didn't think it was a good idea due to my own psychiatric problems, but Louis disagrees.

to be honest, i only care about what Louis thinks.

"i love you," i whisper, the grass tickling the skin on my legs. Louis smells like sweat and sun. "how was footie practice?"

Louis nuzzles his nose in my neck. "tiring. coach made us run extra because apparently i was too energetic." he pauses. "it's really because i was so nervous about you getting your job. my smart little harry."

"let's go home." i blush as he kisses my temple softly.

i let him pull me off the ground, although it results in me leaning into him and he giggles and kisses me, grabbing either side of my head and smiling.

"love you so much," he murmurs. "husband." he reaches one hand to grab my left one, before twisting the ring around my finger. it makes me kiss him harder.

soon he is tugging me towards our house, as i was in the backyard. i love the light blue color of our home that reminds me of the color of Louis' eyes.

"what's for dinner?" Lou asks me as he shuts the door behind us. i place my hands on his waist as we walk towards the kitchen.

"spaghetti," i smile. i already have it set out on the table.

"no macaroni?" Louis is used to me making him a delicious dinner while i eat my usual macaroni and cheese. but, today, with a huge urge of panic in my heart, i set out a plate full of spaghetti for myself. i have to admit, it makes me extremely fidgety when i sit down in front of it, but then when Louis sits across from me, i completely just... don't care anymore.

"i like your hair today," Louis comments. "you look fit in your shirt and shorts. fitter than me, and i'm a footie player." he snorts.

"that's untrue. have you seen my legs?"

Louis' gaze stays fixed on mine. "yes. have you?" i blush at the little smirk playing on his lips, and decide to twirl my fork in my spaghetti.

"zayn's having a party tonight at his flat. he told me specifically to not talk to him when niall was there," i say, smiling knowingly at my husband.

"i knew it was gonna happen. i knew it." Louis takes a bite of spaghetti and groans. "oh my god, angel. this is so amazing. thank you." he leans over the table and cups my cheek before kissing me sweetly. "you're so amazing."

i take a moment to savour the feeling of his lips on mine, putting my hands on my lips and smiling. "thank you," i whisper. "i love you."

"i love you too. now when's this party you're talking about?"

***

"you know," Louis whispers in my ear, "i didn't take my medicine today."

it scares me. one minute me and Louis are taking turns picking each other up and twirling around to the loud disco music, and then he's telling me this.

"really? i put it next to your water this morning," i say anxiously, my eyes flickering everywhere but him, and it helps that he is standing at my side. i can't help but expect him to snap at me again.

"i'm... i think i can control it now."

i step away from him. "Lou. borderline personality disorder is not something that just goes away." i cringe in on myself when a random friend of either zayn or niall brushes past me, their hand touching my waist. Louis glares at them until they're gone.

"harry, are you not listening to me? have i snapped at all today?!" Louis raises his voice, but the music just gets quieter. a slow song. i want so badly for Louis to pull me by the waist into his arms, he's obviously hurt, and i immediately regret everything i said. i feel a rush of panic in my heart as i see the anger flashing in his eyes.

"no, you haven't," i say quietly.

"exactly! now why can't you just be freaking happy for me for once! you have to make everything hard! i can't stand that about you!" Louis takes another step back. "stop being so dramatic, harry. it's annoying."

i feel my breathing quicken. no. i can't do this. i can't deal with this. fights are *not* my strong point. i always end up falling apart.

"please stop, Louis. i'm sorry i ever said anything," i whimper.

"well then stop saying i need medication! i'm so tired of faking everything! why can't you understand that? you're my husband, it's your job to be supportive but you're just.... i can't deal with you."

i stuff my shaky hands in my pockets, biting my lip hardly. "okay. i'll go then," i breathe. i flinch when i feel Louis' hand grab my arm roughly. "ow," i whisper, struggling to get out of his grasp. "Louis, please stop. please please please please please," i say.

he leans in so his lips are brushing my cheek. "i love you angel," he says, kissing my temple, and i shudder, melting against his touch, and the panic fades for a moment. but then he says, "but you're such a baby sometimes."

i rip my arm out of his grasp. "you have no right to be mean to me!" i yell, causing a few people to look at me. "stop! you said you love me! y-y-you love me," i stutter, my breath catching as i struggle to maintain my composure.

"and you love me. so why are giving me so much crap about me not taking my medicine? be a happy person. you just bring me down, so much." Louis shakes his head. these changing personalities make my head spin. now he's not mad, just mean, and it's even worse. i flinch as he walks closer to me, so that his nose is touching mine.

"go away," i choke out, and my head is spinning. every person that dances around us clouds my vision, and when Louis' lips almost touch mine my tears overflow and the lights start to move in blurs as they slip quickly down my cheeks. "g-go away. go away. go away. *go away!*" i scream. my head is throbbing. i can feel a twist in my stomach when Louis glares at me.

"you're embarrassing me. stop," someone who isn't Louis growls, someone mean and dark and not the same Louis that cuddles me and kisses me before i got to bed and nuzzles his nose in my neck while i read books.

"no no no no no." my chest is pounding and i can't catch my breath as Louis continues to grab my gaze, not letting go. i feel lightheaded and faint. no.

i see zayn. he's looking at me. he grabs Louis, who is continuing to say mean words.

"let go!" Louis yells. "he's *my* husband! i can do what i want!"

and then he starts to say things that are even worse than before, and it includes a lot of swear words that i've never heard him say before. when he tries to come closer to me, zayn holds him back.

my vision goes black perhaps the same time Louis' does. when niall comes from behind zayn and punches Louis right across the face.

***

"angel, angel angel angel angel," i hear someone whimpering.

"shut up, louis. you've already said that word a million times. my god. you're gonna wake harry up. he has to go to work tomorrow." it's niall.

"my poor baby angel. he had a panic attack. he was doing so well. he hadn't had one in so long."

harry bit his lip. he didn't know where he was because his eyes were still closed.

"that's your fault, louis. you act ridiculous. you were being such a dick," zayn snapped. "you should never say those things. he's your husband. you have at least a *little* self-control."

"i'm so so sorry," Louis says quietly. "it's just when i get mad, i just... i can't see and i don't even realise what i'm saying until it's too late."

"or until niall punches you in the face," zayn comments and that's when i open my eyes.

"niall punched you in the face?" i ask softly. Louis whips around in his chair to look at me. the left side of his face is red and puffy. i reach out to touch it and Louis squeezes his eyes shut when i run my fingers over his soft skin. "why did he punch you?"

"you don't remember?" zayn asks in disbelief, and he takes my hand off of Louis' face. "if you did remember then you wouldn't be touching him right now, harry."

Louis turned to glare at zayn. "let him do what he wants."

my eyes widen at Louis' hostile tone. "lou?"

Louis looks at me and his face softens. "angel, baby. husband."

i shiver when he leans in and places a gentle kiss to my temple. "don't listen to him. it was just a misunderstanding."

"a misunderstanding?" zayn moves to sit on my bed. "he didn't take his medicine. on purpose. what's so hard to understand about that?"

i bite my lip, trying so hard to find a reason, and excuse, to why Louis apparently acted out. all i can remember is dancing with Louis, nothing more. but apparently, something did happen.

"i love you so much harry. i'll never do that again, swear."

what is he talking about? i don't like this.

Louis turns to zayn. "you act like i do it on purpose. you don't know what it's like, zayn, to have bpd. it's not as easy as you think. you always have control of yourself. i don't. trust me, trust me, harry is the best thing that's ever happened to me, and i don't mean any of the things that i said."

niall, who is sitting quietly on the floor, criss cross, finally speaks up. "he is. he really is." he is looking at his knuckles though, sadly. i feel my heart beat faster at his words. it's odd hearing other people talk about me like this.

"you never mean it," i say quietly, staring into Louis' eyes as he looks straight ahead at the wall. he turns to look at me, and i swear to myself that there's nothing more beautiful than his eyes, the color, the shape, the way his eyelashes frame them in a flawless way. "you never do." i look at zayn and niall. "stop making Louis sad."

niall furrows his brows at me and zayn doesn't tear his eyes away from the floor. "h. you know we love lou. but if you could remember, if you could remember everything he said to you... we're just trying to protect you. we care about you so much, and right when he stopped taking his medicine and went out and yelled at you... that was the first time you've had a panic attack in ages. so long!"

"except for the time we got stuck on the ferris wheel last fall," Louis said softly, and i meet his eyes. i remember that. i remember Louis whispering, "i got you, i got you angel," and cuddling me at the top of it, and i was afraid that i would fall into a million pieces if he had ever let go.

"i love you," i whisper, feeling my heart swell with love for my best friend, my husband.

Louis' eyes widen in surprise, and he reaches out to brush his fingers across my cheek. i lean into his touch, loving the gentle way he traces my cheekbones.

"so are we just going to forget about this?" zayn asks, exasperated. i look at him, trying to read how he's feeling, but all i can see is anger, although if i were him i would be confused.

"i'm going to take my medicine again." Louis looks away. "i thought.... i thought that it would stop after i took it for a while. that i could just keep feeling the way i do now. calm. i don't get how taking a pill makes me lost control over myself. it's scary. i hate it." he gulps. "so much."

i can feel my lip tremble as i watch Louis blink a stray tear out of his eyes. it hurts me, it kills me, to see Louis sad. it's like the pain that hits him hits me too.

i furrow my eyebrows in confusion when zayn leans down and hugs Louis. wasn't he just mad? i really don't understand people. why do they feel so many emotions at once?

Louis, i think. and then i remember. i remember what happened.

and it scares me.

"Louis," i say. "why did you say all those things to me? do you actually mean them?"

Louis pulls out of zayn's embrace, and his face is filled with surprise. "angel... you remember?" when i nod, he starts to speak. "i don't mean it, i don't mean it, you know that. remember in high school? i was always like that to you, even though i had a huge crush on you, a huge one! please believe me when i say that i am in love with you, and everything about you is my favorite thing about you."

this is the last time i hear Louis tell me he loves me before i fall asleep on my bed, snuggled up under the blanket he bought me for our two-month anniversary.

***

i smell pancakes.

i feel lips brushing my forehead, and it pulls me out of my dream. i cuddle further into my blankets though, deciding not to open my eyes. too tired, i think. but when Lou says, "it's six o'clock, silly dilly," i sit up in bed.

"what has happened to my internal alarm clock?" i mumble quietly, which results in Louis laughing and kissing my temple.

"you're so adorable," he says gently, wrapping his arms around my waist and shaking me lightly. i smile and blush.

"thank you," i whisper. "but really, why did i not wake up at six?"

Louis leans in so close his hair brushes my forehead. "it's five fifty-nine. i just wanted to wake you up for once. to see your little eyebrows furrow whenever i interrupt your dream. it reminds me of a kitten." he kisses my lips, and i cringe.

"Louis, i have morning breath."

"well, that's not good." he leans over and pulls me out of my cave of blankets swiftly, despite my protests, and i laugh and whine at the same time as he starts to carry me towards the restroom. the cold air all over my body is not a fun experience, and the fact that my... uhm... is rubbing up against Louis' shoulder isn't so comfortable either. when he puts me down, my whole body is flushed.

"Louis!" i whine, stomping my foot.

"harry!" he mocks me, before squeezing my sides. "you claim you have to be all clean and stuff to kiss me, so i'm giving you your chance," Louis says. i meet his eyes and we stare at each other for a moment.

"i need clothes," i say calmly, biting my lip and trying to control Louis' wandering eyes by catching his gaze and locking it. Louis sighs deeply, dramatically.

"i already trekked you across the mountains-"

"our bedroom," i correct.

"-and placed you right in front of your toothbrush, equipped with it's essential toothpaste. lookie." he picks up my toothbrush, and it indeed has a perfect stripe of blue toothpaste on the brush. i raise my brow.

"i knew my angel would want to brush his teeth, and i was prepared."

"i need to go to the bathroom," i say quietly, trying to contain my smile when Louis comes towards me, before kissing me softly.

"okay, but-" Louis cups my cheek, "i have a problem that i need you to solve."

i'm blushing when he shuts the bathroom door.

***

"Niall, I'm serious, you can't be doing this again. You're making so many people upset," I groan into the phone as I prepare my husband's plate of pancakes.

"Why? Seriously? Why would anyone be upset?"

I can't decide whether I should keep my mouth shut or not. Instead I just say the first thing that comes to mind. "I'm upset that you pick trashy people that you're way too good for." That sounds okay, right?

"Trashy? Lou, she's extremely hot."

"And? What about her personality?"

Niall takes a while to respond. "... She told me she liked my jeans."

I roll my eyes. "Then what'd she do? Offer to have sex with you?" When he doesn't say anything, I continue. "Trashy."

Niall lets out a sad sigh. "Look, Lou. I'm not like you. I can't just stumble into someone who I love-"

"Excuse me, I had to *work* to get Har-"

"and marry them. I just need a girlfriend. Someone! I'm so alone all the time, like seriously! I'm twenty-three and I still live in Zayn's flat."

I smile knowingly. "Yes, you do. Wouldn't you like that forever?"

Niall stumbles over his words. "Yes, I-I mean no, of course not!"

"Think about that, Niall. Now, I have pancakes to serve. You need to talk to Zayn."

"What? Why?"

"Love you!" I yell, before hanging up and shoving my phone in my pocket. "Angel!" I cry.

I'm sitting down at the table when my Harry comes stumbling in, dressed in a pair of cargo shorts and a blue tee shirt. His eyes light up when he sees me, and it makes my heart stutter, just like always.

"Pancakes," I say warmly, and he comes over to me. His curls are wet and they drip a bit on me as he lays his forehead on mine. He smells like Old Spice and his apple shampoo.

"Thank you, Lou," he whispers in response, before placing a gentle kiss to my lips. I kiss him back softly, closing my eyes and brushing my fingers across his waist.

"I love you," I say when he pulls back, and he looks at the ground, smiling.

"I love you too." His voice sounds small, shy.

When Harry is on his final pancake, I speak. "Let's go for a walk, angel." He looks up at me, furrowing his eyebrows.

"It's really early," he responds.

"So what?" I ask. "C'mon!"

Harry laughs, shaking his head. "Okay, Lou," he smiles. I reach out and brush his curls out of his face before grabbing his hand.

"It's a beautiful summer day, angel. Let's celebrate."

When we walk outside, the birds are chirping, the sun is shining, and it *really is* a beautiful day. I can smell the dew on the grass, the freshness in the early morning air. The sound of Harry's converse overlaps the gentle slapping of my vans on the pavement. There isn't anyone in the neighborhood, and for that I am grateful. Peace, quiet, and Harry Styles by my side. Or, Harry Tomlinson.

"Do you have practice today?" Harry asks me quietly, and I reach out to grab his hand. We intertwine our fingers, and I squeeze his hand tightly before loosening my hold just a bit.

"No babe, I'm free all day. You?"

"My first day of work's tomorrow," he says nervously, biting his lip and looking away. "I'm scared, Lou. What if they don't like me?"

I stop on the sidewalk, taking my hand out of Harry's so I can place both of them on his waist. "Harry," I say softly, my accent slow and soft. My voice is a bit hoarse from yelling at the guys during practice. "Harry, you care. About them. You put faith in them." I lean closer and catch his gaze, watching the way the breeze blows his curls out of his face. "Just that will make them love you."

Harry closes his eyes, and the next breath he takes is shaky. "But it's high school, Louis. Nobody liked me in high school then; why should they now?"

I kiss him, softly and gently for a moment before pulling back. "You're not their age. They don't have to be jealous of you anymore." It kills me the way his eyes avoid mine, the way he shakes his head in disbelief.

"Louis," he pushes out. "We both know that's not true. Nobody was jealous of me. Nobody ever *will* be jealous of me, unless it involves you. I.. I can't even get a sentence out without screwing up."

"Yes," I breathe, "yes, you can, angel. You have so many times. And when you can't, it's just freaking adorable." I cup his face in my hands, rubbing my thumb across the soft skin of his cheek. I swear he's the most beautiful person I have ever laid my eyes on.

"I'm just scared," he says nervously, and I place my hands on his waist, pulling him into a hug that's so tight that I can't even breathe. He hugs me just as tightly, placing his head on my shoulder and letting out small breaths as I stand on my tiptoes.

"That's okay. Everybody's scared at first. But... but you can do it. I know you can, I *know it*. I believe in you, and I promise when you get home you'll believe in yourself too." He releases his hold and slowly lowers me back to the ground, and I close my eyes instinctively when he leans in to kiss me.

"Thank you," he whispers against my lips, and I smile a little bit before capturing his lips in mine. We kiss slowly, so slowly and I can hear the small breaths Harry takes through his nose, and I just *love* kissing Harry. His lips are soft, gentle against mine.

I take a moment to catch my breath, to regain my composure, before I speak. "Let's continue this walk, yeah?"

Harry nods quickly, and I grab his hand. I try to match his long strides but it's a struggle. "Stop going so fast!" I whine, pulling him back so that he's almost behind me. "Dumb long legs." I laugh. "Sexy long legs."

I smile when I see the blush on Harry's cheeks. "I love your legs, Lou," he says quietly, shyly. "I love how short they are and I love them and they're perfect."

We're both silent for a moment, and I can hear the breeze ruffle the leaves in the trees, and a lawn mower somewhere close in the neighborhood. The street is still empty, except for the truck with a person throwing out newspapers into people's driveways.

I jump a bit when Harry speaks. "You know my lock screen.. it's still the same."

I turn my head to look at him, and I smile when he clumsily tries to take his phone out of his back pocket while still walking. "S-see, look Lou." He holds it out to me, and I see a black screen. Harry blushes. "Hold on." He reaches over and clicks the lock button, causing the screen to light up.

For some reason, I feel my cheeks burn and a smile grow on my face as I see it.

It's me, in high school, probably when I was a sophomore or junior. I'm laughing, and I see a glimpse of Liam in the picture.

"I look so young," I whisper. "Harry, I can't believe this has been your lock screen all these years."

Harry is still looking at it, his smile so big like it's the first time he's seen it. "I love it," he grins. "Louis Louis Louis."

I grab his phone from him, putting it in his pocket for him before putting one of my hands behind his neck, and the other on his lower back to pull our hips together. I tilt my head and kiss him, I kiss him until I can't breathe and Harry is leaning back against my hand, his head tilting back more and more as I kiss him with everything I have.

"You're so freaking adorable," I laugh as Harry picks me up around the waist and twirls me around, just like in one of those cheesy romance movies that he watches all the time. "Oh my god I love you so much," I breathe out when he puts me down. When I look up into his eyes, it's like I'm falling in love with him all over again. His cheeks are flushed red, his lips red from kissing me. It's breathtaking.

"You know, this feels like the ending to a really girly romantic movie," I say. "Like we've gotten through all of this, and now... everything's perfect." My voice is soft, careful, and I reach over to squeeze Harry's hand. "Angel, this is our epilogue. Our ending. We're perfectly happy."

Harry stares at me for a second, and I wonder why his eyes are searching my face, looking me up and down for so long.

"What?" I ask finally, laughing.

"I don't want it to end," he whispers, and I furrow my brows when I see him frown sadly.

"Angel..." I begin, but he keeps talking.

"I miss being young and I don't wanna die." He glares at me when I start laughing.

"Angel," I push out, "Baby, you do realize that I'm only twenty three, and you're only twenty one. We're not even close to dying." I kiss his lips softly. "And even when we do, we'll still be together."

And then Harry's kissing me so much I can't even take a moment to catch my breath, I just can taste and feel and *breathe* only Harry, Harry Edward Styles.

"I can't believe you love me, even when I have Asperger's," Harry says when I pull back a little, but our foreheads are still touching.

"I love you, and you have Asperger's, and that's part of you. So I love you, and you have Asperger's, and I love that as well." I pause. "I'm the one with BPD."

Harry just shakes his head, insistently. "I love you. Louis Louis Louis. So so much." I jump a bit when he grabs my wrist and places gentle kisses on the faded scars. "I love you."

"Will you marry me?" I ask.

Harry looks at me, and then we both break down laughing, and I can't help but hold his left hand against my cheek so that his wedding ring is brushing my skin.

"Already done, Lou," Harry points out the obvious.

"Will you be mine?" I try.

Harry puts his hands on my waist and before I know it I'm being lifted up off the ground, and my legs wrap around waist.

"Already yours, Lou," he laughs, and Harry, I think, is my angel. My shy, blushing, little angel.

bonus chapter

"Why hello pumpkin!" Louis calls, "and angel, get over here!"

He can't contain his smile when a little girl with bouncy brown curls and an adorable boy, also with bouncy brown curls, walk towards him down the football field. His teammates are kicking balls at each other, usually something they do when practice is over and they are not wanting to get out of the warm summer sun. It's pelting down on Louis' face, and he can feel sweat start to build up on his nose and cheeks, but the flush feels nice.

"Louis Louis Louis," Harry says quietly when they walk over to him. "You will never believe what happened."

Louis doesn't know why, but every single time he hears the honey smooth voice of his husband, he swears his heart melts in his chest and every single rational thought leaves his mind for a few seconds.

"What happened?" He finally asks, leaning over to peck Harry's lips lightly.

"Grayson here got an A on her math test and on her science test!" Louis smiles when Grayson nods her head excitedly, jumping into her father's arms the minute he sticks them out. Louis feels his heart swell with pride when Harry leans over and puts his head on Louis' other shoulder, a small huff of breath escaping his lips. He has a beautiful husband, an adorable daughter, and the best family in the world.

"Honey I'm so proud of you!" Louis says excitedly, kissing Grayson's soft hair before putting her on the ground. "Do you wanna go talk to Niall? He's taking you over to his house for tonight, is that okay?"

Grayson gives a hesitant smile. "Is Zayn gonna be there too?" When Louis nods she lets out a squeal of excitement. "Yes! I love Zayn!"

"So do I," a voice comes behind Louis, and Louis grins.

"Hey Niall!" Harry says, his voice still filled with youth and innocence, and Louis really loves Harry.

"Hey H," Niall goes over and hugs Harry tightly, and the smile Harry has on his face is enough to melt Louis' heart. "And how's my little Grayson!?" Grayson giggles when Niall picks her up, twirling her around and kissing both of her cheeks, tanned from the summer sun.

"Let's make sundaes!" she yells, and when Niall yells in agreement, she lets out a cheer with one fist in the air.

"Well you guys have fun," Louis says, giving Niall the *don't let her get hurt or I'll kill you,* look. "Harry and I will be back around-"

"Tomorrow," Niall interrupts, laughing. "Lou, don't worry about taking her back home tonight. Zayn and I are happy to have her sleep over."

Louis can feel Harry's gaze on his face, and he turns his head ever-so-slightly to meet his shining green eyes. The heat between them suddenly grows when they realise that they have all night together, alone. Harry is biting his lip, almost innocently pushing his curls across his forehead although *wow*, does it make Louis feel so in love with him. "Thanks Niall," Louis says genuinely, but he doesn't break his eye contact with his husband.

"Of course. We're going to go now. Zayn just texted me. Say bye to Grayson, I'm taking her."

Louis is snapped out of his daze when his favorite little girl in the world is at his side, her curly ponytail brushing against his hand. He immediately leans down, grabbing her around the waist, and lifting her to his face. He kisses her over and over, peppering her cheeks and her nose with little kisses. She giggles and holds on by wrapping her arms around his neck.

"I love you, sweetie," Louis coos, before handing her over to Harry, who holds Grayson to him like she's a fragile little baby and closes his eyes as he squeezes her tightly to him.

"My little version of Louis," he whispers, and Louis loves the way his eyelashes look against his light skin as he closes his eyes. "Love you so much." He presses a gentle kiss to her forehead, before placing her on the ground. "Don't hurt her," Harry warns, his voice so sincere, stern, genuine, yet full of fear. Louis strides over to him.

"Angel, it's okay."

"Louis Louis Louis," Harry whispers in response, and when they look at each other, it's like they're teenagers again, just by themselves in this huge world. They're dancing in the cold lake; they're kissing in a car in the middle of winter. And every second that goes by feels like a minute, because when Louis is with Harry, time slows down, the world stops, and they're two hearts beating among many that don't seem as strong, as in love. But now, they've made one more heart that joined their small world.

"What do you want to do tonight?" Louis asks softly, his voice warm and full of excitement. "We can do whatever we want, we can go wherever we want." He lowers his voice, even though by now Grayson is waving at them from Niall's car, which is parked quite a bit away from them. "Let's pretend we're young again."

"Lou, you're only 29. You're still young."

Louis leans forward and kisses him. "Let's be 19."

Harry closes his eyes, letting his lips linger on Louis' for a few seconds before smiling. "Sounds perfect."

***

"Why does this bring back so many memories?!" Louis groans the minute he feels the sand beneath his feet, warm and hot underneath the smoldering sun. "Angel, we used to go here all the time in the summer."

Harry has his arms wrapped around himself, eyes wide, and *god* Louis always always always loved the way he always looked at everything with such wonder, appreciation, and deep thought. No matter how old he got, there was still youth in his heart.

"What do you think angel?" Louis walks towards his Harry, gently putting his hand on the small of his back, where he could feel the slope of his spine and the curve of his hips. "Can you remember too?" By now, his lips are almost touching Harry's ear, and his voice is such a soft whisper that he can barely even hear himself, but he knows Harry is listening by the way he closes his eyes, biting gently on his dark lips.

"Love on me," they say at the same time, laughing when they realize they both thought of the inside joke at the same time. Louis buries his head in Harry's shoulder, and he still has his own distinct smell despite the fact that they've lived together for seven years. That makes him very happy.

The inside joke wasn't coming out of nowhere. It had significant meaning that only the two of them could understand. Of course, that's what an inside joke is. But when they both said it, it was like traveling back in time, to when they were young and naïve, when the world seemed too big for them to tackle on their own.

Louis leads Harry towards the water, gently pushing up against the sand, revealing a new set of odd shaped rocks and tiny shells every time. Although the ocean had better shells than the lake, there were still some pretty cool artifacts you could find at a lake near Harry's old house. Louis rolls up his jeans to his knees, and does it to Harry before Harry has a chance to lean down and do it himself.

"Thanks," Harry smiles, and Louis smiles back at him, gazing into his eyes for a few seconds. The sun shines so brightly on his face that it looks like it's beaming, but before he can say anything, Harry speaks.

"Whoa," Harry breathes, and Louis raises an eyebrow.

"I've never seen so much sun mixed with a sunshine smile." Harry smiles to himself, closed mouth and eyes squinted shut as he hugs himself, swinging his body back and forth. "I like it a lot." His voice is soft, full of warmth and happiness.

"When did you come up with sunshine smile?" Louis asks. Over the long time that they had been together, Harry always murmured it to himself, and Louis never understood where it came from. "Honey, you say it all the time." He leans in and touches Harry's curls gently.

"I do?" Harry asks, and although his cheeks are already flushed from the heat, Louis swears he's blushing, and he squeezes his waist.

"Never be embarrassed around me, angel," he says softly, and Harry blushes even more.

"I- I came up with it, in you know, ehm, high school. When I saw the picture on my lock screen, I thought of, like, sunshine. Like it reminded me of when I was a kid, and I used to sit out on my lawn and drink, the ehm, drink the lemonade that mum made me, and I would love to just sit underneath the warm sun and feel it like, seep into my skin. It made me happy and warm and fuzzy inside. And that's how your smile makes me feel." When Louis doesn't respond due to his absolute adoration for Harry, he continues to speak. "How did you come up with angel?"

Louis laughs, tickling Harry's sides, and Harry squirms away, laughing loudly. "Harold, I've already told you. You're an angel. Everything about you." He reaches in and tickles him again. Harry pushes his hand away, but when Louis begins to pull away, Harry grabs him and pulls him back in.

"You are kind, you're innocent, you're warm and flawless and selfless. Angel. And that's why I call you that, angel. Do you remember that halo you wore on Halloween?"

Harry nods, eyes wide and filled with curiosity. "What about it?"

"Well, that's how I imagine you all the time." He reaches up and pretends to circle it with his fingers. "Right here." Then he touches between his shoulder blades. "There too. Remember?" Harry nods. "Mhm, babe. That's the way it is. Now let's get further in this lake or else my back will roast in this sun."

"You're roasting," Harry laughs quietly, his eyes sparkling from the reflection of the sunlight on the lake. Louis grabs his hand in his tightly, tugging him along, pushing through the water until they has to stand on their tiptoes to be above the water. Well, he has to. Harry is standing flat on his feet. He shakes his head and wraps his arms around Harry's neck, wrapping his legs tightly around his waist. He knows he's light because of the water.

And right when Louis' lips are brushing Harry's, Harry whispers in an extremely voice, "I want food."

"I want you," Louis smiles, trying not to laugh because he's about to kiss his husband and now is not the time for food.

"French fries," Harry replies, smiling and pulling back a little as he laughs. Louis only lets it last for a second, before he's holding the back of Harry's neck and pulling their lips together once more, and he hopes that the way he kisses him, open mouthed and deep, makes him forget about food. He runs his left hand down Harry's wet back.

"Milkshake," Harry moans as Louis squeezes his thighs tighter around Harry's waist.

"Angel, I'm not going to be inside you any time soon unless you stop saying food names," Louis whispers softly, gently into his ear, before kissing his neck slowly and behind his ear.

Harry's breath quickens, and Louis smiles against his neck, kissing his jaw once more before moving back to his lips. Due to the fact that Harry is still holding him, Harry is limited to running his hands all over Louis' back and into the back of his jeans. Louis, on the other hand, his squeezing Harry's sides, pressing their stomach's together and it feels quite amazing with the cool water.

"Louis," Harry whispers, in that raspy voice he gets when he's flustered and turned on. In response, Louis uses his feet to pull Harry's pants and underwear down, careful not to take them all the way off so they don't float away.

There is water dripping of Harry's eyelashes, his bare shoulders above the water strong and muscular as he holds his grip on Louis' waist. His lips are dark and wet, his green eyes pale and bright in the sun, his jawline sharp and quite striking.

Louis stares into his eyes warmly, kissing him until he can't breathe.

2 A.M.

It feels amazing outside.

The wind is blowing, causing the tree's nearby to ruffle with noise, shaking where they stand as each gust passes. Harry's bare back pressed up against Louis' chest is hot, causing warmth to spread throughout Louis' entire body. Louis can hear the splashing of waves up against the shore, the lake going crazy from the wind. He tries to let the sound lull him back to sleep, as it's only two in the morning and no matter how late they wake up nobody can find them.

Harry and he had found this spot years ago, when they were only around twenty and twenty two years old. The lake was surrounded by woods, and there were some trails they could go through. If you followed a trail it led to a big rock, that, from the trail, looked like the edge into the water. But if you climbed over the rock, there was a nice area with sand and trees and the perfect place to hide out for a little bit.

Louis smiles as he remembers Harry's twenty first birthday. Although he was already legal to drink, him and his friends always celebrated the American's age too. Really, it was just an excuse to go out for some drinks and have fun with their mates.

But, on his birthday, Louis took him out for a drink and was watching him take his first sip when he noticed how amazing Harry Styles looked from the neon lights coming from the disco ball in the bar.

"Lights just work with your eyes," Louis had said.

And so he took him outside. It was late July, a hot, breezy night. Louis could feel the sweat on his cheeks as him and Harry walked outside, and Louis admired the way the moonlight reflected off Harry's features and made him look angelic. It brought out his sharp cheekbones and jawline, caused his green eyes to almost glow, and his dark hair contrasted oh so well with his pale face.

"Let's go to the lake and have some fun," he had whispered.

So they stopped at Louis' house, got some towels and a few essentials like clothes, deodorant, and food. The whole time Harry was smiling in excitement as if they were doing something secret, although they were legally allowed to do whatever they wanted and to be honest they didn't really care.

That night on the lake was one of the best nights of Louis' life. They ate marshmallows and only had the light of a couple of flashlights and the moon to see by. They talked for hours, eating until they were stuffed full, and ended it with a bang. And when Harry finally ended up in Louis' arms, his ear against Louis' chest so he could hear his heartbeat, Louis knew why he was so in love with this boy.

Harry Styles knew him better than anybody else. Harry watched him with curious, thoughtful, and loving eyes as Louis spilled all of his deepest, most embarrassing stories and secrets. Harry laughed whenever Louis did, even if it wasn't that funny. Harry put so much thought into everything he said, everything he did, and he even still blushed taking off his clothes in front of Louis.

He also loved Harry Styles because this boy loved him more than anybody else in the world and Louis never thought he would have someone love him like that.

So it's 2 A.M., and Louis is laying holding his husband of almost 10 years. He's reminiscing sweet memories and loving the way Harry's curls tickles his nose as he breathes. The sand is soft beneath them, blanketed by a towel and then by them. Harry's breaths are long and soft, his mouth slightly open. "Love you," Louis whispers softly, kissing his soft cheek.

He doesn't expect Harry to say anything back, but he is caught by surprise when Harry turns over in his sleep, calling his name quietly into the darkness before gathering Louis up into his arms. Louis looks at him adoringly, the way he can barely see his face in the moonlight but he can make out his scrunched up eyebrows, his troubled expression until Louis settles into his hold and his face relaxes. Louis reaches up to touch his face, tracing his lips and cheekbones, his eyelids and nose and forehead.

He flinches when his phone rings on the towel beside him, the screen lighting up with a picture of Niall's face. "Crap," he whispers, worry already growing in his heart. Harry wakes up when Louis sits up, putting his phone to his ear and gently holding Harry's arm with his other free hand.

"Hello?" he says tiredly, stroking Harry cheek when he sees his worried look. "I don't know," he whispers quietly.

"Louis? Louis, Zayn just asked me to marry him." Louis can tell by his voice that he's crying. He stands up in excitement, and Harry tugs on his shirt with a pouty look on his face. He wants to know what's happening. Louis puts it on speaker.

"Finally! Ni, I'm so excited for you! Why did he do it at this hour, though?" Louis asks, laughing, and his heart melts when he hears Grayson's squeal in the background.

"Well," Niall says guiltily. "Zayn woke me up and said that we needed to take Grayson out for sundaes, at that 24 hour ice cream shop, you know?"

"Niall, it's okay if you want to spoil our daughter," Louis chuckles. "Go on."

"Well, we were just eating our sundaes and Zayn was giving me his cherry because he doesn't like cherries, and one minute he was teaching Grayson to tie a knot in the cherry stem and before I knew it he started saying this speech about how much he loves me and he proposed."

"That's so awesome! How's Zayn doing?"

"We're both so happy and right now Zayn is telling Grayson how to kiss a boy."

Harry and Louis say equally worried looks, until Niall laughs and says, "Just kidding. He's teaching her how to correctly insert a tampon." He bursts into laughter again.

"Niall!" Harry screeches, grabbing the phone as if it's Niall. Louis leans over and kisses him. He's too adorable.

And really, when he starts kissing Harry, he never wants to stop. So he doesn't. He pulls Harry onto his lap and kisses him deeper, using his tongue skillfully while holding his sides gently.

"Guys?" Niall says. "I'm here." His voice is muffled, though, because Harry's leg is covering Louis' phone. Louis ignores him. He doesn't get alone time with Harry that much. He has to savor what he has.

"*Grayson! No!*" Niall yells in a terrified voice, and Louis immediately stops kissing Harry.

"Pumpkin?" He says worriedly.

"Sunshine?" Harry says to Louis, as if asking him for reassurance.

"Angel," Louis replies.

"You guys are so weird," Niall sighs. "I just did that to get your attention. Grayson didn't even look at me. Zayn is tickling her like a maniac." As if on cue, Grayson's high pitched shrieks and giggles pour over the phone.

"My baby," Harry smiles, squeezing Louis' hand. "Our baby."

"Hey! I just got engaged here. I haven't been married for 10 years like you."

"I'm really excited for you, Niall. I knew my brother wouldn't be forever alone," Louis laughs, and Niall scoffs.

"I got way more girls than you."

"That's true," Harry nods, laughing. Harry was Louis' only boyfriend, or partner, for that matter.

"I got Harry Styles," Louis replies simply. "That's the best a guy could get." He gives Harry a cheesy smile, hoping to see Harry blush. But instead of a cute little shy blush like he usually gets, Harry tackles him to the ground and begins kissing him deeply, his hand on Louis' side and another behind his neck.

"You guys seriously need to stop. Just because your daughter isn't here doesn't mean you can just kiss whenever you want. I'm trying to have a conversation with you. Do you even hear me? Are you having sex right now?"

***

The air is warm and breezy when the two boys wake up. It blows Louis' hair in his face, whipping around him. He huddles in closer to Harry's warmth, while wrapping their blanket around them. The soft whoosh of the gentle waves of the lake comfort him, mixing with the birds singing a pretty song in the trees surrounding them.

Louis is about to shake Harry awake, but he decides to do it in a way that he would enjoy.

He crawls over the sleeping boy, before leaning in and very, *very* slowly putting their lips together. It's light and tiny and the minute their lips barely touch Louis feels a million butterflies in his stomach. It's odd, that sometimes soft kisses like that can make him more in love and more turned on than the deep ones. Their lips brush with soft ease, until Louis is kissing him completely. Harry's breathing stops it's gentle rhythm as he wakes up, and he lets out a little moan and then he starts smiling when he realizes what's happening.

Louis can't help but smile a little when Harry pulls them tightly together and starts kissing him back.

fin.

author's note

so guys.... this is it.

we're done.

my story is *sniffs* done. okay *gets up and hits head in wall* don't cry kayla. it's just a book kayla. no need to cry.

anyway.

so.

it's been an absolute pleasure writing this book with you guys. notice i say with. because it wasn't all me. i don't think i am intelligent or motivated enough to write a whole like 80 chapter story without you guys. even in the beginning, when my comment goal was four, that meant the whole world to me. every comment pushed me forward, motivated and inspired me to write more. i felt like i had a purpose. so thank you. thank you for (without knowing it) changing the course of the whole book just with an idea you had in a comment. trust me, this has happened like eight times in this story. you guys helped me write this book, you helped me keep up with this book, and push through it to the end.

a lot of people ask me: how do you write so good? and i'm not saying i do, they just ask me that. and i ALWAYS say: write what you would want to read. remember that grammar is important. remember that the way you present it is important. believe me: people judge books by their covers. anyway. get a catching blurb. if you want to make your readers cry, then you better cry while you're writing it. (i have cried while writing many of my chapters). if you want to make them laugh, make yourself laugh, danget.

oh yeah. also people asked me if i decided not to cuss because of the characters. partly yes, but it's also because i don't cuss in real life. no offense to those of you who do, i just don't think they are necessary vocabulary words in my everyday life.

another question: (hey might as well do questions here) how did you get the idea?

to be honest, i originally was just going to give louis bpd and make harry really shy, but my sister hannah (Harry_Styles) told me that harry reminded her of someone with asperger's. i thought about it... and BOOM. i gave that to him. i didn't even realise in those first chapters that harry had all those qualities.

i want to thank you guys so much. my goal when i started wattpad was to get 10,000 reads on a book. after "you changed me" (hopefully at least one of you guys have read this book. it was my first book on here. to save all of you guys from my first attempts of writing, i have taken it down.) i changed my goal to 100,000. i never expected to get it. "since back when" only had about 10,000 reads before i started i sleep naked. and now... now i sleep naked has a million. i cried when i got 100,000, and i screamed and me and my triplet sisters had a freaking PARTY whenever i got 1,000,000. that was so amazing for me. it changed my life, literally. it showed me that i had a chance in the writing world (my favorite world, by the way). my dream is to become an author. and you guys have helped me realise that maybe that dream could come true. so thank you. THANK YOU.

i love you.

all the freaking love.

-Kayla. x

Printed in Great Britain
by Amazon